"Thea Harrison is a master storyteller, and she transported me to a fascinating world I want to visit again and again."
—Christine Feehan, #1 *New York Times* bestselling author

"Smoldering sensuality, fascinating characters and an intriguing world."
—Nalini Singh, *New York Times* bestselling author

PRAISE FOR

Dragon Bound

"Black Dagger Brotherhood readers will love [this]! *Dragon Bound* has it all: a smart heroine, a sexy alpha hero and a dark, compelling world. I'm hooked!"

—J. R. Ward, #1 *New York Times* bestselling author

"I absolutely loved *Dragon Bound*! Once I started reading, I was mesmerized to the very last page. Thea Harrison is a master storyteller, and she transported me to a fascinating world I want to visit again and again. It's a fabulous, exciting read that paranormal romance readers will love."

—Christine Feehan, #1 *New York Times* bestselling author

"I loved this book so much I didn't want it to end. Smoldering sensuality, fascinating characters and an intriguing world—*Dragon Bound* kept me glued to the pages. Thea Harrison has a new fan in me!"

—Nalini Singh, *New York Times* bestselling author

"Thea Harrison has created a truly original urban fantasy romance . . . When the shapeshifting dragon locks horns with his very special heroine, sparks fly that any reader will enjoy. Buy yourself an extra-large cappuccino, sit back and enjoy the decadent fun!"

—Angela Knight, *New York Times* bestselling author

continued . . .

ORACLE'S MOON

Thea Harrison

BERKLEY SENSATION, NEW YORK

THE BERKLEY PUBLISHING GROUP
Published by the Penguin Group
Penguin Group (USA) Inc.
375 Hudson Street, New York, New York 10014, USA
Penguin Group (Canada), 90 Eglinton Avenue East, Suite 700, Toronto, Ontario M4P 2Y3, Canada
(a division of Pearson Penguin Canada Inc.) • Penguin Books Ltd., 80 Strand, London WC2R 0RL,
England • Penguin Group Ireland, 25 St. Stephen's Green, Dublin 2, Ireland (a division of Penguin
Books Ltd.) • Penguin Group (Australia), 250 Camberwell Road, Camberwell, Victoria 3124, Australia
(a division of Pearson Australia Group Pty. Ltd.) • Penguin Books India Pvt. Ltd., 11 Community
Centre, Panchsheel Park, New Delhi—110 017, India • Penguin Group (NZ), 67 Apollo Drive,
Rosedale, Auckland 0632, New Zealand (a division of Pearson New Zealand Ltd.) • Penguin Books
(South Africa) (Pty.) Ltd., 24 Sturdee Avenue, Rosebank, Johannesburg 2196, South Africa

Penguin Books Ltd., Registered Offices: 80 Strand, London WC2R 0RL, England

This is a work of fiction. Names, characters, places, and incidents either are the product of the author's
imagination or are used fictitiously, and any resemblance to actual persons, living or dead, business
establishments, events, or locales is entirely coincidental. The publisher does not have any control over
and does not assume any responsibility for author or third-party websites or their content.

ORACLE'S MOON

A Berkley Sensation Book / published by arrangement with the author

PUBLISHING HISTORY
Berkley Sensation mass-market edition / March 2012

Copyright © 2012 by Teddy Harrison.
Excerpt from *Lord's Fall* by Thea Harrison copyright © 2012 by Teddy Harrison.
Cover art by Tony Mauro. Cover hand lettering by Ron Zinn.
Cover design by George Long.
Interior text design by Tiffany Estreicher.

ISBN: 978-0-425-24659-7

BERKLEY SENSATION®
Berkley Sensation Books are published by The Berkley Publishing Group,
a division of Penguin Group (USA) Inc.,
375 Hudson Street, New York, New York 10014.
BERKLEY SENSATION® is a registered trademark of Penguin Group (USA) Inc.
The "B" design is a trademark of Penguin Group (USA) Inc.

PRINTED IN THE UNITED STATES OF AMERICA

10 9 8 7 6 5 4 3 2 1

ALWAYS LEARNING   **PEARSON**

≈ ONE ≈

Attracting a Djinn's interest is generally not considered to be a good thing, Grace.

The babysitter Janice's pointed words kept bouncing around in Grace's head like a loose football on a field. That football was ten yards away from the end zone, and it had two teams of two-hundred-pound-plus NFL football players scrambling after it with all the intensity of their multimillion-dollar careers being on the line, and if that football could talk, you know it would be whining, "Oh geez this is gonna hurt."

Which was pretty much how the whole day had felt to Grace, including the sense of impending doom.

So thanks for the snark fest, Janice. It wasn't like Grace had any choice about the Djinn appearing in her life in the first place. He had been part of the group that had shown up on her doorstep at three thirty in the morning, because they couldn't wait until a goddamn decent time to talk to her.

She should probably stop calling him "the Djinn." He did, after all, have a name. He was Khalil somebody. According to one of his companions, he was Khalil Somebody Important.

Grace wasn't sure, but she thought his name might be Khalil Bane of Her Existence, but she didn't want to call him that to his . . . well, his face, when he chose to wear a face . . . because she didn't want to provoke him any more than she already had, and she was really, really just hoping he might get bored and go away now that all the excitement had died down.

All the excitement was dying down now, wasn't it?

The killing.

She had never seen anybody killed before that morning.

She shoved the memory aside. Right now she had her niece and nephew to look after, dammit. She didn't have time to react any more to what had happened. It would have to fucking wait until Chloe and Max were in bed.

Maybe the Djinn would be gone when she and the kids got home from getting groceries. Grace could hope. She could hope for a lot of things. There was always the possibility that the grocery store was giving out free steaks today and that a herd of pigs might file a flight plan with air traffic control at the Louisville International Airport.

Actually, she had the suspicion that he had followed them to the store. She couldn't see him, but she could sense his smoky presence at the edge of her mind ever since she packed Max and Chloe in the car and drove to Super Saver. The awareness of his acrid psychic scent jangled her nerves, like the feeling she got when fire trucks roared down a street with all sirens screaming.

It didn't matter if you couldn't see the fire. You still knew something catastrophic loomed nearby.

She managed to get a parking space by one of the cart stations. The humid, ninety-five-degree June day slapped her in the face when she climbed out of the car. In a matter of moments her T-shirt clung to her back, and she wanted nothing more than to tear off her shabby flannel pants above the knees, except she didn't wear shorts anymore, not even around the house, since she couldn't stand the sight of her scarred legs after the car accident.

Grace grabbed a shopping cart from the station and turned back to where the children waited. In the process she caught a glimpse of herself in the car window. She was an average height, with a lean waist and legs, and curving breasts and hips. If family genetics were anything to go by, she would have to take care when she hit middle age, or those curves of hers would become too generous.

Her short, fine strawberry blonde hair was sticking up in tufts because she kept running her fingers through it. Her hazel eyes were dull, and her skin pallid from lack of sleep. She touched her reflection in the window, noting the dark circles under her eyes.

I used to be pretty, she thought. Then she felt angry that it mattered to her.

Screw pretty. I'd rather be strong. Pretty fades over time. Strength gets you through the bad shit. And that matters, because sometimes there's a lot of bad shit.

She lifted Chloe into the cart. Then she transferred Max over into his baby carrier. Chloe sat in the shopping cart, folding her delicate four-year-old body into a tiny package. She was singing softly to her miniature Lala Whoopsie doll, or whatever the hell the doll was called, and making it dance along the rim of the cart.

Chloe's pale blonde hair was fine and silky. It was a lot like how Grace's and her sister Petra's had been when they were small. Both Grace's and Petra's hair had darkened as they grew older. There was a good chance Chloe's hair would deepen into the same shade of strawberry blonde, while Max had inherited his father's Mediterranean-style, dark good looks.

Chloe's curls were now floating around her head, except, Grace noticed with embarrassment, for a tangled knot at the back. She had forgotten to comb Chloe's hair before they went out. Well hell, she'd forgotten to comb her own hair too. That's what she got for trying to stagger through her day in a half coma. She tried finger-combing first Chloe's hair then her own, with limited success.

Nine-month-old Max was sound asleep and snoring in his carrier, his little rosebud mouth open. After being so sick through the night, the poor baby boy was exhausted.

Pushing the cart with the children loaded into it, Grace limped into the grocery store. Super Saver was a no-frills discount grocery store, with goods stacked in the aisles in cardboard boxes, but they had a refrigerated and freezer section, and the store was air-conditioned. Grace sighed with relief as cool air licked her skin, even as the change in temperature made her exhausted head spin.

She gritted her teeth. All she had to do was get the groceries home and put away the stuff that needed refrigeration. She could put everything else away later. Maybe she could coax Chloe into watching a *Dora the Explorer* DVD while Grace stretched out on the couch and napped. Sometime that day she had to figure out which of the red-inked bills she could pay, but that could wait until she had at least part of her brain back in working order.

She frowned at the stack of boxes in front of her. Should she get two cans of tuna or three? They were down to the last of their food stamps for the month, and every small decision mattered.

Once, neither Grace nor anyone else in her family would have dreamed of going on food stamps. Her lineage was a very old, proud one with its roots in ancient Greece. The Andreas family had a unique Power among human witches, the Power of the Oracle that was passed down from female to female over countless generations.

Once the Oracle had been located in a sacred temple complex at Delphi. Kings and queens, Roman senators and emperors, humans and all sorts of creatures from the Elder Races came as supplicants to petition for her prophecies. In return they laid a fortune in gold and jewels at her feet. It was all part of an ancient social contract that almost nobody remembered to honor any longer.

The Oracle spoke for the people, and the people were to support her. Petitioners were to give offerings to the Oracle. The Oracle could not ask for or demand money. If she did, she would be charging for her services, and legend had it, the moment she did that, she would lose her Power of prophecy.

Other family members could speak on the Oracle's behalf,

but unfortunately the family had gone through several generations of financial decline, ill-health and just plain bad luck. Grace's parents had died when she was a small child. Her grandmother raised her and Petra, and taught them the old traditions. Five years ago, when Grace was nineteen and Petra twenty-six and newly married, their grandmother died of cancer. Niko had been Petra's champion when the Power had passed on to her. Niko'd had no problem reminding petitioners of their obligations to his wife. Then earlier this year, Petra and her husband, Niko, had been killed, and the Power moved on to Grace.

Now there was only Grace and the children, and Grace was only twenty-three. She was facing something she should never have had to face alone, and she had her niece and nephew to feed, two small children for whom she would do anything. Hell yes, she applied for food stamps. Just as soon as she was able to leave the hospital, she had applied for everything they were eligible to apply for.

As far as her holding on to the Oracle's traditions went, that decision was touch and go. When she was in the hospital recovering, Grace had promised herself she would not make any long-term decisions or commitments to anything or anyone other than Chloe and Max. If anything else became intolerable, she would drop it.

For now it was one foot in front of the other, one day at a time. She gently touched the back of Chloe's tangled, shining head.

Chloe looked up and smiled.

"Gracie, did we have company when I was sleeping?" Chloe asked.

"Yes, baby girl," Grace said.

"Why didn't you wake me up? I like company. Did they miss me?"

"I'm sure they would have if they had known about you," Grace said. "But this was adult company. This was not Chloe company."

"I'm a big girl," Chloe scolded. "I'm very big now."

"I know you are," Grace said. She chose two cans of tuna

and put them in the cart by Chloe's tiny feet. "I can't believe how big you've gotten. Pretty soon you're going to push the grocery cart, and I'm going to ride inside it." Chloe giggled. "But this was Oracle-adult-business company. It wasn't Chloe-big-girl company. That's why Janice came over to stay with you and feed you breakfast until I got back."

As soon as Grace said "Oracle," a darker, knowing look shadowed Chloe's eyes. Or maybe that was just a product of Grace's exhaustion. In either case, Chloe simply nodded, bent her head over her doll and fell quiet for a time.

Grace added a gallon of milk and a dozen eggs to the cart. A few steps down the aisle she grabbed a couple of canisters of Max's formula. He also loved bananas, so she looked at the fresh produce. Super Saver didn't have a great selection of fresh fruits and vegetables, but the bananas looked nice enough so she put a few in the cart.

"Can we keep the doggie?" Chloe asked.

Grace had difficulty processing the words for a few moments because they were so random and disconnected from anything else that was happening. But that was what talking to a four-year-old was like, and she soon caught up. "What doggie?"

"He says sometimes he can be a cat if I want."

Grace grinned. "You want to keep a doggie that's a cat."

"Uh-huh." Blonde curls waved in the air as Chloe nodded. "He likes me."

"Of course the doggie-cat likes you." Grace moved around the cart to drop a kiss on the girl's forehead. Chloe looked expectant, so Grace told her, "You're wonderful and likeable and loveable and very, very big."

Chloe's eyes rounded. "I am, aren't I?"

"Yes, you are. And if we ever manage to find a talking doggie-cat, I would love to keep him. But for now, why don't I see if we can get Joey and Rachel over for a playdate. I'll make apple juice Popsicles. Would you like that?"

"Uh-huh."

"Okay, sweetie." She paused to search for a scrap of paper in her purse and scribble a note on it. Joey and Rachel were

Petra's friend Katherine's children. Katherine had been an immense help since Petra and Niko died, and Grace owed her a good six months' of regular playdates, but she would never remember to make that call if she didn't write it down.

Her leg was hurting worse than ever, and she was limping badly by the time she got the children and the groceries out to her battered car.

Instead of using the car insurance money from the accident to buy a new car, Grace had decided to fix up her own 1999 Honda Accord so that it ran more reliably. Then she spent the rest on replacing a leaky water heater. The property was a money pit. The house was not quite falling down around their ears, but a building that was over a hundred and fifty years old had constant issues.

At least Petra and Niko had replaced the old monster of a furnace last year with an energy efficient one, but the roof was in such poor shape, Grace didn't think it would last another winter, and she honestly didn't know what she was going to do about it.

The trip home was lost in a fog of exhaustion. She got the children inside first and set Max in his carrier down gently on the floor by the couch. Then she put some pretzels in a small plastic bowl for Chloe, along with milk in a small cup. Chloe was delighted to watch Dora for the ten thousandth time. Grace limped through the house to make sure that the child gate was secured properly at the foot of the stairs and that other doors were shut throughout the ground floor.

She left the door to Chloe and Max's bedroom open so that Chloe could get to the toys stored in that room if she wanted. Then Grace turned on the floor fan in the living room. Running a fan was cheaper than running any of the three window air-conditioners in the house. After that she carried in the groceries.

There were four steps up to the porch. She thought of all the times she had blithely run up and down those steps, her young, strong body working so smoothly she never gave it a second's thought. She would never take anything like that for granted again.

She had gone up the steps once with the children. If she

stacked all of the grocery bags on the porch first, then she only had to climb up those four steps one more time. She stopped trying to think and let her mind float away on a sea of pain.

She had pushed too hard today. She would have liked to soak in the tub, except the tub was on the second floor. Getting herself and the kids up a full flight of stairs, along with the baby gate, sounded like climbing Mount Everest. She could wait until she put them down for the night and take the baby monitor upstairs with her, but she didn't think she would last that long. She had a feeling that once she got the kids to bed, she would go out like a light. Thank the gods they were so small she could bathe them in the large, old-fashioned kitchen sink that evening without having to bend over or kneel. As for herself, she would have to wash again at the sink as well.

On the television Dora went in search of her lost teddy bear. Chloe ate pretzels, pretended to feed her doll and sang along with the show. The psychic air around the property seemed restless and full of spirits. Something about the Oracle's presence, or the property, attracted them. The house was crowded with ghosts.

For some reason, a group of elderly women had been hanging out in the kitchen for the last couple of weeks. Grace didn't recognize them, and she couldn't quite make out what they said. Either the ghosts weren't strong enough, or they didn't have anything they felt passionately enough about to communicate clearly to her. She suspected they just enjoyed the children and the atmosphere of the old kitchen. Whatever the reason was for their presence, she liked their companionship. They felt worn, comfortable and faded, like an old, warm blanket. Concentrating on them helped to take her mind off her body's misery.

Sometimes the ghosts that came to the house weren't comfortable. Sometimes they were jagged presences, serrated with old malice and resentments, or still reverberating with the traumas from their lives.

Sometimes there was nothing else to do but chase the dark

spirits off the property. She wasn't Jennifer Love Hewitt, and this wasn't the *Ghost Whisperer*, where angry ghosts some- how turned into nice people once they had a chance to settle misunderstandings or get grievances off their chests, and then all the happy ghosts moved on to a shiny afterlife at the end of an episode. Dark, angry spirits tended to be dark and angry because they held on to things. Given half a chance they also tended to linger, spreading their ill will and nega- tivity throughout the property like a malaise.

The Power of the Oracle was the Power of prophecy. Prophecy, as it related to the Oracle, was neither fortune- telling nor divine revelation, but involved a sense of clair- voyance, or the ability to see beyond the five senses. If the petitioner asked after those who had passed, occasionally it could involve channeling the dead. The Power always passed to a female in the Andreas family, but not every female was an eligible candidate. The abilities of those who had the potential to become an Oracle often manifested in either a strong second sight or a connection to things of spirit, and the veil of time could become thin in odd ways.

Both Grace and Petra had shown potential very early, so their grandmother had taught them both the skills and tradi- tions they would need if the Power passed on to them. Grace had her own suspicions about Chloe. The challenge in iden- tifying the ability was that every small child had an active imagination and often chattered to invisible friends. Usually a potential was identified by the time the candidate was around five years of age, because by then it was possible to have enough of a coherent conversation with a child to con- firm the presence of the ability.

Whatever might happen to Grace, whether she lived a long life or died young, little baby Max would never become the Oracle. The Power never transferred to the Andreas males, and they never demonstrated the ability, although they could father daughters who were potentials, and some of the men in the family tree had become Powerful witches in their own right.

Grace envied Max for a lot of reasons today.

She put away the groceries that needed to go in the fridge then stood for a few minutes with the door open, relishing the frigid air. She poured herself a glass of cold water, swallowed prescription-strength ibuprofen and limped to the living room. After locking the screen door, she left the front door propped open in the hope of catching wayward breeze.

Next she checked on Max. The little man was still sawing logs, a chubby fist held over one closed eye. Now that was an intense nap. She gathered up his lumpy nine-month-old body. He seemed heavier when he was a dead weight. She took him into the children's bedroom and eased him into his crib. He didn't even stir to roll over.

All her immediate tasks were done. She made her slow, tired way back to the living room and sat on the couch with a grunt.

Her gaze fell on the textbooks she had left stacked on the coffee table.

She hadn't felt ready to go to college directly out of high school. Instead, she had kicked around for a year, dated a few guys and driven across the country with her friend Jacqui so they could dip their big toes in the Pacific Ocean. Then they had driven home again, and Grace had worked in restaurants and saved a little money. She had started college a year late, and as a result, she still hadn't finished.

This past spring was supposed to be her final semester. Petra, Niko and Grace had been happy when they had gone out to eat that rainy Friday night. Grace's spring break had just begun, and Niko had found out he had gotten a raise at work.

All it had taken to smash their lives apart was one independent trucker who had fallen asleep at the wheel and crossed over the median line into oncoming traffic. The accident killed Petra and Niko, and it had nearly killed Grace as well. If Chloe and Max had been in the car as originally planned, the last of the Andreas family could well have been wiped out in one freak crash, but Petra had decided she wanted dinner out without the children, so at the last minute she had arranged for a babysitter.

Grace didn't remember the collision. She was glad. She didn't want to remember.

When she had awakened in the hospital, she had been disoriented and groggy with painkillers. Even so, she had felt it immediately, that old Power nestling deep inside of her, and it was one of those things that you can't unlearn once you know it. She knew her sister was dead and nothing would ever be the same again.

Now she had five incompletes from very understanding professors, no Bachelor's degree and a load of student debt that would come crashing down on her shoulders at some point in the near future. She had accumulated a monstrous pile of bills from multiple surgeries on her knee, along with a hospital stay, a tangle of car and life insurance policies but no health insurance coverage, and she had received nothing at all from the dead trucker who had let his insurance coverage lapse. No matter how she wrangled the numbers, the assets she had were nowhere near enough to cover all the bills.

Somehow she had to create a life for herself and the kids. She had to try to finish those classes, get her degree and find a paying job that would cover both living and childcare expenses. And no matter how much she resisted the idea, it was becoming clear she was going to have to file for bankruptcy. Maybe she could qualify for a waiver for the court fees.

"Got everything you need, baby girl?" she mumbled to Chloe.

"Uh-huh," Chloe said, her blue eyes glued to the television.

Sorry, Petra and Niko, she thought. *I know you didn't like using the TV as a babysitter, and I try, I really do. But my gods, I can't keep my eyes open any longer.*

She eased her sore body flat and fell into a black hole.

·

≡ TWO ≡

Grace dreamed she was running along a dark paved road. The night was full of shadows, the new moon hidden from the naked eye. The full moon at its zenith was a witch's moon, a time for incantations and Power. The new moon at its darkest was the Oracle's moon, a time when the veil between all the worlds and all the times thinned. A brilliant spray of stars like Djinns' eyes pierced the dark purple sky, and the wind whispered secrets to the shadowed, swaying trees.

Her running shoes slapped the ground rhythmically. They struck a pagan tempo for the song in her coursing blood. She loved how her body felt, sleek and strong as it moved along the paved road. Perfect. She felt perfect.

A gigantic black panther ran along beside her. His broad shoulder was as high as hers, and his long, powerful body ate the distance with effortless, fluid grace. As soon as she became aware of him, the panther turned his head and looked at her with diamond eyes that were as piercing and shining as the stars. Shocked, she jerked and stumbled. . . .

And she slipped into another dream. This time she climbed the side of a steep rocky bluff. She had to use her hands, and the burn in her muscles felt good. The sun was perched high in the sky and beat down on her head, and she dripped with sweat.

An immense black dog climbed at her side. He was easily twice the size of a mastiff, all muscle and power, yet he climbed up the side of the bluff with impossible agility. As she stared, he turned to look at her with radiant diamond eyes that startled her so badly, she lost her grip on the rocks.

Gravity yanked. She fell, and the ground hurtled toward her.

She woke with a start, her heart hammering. Her clothes were clammy with sweat. The sun had shifted, and she was alone in the living room. The television was off. So many things were not right with the scene, but before she had a chance to panic, she heard Max and Chloe giggling in their bedroom.

"I want you to be a doggie now," Chloe said.

A male voice said, "But at the moment I am a cat."

Grace knew that voice. She had only heard it for a brief time, but she would never forget it. It was the voice of the Bane of Her Existence. It sounded deep and clear, with a kind of purity that somehow hurt the heart, and it held the power of a cyclone.

It belonged to a creature whose whirlwind arrival on her doorstep had heralded confrontation and violence.

And the killing.

And it was visiting with her kids.

She was off the couch and moving down the hall before she fully knew what she was doing.

Chloe said, "I want to ride the doggie!"

"I believe what you want would then be called a horse," said the Bane.

Max shrieked, a happy sound that escalated so high it could shatter glass.

Sharp pain shot up her leg. Just as it threatened to give out from underneath her, she reached the children's bedroom and grabbed on to the doorway as she looked inside.

Max stood in his crib. He couldn't walk on his own yet, but he could stand when he held on to something. The single wisp of dark brown hair at the top of his head waved as he bobbed up and down. He was grinning from ear to ear and watching Chloe, who sat on the floor along with a black cat, who sat in front of her.

The cat had to be the Bane of Her Existence. The Djinn. Khalil Somebody Important. Visually, it looked like a normal, fairly large cat, perhaps twenty pounds or so, but to her mind's eye, it felt immense with a shadowy, hazardous Power.

The cat said, "For something so small, you emit a great deal of noise."

Chloe grabbed the cat's tail and yanked on it. "Doggie!" Chloe shrieked. "Doggie! Doggie!"

"That is my tail," the cat remarked. The little girl stabbed at his furred face with a plump finger. "Now you have discovered one of my eyes. Oh look, you have discovered the other one. I think you have awakened your aunt. I told you we should be quiet."

The trio turned to look at her as she stood frozen. Two delighted children and what appeared to be a normal black cat but was instead an alien, enormously Powerful, infinitely dangerous creature.

"Look, Gracie!" said Chloe. "It's the doggie-cat! You said we can keep him."

The cat's strange, wrong eyes narrowed. "Did you?" he said. His triangular face looked distinctly unfriendly, whiskers held awry. "That wasn't what you told me earlier."

Grace lunged forward to snatch up the cat, and he allowed it. His body hung boneless from her grip just like a real cat would. "I had no idea you meant this doggie-cat, Chloe," she said, her voice hoarse. "That changes everything."

"Which other doggie-cat could she possibly have meant?" said the cat. "You don't exactly have a plethora of them hanging around."

Grace growled to Chloe, "Stay here."

Chloe pushed to her feet and whined, "But I want to play with him."

Grace looked at the little girl. "I said stay here, young lady."

Something in Grace's expression must have made it clear she meant business, because Chloe kicked her toys on the floor. "You never let me do anything fun. I'm never going to live here again."

"Fine," Grace said between her teeth. "Just do as you're told."

She limped out of the bedroom. Max gave a wordless yell, clearly displeased at recent events. Chloe shouted, "Horrible! He's *MY* doggie-cat! I found him first. You're not fair! I hate everything and everybody!"

Grace hissed at him. "Thank you. Thank you so much for that. There are so many things wrong with what just happened. What the hell is the matter with you, anyway? Have you got no sense?"

"You are every bit as impudent and disrespectful as you were earlier this morning," he said in a cold voice.

The cat grew as she walked down the hall, until suddenly she held on to a weight that was much too heavy for her to carry. She dropped him, and he continued to grow until he became the massive black panther from her dream. A thrill of shock iced her skin. Her gaze slid sideways to look at the impossible behemoth slinking along beside her. He was the size of a large pony, yet he still seemed small compared to what her mind insisted was the immensity of his true presence.

She would not give in to what she was feeling. She would *not*.

"Stop it," she snapped.

"I have no idea what you're talking about," said the monstrous feline. He turned his head to look at her with bizarre eyes that sparkled with malice.

They reached the living room. Grace rounded on him. She used her fury to propel her forward. She shoved at the giant creature. It was like trying to push a mountain. She shoved at him again. "You're trying to intimidate me. Well, guess what, asshole? It isn't going to work. This is my home. Those two kids are my niece and nephew. And I did not give you permission to spend time with them. You are trespassing, and it is not okay."

The giant panther morphed into the upright figure of an angry man, and finally she came face-to-face with the Djinn she had met when he and his two companions had knocked on her door.

The form he wore this time was tall, somewhere close to six and a half feet. Long, raven black hair was pulled back from an elegant, pale face. That face had all the same things that a human face had, two eyes, a nose and a mouth. It was even lean-jawed and handsome, yet somehow it was clearly not a human face. His strange eyes were the same in every form he chose to wear, crystalline and diamondlike. He had a lean, graceful frame that matched his face, and he wore a simple black tunic and trousers, and a fierce, regal pride.

This, as much as anything, was his real physical form. At least it was his go-to form. At his essence, he was a spirit of magic and fire. No physical form could contain him in his entirety. His Power filled the house.

My gods, there's so much of him, she thought as she stared up at his sparkling, angry eyes. What a calamity he is. Standing in front of him, she felt absurdly young, very small and stupidly, excessively fascinated.

"I offer you a gift beyond price, you foolish creature," he said between his teeth. "And you throw it back in my face."

"What do you think you're offering me?" she asked. "I wake up and I find you with my kids in their bedroom. And I'll say this again: without my permission. Do you realize how offensive that is? Maybe you don't. Maybe that's something Djinn would do all the time. You know what, I don't care. And I'm not even going to get into all the wrong lessons you were teaching them. Wait a minute, yes, I am. You were a talking cat with children who are much too young to differentiate between that and reality."

His eyes narrowed. "What nonsense are you spouting, human?"

"What do you think is going to happen the next time Chloe sees a black cat?" Grace demanded. "Do you think she's going to say to herself, oh this is not like the freaky black cat that talks to me and lets me yank its tail and poke it in the eye? No. Do you know what she's going to try to do?

She's going to try to talk to it and pull its tail and maybe poke it in the eye. And you know what *that* cat is going to do—because it's a real goddamn cat? It's going to scratch her. It might bite her. Cat bites are filthy things. Usually the puncture wounds go deep, and they get infected. And then suddenly, I'll be taking a confused, crying four-year-old girl to the ER for a three-hundred-dollar doctor's visit to get antibiotics, all because of your ignorant arrogance!"

He regarded her with a supercilious expression. "Do all your thoughts proceed in such a fashion?"

"What are you talking about?" Grace blinked, thrown off balance. "Do my thoughts proceed where?"

He gestured with a long hand. He made it look impossibly graceful. "To conclusions of disaster, of course. No doubt there will also be brain-eating parasites in the cat bite, or perhaps a troop of rabid monkeys will escape from a nearby zoo and cut a path directly for your house."

She stared. "You think I'm making this stuff up? That cat bite happened to me when I was little. I have the scars to prove it. Do you know what I caught Chloe trying to do yesterday? She was climbing on top of the kitchen table. She thought she could jump off and fly like Clark Kent, because we had just watched an old movie rerun with Christopher Reeve, and if Superman could fly, she thought she might be able to too. Maybe she wouldn't have broken her leg if I hadn't caught her, but she probably would have hurt herself somehow."

The curve of his elegant mouth turned cruel. He looked around the living room, his gaze cold and judgmental. "How unfortunate then for your children that you choose to nap in the daytime instead of watching out for them the way you should."

She flinched as if she'd been slapped, and she looked around the living room too. Her textbooks were stacked on the coffee table. Toys littered the floor. A basket of unfolded laundry sat on the floor by the armchair. Chloe had spilled some of her pretzels on the area rug in the living room then walked over them. Crumbs were everywhere.

Grace thought of the tangle at the back of Chloe's head that she still hadn't brushed out. Embarrassment and fury clogged her throat so that she couldn't speak. After a moment she managed to whisper between clenched teeth, "You have no idea what you're talking about. You have no real under-standing of me, my kids, or any of the issues we face. That lack of understanding alone makes you dangerous to us."

"How dare you?" He thrust his angry face close. "*I would never cause harm to a child.* The whole reason I stayed was to protect them!"

His rage curled around her, manifesting as black smoke. She felt as though she stared into an inferno.

She would not flinch. She would *not.*

There was simply no point in trying to reason with him. They were too different from each other, and he was too arrogant to listen to anything she said. She dug down deep and found enough composure to say, "I get that you don't mean us any harm. Thank you for staying this morning to make sure Chloe and Max were protected. If you don't wish to petition for a consultation with the Oracle, I'm telling you now to leave my house."

He scowled and opened his mouth, clearly intending a scorching reply, but a small, sad voice beat him to it. Chloe said, "No more fighting. Don't be mad anymore, okay?"

Khalil's diamond gaze flickered. He looked down, as Grace did, at Chloe's worried face. Then Grace witnessed a remarkable thing, as his elegant, malicious expression gen-tled. He went down on one knee so that he could come face-to-face with Chloe. The girl regarded him gravely. Some-thing in Grace's chest twisted. He was so enormous, and Chloe so tiny.

"I will not be mad anymore," Khalil said. He did some-thing to throttle back the Power in his voice and spoke quietly.

"Promise?" Chloe asked.

His gaze slid sideways and up at Grace. He looked sour. Wow, Grace thought on a sudden spurt of hysteria, he really doesn't want to give up on his grudge. But he wasn't talking to Grace any longer. She raised her eyebrows and nodded toward Chloe, telling him with the silent gesture, you're answering to her, not to me.

His strange, unfriendly gaze pledged something to her, but she didn't know how to read unspoken Djinn messages. With an air of decision, Khalil turned to Chloe. He said, "Yes, we both promise."

Wait, what? Grace straightened. She hadn't given him permission to speak for her.

"We will not fight anymore," he continued. "It is too upsetting for small people."

Chloe said strongly, "It's upsetting for big girls too."

"Indeed," said Khalil. He held out his hand and Chloe put hers into it.

Chloe was so small, Grace thought, biting her lip. So fragile, so precious. Grace held herself so tensely her muscles were starting to ache again.

He brought the girl's fingers to his lips and kissed them. Then he let her go and straightened to his full height before he vanished.

Grace stared at Chloe, looking for some kind of reaction to his sudden disappearance. Other than wiggling the fingers Khalil had kissed and looking intensely thoughtful, the little girl didn't appear to have much of one. Maybe Chloe was concentrating on trying to disappear too, and she was discovering that she couldn't do that either.

Max shouted angrily from the bedroom. Normally good-natured, he'd apparently had quite enough of being left out.

Grace sighed and went down the hall to collect the little man. Chloe had eaten her pretzels snack, but Grace and Max had missed out on lunch. He had to be starving. She knew she was. She changed Max's diaper and tickled him until his bad mood vanished, and he kicked and giggled. Then she settled him on the hip on her good side and turned to Chloe, who had followed her into the bedroom to watch.

"Think it's about time we had some supper?" she asked.

Chloe gave that proposal due consideration. "Indeed."

• • •

Grace fixed macaroni and cheese for supper. Chloe liked macaroni and cheese. Janice said Chloe had only picked at her breakfast, and the only other thing she'd had to eat that day were the pretzels.

Chloe liked applesauce too, and so did Max. What the hell, Grace thought. Let's get wild and crazy, and switch things up. We'll have applesauce tonight instead of a vegetable.

A bout of trembling hit as she pulled a jar of applesauce from the fridge. She left the jar on the counter and sat at the table while her limbs shook as though she had a fever.

In the living room, Chloe danced and sang while she watched a Disney DVD. Grace couldn't remember the name of the movie. It was another story about a spunky princess with a requisite sidekick. Max sat quietly in the middle of the kitchen floor, happy to chew on a soft plastic baby book. Grace rubbed her forehead as she watched him. Apparently she was going to have her reaction before the kids went to bed, whether she liked it or not.

The killing.

For her, the events that led up to the Djinn's arrival, and then to the killing, all began with Max's ear infection. He had started to act cranky yesterday, which was enough of a change from his normal, happy personality that she took note and began to watch him closely.

He had worsened until he was up half the night, feverish and crying, until a strange and extremely dangerous trio came knocking on their front door.

If there had ever been a time when she had not wanted to answer the door, it had been at three thirty that morning. She had been walking the floor with a crying Max and trying not to pull her hair out. Unused to handling such crises, she didn't know if she should tough out the night and take him to his regular pediatrician in the morning, or if she should wake Chloe up and take him right away to an urgent care facility.

But whether it was convenient for her or not, she had to

answer the door. Her newly inherited position as the Oracle of Louisville demanded it.

Grace, Chloe and Max lived in the sprawling, old farmhouse where Grace had grown up. The house had been in the Andreas family ever since they had come to the States. It sat on a five-acre stretch of land that bordered the Ohio River. By inter-demesne law, the entire property was supposed to be a place of sanctuary for all who came to consult with the Oracle, and the Oracle had the obligation to welcome all petitioners.

But the Oracle should have been either Grace's grandmother or her sister, Petra. Grace had never really believed that the Power would pass to her. Ever since the accident, she had been close to chucking away an ancient family heritage that had spanned thousands of years, but she'd held on to the impulse so far.

Barely.

So when the knock came in the middle of the night, Grace opened the door. She found Carling Severan, Rune Ainissesthai, and Khalil standing on her doorstep. Carling was one of the most Powerful witches in the world, a Vampyre, and she had once been Queen of the Nightkind. She was also newly retired from her most recent role as Councillor on the Elder tribunal. Her partner, Rune, was not just any Wyr. He was a gryphon, and he had been First sentinel for the Wyr demesne, although he too had just recently retired.

Then there was their companion, the Djinn. Khalil Somebody Important.

It almost sounded like the setup of a classic joke. Do you know what happens when a Vampyre, a Wyr and a Djinn walk into your house . . . ? Only Grace found out that the punch line wasn't funny.

Max's illness was one of the reasons why she had tried so hard to persuade Carling, Rune and Khalil to come back at a more reasonable hour, but they couldn't be dissuaded. At least Carling had healed Max's ear infection before formally petitioning to speak to the Oracle.

Thankfully, nighttime petitions to consult the Oracle were

rare. When they did occur, they tended to involve matters of some urgency. Such was the case with Carling and Rune. Rune had been wounded, and apparently their mission was urgent, and shit just sometimes happened.

The shit that had happened this morning just before daybreak had been big and bad enough to attract some of the most Powerful creatures on the North American continent. All but one of the seven Elder tribunal Councillors had converged in a tense confrontation with Carling and Rune. Two of the seven demesne rulers—Dragos Cuelebre, dragon and Lord of the Wyr from New York, and Julian Regillus, Vampyre King of the Nightkind demesne from San Francisco—had also been present.

Catching sight of the dragon that had filled up the back meadow before he shapeshifted into his human form—now that had been a helluva kick in the head.

Nothing Grace had ever seen on television or in movies or in her own imagination could have prepared her for the sight of the dragon in real life.

She had already been struggling. She'd had the sleepless night with Max. Then she summoned the Power of the Oracle in an intense session with Carling and Rune that had left her with a blackout of blank time in her head. And to top it all off, Rune had shoved Carling—he had meant to get her out of danger, but Grace had been in the way. Carling had fallen into her, and Grace had been knocked on her ass hard enough to jar her whole body.

And things kept going from weird to worse, like some sort of high-speed hallucinogenic car chase. Picking herself up after the fall, Grace had watched from one side, largely unnoticed, as the scene unfolded.

She hadn't understood everything the group discussed. For some reason, Carling was under a death sentence. Then the Elder tribunal decided to put her in quarantine instead. Except Grace was pretty sure Carling didn't have anything contagious. Where the tribunal would hold Carling was also under some debate. Grace couldn't figure out if the tribunal meant to put Carling in a hospital or a jail.

To complicate things, Rune had also taken Carling as his mate and refused to be separated from her. They couldn't go to the Nightkind demesne—there was some kind of bad feeling between Carling and her progeny Julian, the King—and nobody liked the idea of the pair going to the Wyr demesne.

Meanwhile, image upon fantastic image careened by in front of Grace's astonished gaze.

The Councillor from the Elven demesne, standing tall and shining and ageless. Holy crap, that woman had been riveting. The Djinn Soren, Demonkind Councillor and head of the Elder tribunal, with white hair and stars for eyes, whose Power was a tower of flame so intense it burned her mind. The trio of Vampyres: the Nightkind King with his pleasant-faced companion, Xavier del Torro, who was so notorious even Grace had heard of him, and the blonde woman with them who had *pulled a sword on Carling while in sanctuary*. That single act confirmed everything Grace had ever known, that the laws protecting the Oracle, her petitioners and her land were simply not enough.

Then the strangest thing of all happened. Everything around her slipped a groove. If reality was an old 45 vinyl record playing on a turntable, the needle had jumped, skipping an important part of the song.

And suddenly Rune shapeshifted into something monstrous. He killed the blonde Vampyre, who disintegrated into dust and blew away on an early morning breeze.

Grace had thought the group had argued a lot before, but that was nothing compared to what came next. She was reeling from exhaustion and shock but glued in place, because what those deadly, immortal Power brokers decided mattered a whole hell of a lot to her.

When at last the Demonkind Councillor turned to her and asked for her opinion, she was all too happy to give it. She knew she hadn't seen everything that had happened, nor had she understood all of the arguing, but she saw one thing clearly enough, and she knew how she felt about that.

The Vampyre woman had *drawn a sword* on her land. As far as Grace was concerned, whatever Rune had done after that point was only what the woman deserved. Grace would have killed the woman herself if she'd had the opportunity.

Once she had said her piece, the whole thing had been over.

To a young, inexperienced human Oracle, the morning had been extraordinary, dangerous, confusing and terrifying. And she hadn't had a chance to talk it out with anyone or process what had happened. The events kept swirling in her mind like a funnel cloud.

The fact that Grace hadn't had to kill the woman in self-defense was beside the point. The early morning's violence hadn't even been directed at her, but witnessing it had changed everything. Grace's quiet home and her small life had been indelibly marked.

Her world had already been shaken to its foundations these last four months. Now she felt like she and the children lived in an unimaginably fragile house of glass, and she did not know how she could stand for them to stay there.

At least all the covens in the witches' demesne recognized what an unmanageable position Grace had been in ever since the accident. It was impossible to meet the obligations and uphold the traditions of the Oracle's position while also acting as a single parent.

At the instigation of Isalynn LeFevre, the Head of the witches' demesne, a roster had been developed of witches who were on call to babysit whenever Grace was petitioned to act in her new role as the Oracle. The witches donated their time as part of their tithe of community service. The tithe was required of all actively practicing witches in the demesne, but sometimes the help they gave Grace was grudging. In any case, the babysitting roster was only a stopgap solution. It didn't solve any of her larger problems.

Or alter the fact that something, somehow, had to change.

It had to, because continuing like this was inconceivable.

The oven timer dinged. The pasta was done.

Grace stood and fed the children supper.

≈ THREE ≈

Khalil reformed on the roof of the house, not necessarily because he felt any particular desire to take physical form again but more to give his roiling energy a focal point. He crossed his arms and leaned back against a dormer. The roof was shabby and missing a few tiles, he noted with disapproval. The land was as unkempt as the house, with grass that was too long and weeds that sprouted around fence posts. They were overtaking once well-tended flower beds. Everywhere he looked there was evidence of neglect, while the lazy, contentious human napped. He did not approve of how the property was maintained or how she cared for the children. He tapped his fingers on his biceps and thought.

The Djinn were among some of the first creatures that came into being at the Earth's formation. Born of magic and fire, they were beings of pure spirit. They gained nourishment from the energy of the sun, from the living things of the Earth and from sources of Power. Any form Khalil chose to take was like donning a suit of clothes. He did not need to eat food or drink liquids. This body would not grow hungry, or grow old and die. Easily assumed and easily discarded, it would fade into nothing as soon as he let go of it.

He was not the oldest of his kind, the first generation of Djinn born at the keen, bright morning of the world, but he was of the second generation and, therefore, considered old among his people. He was an authority in his House and a voice to be reckoned with among the five Houses of Djinn. This young human creature was nothing more than a single breath of time in his ageless existence, and the fact that she called *him* ignorant was insupportable.

While he certainly knew why she irritated him, he did not know why she interested him. Her facial features and physical form were pleasant enough, at least as far as humans reckoned such things. She was pale and wore shadows on her face like the haunts of memory. Those shadows were intriguing. They told a tale but in a language he couldn't read. He wondered what they said.

Her hair. Now her hair interested him. It was a light reddish blonde, like captured fire and sunlight, and her hazel eyes held flecks of green, blue and honey brown. What he found most interesting about her was her energy, which crackled with intensity. She had a temper as fiery as her hair, and she held Power in that slender body of hers too, a great deal of it. It was an odd thing that such a young creature held a Power that felt so old to him. The land itself held echoes of the same Power. He wondered what it meant.

He sensed movement and other flares of ancient Power in the nearby city. Even though his focus had been on the children and he had remained at the house, he had sensed the gathering earlier on the property. He knew that several of the entities were still in the area. Carling and Rune, Elder tribunal Councillors, the Nightkind King and the dragon were somewhere close by. Khalil was curious to discover who might leave and if any of them might return to speak again with the Oracle.

Shadows lengthened across the land. The Midwestern air felt heavy and full of water, like it was pregnant with some kind of storm. From his position on the roof he could see the Ohio River that bordered the western edge of the property. One of the great rivers of the North American continent, the water captured the sunlight along its surface until it seemed to shine with its own light.

He listened to the sounds from within the house, small domestic things like the clink of cutlery against dishes, the baby's infectious giggle and Chloe's light voice. The child chattered about anything that took her fancy, and when she wasn't talking, she sang. She asked questions unceasingly. Despite the temper Grace had displayed to him, she always answered Chloe's questions with patience.

They were like a small nest of birds. Khalil grinned when he thought of it. *Chirp chirp chirp.* Then there was the sound of water running and much flapping of wings. The chirping grew louder. Giggling was punctuated with Chloe's *tra-la-ing* and Max's cheerful yodel. The noisiness moved from the kitchen to another part of the house. Grace was putting the children to bed. She lavished love on those babies. While he did not approve of her and he was almost certain he didn't like her, he would have to give the human female credit for that much.

He thought back to a time long ago, when his own child, Phaedra, would have made such light, happy sounds. All forms of children were rare to the Elder Races, as if nature were compensating for giving the Elder Races such long lives.

Djinn children were not born like humans or other embodied creatures, but were occasionally formed as two Djinn mingled energies. Their children also did not require as much intensive caretaking as the creatures of other species. They came into existence with their personalities well formed, and they inherited quite a bit of knowledge from both parents. Still, Djinn children were innocent, new to the world and filled with a mischievous lightness of being.

Phaedra's mother, Lethe, had been even more Powerful than Khalil, a first-generation Djinn who remembered the dawn of the Earth. Over time he and Lethe had become enemies, and to hurt him, Lethe took their child and tortured her. Khalil, along with a select few allies that included Carling, had rescued Phaedra and torn Lethe to shreds.

His daughter lived but didn't laugh any longer, not like

these bright, innocent humans. Occasionally Djinn sustained so much damage they became malformed. Phaedra was like that, her energy jagged and twisted. She shunned contact with others, and she was quick to lash out and cause damage. He did not know how to help her. He had never known how to help her.

At last Grace left Max and Chloe's bedroom. He heard her move back to the kitchen. She ran more water, and there were more sounds of dishes clinking and splashing. Then she moved to another room, the left room in the downstairs. That would be the office area. She was silent for a while, and then she went into the living room. He noticed how her gait changed at times. She would start walking at a smooth pace, but she quickly slowed down, and her footsteps became arrhythmic, ungraceful. It was another oddity.

She turned on the television, and that was when he slipped silent as the summer breeze through the open window into the children's bedroom.

The toys had been picked up. The floor was clear, and the room tidy. The bedroom was not quite dark because the door was open, and indirect light shone from the living room down the hall. The two beds were at opposite sides of the room. Colorful posters adorned the walls. A cheerful green frog hung over Max's crib, and a pink pig wearing a blonde wig and pearls hung over Chloe's small bed.

Khalil added the pig in the blonde wig to the growing list of things he did not understand. He hated to admit it, but the human female might have had a point.

Khalil moved silently over to check Max's still form. The baby smelled clean and was fast asleep again, his round cheeks flushed. Khalil picked up Max's hand and studied it curiously. It was even smaller and more delicate than Chloe's, a soft little starfish of flesh. These humans were such odd creatures.

When he moved over to Chloe's bed, he saw that she lay on her stomach, sucking her thumb. She smelled clean too, and her shining curls were combed. Then he saw the shadowed sparkle of her eyes, and he realized she was awake and watching him as he watched her.

He crouched to look at her. She smiled at him around her thumb. He whispered, "Do you know that I am the doggie-cat?"

She nodded.

"Clever girl." He thought a minute, trying to come up with words she might understand. It was surprisingly difficult to try to think like a small, new human might. "Do you know that I am not really a doggie or a cat?"

She nodded again.

Good. That was good. He patted her back. She felt warm and soft and a little lumpy under a light summer blanket. "Do you know that you should not pull a real doggie's tail or a real cat's tail either? And you should not poke them in the eye?"

She popped her thumb out of her mouth and whispered, "Indeed?"

He frowned, suspicious. "Do you understand what that word means?"

She shook her head.

He sighed. "I see we have things to work on."

She asked, "Can you be a horsie too?"

Ah. Small, noisy and remarkably tenacious. He was learning a great deal about new humans.

"I don't think we should be having this conversation right now," Khalil whispered. He wanted to pick her up and hug her but restrained himself.

She snickered sleepily. "Indeed."

He patted her back again.

Indeed.

The Bane of Her Existence might have disappeared from sight, but he still hadn't left. Grace could still sense his presence hanging in the air, like the aftermath of a bonfire.

Why hadn't he gone? What attracted him, and how could she change it, so that he would lose interest and leave for good?

Grace considered the problem of the unwelcome Djinn, while the matronly ghosts murmured to each other and she cleaned up the kitchen.

The babysitting roster wasn't the only assistance Grace received from the witches. Jaydon Guthrie, the head of one of the oldest covens in Louisville, had arranged for a quarterly community work day to help her with basic maintenance on the property. As Jaydon said, the work days would benefit more than just Grace. They would also provide a way for witches to volunteer several hours at a time, which would help those who were behind on their community service tithe. Grace had been too desperate to consider turning the offer down.

On the first work day, she had used their help to arrange things so that she and the children were mostly using the ground floor. The kitchen was spacious and had a dining nook with a table, a high chair and four chairs, so they didn't need a separate dining area. When Petra and Niko had decided to have children, they had installed a stacked washer and dryer in the kitchen so that Petra wouldn't have to go into the basement very often. The ground floor also had a half bath.

Grace had the large dining table and chairs stored in the garage, the downstairs office moved into the dining room and Chloe and Max's bedroom set up in what had once been the office. She slept on a futon in the office/dining room. That meant she only had to climb the stairs when it was bath time or when she needed to get a change of clothes. The downstairs was cooler in the summer, and it was easier on her leg, so the solution worked for now. Gradually her clothes were coming down the stairs and not making it back up again. She had started storing things in a filing cabinet in one corner of the office.

Saturday was the next work day. Maybe she could get someone to move a dresser downstairs. Simple things like that could make a hard situation a lot more bearable. She put the wet load of clothes from the washer into the dryer. Then she washed up at the kitchen sink, sticking her head under the faucet and soaping her fine, short hair with the baby shampoo she had used on the kids.

Even with two fans running downstairs, the house was too hot. She gave in and went into the office to dig through the filing cabinet for lighter clothes, slipping on a tank top and cutoff shorts made from a pair of old, soft sweatpants. After all, she wasn't expecting company, and she didn't have to look at herself if she didn't want to.

Anyway, it was time she got used to how her body had changed. Maybe she shouldn't ignore how she looked. Maybe she should look at herself until the scars didn't matter anymore. They would fade over time and become less noticeable. At the moment they were still an angry, raw-looking red.

Grace had been riding in the backseat of the car at the time of the accident. That had saved her life. The head-on collision had driven the front seat back into her. She had scars on both legs, but the real damage was to her right leg, where she had suffered extensive tearing in the cartilage of her knee. The surgeon had done what she could to repair the damage, but Grace, who had once run track in high school and had considered training for Louisville's half marathon, would never run again. The surgeon had also warned she might still have to have a knee replacement at some time in the future.

A knee-replacement surgery could cost as much as $35,000, if not more. Yeah, that wouldn't be happening anytime soon. Grace did her physical therapy exercises religiously, and when she had to, she wore her knee brace. When all else failed, she used a cane. The fall from earlier was still bothering her, so she strapped on the brace and felt relief from the extra support immediately.

She sat at the desk and turned on the computer to scroll through the database on the Elder Races that Niko had created based on the journals and books written by previous Oracles. Ah, she knew there was an entry on the Djinn. She clicked on the subject to open it up and read through it quickly.

In the Demonkind demesne, the Djinn social structure was made up of five Houses—the Shaytan, the Gul, the Ifrit, the Jann and the most Powerful of them all, the House Marid. The Houses were based on relationships, much like humans conceived of clans or extended family groups. Large decisions that affected an entire House were made through consensus, with the older, more Powerful Djinn having the final say.

Djinn were creatures of magic and fire, and almost unimaginable Power. They did not value physical things or money, but traded in favors. To the Djinn, a bargain was a sacred thing, and to break a bargain was a serious crime. They were not known as forgiving creatures. Many human legends told of Djinns' malicious or mischievous behavior toward anyone who was foolish enough to make a bargain with them and then break it.

She hadn't expected to find the information quite so absorbing, but interesting though it was, the article didn't say anything about how to get rid of a Djinn that insisted on hanging around.

Thanks to her grandmother's teachings, Grace knew the steps she would take to get rid of an unwelcome ghost or a dark spirit, but a Djinn was an entirely different class of creature. Most ghosts were little more than a dead person's memories, and they tended to fade away on their own. Dark spirits like poltergeists were rudimentary things. They were residual energy from a particularly strong, malicious ghost, and while they could create physical chaos and cause harm, there was relatively little personality left with which to reason. As actual living creatures, the Djinn were much more sophisticated and Powerful. Sighing, she switched off the computer and moved to the living room.

She turned on the television to catch the tail end of the local news while she straightened up the room, picked up toys and folded laundry. When she heard the current news segment, she turned to stare at the screen. The two anchors, a man and a woman, speculated on the sudden appearance of several Elder Councillors in Louisville, but the main focus of the segment was on Dragos Cuelebre, Lord of the Wyr, and his new mate as they checked into the luxurious downtown Brown Hotel.

Cuelebre was a massive black-haired male who stood head and shoulders above almost everyone else around him. He had turned his rough-hewn face away from the camera. His arm was around a tall, slender woman with pale blonde hair. Grace recognized her from the confrontation in the meadow earlier that morning. In the aired segment she wore sunglasses that covered half of her triangular face. The woman said something to Cuelebre as they entered the hotel, and he nodded in response. They both ignored the cluster of reporters and camera crews surrounding them.

The female news anchor was speaking. "So far no one has released an official explanation for why so many Elder Races dignitaries have gathered in Louisville, other than Councillor Archer Harrow's secretary, Tara Huston, who spoke to the press this afternoon. Reading from a prepared statement, Huston said the gathering involved a private matter and had nothing to do with the sometimes tense interactions between the demesnes. However, what could that private matter be, Todd? Why would it necessitate Dragos Cuelebre's sudden presence, along with his mysterious escort who, inside sources inform us, is his new mate?" The woman's blonde hair was lacquered with so much hairspray that when she turned to face her coanchor, her entire head of hair, like a helmet, turned with her.

Todd gave the camera a practiced smile. "Good question, Joanne. Cuelebre has been under a great deal of pressure recently. Like the rest of the world stock market, Cuelebre Enterprises has taken some serious financial hits lately, although no doubt the corporation will remain in *Fortune*'s top fifty for the year. There has also been increased tension between the Wyr and the Elven demesnes. In one of the most surprising announcements of the year, Cuelebre has also lost one of his seven sentinels, Tiago Black Eagle, who resigned from his position to work for the new Dark Fae Queen, Niniane Lorelle. Cuelebre's seven sentinels are the lynchpins in

Wyr governance, so not only is Cuelebre facing financial challenges and border strife, he is also critically short-staffed. Whatever the 'private matter' is here in Louisville, it must be something urgent for him to be called away from New York on short notice. . . ."

As she listened, Grace realized that the news channel didn't know anything of what had really happened earlier. They didn't mention the gathering at her property, and they stated that Cuelebre had lost only one sentinel, not two. Apparently Rune's resignation as Cuelebre's First sentinel had not yet been made public. The segment was really a gossip piece that focused on Cuelebre because he was one of the media's favorite subjects.

She lost interest in the talking heads and switched off the TV. Sweat trickled between her breasts. She limped to the floor fan to position it in front of the screen door so it would pull in the cooler air from outside.

As she did, she glanced out at the deepening dusk.

Two tall figures wearing cloaks were walking up the gravel driveway to her house. The taller, broader figure glanced at the setting sun and pushed back his hood to reveal strong, aquiline features and dark hair sprinkled with flecks of white at the temples. It was Julian Regillus, the Vampyre Nightkind King. The second figure pushed back his hood as well. That man had shoulder-length, nut brown hair and a pleasant, nondescript face, and he was one of the most feared hunters in all the Elder Races, Julian's right-hand man, the Vampyre Xavier del Torro.

Vampyres were walking up her driveway.

She had met Vampyres before. Not often, but she had. Those she had met seemed like perfectly pleasant people.

The two Vampyres approaching her house were not perfectly pleasant people. They were two of the most Powerful Vampyres in the world. And their companion had been the one to pull a sword in a place that inter-demesne law had decreed a sanctuary for all races and people.

Laws were a lot like locks; they were only as effective as the people who chose to allow them to work.

Adrenaline roared along her veins as if shot from a rocket launcher. She shifted the floor fan out of the way, closed the front door and, ridiculously, locked it. An invisible vise squeezed her ribs, and she couldn't breathe. Stupidly, she thought of Niko's old shotgun, which was unloaded and stored at the top of the kitchen pantry. She knew how to use the shotgun, but even if she had time to retrieve and load it, the only thing she would accomplish by waving it around would be to piss the Vampyres off. It couldn't cause them any real damage.

Her gaze fell. She hadn't had time to vacuum before putting the children to bed, and the floor was still sprinkled with crushed pretzels. The crumbs outlined a shoeprint the size of Chloe's foot.

Vampyres are coming to my house, she thought. And there's no one here but me, two little children and assorted ghosts.

Along with one arrogant, child-loving Djinn.

Khalil is one of the oldest and strongest of the Demon-kind, Carling had said to her earlier that morning. *If he promises to keep your children safe, he will keep them safe.*

"Um, hello?" she said to the silent, empty-seeming house. Her voice was shaking as much as her hands. "Can we talk for a minute?"

The silence acquired a listening attitude. Khalil, however, did not appear.

"There isn't much time, and I know you can hear me," she whispered. *"Please."*

Black smoke drifted across the living room floor. A tendril of it lifted in front of her and formed in the semblance of Khalil's face. The face regarded her with about as much friendliness as the black cat had earlier.

She clenched her hands into fists. The article might not have told her much about Djinn, but it had said they loved to bargain. Material things meant little to them. What they traded in were favors. She said in a low voice, "We may not like each other much, but we both care about my niece and nephew, don't we?"

Khalil raised a dusky, elegant eyebrow.

A firm knock sounded at the door. She startled violently. She switched to telepathy and spoke fast. *I would like to offer you a bargain. If you protect me and the kids from the Vampyres, I'll owe you a favor.*

The smoky Khalil-face cocked to one side as he considered the human female's words. She really was a foolish creature, he thought. He had said he offered her a gift beyond price that she did not value. Now he realized she truly did not understand what he had meant. He had already promised he would look after the babies, and he had not put a time limit on that offer. And part of looking after the babies meant ensuring the safety of their caregiver, whom they loved and depended upon so much.

Now she meant to bargain for something he had already given freely? He almost laughed. He took note of her rapid heartbeat and dilated eyes, and he realized she was truly in a panic.

A compassionate creature might have cared about that and not taken advantage of it, but the Djinn weren't known for their compassionate natures.

And he certainly was not responsible for her poor bargaining skills.

Another, louder knock sounded. "Ms. Andreas, please answer the door," del Torro said. His voice was as pleasant and nondescript as his appearance. "We know you are in there."

You and the babies have my protection from the Vampyres, Khalil said, his mental voice as smooth as a rope of silk slipping over her neck. *At a time of my choosing, you will do anything I ask you to do, for the sum of one favor. Agreed?*

She gave him a jerky nod. *Agreed.*

Khalil gave Grace a sulfurous smile. Intending to take on a full physical form with which to greet the Vampyres, he let the smoke-face dissipate and . . .

Grace straightened her spine, assumed a calm if tight expression and turned to open the door.

Khalil had to admit, that surprised him a little. After the

human had evidenced such panic, he hadn't thought she had
it in her. She still smelled of fear, but her energy crackled
with anger too. She clearly didn't like how the Vampyres had
frightened her. Since it was also clear she had the ability to
sense his presence, he decided to hold off on materializing
to see how she dealt with what waited on her doorstep.

Grace felt Khalil looming behind her as she looked
through the fine mesh of the screen door at the two Vampyres on her porch. Earlier that morning in the clearing,
there had been so much concentrated Power from so many
entities, she'd had trouble sensing which Power belonged to
whom. She'd felt surrounded by a formless heat, as if she
had been engulfed by a solar flare.

Now she had no difficulty sensing the intense Power that
the Vampyre males carried. She faced two disasters dead
ahead with a calamity at her back, and that was more than
enough to dry out her mouth and keep her heart racing.

"What do you want?" she said to the Nightkind King.

Wow, listen to me, she thought. I sound kinda rude, don't
I? Get me a Djinn like a gun in my holster, and I lose all my
manners.

Julian Regillus's dark gaze met hers. She felt the draw
from his eyes through the screen door. "I want to talk with
the Oracle, of course."

The Nightkind King's voice was deep and rough, like a
shot of raw whiskey. He had opened the front of his cloak to
the warm summer night, and he wore a plain black shirt and
black trousers underneath. He was broad across the chest
and shoulders, flat through the abdomen and heavily muscled. This close, she could see that when he had been mortal,
he had not aged particularly well. He looked like he was in
his late forties when he had been turned, so he had probably
been in his midthirties. His rough features were weather-
beaten, lined at the eyes and at the corners of a stern mouth.
Though he kept his hair military short, somehow he gave the
impression of a shaggy wolf that watched her every move.

In contrast to his King, the killer that stood beside him
appeared almost slender, del Torro's long, lean body disguis-

ing what must be a terrible whipcord strength. Xavier del
Torro looked like he had been turned in his early to mid-
twenties. He could still embody the illusion of youthfulness,
with eyes that were somewhere between gray and green, a
clear complected skin and refined features that somehow
missed being either handsome or delicate.

Del Torro's turning had been a famous event in history.
A younger son of Spanish nobility, he had been a priest until
the Tribunal of the Holy Office of the Inquisition tortured
and destroyed a community of peaceful Vampyres near his
home in Valencia. The Vampyre community had included
del Torro's older sister and her husband. After the massacre,
del Torro walked away from the Catholic Church and approached Julian, who turned him into a Vampyre and set
him to cut a swath through the officers of the Inquisition.
The ten years that followed were some of the bloodiest in
Spanish history.

While in theory Grace didn't have a problem with someone who had decided to go after the Inquisition, um, yikes.

Grace turned her attention back to Julian. "What do you
want to talk about?"

Del Torro turned his attention from studying the front of
her house and gave her a pleasant smile. He asked, "Is this
how you offer sanctuary to strangers?"

"You're rich and Powerful," she said. "You don't need
sanctuary. You need a luxury hotel suite downtown. And you
lost any right to sanctuary this morning when your friend
pulled a sword on my land."

Behind her, Khalil's presence flared in surprise, and she
realized he hadn't known what had happened. His attention
must have been focused on the house. He coiled tightly
around her.

Julian shifted, a sharp, abrupt movement, and del Torro
lost his easy smile. "We did not know that she came armed
or what she intended to do," Julian said.

"That seems somewhat careless of you," Grace said. "Is it
supposed to make me feel better about letting you into my
house? Because it doesn't."

"We had no argument when the Wyr killed her," Julian said. "We agreed that was justice."

Was that sincerity or expediency? Something was in the Vampyre's voice, but whatever the emotion was, it was more complex and nuanced than she knew how to name. He was thousands of years old, and she was twenty-three. She wasn't even going to try to understand him, because she knew she couldn't.

"Still not feeling reassured," Grace told him. "I'm not up to a second consultation in one day. Why don't you just ask me whatever it is you want to ask me, so I can answer, and you can go away?"

Julian said, "I want to know what you and Carling talked about."

Del Torro's gaze lowered. He moved suddenly and muttered under his breath. *"Madre de Dios."*

She looked down.

Black smoke wafted around her, covering her from the waist downward. She drifted fingers through the top of it. It curled and eddied just like real smoke. Khalil was making his presence known to the Vampyres in no uncertain terms. She stirred the smoke with a forefinger. It looked really neat, actually, like she was standing in the mouth of a volcano. Or maybe in the mouth of hell.

"Meet my companion," she said. "He's not very friendly."

Khalil Somebody Important. Which probably meant he was the Bane of More Than One Person's Existence. He might possibly be the Bane of Quite a Few Peoples' Existences. For the first time since meeting him, Grace felt almost cheerful.

Khalil's presence expanded to fill the room behind her. She glanced over her shoulder. Black smoke lifted like gigantic wings over her head. Out of it wicked crystalline eyes watched the males.

Well, ain't that another kick in the head.

"There are small children asleep in this house," hissed Khalil. "And the Oracle has made herself quite clear. You are not welcome here."

She turned back to face Julian, who stood with blazing eyes and his jaw clenched. He stepped forward and moved his angry face closer to the screen. The black smoke that was Khalil came down over her in a transparent veil. Julian said icily, "We do not hurt children."

Grace rubbed her forehead and tried to think. She could live with not making friends with the Nightkind King, but making an enemy of him would be downright foolish.

"Look, you might not know what happens when the Oracle speaks," she said bluntly. "But we aren't really in control of the experience. Sometimes we remember what is said, and sometimes we blank out. I don't remember what happened with Carling. I went blank, and the next thing I knew, I was on my knees and the whole thing was over. You have truthsense. You must know I'm telling the truth. Supposedly those of you who are so much older than I can tell that sort of thing, so there's no point in you returning. I've got nothing to tell you."

Julian gave her a long, hard look. She felt the weight of his personality and his age in that look. Surrounded as she was in Khalil's veil of protection, she still shivered. Then Julian inclined his head and walked away. Del Torro did not linger either but turned on his heel and followed.

Grace watched as the two men traveled down her driveway to disappear beyond the bushes and trees that bordered the front of her property. The veil of black smoke pulled away from her. She could sense Khalil shooting after the two Vampyres, hopefully to make certain they actually left. The rigidity left her spine, and she shook so hard she staggered and might have fallen if she hadn't clutched at the doorknob.

She felt a sudden need to look in on Chloe and Max. She grabbed the cane that she left by the front door and turned to hurry down the hall as fast as she could.

Their room was shadowed and quiet. She eased over to Chloe's small bed first and bent down to check on her. Chloe was sound asleep, her thumb half out of her mouth. Grace swallowed hard, tucked Chloe's light summer blanket around her and eased over to check on Max. He had crawled to the head of his crib and lay sideways, his feet propped up on the side bars. He was also sound asleep.

Her eyes watered. She hated when that happened. She pushed the edge of her fist against the bridge of her nose as she touched the downy wisp of hair on Max's head. His hair hadn't really started to grow in yet; he looked like a bald, happy little Charlie Brown.

Maybe the Nightkind King had spoken the truth. Maybe he hadn't known or approved of what the other Vampyre had done. Maybe they didn't hurt children, and Chloe and Max had been perfectly safe the whole time. Maybe she had over-reacted.

But she couldn't afford to risk Chloe's and Max's lives on a string of maybes. And she couldn't afford to risk her own life either, not when they depended on her so much.

Khalil coalesced beside her and looked down at Max too. She turned and gripped his forearm. "Thank you."

A creature that was not known for having a compassion-ate nature also did not suffer from an overabundance of con-science. But as Khalil looked into Grace's full gaze and sincere, grateful expression, he might have experienced a twinge or two.

He turned his gaze to the sleeping baby. *Thank you*, she said, and that was not something a Djinn heard often. A bar-gain kept the scales balanced. There was no need for grati-tude in such an exchange.

He frowned, reluctantly searched for foreign words and found them.

"You're welcome," he said.

⇒ FOUR ⇐

Once Khalil disappeared, all the tension spilled out of Grace. Suddenly her body ached twice as much as it had before. She stopped in the half bath to brush her teeth. Then she turned off the lights as she made her way to the office/bedroom, and she stretched out on the futon. She didn't bother to put down the futon or take off the brace, even though it felt hot and tight on her leg. She had learned the hard way that when her knee ached this badly, just rolling over in her sleep might make it flare with a burning, grinding pain.

A gust of wind rustled through the trees, billowing the lace curtains in the nearby window and licking along her sweat-damp skin. The scent of green growing things drifted into the house, along with a hint of the nearby river. She stared at the shadowed ceiling, listening to the small familiar sounds of the old house settling into place. She wasn't sure how she knew, but she sensed that, while Khalil had left, he had somehow kept a tendril of connection with them. She could feel his presence in the distance, like a touch of brimstone.

A ghost walked through the downstairs. She hardly paid attention, other than to note that it was one of the old women from the kitchen. For the first month after the accident, she had gone through her days braced for the terrible possibility that Petra or Niko might appear, but neither did, and after a while she had stopped looking for them.

Her eyes were dry and felt full of grit. She closed them and willed herself to sleep. She was wretchedly tired. She was always wretchedly tired. According to the doctor, that too would pass, as she healed emotionally and physically.

The children were recovering from their own loss. Petra's friend Katherine had kept Chloe and Max while Grace had been recovering in the hospital. Too young to understand why Mommy and Daddy were never coming home again, they had been subdued and clingy when Grace had been well enough to bring them home. Now, months later, they had recovered enough to laugh and play, but they were each still prone to crying jags, and sometimes Chloe retreated into herself and refused to talk. It broke Grace's heart to see her that way.

Outside, something snapped. Grace bolted into a sitting position and yanked the curtains aside to stare into the night. Her pulse thundered in her ears.

—*pulled a sword*—

—*Vampyres, walking up her driveway*—

The killing. The golden monster that Rune had become had split the Vampyre's body with claws as long as scimitars. For one moment bright red liquid sprayed everything around them. Then the blonde Vampyre's body, along with her blood, had disintegrated to dust, and Grace had been left staring at the empty space where the woman had stood.

Just outside her window, a raccoon waddled out from the bushes underneath the nearby trees, followed by three half-grown kits. The breath shook out of her as she watched the animals wander across the lawn. She knew where the raccoons were headed. They were going to check out the trash bins beside the garage. Living on a five-acre property meant

the wildlife was opinionated and abundant. Just as the rest of
her family had done for years, Grace kept the trash bins
latched, but the raccoons never gave up hope.

She let go of the curtain and put a hand to her forehead.
Then she clenched that hand into a fist.

Get a fucking grip, already, she told herself.

Okay, but how?

Confront the problem head-on. Solve it.

She pushed off the futon, limped over to the desk and
turned on the computer. Then she composed a draft of an
e-mail outlining her problem. Who should she send it to—
Isalynn LeFevre? As the elected Head of the witches' demesne
and a U.S. senator, LeFevre was one of the most powerful
legislators in the States. Or should Grace send the e-mail to
the Elder tribunal, care of Councillor Archer Harrow? Most
of the Elder tribunal had been here when sanctuary was vio-
lated; they already knew what had happened.

Grace sat back in her chair, staring at the screen. The computer clock read 12:17 A.M. She had no business e-mailing
anybody after midnight, let alone powerful and sophisticated lawmakers. Slowly she clicked to save the e-mail as a
draft.

She needed to think this through. She knew her own faults.
She was young, inexperienced, and she was well aware that she
was a hothead and prone to impulse. If she was Catholic, she
should probably take up permanent residence inside a confessional booth. She did not need to splatter all of that onto a
page and then make it public.

In any case, what did she really want to gain? Those
ancient, deadly creatures on the Elder tribunal lived lives
that were far more violent than anything she had ever known.
Their lives were written on large canvases, their dramas
playing out on the world stage. Inter-demesne politics, treaties and alliances, old grudges and betrayals, keeping the
peace and fighting wars. And, sometimes, murder.

So there was a violation of sanctuary. It was a single incident in more than a hundred and fifty years of her family
living on this property. As a crime statistic, one incident was

less than compelling. She imagined one of the tribunal Councillors reading her e-mail and patting a yawn.

Grace needed to be taken seriously when she spoke and not dismissed or marginalized—or at least not marginalized any more than the Oracle was already.

Besides, changing the law wouldn't do a damn thing.

So if the law couldn't offer any real solutions to her problem, she needed to find her own.

What she really wanted was to keep the children safe and to have protection when they needed it. If she only had money, she could hire a bodyguard or a security service, someone who was Powerful enough that his or her presence alone would be a strong deterrent to any potential lawbreakers.

She . . . could hire somebody . . .

She sighed, tilted her head back and closed her eyes.

She could eat humble pie, is what she could do.

"Hello, are you still there?" she asked.

Even though she spoke softly, the sound of her own voice shattered the deep, late-night silence. She couldn't sense Khalil's presence in the house or even on the property, like she had earlier. But now that she had turned her attention toward him, she could feel a tenuous thread of connection that streaked through the air like a vapor trail left from an airplane.

Still, she got no response when she called his name, not even a shift in the air. Terrific. He wasn't paying attention.

She felt the impulse to pace but stifled it. Pacing had become more trouble than it was worth. Instead, she spun the office chair in circles. Of all the foolishness she had been guilty of in her life, feeling peeved that Khalil didn't respond when she called him—especially after she had been so insistent that he go away—ranked high on the list.

Maybe he was on a date. Maybe he had a mate. Maybe he had several mates. Maybe he was watching TV. Hell, as far as she knew, maybe he didn't even need a television set, he just sucked up the information on the airwaves.

She pinched her lower lip and spun in more circles, watching the shadowed room go round and round.

An affinity to things of the spirit meant sometimes going

past the teachings from her childhood, to an understanding that resided deep in her gut. She patted along the edges of the connection, learning as she explored the thread. When she was confident she had a good sense of it, she wrapped her awareness around the thread and *yanked*.

Far in the distance, an immense cyclone whipped around to give her its full, startled attention. She stopped spinning and sat back in her chair as it streamed toward her, spitting with fury.

The cyclone exploded into the house. The window curtains spun into a knot, and all the loose papers on the desk blew around the room. Black smoke seethed in the office and coalesced into the figure of one outraged Djinn.

He wore a dark crimson tunic and trousers, his raven hair pulled ruthlessly back from that elegant, inhuman face. His ivory skin was luminous against the rich red, and his diamond eyes shone brighter than the backlit computer screen, casting the shadowed office into even deeper darkness.

Yeow. He seemed bigger when he was angry.

He snarled, "You dare?"

Well, that experiment went well. She raised her eyebrows and pinched her lower lip again. "Would you rather give me a cell phone number that I can call?"

He gave her an incredulous glare. "How did you know to do that?!"

"I'm good at what I do?" she offered. What exactly had she done? She patted the air, found the thread of connection and gave it another small, experimental tug. Sulfurous anger boiled the air. Okay. Whatever it is, it must be like pulling the tail on a cat.

He bared his teeth and hissed at her. *"Stop doing that!"*

She muttered, "Also? Apparently sometimes I can be kind of stupid."

Maybe he had been, well, having sex with his date. Mate. Mates. How inopportune was that.

If Djinn had sex. If they didn't, it might explain his perpetual bad mood. Driven by a compulsion she couldn't control, she asked, "Do you ever watch TV?"

Suddenly he was across the room and bending over her, huge hands clenched on the arms of her chair. "What do you want, human?"

She frowned, starting to get angry herself. "First you butt in where you don't belong. You trespass and visit with my kids without permission. Now you yell at me simply because I want to have a talk with you? You are an inconsistent, irascible son of a bitch, aren't you?"

He cocked his head, his eyes narrowed, and growled, "Baiting me is more than kind of stupid."

She threw up her hands. "I'm not baiting you! I called but you didn't answer! If you didn't want to be interrupted, why did you leave that thread? I had no idea Djinn were so fragile. I certainly didn't mean to hurt you when I yanked your chain." She shrugged and made a mea culpa gesture. "Okay, maybe *that* bit was baiting."

Somewhere in the house, one of the ghosts chuckled. Khalil didn't seem to notice either the ghost's presence or Grace's digs. Instead he lifted his head and stared in the direction of the hall. "Are the children all right?"

Her angry sense of mischief melted into a confused twist of emotion. This glorious, strange entity really cared about the welfare of her kids. She said quickly, "They're fine."

Those fierce diamond eyes came back around to her. "You will now tell me why you summoned me," he said in that low, pure voice of his that held not a hint of softness, "or I will make you sorry."

She lost her breath. She felt as if a five-hundred-pound Bengal tiger had padded up to growl in her face. In a way, it had. Her gaze turned wary as she searched his hard ivory face. "I . . . summoned you? I didn't realize that's what I was doing."

Khalil's penetrating eyes searched her expression. "You have no idea what you did," he said, his tone suspicious.

She rolled her eyes in exasperation. "Are you telling me you have no truthsense?" she said. "Because if you are, I'm going to ask you to pull the other one."

"Pull the other what?" he said, his face going blank.

"Pull the other leg?" He still looked mystified. She shook her head. "It's a human saying, never mind."

"I can tell you are telling the truth," he said. "I just find it hard to believe. Humans are conniving and always on the search for greater Power."

"Wow, that's pretty bigoted," she said, taken aback. He had made no secret of his dislike for her, but she'd had no idea that dislike might be part of a bigger picture. "If you think that badly of the human race, why did you promise to keep the children safe?"

"They have not yet been corrupted," he said with a scowl. "They are innocent."

Grace's neck was beginning to ache from tilting her head so far back, but she didn't want to look away for fear Khalil would take that as a sign of deception. She needed to remember what she was supposed to be eating here, and serve herself a big, delicious helping of humble pie. "Yes, they are, and I'm grateful for what you did when you promised to keep them safe," she said. "Both this morning and this evening when the Vampyres came."

Somehow what she said made him angry again. He scowled. "There is no need to thank me. You paid with a favor, and you still owe me."

She frowned. "Yes, but that doesn't mean I'm not grateful too—because I am. Maybe the Nightkind King and del Torro really didn't intend any harm, but I couldn't risk that. Chloe and Max are so vulnerable. They can't defend themselves." Bending over her chair as he was brought him too close, and his energy surrounded her. She felt like she sat in the middle of a pure argent flame. The sensation was exhilarating and uncomfortable. She broke down and put a hand to his broad, too-perfect chest and pushed lightly. "Do you mind? I could use a little space."

He frowned but straightened and backed away from her chair. It didn't help much. His physical form was the smallest part of him, like the visible tip of an iceberg. At least she could sit up in her chair and ease the pressure on her neck.

Still working on swallowing that piece of pie, she said gravely, "Thank you."

He threw her a narrow-eyed glance, and a lightbulb winked on.

Oh-ho. He didn't like to be thanked? She watched him carefully as she said, "I really appreciate it."

He threw her a glare and started to pace, and she had to suck on her cheeks to keep from letting a grin break over her face. He *definitely* didn't like to be thanked. There had to be a reason for that. And she was more than a little stupid, if she could enjoy teasing such an irascible, Powerful creature. That might put her in the unforgiveable range of TSTL— Too Stupid To Live.

The massive form he chose to wear made short work of the office floor space. She wondered if he wore the dark crimson because he enjoyed the color or if there was some other reason. It suited him, turning his tall figure into a tower of flame that matched his true, invisible presence.

She rubbed the back of her sore neck and tried to focus.

Khalil said, "You were right not to take chances with the little ones' lives."

She took a quick breath. "Do you know something I don't?"

He shook his head and said, "I know nothing more than you do about the Nightkind King's intentions, good or otherwise." His sparkling gaze moving restlessly over the chaos he had created in the room. He waved a hand impatiently. She flinched back as all the scattered papers flew through the air to land in a haphazard pile on her desk. "But you should not take risks with the children."

"Of course not," she said, looking sideways at the pile of papers. The paper on top of the pile was an upside-down electric bill. She pinched her nose and sighed. With one thing and another, she had forgotten to pay bills earlier. She had better work on that first thing in the morning.

Khalil lifted a finger. "I propose another bargain, of sorts," he said.

Her attention snapped back to him. His words echoed so closely the reasons why she had called him, she was taken aback. "You do?"

"Yes," he said. "You will ask me a question, and I will answer. Then I will ask you a question, and you will answer. The conversation is balanced. At the end, we both walk away without owing each other anything."

"You want to play a truth game?" She stared. "But that's a silly college game." The version she had seen at parties was a variation on a truth-or-dare game. Usually it involved drinking beer when one didn't want to answer.

Khalil wandered around the office. He stopped to pick up a plastic container of blank CDs from the top of the filing cabinet and examined it curiously. "Versions of that silly college game, as you call it, were played at the crossroads on the ancient passageways that led to Damascus. Men played for the chance to win riches, and they lost their heads if they dared try to lie."

She blinked rapidly several times and cleared her throat. "That brings up a good point," she said, her voice strangled. "What would be the forfeit?"

He turned to face her and bared his teeth. It was not really a smile. "Why, are you thinking of trying to cheat?"

"No, I just—I think that if we decide to do this exchange, a forfeit should be named, that's all." Was she actually considering playing a truth game with a Djinn who so obviously disliked her? She needed her head examined. Like, right now.

Those diamond eyes studied her. It was like being pinned by twin laser beams. Khalil said, "If either one of us refuses to answer, the other one will be owed a favor."

She scratched her fingers through her hair, massaging her scalp as she considered. She could see that road to Damascus in her mind's eye. The signpost had an arrow pointing one way that said SMART ROUTE and another arrow pointing the opposite way that said DUMB ROUTE. Hmm, which way to go?

In her imagination the signpost morphed into a coin flipping in the air. Smart route. Dumb route. Smart. Dumb.

She could tell by the look on his face that Khalil thought

she would be too afraid to enter into the bargain. He would almost be right about that. Clearing her throat again, she said, "The children need me. I can't enter into any agreements that would jeopardize my own safety. That goes for the other favor I owe you as well."

Sleek dark eyebrows lowered. Clearly she had surprised him. After a moment, he said, "No bargain we enter into will cause jeopardy to the children. But one can only stop when both of us have asked a question and a round is complete."

She tugged at her lower lip, considering him. She didn't really have any secrets. As the Oracle, she wasn't actually a head of state or a real Power broker in the Elder demesnes. She probably would have told him anything he chose to ask anyway, not that he necessarily needed to know that.

When else would she ever get the chance to ask a Djinn questions of her own, about dating and mating and sex and TV?

How could she ever justify this later to anyone else, much less herself? It was late, she had poor impulse control, and he was interesting. That sentence probably encapsulated every mistake every female had made throughout the history of relationships.

Even though she wasn't Catholic, she wondered if she should find a confessional booth somewhere and sit in it for a while, just for the principle of the thing. Maybe she should lock herself in the booth and throw out the key.

In a last-ditch effort to grasp hold of her sanity, she asked, "Why do you want to do this?"

He crossed his arms. "I wish information, and I will not be beholden to you for it. Enough prevaricating, human. You will either enter into the bargain or not. Choose."

Information was a valuable commodity, especially to one who was not interested in material things.

Smart. Dumb.

The coin landed.

"Okay?" she said. She hadn't meant to sound so uncertain. "Who goes first?"

"I offered the bargain," he said. He placed the plastic container of CDs back on the filing cabinet. "I ask first."

She shrugged and waited. Her idiotic heart picked up its tempo as he studied her, and the silence stretched taut between them. All the ghosts were quiet, as if waiting and watching. She felt like she was standing in a combat arena, and the audience was watching closely to see if blood might spill on the sand.

"What exactly do you know about summoning?" he asked. His laser-sharp gaze dissected every inch of her expression.

She opened her mouth and closed it again. Of course he would ask that.

She said, "I've seen summoning rituals in movies and read about them in novels, of course, but those tend to be silly, like portraying witches' covens as child-sacrificing Satanists. There are a couple of spells that witches can use to summon a boost in Power, but they don't make other creatures show up in a pentagram or compel them to obey. One calls upon the five elements—fire, wood, water, metal, earth. The other one is a spell that a witch can use to call on her own Power. I've heard that one is like calling up a rush of adrenaline. The problem with those is that they give a temporary boost, but they also drain the witch, so they can be dangerous to use, especially if the witch isn't in a safe environment to recover afterward. When I'm petitioned, I call on the Oracle's Power. I guess that's a kind of summoning too."

Khalil strolled over to the futon. Her pillow was at one end, a sheet crumpled at the other. He flicked the sheet onto the floor, tossed the pillow on top of it, and sat with as much regality as a sovereign assuming his throne. "You talk of witches as though they are different from you," he remarked.

She looked sourly at her sheet and pillow on the floor. "I don't hear a question in that," she said. "And I wouldn't have to answer if I did, would I?"

"Not for this round," he said. "Are you finished?"

"Yes," she snapped.

"Proceed with asking your question," he commanded. He crossed his arms.

He looked powerful, exotic and oddly beautiful, and his

Power filled the house again like it had the last time. It felt very male and altogether indifferent to her. By contrast, she felt sweaty, inelegant in every way and, even though she had bathed just a few hours ago, grubby. Disliking the feeling intensely, she mirrored his action, crossing her own arms, and scowled at him. "What do *you* know about summoning?"

He raised an elegant, supercilious eyebrow. "I shall assume that you do not want to hear me lecture for a month."

She could have negotiated sarcasm out of the bargain, except if she had, she would have tied her own hands as well. She spun the office chair in a circle and informed him, "I'm bored now."

"You must have the attention span of a gnat," he said.

That surprised her into laughing out loud. He looked startled and grinned. The expression brought a shocking change to his hard face. Even as she hiccupped a little and stared, the grin vanished. He said, "For the purpose of this bargain, I shall try to answer your question in a way that is complete but also with some brevity."

"I had no idea Djinn were this pedantic," she said. "It must come from all your preoccupation with bargaining."

He said between his teeth, "Do you want me to answer or not?"

She gave him a sly, sidelong look. "If you don't, doesn't that mean I get a favor? If you owe me a favor, does that cancel out the one I owe you?"

He chuckled, and that was the most dangerous sound he had made thus far. "You wish, human."

Attempting to mimic his regal, preemptory attitude, she rotated her hand in a *get on with it already* gesture, and he grinned again. He sobered and said, "I made the connection with your house when I said I would protect you and the children. Older Djinn who owe and own many favors have connections all over the world. You startled me when you pulled on it. Summoning a Djinn is calling upon any obligation they may have or favor they may owe to you. You do not compel a Djinn when you summon them, but you do . . . shall we say . . . call upon their honor. A Djinn who refuses to answer a summoning should have an overriding reason, such as answering a prior commitment, or they will be seen to have no honor, in which case no other Djinn will have anything to do with them. An honorless Djinn has no House and becomes a pariah. Since you apparently know so little about Djinn, to the point where it could be hazardous for your health, I offer you this advice for free: do not have anything to do with a pariah. Our Houses are built on our associations, and our associations are built on our word. The pariahs go against this fundamental truth. They are very dangerous. They are also, thankfully, rare."

She frowned. "I didn't know what I was doing. I could feel the thread, and I pulled on it to get your attention."

"Well," he said drily, "you did that. You pulled quite hard."

She frowned. "I'm sorry. It didn't hurt, did it?"

"No, it did not hurt. It was more like you suddenly shouted in my ear. Very disruptive and annoying."

As they talked, he appeared to relax. Or at least he was less menacing. He might be indifferent to her, but she wasn't indifferent to him. She wished she didn't enjoy the sense of being immersed in his intensely male presence, but she had to admit she did. To be honest, she wanted to roll around in the sensation like it was catnip.

Instead she sighed, tugged her lip and spun the chair. She said, "That's why you were Mr. Grumpy Guts when you showed up."

"Mr. . . ." He shook his head and snorted. "Stop doing that."

"Stop doing what, spinning the chair?" Feeling childish, she put a bare toe to the floor and deliberately shoved the chair into another rotation.

"Stop pulling at your lip," he ordered. "It is time for a new round of questions, and it is my turn to ask you something."

She sighed and stopped pulling at her lip. Inwardly, she was rather pleased with how the whole truth game had gone so far. Not only was she learning something, but Khalil was unexpectedly entertaining . . . in an entirely rude and insufferable sort of way. It wasn't as though she liked him. But conversing with him beat lying sleepless on the futon and freaking herself out at every stray nighttime noise. And frankly, she couldn't remember the last time she'd had this long of a conversation with another adult. She would pay for it in the morning when the children woke up at the crack of dawn, but she would have paid for her sleepless night one way or another.

She said, "So ask."

Khalil regarded her with a heavy-lidded gaze. He took so long, she stopped her chair and scowled at him. That was when she noticed he was looking at her brace, his expression curious. He asked, "Why do you wear that black contraption on your leg?"

Her gut clenched. His question was as artless as a child's, but it still hurt. She breathed evenly through pinched nostrils until she could unclench enough to answer. She said shortly, "I was in the car accident that killed my sister and her husband. My knee is damaged, so sometimes I have to wear a brace."

He frowned. "This is also why you use a cane."

She looked down at her leg, nodding. Suddenly he was crouched in front of her chair. She nearly jumped out of her skin. "Don't do that!"

But his attention was on her leg. He was still frowning. "I want you to show me."

She almost lashed out at him, physically as well as verbally, but his fascination was so alien, so outside normal human boundaries of behavior, it caught her own attention. Slowly she unbuckled the straps on the brace and pulled it off. Her slender leg was bare from the ragged edge of the cutoff shorts to her naked foot.

Khalil took hold of her, one huge hand at her ankle and the other slipping underneath her knee, and he pulled her leg out straight. His hands were quite careful and inhumanly hot, as if his physical form contained an inferno of energy. While he studied the mass of red scars, she studied him by the indirect light of the computer screen. Her stomach clenched again as he probed her knee with a light tendril of Power, but she let him explore the injury in silence.

He wasn't exactly compassionate. If he had been, she

would have shoved him away. No, his impartial attitude had a strange effect on her. She found herself relaxing and studying her own knee with dispassion, as if it belonged to someone else. It was the first time since the accident that she had been able to do so.

"This has been cut open," he said. He sounded shocked.

"I had to have a couple of surgeries," she said. His quick diamond gaze met hers, and she shrugged. "I'm lucky to be alive, but that doesn't stop me from complaining."

"Your flesh is so fragile," he murmured. "And even though you are still healing, it is too late to repair your knee by Powerful means."

She said drily, "Even in the witches' demesne, doctors with that kind of Power are rare. I didn't have health insurance or the money to pay for that kind of treatment. I guess the concept of permanent physical damage must seem pretty foreign to you."

He shot her a quick, upward glance from under frowning brows. "I understand permanent damage," he said. "I have struck down my enemies before, both those bound in flesh and those who are folk of the air. Djinn can be damaged. My daughter is."

Surprise pulsed. She said, "I'm sorry."

Instead of replying, he took the brace and fitted it around her leg again. She took over to strap it into place. Her voice was a little hoarse as she said, "It's my turn to ask you a question."

"Yes," he said. He sat back on his heels. His expression had turned inscrutable.

It was her turn to fall silent. Somehow asking him about dates, mates, sex and TV seemed too childish given the turn in their conversation. She studied him, considering questions and casting each one aside. Either one of them could put an end to the truth game after she asked him her question and this round ended. She wanted to make sure she asked something as useful as possible.

His expression turned irritable. "Are you going to ask me something or pay the forfeit?"

She raised her eyebrows. "Don't try to rush me. We didn't negotiate a time limit on asking our questions."

"Very good, human," said Khalil. He sounded surprised and somewhat amused. "You might learn to be an effective bargainer, given enough practice."

"The more you talk and distract me, the more time I might need to think," Grace warned.

He laughed as he stood. The laughter was real, and it danced through his energy along with a physical ripple in his low, pure voice. She shivered, and a sprinkle of goose bumps rose along her skin. She'd had no idea that a Djinn could be so fascinating.

She shoved that thought aside as she spun her chair in another circle, more slowly this time. Then she caught sight of her computer screen. The saved-as-draft notification still showed on her e-mail program, reminding her of why she had called Khalil in the first place.

She turned back to face him. She needed to phrase this carefully so she didn't waste an opportunity. Making sure that she said a statement and didn't frame it as a question, she said, "When the Vampyres were here, we spoke of someone who was killed on the property earlier today."

He gave her a thoughtful look. "Yes. I have since learned the details of the incident."

She gripped the arms of her chair until her knuckles whitened. "What happened was an excellent example of how meaningless the law of sanctuary can be."

"I cannot argue with that."

Grace licked her lips. "The Oracle's Power doesn't work like other witches' Power, and I don't have offensive spells. I would like to . . . hire you, I guess, for lack of a better term. Do I have anything you might value enough that I can bargain with you for continuing protection for me and the children?"

Khalil's expression shuttered. "Yes," he said.

≡ FIVE ≡

Khalil watched with interest as Grace's expression fell. Usually he enjoyed that look of disappointment on humans' faces. He wondered why he didn't this time.

She said, "I didn't phrase the question right, and you answered me." She rubbed the back of her neck and slumped in her seat.

For a moment, all the young human's spitfire was doused. She looked so weary and discouraged, Khalil felt moved to . . . something.

He was not moved to point out that she was asking for something he had already granted her, nor did he see any reason to inform her that she'd already thrown away one favor. That went against every Djinn instinct he had. She needed to learn to pay better attention. Bargaining and negotiation were skills that every youngling Djinn had to work to acquire, and there was no better way to learn that than practicing in real life.

He might not have recognized "pull the other one" but despite how he had baited her earlier, he had in fact associated amicably with quite a few humans throughout his long existence, and he knew some slang and colloquialisms. He believed there was an appropriate saying for a time such as this. It was called learning from the school of hard knocks.

No, he felt moved to something else, something strange that he poked at curiously. He pointed out, "You are too tired to continue this conversation properly."

She lifted a shoulder in a desultory shrug, her gaze unfocused. "I suppose you're right. It's been a hard day, and a rare one. I've never seen anybody killed before."

That jolted him. Was she really that young and innocent herself?

She continued, drily, "Even though it was justified, I'm still rattled, although I doubt a troop of rabid monkeys is going to escape from the zoo and attack in the next few hours. I will try to come up with a bargain that interests you another time."

What would it be like to watch someone else get killed for the first time and to know you did not have the Power to prevent something like that from happening again? His own Power roused and twisted upon itself at the thought. He would not like it. He would not like it at all. That was when he realized she had been so angry and contentious throughout the day because she had been frightened.

Perhaps this human was not quite so awful after all. He wouldn't go so far as to admit he liked her. But even though the damage she had sustained clearly pained her, her lack of self-pity was respectable enough. And her cheeky attitude was unexpectedly amusing.

Then there were the children to consider.

He crossed his arms and sighed. "You will let me visit with the children anytime I wish."

Her gaze shot up to his. She looked startled and suddenly very alert, and a touch of fire came back into her energy. Ah, that was better, Khalil decided. He had to admit: he did like her fire.

"No," she said.

He lifted an eyebrow. "You're the one who wanted to bargain with me," he pointed out. "I am merely presenting a term that would be acceptable to me."

She watched him with the kind of wariness with which one might watch a poisonous snake. "You can visit with Chloe and Max anytime you like," she said, "but only when I'm present. I don't want to see anything else happen like this talking cat nonsense."

"That was not merely nonsense, as you say," he said irritably. "I did have a reason for doing it." Really, he was not usually so irascible. This female had a talent for bringing that out in him.

Grace's slender eyebrows rose. She said, "I hardly dare to ask."

His mouth tightened. He was not inconsistent either, and stating a reason for the purposes of making an argument was not the same thing as acting defensive. He said, "I merely wished to develop a rapport with the children, so that I would not frighten them whenever I might show up."

Small indentations appeared on either side of her shapely mouth. What were those indentations called again? Ah, yes. Dimples. She said, "Aw, you wanted to make friends with them. You wanted them to like you. You were bribing them."

"I was not bribing them." He glared.

Her dimples disappeared as quickly as they had appeared. She said sternly, "What I say goes for anything that has to do with the kids. You may know a lot of things—and believe it or not, I mean this with respect—but you do not know human children well enough to know what's good for them. If you have questions or concerns, you can talk to me telepathically or some time when they're not around, so we don't argue in front of them again and upset Chloe. That's the only deal I will accept that involves the children."

He sucked a tooth to avoid a sudden smile. She went from dejection to dictating in a matter of seconds. He approved. He also approved of her protectiveness for the little ones. "Agreed," he said. "The connection is in place. You've already shown yourself to be proficient at . . . how did you say . . . yanking my chain. You may summon me at any time if you feel alarmed or in need. I will stop by some time tomorrow to begin collecting on my end of the bargain, so plan for my visit with the little ones. Now, go to bed."

He lingered just long enough to watch for her reaction to his order. She sat very straight, and a sarcastic, angry look crossed her face. As she opened her mouth, he chuckled to himself and vanished.

Khalil might have a talent for rubbing Grace the wrong way, but she had to give him credit for one thing: once he disappeared after their talk, she was able to stretch out on the futon and fall asleep.

That didn't last nearly long enough. Something squashed her nose.

Her eyes popped open. She stared into Chloe's upside-down face as the girl hung over the end of the futon. Chloe was grinning. Her blonde hair stood around her head in a nimbus. Some might even compare it to an angel's halo.

Grace knew better. She said groggily, "Pushing my wake-up button never gets old for you, does it?"

Chloe giggled and shook her head. She pushed Grace's nose again with a forefinger. "Wakey, wakey, Gracie," Chloe said. "When am I going to get a big-girl bed?"

Grace sighed. Chloe had a small toddler bed, which wouldn't be suitable for much longer. She needed a regular twin-sized bed soon. "I've told you before, baby girl, we'll get you a new bed as soon as we can afford one."

"Yeah, but when will that be? I'm too big to sleep in a little bed anymore."

"I know you are, honey," Grace mumbled.

The only other beds in the house were upstairs. Grace had lived at home while she went to college, so she had a double bed in her bedroom, and the bed in Petra and Niko's old room was a queen. Not only were those too big for Chloe, but they wouldn't fit in the children's downstairs bedroom. Maybe she could trade Chloe's toddler bed to somebody for a twin-sized one. Petra's friend Katherine ran a daycare.

Katherine might know of someone who needed a toddler bed and was interested in a trade.

Grace put an arm around Chloe and hugged her while she looked at the window. The lace curtains still hung in a knot from Khalil's furious entrance last night. Outside, the morning brightened past dawn, and birds were yelling at the top of their lungs. In Grace's experience, early morning birds never sang. Instead, they bellowed. Grace had gotten perhaps five hours' sleep. It was going to be another long day.

She asked, "Is Max awake?"

"Uh-huh," Chloe said. "Can we have pancakes for breakfast?"

"If we do, will you eat the other half of Max's banana?" Grace asked. Getting Chloe to eat fruits and vegetables was a constant challenge.

Chloe tilted her delicate jaw. "Bananas disturb me," she said.

Grace burst out laughing. "Where on earth did you learn that?"

Clearly pleased with herself, Chloe grinned. "Pancakes, one bite of banana," she offered, with a bargaining wiliness worthy of a Djinn.

"No, Chloe."

"Fine! Ugh! You never let me have anything I want!" Chloe turned to stomp out of the office.

Grace called after her, "You're getting pancakes, aren't you?"

"Just wait until I'm big enough to push the grocery cart around!" Chloe shouted from the living room. "We're never going to buy bananas again!"

Grace burst into a fresh peal of laughter. Chloe in a temper was a sight to behold.

Max was as sunny natured as his sister was tempestuous. Grace found him humming and burbling in his crib. "Eeeee!" he said happily when he saw her.

"Good morning to you too, sunshine," she said. She changed his diaper then picked him up to kiss him all over his soft, round face. He giggled and threw his arms around her neck. She held him tight for a moment. Sometimes she felt like she couldn't breathe for worrying about how she would take care of these kids. She felt too young and far too inadequate, but gods, she loved them with all of her heart.

In the kitchen, she settled Max into his high chair while Chloe climbed into her booster seat, the Lala Whoopsie doll dangling from one hand. Chloe set the doll on her lap and looked expectant. Grace peeled a banana, and Max's eyes lit up. He had developed enough dexterity to pick up bites of food with his thumb and forefinger, so she cut up part of a banana and set it in a bowl in front of him. "Mmm," he said delightedly and set to work.

When she set the other half of banana in front of Chloe, the little girl scowled. "Why can't we have pancakes first?"

Grace said, "Because I haven't cooked them yet. Besides, you need to eat your banana first."

Chloe said, "You're bad."

That was going too far. Grace said sternly, "That's enough, young lady. You have two choices. You can choose to eat your banana and be nice and get pancakes, or you can choose to get cereal and go to your room after breakfast."

In Grace's mind, the coin from last night tossed into the air. Smart. Dumb. Poor Chloe was going to be living in the confessional booth beside Grace's if she didn't watch out. Grace understood her niece probably a lot better than Chloe thought.

"But you promised!" Chloe wailed.

"I never promised to cook pancakes for girls who try to get out of eating their banana like they said they would and who say mean things to me," Grace said. She looked at Max. His cheeks were full, and he already had fruit smeared in his wispy hair. Okay. Another bath after breakfast for that one. Chloe turned red and started to cry as she ate her half of the banana in fast, furious bites. And a meltdown for the eldest one, and it wasn't even seven o'clock yet.

Grace headed in desperation for the coffeemaker. Apparently it was going to be one of those mornings. Funny how often those happened after a short night's sleep.

She set the machine to brew an extra-strong pot, because these days caffeine was her best friend. The coffeemaker sat on the worn countertop beside the kitchen window. As she switched on the machine, the sunny morning darkened. She leaned over the counter to look at the sky.

The sky was blue, dotted with fluffy cumulous clouds, and directly overhead a huge portion of it rippled. Wow, was that wrong.

Before she could do more than stare, the rippling mass of nothingness descended onto the wide, neglected lawn, and for the second time in as many days, a dragon appeared on her property.

Not *a* dragon. *The* dragon. Dragos Cuelebre, the only known dragon in existence.

Cuelebre was easily the size of a private jet. He was a deep bronze color that gleamed in the early sunlight. The bronze darkened to black at the ends of his gigantic wings, tail and long, powerful legs. He turned an enormous, triangular horned head to look around the clearing with fierce, metallic gold eyes before he shimmered into a shapeshift. His form shrank into that of a massive man, almost seven feet fall in height, with bronze-colored skin, inky black hair and gold dragon's eyes.

She had to stop getting kicked in the head like this. She had to.

She looked at the brewing coffee with equal parts panic and despair. Then she looked at Chloe and Max. Chloe was tearfully muttering to the last of the banana in her hand. Max kicked a tiny plump foot as he licked his fingers.

Grace's appalled gaze traveled back to the scene outside the window. Cuelebre strode in the direction of the front of the house. He had a brutal handsomeness, as though he had been hewn out of granite, and to her mind's eye the air around him boiled with the force of his presence.

Violence is forbidden here. She had said that to Cuelebre just yesterday morning, when he had come to confront Rune and Carling, and eventually the Elder tribunal as well. Cuelebre's mate had accompanied him yesterday, but this morning the dragon was alone. He was more frightening when he was alone.

People can be taken from this place, Dragos had said. *And violence done to them elsewhere.*

Grace started to shake. She fumbled for the thread of connection to Khalil and pulled on it. She sensed him streaking toward her, his bright Power arcing like a shooting comet, then he filled the kitchen with his presence as his form coalesced beside her.

Max crowed in surprise. Chloe said, "Hello there, doggie-cat. Would you like a bite of my banana?"

Grace turned to face Khalil. He had looked powerful and exotic last night, ivory and crimson, and gleaming raven black hair. In the full light of morning he appeared more alien than ever. He wore undyed linen this time, and his ivory skin was poreless. Those piercing diamond eyes focused on her then he glanced sharply around the cheerful, domestic scene.

He gripped her shoulder in one huge hand. "What is it?"

A sharp knock sounded at the same time. Dry-mouthed, she whispered to Khalil, "Would you mind answering that, please?"

His hard, elegant face turned toward the front of the house. Then he vanished. She felt him streak toward the front door.

Grace looked at Chloe, who assumed a pious expression as she held up the last of her fruit. Chloe said, "I was only trying to share."

Grace leaned back against the counter and slid to the floor. Her bad knee protested, so she stretched out her leg. She leaned an elbow on her other, upraised knee and rested her head on the heel of that hand. Her blood pounded through her body in great sledgehammer thuds. She felt it throbbing in her eyes, at her temples. Male voices sounded in the background, but her heartbeat pounded too loudly in her ears for her to make out what Khalil and the dragon said to each other.

I can't do this, she thought. Oh, Petra, you're the one who always wanted to be the Oracle. I never wanted this. I was never supposed to *be* this. I'm not big enough, strong enough or smart enough to be the Oracle. It's too much.

So that's it, I'll quit. If I stop talking to people, the Power will go away. Won't it?

Small fingers touched lightly on her arm. Grace looked sideways under the support of her hand. Chloe knelt beside her, her blue eyes wide. "I'm sorry, Gracie," Chloe said. "You're not bad. You're good, and I love you."

Grace smiled. "Thank you, baby girl. I love you too."

"You don't have to make pancakes if you don't want." Chloe showed her other hand, which was empty. "See, I ate all my banana."

"What a good girl you are." Grace felt her eyes grow damp. She gathered Chloe up and hugged her. "You're such a good girl."

What if she rejected the Power and it did go away, just as all the family legends said it would? What if it found its way to her niece? Chloe was the only other surviving female of the Andreas family. Grace was already pretty sure Chloe was a potential.

If the Power did not pass to Chloe, was it possible for it to go dormant and wait? Grace couldn't imagine having any children of her own—Chloe and Max were more responsibility than she had ever expected to take on—but sooner or later, they would grow up and possibly have children of their own. Could the Power move on to one of their children before that girl was ready for it?

She turned her face into Chloe's soft floating hair. Like hell it would.

Woman up, Gracie. Take responsibility. Do your job.

You never have accepted this. You grew up hoping you would never have to be the Oracle, and you've been kicking against it from the moment you knew your big sister was dead. Like the accident, it just happened to you. If you can't take this on for the people like Rune and Carling who might need the Oracle's help, do it for the children. And make damn sure you live a good, long life while you're at it, so Chloe can have the same kind of happy, carefree childhood you had.

Her arms tightened protectively on Chloe's delicate body. "I am going to make you the best pancakes you ever had," Grace said. "The very, very best. But first I need for you to be a big girl for a few minutes. Would you keep your brother busy so I can go talk to the man at the front door? You can show Max your doll."

Chloe smiled. "Okay."

"Thank you, sweetie."

"Welcome."

Chloe scampered to the table, grabbed up her doll and shoved it in Max's face. Max had been fingering the top of his sticky head thoughtfully. He laughed and reached for the doll as Chloe danced it around on his high-chair tray.

Feeling twice as clumsy as usual, Grace grabbed hold of the counter and used it to haul herself to her feet, balancing all of her weight on her good leg. She hurried toward the front of the house. Tension and antagonism crackled in the air like thunder and lightning. Khalil stood in front of the screen door, arms crossed and expression stony. On the other side of the flimsy barrier an angry dragon towered in human form.

"I see we're not getting along," Grace said breathlessly as she came up beside Khalil. She put a hand on Khalil's bicep and said telepathically, *Thank you.*

He threw her a disgusted glance.

Hilarity bubbled up. Oh, yes, that's right, he didn't like to be thanked. Well, that was his problem. She kept her hand on Khalil's arm and turned to the Lord of the Wyr. "Good morning. What can I do for you? Can I help you quickly, or did you want to consult with the Oracle? I'm in the middle of feeding two children, so if you want a consultation, it will have to wait until after breakfast."

The dragon's hot gold gaze shifted from Khalil to her, and she felt the impact to her bones. "Interesting," said Cuelebre. "How did you get a prince of the House Marid to answer your door like a servant?"

"Do not answer that," Khalil said between his teeth. "It is none of his business."

Grace had, in fact, been about to answer Cuelebre's question. Her mouth hung open for a moment before she shut it with a snap.

According to the database article she had read, the House Marid was the most Powerful of the all the Houses of Djinn. So Khalil was a prince? The article hadn't mentioned anything about royalty, just that the Houses used consensus in decision making. She filed the observation under "irrelevant at the moment but interesting enough to pursue at a later time."

"Hungry kids," she said to Cuelebre. "Ticktock."

This was the second demesne ruler that she had been rude to in as many days. Clearly she was on a roll. She had just five more demesne rulers in the United States to go. Give her to the end of the month, and she would have plenty of time to piss off everybody. Probably the confessional booth she would soon call home should be in a foreign country where no one knew her name.

Underneath her fingertips, laughter danced through Khalil's energy. She glanced up and was startled to discover his expression was as stony as ever.

Cuelebre said, "I do not consult with Oracles."

Her attention returned to the dragon's brutal, impenetrable face. She thought, I bet you don't. You would not let yourself become that vulnerable to a stranger.

Cuelebre continued. "I came to find out what happened between you, Carling Severan and my First sentinel yesterday."

"Funny how many people want to know about that," Grace muttered. Even though Rune had made his resignation clear yesterday morning, apparently Cuelebre was still not acknowledging it.

Khalil said coldly, "You should have told me what you wanted when I asked why you were here, dragon. I could have told you the Oracle doesn't remember anything from that consultation."

Cuelebre's gold gaze did not waver from hers. "Is this true?"

She sighed. "Not that it's any of your business—it wasn't

any of the Nightkind King's business either—but yes, that's true. I don't remember what happened."

Just as Julian had reacted, something flickered over Cuelebre's face, only this time Grace fancied she understood a little of Cuelebre's expression. There was a touch of weariness, perhaps, or maybe disappointment. Cuelebre's broad shoulders might have sagged a fraction of an inch.

Of all the challenges the Lord of the Wyr faced, he had chosen to take the time to come here and to ask her this question. She wondered if he would miss his First. She thought maybe he would. Or maybe she imagined all of it.

Ignoring Khalil, Cuelebre gave her a curt nod and turned to go.

Something stirred deep inside, a familiar, Powerful leviathan. Shocked, she sucked in a breath and called out, "Wait!"

Cuelebre had reached the path. He pivoted on one heel, inhumanly fast for someone so large.

Grace said to Khalil, "Stay with the kids for a few minutes? Please?" Her own voice sounded strange and disconnected from her.

His eyes narrowed on her, but he said, "Very well."

She unlocked the screen door and walked down the porch steps toward Cuelebre.

As she approached him, a shadowy, ancient tide welled. It came from an endless ocean that touched everything, flowed everywhere. Even though the bright morning was sunlit all around, this tide came from the dark of the Oracle's moon.

Part of her remained astonished. She had been taught that the Oracle's Power was something so deep, they must access it from the recesses of the Earth. The most ancient traditions from Delphi held that the Oracle must speak from a temple in a cavern. Of the seven Elder Races gods, Nadir was the Oracle's goddess, the goddess of the depths. Grace had never heard of the Power rising, uncalled, in the full light of day.

The tide filled her up, covered her eyes, spilled out of her mouth. She heard words and knew she was talking, but she could not focus on what she said, because someone else was speaking quietly. That quiet voice grew in strength until it became a gigantic noise, like the roar from an invading army.

"Nevertheless, the question remains unanswered. Do the stars feel pain? When the sun flares to its death, will it do so in agony? We must choose to believe it will, for the Light is a creature just as is the Dark. . . . It is impossible for those living to look upon me and not to speak of the nature of evil, for the living cannot grasp the true meaning of who I am. Lord Death himself has forgotten that he is but a fraction of the whole, for I am not form but Form, a prime indivisible. All these things were set in motion at the beginning, along with the laws of the universe and of Time itself. The gods formed at the moment of creation, as did the Great Beast, as did Hunger, as did Birth along with Finality, and I am the Bringer of the End of Days. . . ."

Then a vision came hurtling out of nowhere, and a vast scene slammed into Grace. She vaguely sensed her body tilting as she lost her balance, but it felt as though it happened from a great distance.

She saw an exquisite infinity of stars, strewn across unimaginable distances, colossal shining clusters of galaxies spiraling with outstretched arms. As the voice spoke, one by one the stars vanished, swallowed by a black figure that walked a scorched land. The horror that washed over her was indescribable. She tried to scream, but she had no voice of her own, drowned into silence by the words that were spoken in a cadence that drummed the world out of existence.

Stars.

Two ageless, shining stars, crowned by raven hair and surrounded by a corona of sunshine. The purest Power she had ever known surrounded her, scorching and fierce, and finally, finally the dark, inexorable voice was extinguished. She could have sobbed from the relief.

Her world rattled. Gradually she became aware that she lay on the ground, looking up at Khalil, who bent over her. He held her in his arms and blocked out the sun with his body, just as he blocked out the voice with his presence. He shook her and said her name. She received the impression he had been calling her name over and over.

Cuelebre knelt on her other side, staring at her. His rough-hewn features looked bloodless, his gold eyes molten.

"Stop," she croaked to Khalil. "I'm here. I'm back."

Looking wild-eyed, he stopped.

"What the unholy fuck was that?" Cuelebre asked. He sounded quite calm and utterly terrifying.

Grace shook her head. "I have no idea," she said. "All I know is that the Oracle's Power roused for you, and that just doesn't happen, unasked in daylight." She shuddered. "Did you hear a . . . really bad voice?" Khalil's arms tightened, and the two males exchanged a glance.

"We both heard it," said the dragon.

"I was in the kitchen with the children," said Khalil. His own voice did not sound pure in that moment. Instead he sounded rough and shaken. "And I still heard it."

Grace sucked in a breath. "They didn't, did they?"

Khalil shook his head. "No. They were unaware."

Cuelebre looked at Khalil. "I must get back to my mate. You are staying?"

"Yes," said Khalil.

Cuelebre dug into his shirt pocket and handed a heavy white card to her. She turned it over to look at both sides. There was no name, just a phone number printed in heavy, embossed black. Cuelebre said, "That's my personal cell number. Call me immediately if you see anything else."

She nodded numbly and tucked the card into the pocket of her cutoffs.

As Grace and Khalil watched, Cuelebre stood and walked away without another word. Several feet away he shimmered into his dragon form and launched into the air.

Grace shuddered again. She whispered, "I can never let this Power go to Chloe. She can't ever know anything as horrible as that voice."

If anything, Khalil looked even wilder. He picked her up in his arms, stood and with long, swift strides he carried her into the house. He said, "So be it. We protect the child from whatever that was at all cost."

When they were in the living room, she said, "Stop."

He stopped instantly.

"Please put me down," she said.

He didn't move. He said slowly, "You fell."

"I didn't hurt myself," she told him. "I just lost my balance in the vision. And I will not frighten the kids because you're carrying me, and it looks like something might be wrong."

He stared at her, his mouth tight. After a moment he let her legs slide to the floor but kept his arms around her. When she straightened and pulled away, he let her go and followed her into the kitchen.

They found Chloe on her hands and knees. A plastic gallon milk container lay on its side on the floor, in a lake of white liquid. The lid had been removed, and the container was nearly empty. It had been almost full at supper the evening before. Sodden paper towels lay in heaps everywhere.

Grace stopped in her tracks so suddenly Khalil ran into her. He grabbed her shoulders to steady her.

"Oh, Chloe," Grace said. "That was our only gallon of milk."

Chloe looked up, wide-eyed. "I didn't do it. I found it this way!"

Max turned around in his seat. He was sucking on one of the Lala Whoopsie doll's feet.

Khalil muttered something under his breath in what sounded like an alien language. He said aloud, "I only left them for a few minutes."

"I will clean up the floor, honey," said Grace in a strangled voice. "And then I will make you those pancakes I promised. I swear it. Just please, pretty please with sugar sprinkled on top—please let me have a cup of coffee first."

⸗ SIX ⸗

"No," said Khalil.

He surprised himself. He hadn't meant to speak, but he looked from Chloe, who was trying not to cry, to Max in his high chair. The baby wore a worried, confused expression. Clearly Max knew something was wrong. Khalil still gripped Grace's slender shoulders. He could feel her muscles quivering, and somehow the word just fell out of his mouth.

He released her as she turned, and all three of them, Chloe, Max and Grace, stared at him. He said to Grace telepathically, *You asked me to stay with the children, and I didn't. This is mine to address.*

She looked at him gravely. He noticed again the rich flecks of azure, jade and honey brown in her eyes, and for the first time, he realized with surprise that she was actually beautiful.

The fear she had shown outside still shadowed her gaze. He added, more gently, *We will talk of what happened at a later time when the children are not around. Yes?*

She nodded hesitantly. *All right.*

For now, sit, he said. *Take time to recover.*

She did not protest, and he thought it was a measure of how the vision had shaken her. He looked at Chloe. "Come over to the table. Sit with your aunt. I will clear away this mess and . . . I will achieve pancakes."

Grace's lovely, tired face wobbled with what looked suspiciously like mirth, but she had been under so much stress he decided his first impression could not be correct. "You'll *achieve* pancakes?"

"I do not see why not," he said.

"Have you ever achieved them before?" she asked. A touch of liveliness came back into her vivid eyes, and they sparkled.

"That question is irrelevant," he told her, while his eyes narrowed in suspicion on her tired face. On a Djinn, her expression would definitely be laughter. "I will achieve pancakes now."

Grace turned to Chloe. "I'm the one who made the promise. Is it all right with you if Khalil cooks pancakes instead of me?"

"Uh-huh," Chloe said. She hopped to her feet and splashed through the milk puddle to reach Grace. Liquid soaked the hem of her nightgown.

"You are both getting another bath after breakfast," Grace said. She picked up Chloe and set her in her booster seat then tiptoed around the milk to pour a cup of coffee.

"I never said I was going to cook," Khalil corrected.

Two sets of dismayed female eyes turned to him. He was at a loss to pick which of them looked more betrayed, and he had to bite back his own smile. He told the youngest female, "Do not jump to hasty conclusions. Just watch. You will get your pancakes. I have said it."

He was unsure whether the little girl understood either "hasty" or "conclusion," but she seemed to get the gist of what he had said, for she smiled and looked eager. Grace looked much more skeptical. Out of the corner of his eye, Khalil watched as she quickly prepared a bowl of something that looked sticky and white, like porridge. The baby began to bounce in his high chair and squeal. Grace took her coffee and the bowl to the table, and began feeding Max his breakfast.

Khalil wanted to tease Grace awhile longer and watch her

too-pale face flush with temper, but he could not bring himself to put Chloe through any more waiting. He turned his attention to the vast, invisible web of connections that surrounded him. Reckoned in Djinn terms, his wealth was immense. Many Djinn from all five Houses owed him favors, and many creatures other than Djinn did also.

He chose one of the oldest connections in his web. It led to Mundir, an elder in House Gul who had owed him a favor for millennia. Khalil plucked the strand politely. He sensed the other Djinn in the distance, bristling in surprise, but Mundir streaked toward him at once. The other Djinn coalesced in front of him. Mundir's physical form looked like a slender human male teenager, with blonde hair and arrogant, starred eyes that revealed his inhumanity.

Khalil disliked Mundir. He asked, "Are you able to pay your debt?"

Mundir curled his lip. The dislike was mutual. "Of course."

Khalil smiled at the other Djinn. The debt had been a long inconvenience for Mundir, and holding it over his head had been most enjoyable. Now it was time for another pleasure. "You will clean this kitchen floor with . . ." He looked at his small nest of human birds, who were staring openmouthed at the new arrival. Khalil asked Grace, "What does one use to clean a kitchen floor?"

She gave both him and Mundir a wary glance. "A mop and bucket?"

Khalil waved a hand and finished giving Mundir his order. "For what you have owed me, you will clean this kitchen floor as humans do, with a mop and bucket, and I suppose that means soap and water as well." He added telepathically, *And you will go gently as you do so, House Gul, for young ones live in this place, and they are vulnerable.*

The tight, incredulous expression on the other Djinn's face alone was worth the cancellation of his ancient debt. Fury shook in Mundir's voice as he hissed, "This will pay in full what I have owed you."

Khalil opened his eyes wide. "Of course."

He caught sight of Grace shaking her head slowly, her

gaze wide. He gave her a gleaming smile. Associating with this young Oracle was proving to be beneficial on many levels. So far this morning he had quite virtuously obstructed the path of the Great Beast—an opportunity that did not come around often—and he had also provided a great source of irritation to another Djinn whom he had disliked for countless years. Now he saw that he had rendered the Oracle in a rare state of speechlessness. Aside from her disturbing and mysterious vision, the subject of which he intended to pursue as soon as the little ones were not present, this morning was turning out to be truly fine.

It put him in such a magnanimous mood, he felt like splurging. What the hell. He plucked another connection, and another startled Djinn appeared. This one was Ismat, of the House Shaytan. The form she chose was pleasantly rounded and dark skinned, with hawkish features.

After verifying she was available to pay her debt, Khalil said, "You will go to a respectable restaurant." He tried to think of a good one. He didn't know very many restaurants. Finally he said, "The Russian Tea Room in New York will do. You will bring back pancakes for these humans, along with an assortment of other breakfast dishes, and you will create a fine table from which they will dine. The small female has been waiting some time for her breakfast, so do this quickly." His thoughtful gaze fell on an infuriated Mundir who mopped the floor, and he added, "Oh yes, and bring back a gallon of milk while you're at it."

Ismat looked around the kitchen. She grinned as she caught sight of Mundir with a mop and bucket. Eyes twinkling, she said to Khalil, "I see you have finally loosened your tight fist on all those many debts you own. This will pay in full one of the favors I owe you."

"It will indeed," he said.

Ismat vanished.

Khalil turned back to his audience at the kitchen table. Excited by the comings and goings, Chloe climbed out of her booster seat and hopped around, squealing. Grace had taken Max out of his high chair to cuddle the baby on her lap.

She looked dazed. "I think I'm beginning to see how pancakes could be viewed as an achievement."

Khalil nodded. He noticed her coffee cup was empty. He fetched the carafe of dark, steaming liquid from the apparatus on the counter. On impulse he searched cupboards until he found a collection of mugs, and he took one for himself. Then he strolled over to sit at the empty chair at the kitchen table and enjoy the fruits of his labor. He poured coffee, first into Grace's cup and then into his own, and he stretched out his legs.

"I was going to fetch breakfast myself," said Khalil. "But I decided to drink a cup of coffee and enjoy watching Mundir mop instead."

Grace had studied the children carefully when she had returned to the kitchen. Aside from Chloe's upset at having spilled the milk, they acted normally. Khalil was right; they hadn't heard the voice. She relaxed somewhat, but she hadn't thought she would be able to set aside the disturbing vision and eat anything. Then Ismat arrived with the food and set a feast of exotic dishes on the table.

Pecan-studded pancakes with macerated strawberries and maple syrup. A superb quiche, cooked with bacon, leeks, black truffle, potato and Gruyère cheese. Russian yogurt with fresh berries and spiced roasted almonds. Cherry and cheese blintzes, and apple smoked sausage. Smoked salmon with chives, creamed goat cheese and a cherry tomato, and micro green salad.

Linen napkins. And milk.

The bounty from the famous Tea Room was so rich, strange and plentiful, even Chloe fell silent.

Grace's reaction was just as rich, strange and plentiful. She shouldn't have agreed to allow any of it. The whole thing was as bad as the talking-cat nonsense. Or maybe it was worse? She couldn't decide, and the dilemma was making her feel a little too much like the witch Samantha's cranky, disapproving husband Darrin from the TV show Bewitched.

But the fragrance of the steaming gourmet food hit Grace where it truly hurt. Still shaken from the vision, too tired and hungry herself, Grace took one look at Chloe's wide, shining eyes—and reached for the nearest serving spoon to place small heaps of the delicacies on Chloe's plate.

After Chloe had plenty, Grace served herself, took her first bite and was transported with delight.

Her enjoyment was helped immensely when Mundir finished mopping shortly after the food arrived and disappeared with a sneer. She was grateful when the hostile Djinn left. It was a little difficult to try to eat while he cleaned her kitchen floor.

Who was she kidding? She would have wanted to eat that breakfast in the middle of tornado warnings with smoke alarms going off. The fact that she relaxed and stuffed herself in Khalil's presence kind of proved her own point.

Oh gods, the smoked salmon.

She gave Max his bottle, and he drank contentedly while she savored each bite of the rich, exquisitely prepared food. While she had accessed the Oracle's Power only a few times since she had inherited it, she found the stories her grandmother and Petra had told her about the aftermath were true. She felt shaky, like she was loosely attached to the physical world. Eating breakfast helped to anchor her more fully in her body. The intensity of the vision faded, and the reality of her own life came to the forefront of her mind where it belonged. She set the whole experience aside, to examine it later. For now she focused on the children and the present.

Khalil lounged in his chair, a massive, regal figure, his presence crackling against her hypersensitive awareness. She watched him out of the corner of her eye. His arms were thick, and his chest was wide with the appearance of muscles. He watched Chloe eat, his radiant eyes lit with an indulgent expression. He chatted with the little girl, asked her questions about her doll and friends, and from time to time he sipped coffee or chose to sample a bite from one of the dishes. Once or twice he glanced at Max with a slight smile.

Did his smile hold a touch of wistfulness? She thought of

his brief, tragic statement about his daughter who had sustained some kind of damage and had apparently not recovered from it. For a moment he had shown an immense rage and deep grief before his expression smoothed over.

He clearly liked creating mischief, and he carried more arrogance in his little finger than anybody else she had ever met. But she did not sense any true malevolence in his actions. Despite his acerbic and high-handed manner, all in all he had treated her far better than she had expected.

Then there were the children. They were her anchor, her terrifying responsibility, and now somehow they had become a bridge to this Powerful creature.

Aware of their bargain, she said hesitantly, "Would you like to hold Max?"

Surprised pleasure lit Khalil's hard face. He said, "If the small gentleman would deem that acceptable."

"Let's see, shall we?" she said. "He's pretty easygoing, and he likes people."

She handed Max over to Khalil, sticky banana-coated hair, bottle and all. Max grinned, kicked his legs and burbled conversationally. Khalil held the baby straight out in both hands, staring at him. Now that he actually had hold of Max, he seemed frozen and unsure about what to do.

Grace covered her mouth to hide her smile. She suggested, "Set him on your lap."

Khalil's gaze shifted to hers. He settled the baby on his lap. Max leaned back against his arm, tilted his bottle up and waved a foot in the air as if drinking his bottle while hanging out with a Djinn was an everyday occurrence. Grace patted the baby's shoulder. She might be biased, but she thought her nephew was one pretty-cool guy.

"Do you think he likes me?" Khalil asked, his black brows drawn together.

His uncertainty was so unexpectedly endearing, Grace bit her lip. She opened her mouth to reply, but her niece beat her to it.

"Sure," said Chloe as she chewed on the end of a sausage. "I like you too. But I'd like you better as a horsie."

Khalil grinned, and Grace murmured warningly, "Chloe."

"What?" Chloe said, wide-eyed again. "Was that bad?"

Grace noticed that Chloe wasn't really eating the sausage, just chewing on the end of it. "Are you done eating?"

"Uh-huh."

"Then stop chewing on that. It's time for you to have that bath." She stared at all the food on the table. It could wait for fifteen minutes. She would put it away after she got the kids clean. She turned to Khalil. "Thank you so much for breakfast."

He looked resigned. "You are welcome."

She gave him an evil grin as she nudged Chloe. "Come on, honey. Say thank you to Khalil for the pancakes."

Chloe knew how to turn on the charm. She gave Khalil a high-watt beam worthy of a beauty-pageant queen. "Thank you!"

Khalil held Grace's gaze as he returned her smile, his own laced with a grudging amusement. Then he turned his attention to Chloe. He said to the little girl, "You are welcome. Did you enjoy them?"

"Yes!"

"I'm glad."

Grace held out her arms for Max, and Khalil handed the baby over to her. "Well," she said, somewhat awkwardly. What now? Should she tell him to go, only much more nicely than she had before? "I really appreciate you coming when I called."

He gave her an exasperated glare. "Shut up."

She hadn't actually meant to tease that time, so she burst out laughing. Sobering quickly, she said to Chloe, "It's not okay to tell someone to shut up. It's very rude, especially if they're only trying to be nice."

Chloe rolled her eyes. "Even I know that."

A clean kitchen floor, and an excess of caffeine and carbohydrates, must have gone to Grace's head. Feeling giddy with her own mischief, she turned back to Khalil and told him, "So you should actually apologize to me."

His eyes widened. He looked from Grace to Chloe's

upturned, expectant expression, then back to Grace again. She thought for the first time since they had become acquainted, real respect entered his expression. "I apologize for telling you to shut up," he said gravely, while his gaze promised her some kind of retribution for her impudence.

But he would not do anything to hurt either her or the children. He had said so, and his associations and his word meant everything to him. No wonder Djinn considered information to be so valuable they would trade for it. Grace blinked at him with a creamy, innocent smile and once again chose the dumb route to Damascus.

"Why don't you make yourself useful and clean up the kitchen while I bathe the kids?" she said to the Djinn prince of the House Marid.

Retribution? He could bring it.

She took the children to their bedroom to gear up for the bath. Chloe could carry her own summer outfit, shorts and a daisy-patterned T-shirt, along with Max's diaper and a shirt that read: BAD TO THE BONE. They would be getting another wash in the kitchen sink.

She wanted to find a way to make the upstairs more accessible. Some of that would come as her leg strengthened, which was a good thing since Max got bigger and heavier every day. She grabbed baby shampoo, a washcloth and a towel from the cabinet in their room that she used as a linen closet.

The safety gate at the bottom of the stairs had a frame that could be left pinned in place while part of it opened like a real gate. When she had the funds, she could get a second gate to put at the top of the stairs. Then they both could stay fastened in place, and she wouldn't have to keep hauling one gate up and down the stairs. She added a second gate to her wish list, along with getting Chloe a twin bed, although moving a dresser downstairs on Saturday topped the list.

Chloe scampered ahead of her and rounded the corner to the kitchen. With Max on her hip, Grace paused to tuck Cuelebre's card carefully in her spiral-bound phone book in the living room then joined Chloe. Of course the kitchen was still a mess, and Khalil was nowhere in sight.

That surprised Grace. Not the mess—she had expected that he would ignore her cheeky order to clean up the kitchen, but she could have sworn she still sensed Khalil's presence, and she had been geared up to continue their argument.

Frowning, she bathed the children with swift efficiency. She set Max on the clean floor afterward while Chloe skipped off to play in the living room.

Then she turned her attention to the kitchen table. There was quite a bit of food left over, and a lot of it would freeze well. She put it away, enjoying the thought of a few easy, delicious meals.

Had Ismat paid for all this food, or had she simply whisked into the restaurant and taken whatever dish she fancied? If Djinn went around stealing things all the time, they would be prosecuted like any other thief—but the trick would be to catch them.

And was Grace really going to look that gift horse in the mouth? She decided not to this time, especially since she had eaten and enjoyed so much of the evidence.

Apparently she also now owned several gleaming metal serving platters, complete with lids, along with four heavy linen napkins. Once the serving platters were clean, she stacked them and set them aside on the counter until she could figure out what to do with them. Maybe she could sell them or give them to somebody. Katherine would enjoy having them, but Grace wasn't sure she wanted to explain how she got them in the first place.

Then she paused to assess the area. Damn, she could have sworn she still felt Khalil's presence. Pretending to more confidence than she really had, she said telepathically, *I know you're here.*

Did somebody just sigh in her ear? Khalil replied, *I still wish to discuss your vision, but not in front of the children.*

She hunched her shoulders. She didn't want to think of what happened earlier or remember the voice from her vision. She would rather pick a fight with him and pretend everything was fine. Reluctantly, she said, *Come back when they're asleep.*

Yes, said Khalil. His presence faded.

Grace expanded her awareness. She felt nothing unusual, either in the house or on the property, just the faded edges of the occasional ghost. This time she really was alone, except for the children. It had become just another normal summer morning.

She told herself she was all right with that as she listened to the silence.

⇒ SEVEN ⇐

Figuring out which bills to pay was a bit of a joke.
Grace put Max down for a morning nap, started a load of the never-ending pile of laundry and built Chloe a "castle" in the living room with a sheet spread over the back of the armchair and across one of the straight-backed chairs she brought in from the kitchen.

While Chloe played happily in her castle with Lala Whoopsie and several stuffed animals, Grace looked through the bills twice. She came up with the same answer both times. Keep the water, electric and phone bills paid. All the medical bills got stacked on top of a neat, growing pile. She put student loan deferment notices in another pile. Each one was like the ticking of a time bomb that would eventually blow up in her face. Then, her stomach in a clench, she spent a half hour calling around to bankruptcy lawyers. Fun times.

She folded laundry, looked through her unfinished senior history project and set it down again, fed the children lunch and found the note in her purse about calling Katherine to set up a time when Joey and Rachel could come over for a playdate. Feeling guilty about asking Katherine to babysit yet again, Grace picked up the phone and stepped into the kitchen so Chloe couldn't hear the conversation. No point in getting Chloe excited if Katherine couldn't take them. She hit Katherine's number on speed dial.

Katherine picked up on the third ring. "Gotta love caller ID," she said. "Hi, Grace, how are you doing?"

Grace could hear the cheerful shouts of children in the background. She said, "Hi, Katherine, we're doing all right. I know you're working, so I want to keep this brief. Is there any chance you could take Chloe and Max on Saturday? The second quarterly work day is coming up, and last time I had a hard time keeping track of them while I dealt with everybody's questions about what needed to be done."

"Of course," said Katherine immediately. "You know how much I love them. Why don't they spend the night as well? That way you can just crash when everybody leaves."

Grace felt a rush of love for the older woman. Katherine had grieved almost as hard as she had at Petra's death. Katherine was always willing to help out in any way she could, while Grace's friends had drifted away after the accident. Grace tried not to take it personally. Her friends were as young as she was, and when Grace had taken on the children, she had been catapulted into a completely different reality from theirs. Still, the lack of connection with her old friends felt like an abandonment.

"That's so good of you," Grace said to Katherine, her voice thick with emotion. She would pack up the serving platters and give them to Katherine as a thank-you, and if Grace had to explain how she got them, so be it. "I wanted to ask you about something else too. I'm looking to trade Chloe's toddler bed to someone for a twin-sized one. Would you be willing to tell the parents of your daycare kids, to see if any of them might be interested?"

"Be delighted to," said Katherine. "I'm sure we'll find someone who'll be happy to trade."

"Great, thanks so much," Grace said. "Can I bring the kids over at eight? The work day is supposed to start at nine, and that will give me time to get ready."

"You bet."

Grace ended the call quickly and turned her attention to other things. She washed the lunch dishes. Their stack of library books were due in a few days. She bagged and set them by the front door. Then she put the kids down for an afternoon nap. That sent Chloe into another meltdown, and when things finally quieted down, Grace did her physical therapy exercises. After that she worked on her resume. She had two versions going. One of them listed her actual college credits. The other was a resume built on hope and included the bachelor's degree she had not yet earned. Louisville was still hurting from the long recession. Jobs were hard to find, and she had to make her resumes look as good as she could.

Something had to give, somehow, sometime. The law of averages said it had to. Meanwhile, Grace felt like she had been locked in a pressure cooker and set on a burner that was turned on high. It wasn't going to be a pretty sight when that pressure cooker exploded.

She hit another wall, staggered to the couch, and a black hole sucked her down again. She slept hard, and when she woke a half hour later, the house was still silent. When she checked on the children, she found both still sleeping.

My goodness. Could she actually grab some time for herself?

She went to the kitchen and used the leftover coffee from that morning to make herself a glass of iced coffee, then she sat to stare blankly at the clean table.

She wondered what her high school friend Jacqui was doing this summer. The last time they had talked, Grace had just gotten home from the hospital. Jacqui had stopped by the house to say hi. The visit was awkward. Grace watched as Jacqui looked everywhere in the living room except at Chloe and Max, who were playing on the floor. Jacqui said she couldn't stay long because she had to study for a test the next day, then she looked stricken. After that, they had exchanged a couple of e-mails. Then silence. Grace wondered if Jacqui was even still in the area or if she had gotten a job somewhere else after graduation.

The ghosts were silent. Nothing moved, either in the

house or outside. The summer heat blanketed the land like a lover.

She didn't want to have quiet time to herself. She didn't want to think about that terrible vision, not when she was alone. She closed her eyes, wrapped her arms around herself and huddled in her chair.

This time when Khalil appeared, he did so gently. His presence curled into the kitchen like a tendril of soft breeze. Her heart leaped, but not from irritation. She opened her eyes and turned in her chair and tried not to show how glad she was that he had come.

Khalil wore black, and once again his long raven hair was pulled back. The afternoon sun slanting through the kitchen window touched his ivory features with gold. His regal face was grave, contemplative. For a moment he looked like a sculpture created by one of the masters, his impossibly graceful form freed forever from priceless marble by Michelangelo's genius.

She cleared her throat. "I thought you were coming tonight."

He walked toward her, pulled out a chair and sat down. "You said to come when the children were asleep. They are. You have also rested."

Just as before, he filled the entire house with his presence. She took a deep breath and let go of the tension that had built up between her shoulder blades throughout the day. She asked, "How did you know I rested?"

"I checked in earlier. You were asleep on the couch." His too-keen diamond gaze focused on her face.

She nodded and looked away, feeling awkward under his scrutiny. She could waste time feeling strange about him looking in the house when she was asleep, but that seemed like a little too much, too late, when he'd already shown he didn't have human sensibilities or boundaries.

What should she say or do now? Her social skills were not the most refined at the best of times, and she had no idea how to behave with him if they weren't sniping at each other. She noticed her glass of iced coffee, sweating rivulets of moisture in the heat of the day, and she started to rise to her feet. "I'll get you a drink. What would you like?"

His hand came around her bicep. She looked sideways at the long ivory fingers curled around her arm as he eased her back down into her chair. "I do not require refreshment," he said. "We must discuss what happened this morning."

She nodded again. He had not removed his hand from her arm, and she decided not to remind him of that. His grip felt heavy and reassuring. She noticed again how hot his touch was, as if his presence was a fire his skin barely contained. With her free hand, she touched her cold, sweating glass then took a quick swallow.

She said, "I'm scared to look at it too closely."

"Do not be frightened," Khalil said quietly. "You and the children will be safe. I have said so."

At that, she turned to face him and met his crystalline gaze.

Those ageless, inhuman eyes held such piercing clarity, when she looked into them she felt as if she fell into forever. She couldn't look away, and he didn't. With the whole of her attention on him, she felt her own energy settle into alignment with his, and it was an entirely new experience that felt right somehow, comforting and good. It held a completeness she had never known before, his maleness to her femaleness, his Power touching the Oracle's Power that resided inside her, along with her own, unique Power of the spirit. She felt enfolded, warmed, almost as if he had physically reached out to put his arms around her. A strange expression flickered across his face. He frowned slightly, tilting his head as he stared at her.

Up this close, the shining flame of his own Power was fierce and inexhaustible, a pure, unceasing roar that was . . .

It was sexy. Not just a little sexy. Awesome, kick-in-the-head sexy.

For the first time in months, she felt a pulse of arousal.

What?

Shocked and disconcerted, she pulled away. His hand fell from her arm. Breathing unevenly, she sat in a rigid, upright position and stared straight ahead. She could feel the blood rush to her cheeks.

His fiercely male presence filled the house, just as it had last night.

And he was no longer entirely indifferent to her.

"Now you have interested me," murmured Khalil.

"I have no idea what you are talking"—she could barely squeeze enough air out of her lungs to get the words out—"about."

He chuckled, and the husky sound was even more dangerous than that from the night before. It shivered along her exposed nerve endings with as much sensuality as if he had trailed his fingers along her bare skin. "I think I might like it when you lie," he said. "It makes my truthsense feel so superior."

She tried to glare at him but was afraid she might have just ended up looking panicked and confused. Outrage, where was her outrage when she needed it? "Of course superiority would matter to you." Her attempt at scoffing came out more like a squeak, and she had a sudden impulse to get her sheet from the futon and pull it over her head.

She never saw him move. Suddenly he was bending over her from behind. He whispered in her ear, "You know, our truth game is still open, and it's my turn to ask a question."

She started shaking her head then her whole body decided to join in, as she shivered. They were supposed to be talking about something scary, but there were so many scary things in her life right now, she had lost track. What were they supposed to be talking about again?

"We're on a new round of questions," she whispered back, unsteadily. "So it's only your turn if I don't end the game."

"Are you going to end it?" Tiny puffs of air from his words tickled her ear.

She shivered harder. Smart. Dumb. Oh, Damascus. "I–I don't know."

He cupped her shoulders. "Are you cold?"

She looked over her shoulder at him, wide-eyed. His eyes shone, and his expression was heavy lidded, languorous and wickedly knowledgeable. This time she didn't even try to verbalize, but instead shook her head again. She felt as if she had lost contact with gravity and was floating in midair.

Khalil gave her a slow, keen smile. "What are you, then? You're shivering."

She fought to get some grounding, to push back. "You've just asked three questions, and I've answered two of them. No matter how you look at it, it's my turn now."

His smile widened into a grin. The look was stunning with his elegant features. He was not just prince of his House. He was also prince of mischief. "I concede," he said. "It is indeed your turn."

"I won't be rushed," she warned. This time she would be sure to make her question count, if she had to sit down at the computer and write drafts until she got it right.

"Take your time," he purred. The pure sound licked over her skin. "I am in no hurry."

Where had the irascible, antagonistic Djinn gone? He had been replaced by one who oozed sensuality and sin. She heard herself blurt out, "Do Djinn even like sex?"

Oh, God, she didn't just ask him that. Why did she *always* have to take the dumb route? She squirmed and felt herself flush, not just on her face but all over, so that she could actually feel heat pulsing off her body. She would give anything to hide under her sheet.

If he was stunning before, the expression on his face now turned downright electrifying. "With the right person, we enjoy sex very much," he said in a gentle, unhurried reply. "We enjoy it in a leisurely fashion, and we devote all of our attention to it. And our lovers crave it."

Grace felt like she was about to leap out of her skin. He still bent over her as she sat in her chair, and he had braced one hand on the edge of the table. The memory of every boy she had kissed in high school, along with the lovers she had taken in college, burned away under Khalil's intense, incendiary attention, and all he had done was flirt with her.

What would kissing him be like? Her mind whited out,

and she coughed. It sounded suspiciously like a whimper. "Well, okay. I guess I blew that round again, didn't I?"

"I don't know," he whispered. "Did you? I found your choice of topic extremely interesting."

She shook her head. "I just blurted it out." Her voice sounded jerky, the words disjointed. "I was going to ask you something really clever and useful."

He laughed. The deep sound of his mirth filled the room. "We have both been caught using our questions poorly. I have not been so foolish in a long while."

If she were to choose how she viewed what just happened, she decided she would feel a small, sneaky sense of triumph for goading (coaxing? *flirting*?) him into the foolishness, because excuse me, at his age, he really should know better. She wasn't sure that it made up for her own foolishness, and she suspected she had been quite a bit more foolish than he, but she wasn't too proud to take any victory where she could find one.

And their whole exchange had been too strange, too intense. A strategic escape might be in order. She swiveled around in her chair to face the table again, grabbed her iced coffee and buried her nose in the glass.

Still chuckling, Khalil moved back to the table to take his seat. With her head bent, she took small sips, watching him out of the corner of her eye. He sobered and grew thoughtful. After a bit, she thought it might be safe to put down her drink, but she didn't let go of it. Talk about foolishness. As if holding a glass of anything would ward off a Djinn who was determined to do something.

Khalil's gaze darkened. "As much as I have enjoyed teasing you, we still must talk about this morning."

All thoughts of flirting blew away. Her shoulders sagged even as she nodded. "Yes, of course."

She put her elbows on the table, her forehead in her hands, and turned her attention to what she had been circling around since it happened, the memory of the voice that tore down the stars.

While she appreciated that Khalil had been trying to reassure her in his own way when he told her not to be frightened, she didn't think he understood that the vision itself had been terrifying, and she was reluctant to open herself up to the possibility of having another one.

Her hands clenched into fists as she poked at the memory. To her immense relief, it remained distant, disconnected from her.

She hadn't realized how much she had tensed until Khalil put a flattened hand to her back. He said, "Talk."

"I'm not getting anything else," she said. "It's gone now. The vision definitely came for Cuelebre."

Khalil said, "The voice mentioned the Great Beast."

"Whether he wants it or not, it's his prophecy." Her forehead crinkled. "Although I think whatever the vision is about, it might be bigger than just Cuelebre. It felt global or elemental in some way. I had a vision of stars being blacked out in the night sky." The sight was so unnatural, she couldn't stop another shudder.

His gaze sharpened. "I did not see anything. I only heard the voice. Did you recognize the landscape?"

She shook her head. "No. It might have been symbolic, but I'm not sure. Oracular visions can come in a variety of ways. They can be from the past or from possible futures, or they can be a dreamlike sequence of images that has particular significance to a petitioner. My grandmother and Petra could tell the difference, but I haven't had enough experience yet. This was only the third time I've accessed the Oracle's Power. My second time was with Carling and Rune." She gave him a twisted smile. "Both my grandmother and my sister, Petra, said the same thing. The Oracle sees a lot of weird shit. They also said they—we have a kind of built-in defense mechanism that helps us gain distance from the visions after we have them. The visions we see come for other people. We've got to let go of them or go crazy. Petra thought that might also be why the Oracle sometimes blacks out. I think I'm starting to understand what she meant."

"Is it normal that both Cuelebre and I heard it?"

"Yes and no." She grimaced at him. "Sometimes the Oracle can channel someone who has died for those who are in mourning and who need to say good-bye, and when we prophesy, the Power has its own voice. Several people might hear it, but usually that's when we're all together. And usually the Oracle only prophesies from a place deep in the Earth."

"Why is that?"

"I think part of it is tradition. That's how things have always been done, so we continue to do it that way. Also, the Power that comes to each Oracle is inherited." She frowned as she fumbled to explain something she knew so intimately. "Just like anybody else, we each have our own wellspring of Power, talents and affinity to things. My sister was really good at a kind of clairvoyance called farseeing, which is a kind of seeing at a distance but in real time. My talent is an affinity to spirit. I've always had it. I have a facility with ghosts and other spirits, and I know when you're around even when you're not visible or in physical form. I could also feel the connection you created."

"Yes," he said thoughtfully. "That is quite unusual. I have never heard of another human able to do so."

"In our family, our talents make us potential Oracles, but the Power of the Oracle itself is an inherited Power." She swallowed a sudden lump in her throat. "I knew my sister was dead when I woke up in the hospital, because the Power had come to me. I know this sounds strange, but we never know who will inherit it, except that it always moves from female to female. For example, theoretically it could have moved to Chloe when her mom died, although I've never heard of it going to someone so young. But it wouldn't have gone to Max."

His eyes narrowed. "So you didn't have a choice about it coming to you."

"No," she said. She felt a sudden impatience and brushed that aside. "But that doesn't matter. It's mine now, and it's up to me to see what I can make of it. Basically what I'm trying to say is most people have one source of Power. I have two sources, the one I was born with and the Oracle's Power that

I inherited earlier this year. That is a very old Power, and it runs deep."

He watched her face closely. "What do you mean?"

"It's always present. I can feel it, but it sits just on the edge of my consciousness." She tried to sift through the life-time of teachings in her head to distill things for him quickly and easily. "Did you know that human witches often take a patron god or goddess?"

He shook his head.

"Our goddess is Nadir, because she's the goddess of the depths. There's one family legend that says Nadir gave us the Power of the Oracle. There's another that says it came from someone else, another god or Powerful creature. Whatever the truth of that is, the original temple at Delphi was in a cavern below ground, and we have a small cave system here on the land. When someone petitions to speak to the Oracle, that's where we take them. Going there helps us to reach down into that deep part of us, so we can access the Power." She thrust her fingers through her hair again. She muttered, "I'm giving you too much information."

"Do not trouble yourself about that," he said. He was still frowning. "So this Power might leap from you to Chloe."

She shook her head grimly. "Not while I'm alive," she said. "When I die, it will pass on to another female in the family. That may be Chloe. She's the only other living female relative that I have right now. Or maybe by then we'll have more family, if Chloe and Max grow up to have kids."

"And what happened this morning was different from how the Power usually manifests?" he asked.

"Well, I'm no expert," she said. "But yes, it was different from anything I've experienced or anything Petra or my grandmother talked about. What happened this morning came out in full daylight. I was taught that we have to reach for the Power, to call it up, but this morning it just spilled out. I don't know if that was because Cuelebre's presence triggered it, if the vision was urgent, or if it had something to do with me and how I connect to the Power. I'm just grateful Chloe and Max didn't know what was happening."

He pressed his palm against her back, almost as if he would press strength and calm into her body by willing it to happen. "Did the voice take you over?"

She lifted up her head to frown at him. He was watching her closely. She fumbled for words. "It was more like I tuned into a radio frequency, and the voice came through on that channel. I don't know how else to explain it. It couldn't have been physical, or the children would have heard it too. Right?"

He nodded, frowning as well. The brilliance of his gaze was muted into shadowed diamond sparkles. "Your radio frequency analogy is a good one. I heard it like telepathy, but it felt on a different level somehow than normal telepathy."

"Chloe's telepathic," Grace told him, her throat constricting. "She isn't very good at it yet. Most human children develop the ability after they develop physical speech patterns. Petra always used to say it was nature's way of protecting young parents. Just think what it would be like to have a telepathic two-year-old having a screaming tantrum in your head."

He gave her a small smile. It faded almost at once. "If you feel something like that vision coming again, you call me immediately. Pull hard at the connection, and I will know your need is urgent."

She nodded. She didn't see how she had any choice. As fast as the earlier vision had taken her over, he was the only entity she knew who could get here quickly enough to make some kind of difference. "I can't lose control like that and leave the children unsupervised. You saw what happened with Chloe and the milk. If I pull really hard, when you come, look after the kids, do you hear? Make sure they're safe."

His expression turned fierce. "I have promised both you and the children protection, and you will all have it."

Her eyes grew moist. She wouldn't thank him again. She had thanked him enough, and anyway, he didn't like it. Instead she leaned back against his hand.

He tilted his head as he studied her. "You are doing all this on your own, while looking after the children."

She lifted one shoulder. "Not quite. Petra's best friend,

Katherine, kept the kids until I got out of the hospital and could bring them home. Remember Janice from yesterday morning, the one who babysat when I spoke with Carling and Rune? Janice belongs to a roster of witches who are on call to babysit whenever someone petitions to speak to the Oracle. They do it as part of their community tithe. More people are coming on Saturday to put in a quarterly work day. They'll beat back the worst of the weeds and mow."

She braced herself for another one of his contemptuous looks. That had stung when she didn't even like him very much. Maybe she did like him after all, now that she had gotten to know him better. Now his disdain would hurt worse than a sting.

But he didn't look contemptuous. Instead, his face tightened. He said, "It is good that you have some help. And now both you and the little ones have me for protection. But you are still too much alone in all of this. You should be surrounded with a House filled with associations."

She had to press her lips tightly together and look away before she could say, after a moment, "Well, nobody expected things to turn out this way."

The afternoon sunlight had deepened as they talked. From down the hall, Chloe started to chatter. She was talking to her toys, but Max burbled a wordless reply.

Grace turned back to Khalil. His hard face had eased into an indulgent smile again. "Thank you for the talk," she said. As the words fell out, she clapped a hand over her mouth. "I swear, that one just came out. I'm sorry."

Instead of looking angry or disgusted, this time he looked amused. He stood. "I will come back tomorrow to visit with the little ones."

Grace stood too. "We're going out. It's story time at the library, and we have books to return, and . . ." He was listening to her with such close attention, she grew self-conscious. She ended, awkwardly, "Well, you don't need to hear about all that."

"What is their schedule in the evening?"

"Dinner at five, bed by eight."

He raised his eyebrows. "May I come to visit with them before they go to bed?"

Grace was impressed. He actually asked; he didn't dictate. She said, "Sure."

He studied her for a moment, his gaze unreadable. Then she felt his presence slide along hers in a scorching, invisible caress. As she sucked in a breath, he inclined his head and disappeared.

She shut her mouth with a click. What *was* that—his version of a hug good-bye?

"Even Samantha was surprised when people appeared and disappeared without warning," she muttered. "And she was a witch too. I am not Darrin. I'm not."

There was nobody around to argue with her, so she went to get the children up from their nap.

As entertaining as arguing with Khalil was, she had enjoyed talking with him even more. She tried not to dwell on that too much, either that evening or the next day.

After she put the kids to bed, she took the baby monitor and tackled the stairs to dig through her wardrobe for more clothes. She seemed to have broken through some sort of emotional barrier about the scars on her legs. Not only did she collect several pairs of shorts, she also rediscovered a couple of pairs of capri pants she had forgotten she owned. She shook her head, exasperated with herself. If she hadn't been so frozen over examining her summer wardrobe, she could have been wearing those all along.

In the morning, she took the children to the library. The early learning program for babies Max's age was at nine o'clock. It involved little more than sitting in a circle, playing with soft, plastic-coated books and singing nursery rhymes, but he adored it. Chloe declared she was too big to sit in the circle and sing with the babies and their caretakers, so she usually sprawled nearby with a coloring book and crayons, and hummed along with the songs.

On the way home they stopped at a few stores to pick up

some essentials that Super Saver didn't carry. Then it was nap-time for Max, lunch, back to the library again for Chloe's story time, home again and a nap for both of the children in the afternoon. While Max and Chloe slept, Grace finished polishing one resume and worked on tweaking the other version.

A knock sounded hesitantly at the front door. She peeked out the office window. A middle-aged couple stood on the porch.

She braced her shoulders and stifled a sigh. When an Oracle died, the witches' demesne sent out a public notice to ask that people grant the new Oracle three months' transition time before approaching her with a petition. For Grace, that transition time was now over. More and more people would begin to petition for a consultation. She went to answer the door.

The couple turned out to be a brother and sister, Don and Margie. Their mother had been deceased for many years, and their father had died of a heart attack the week before. Shocked and grieving, they hoped to say good-bye.

Grace couldn't help but soften. She invited the couple in and called Therese, the next witch on the roster for babysitting duty. When Therese arrived, Grace took the couple out to the cavern. "I want you to understand, I can't guarantee that your father will come," she told them as they walked the overgrown path. "We can only try."

"Trying means everything to us," said Don.

They reached the back meadow where the cavern was located. The Ohio River ran along the western border of the property. Sparkling glints of blue water were visible through a tangled border of trees and underbrush.

Earlier in the summer, she had explored, briefly, trying to sell some of the riverfront acreage in order to raise some cash. The Oracle's Power had bristled, clearly antagonistic toward the idea, but it wasn't writing the checks for her monthly bills, so she shoved it aside and made some phone calls.

The venture quickly became too complicated to pursue with any real hope of financial return. The real estate agent she had spoken to had been blunt. Granting access rights to anyone who potentially built along the shoreline meant they would be driving past her house in order to get to their patch of land, and she would lose any hope of privacy. Also, the land had too much of a reputation for being haunted to have any wide market appeal. In the current housing slump, it was unlikely the agent could move the parcels of land at all.

The path to the cavern cut north through the meadow then veered a little east, where the land rose into a short, rocky bluff that was dotted with trees and bushes. The entrance to the cavern was set into the bluff.

When Grace was a child, she used to climb the bluff and have picnics on the squat, flat rock at the summit. The bluff was tall enough, and the land sloped downward at a steep enough angle, that she could see over the tops of the trees that grew down by the shoreline and watch the river for boats and barges.

She gave the bluff a wry glance. It was unlikely she would ever see the top again. She could probably take her time and climb up the way she climbed the stairs, using her sound leg to haul herself up, but that seemed like a useless expenditure of energy when she had so many other things that needed her attention.

She led Don and Margie across the meadow to the old doorway that had been built into the side of the bluff. The door was locked to keep exploring children out, and the key was stored in a small rusted coffee can that rested on the top of a wooden lintel.

The doorway opened to a tunnel that led down to the cavern. Grace was familiar with every inch of the property. She had played in the meadow, walked that tunnel and had been down to the cavern more times than she could count, but Don and Margie were wide-eyed and stared at everything.

Grace collected a couple of flashlights and the mask, from which the Oracle had spoken since the temple at Delphi, and that was when Margie broke down in tears. "I can't do this," the older woman said to her brother. "This is too much, too strange. I just can't."

Grace was unsurprised. It happened sometimes. People might travel from all over the world to consult with the Oracle, only to balk at the last minute. She said, "I'll wait outside while you decide what you want to do. Just remember while you talk this over—you don't have to try this right now. Your father just passed. You can give yourself some time and come back when you're ready. The tunnel is quite roomy, and the cavern looks just like the ones at Mammoth Cave National Park or the cave systems in southern Indiana."

Don said, "We read about it on the Oracle's website, and looked at the photos." He looked at his sister sadly. "I guess it's all a bit much in real life."

Niko had created a simple website in an attempt to prepare petitioners. It had a brief section on the Oracle's history and another one on what to expect when they arrived. There was also a page that explained the ancient social contract, that while the Oracle acted in service and did not ask for payment, donations were essential for the upkeep and maintenance of the property. He had even set up a PayPal button. The website pulled in between two and three hundred dollars every six months.

Grace said again, "You don't need to do this right now. You can come back when you're more ready."

She stepped outside and waited in the sunshine while Don and Margie talked. While she tried not to listen, she could still make out snatches of their conversation. It was difficult to hear their struggle, and their grief touched too close to home. She crossed her arms and scowled at the tall grass. The meadow was dotted with bright colors, mostly yellow from dandelions, but also white and purple wildflowers.

Going into the cavern *was* strange for people who were not used to it. The old stories told of petitioners approaching the Oracle of Delphi in awe and supplication.

But the Power had come so strongly the other morning. She could not think of a single reason why it could not do so again.

She felt along the edge of her consciousness, and there it

was, nestled inside of her, deeper than gut instinct, an ancient well running through her like a dark subterranean sea. Was it really a gift from the goddess of the depths, or was it from some other strange, Powerful creature? The oldest stories her grandmother had told were a tangle of superstition and myth. The earliest Oracles had worshipped the Power and believed they spoke the words of the gods themselves. Over thousands of years, that attitude had evolved and changed, but Grace's grandmother, and even Petra, had talked about serving the Oracle's Power as if they were subservient to it. Without having any real experience herself, Grace had listened and accepted what they said, pretty much without question.

Until now. She patted along the edges of the Power with her awareness, really exploring it for the first time since it had come to her. It felt unruly and untamed, almost as if it had a mind of its own, except it wasn't quite a person. She knew what personalities felt like from the ghosts she had encountered and the dark spirits she had driven off the property. Growing familiar with Khalil's presence had only sharpened her understanding. She could see clearly that even though the Oracle's Power seemed vast, it was too incomplete to be a personality.

She thought, how could you have Power without a person? You couldn't, like you couldn't have the ability to draw without someone to manifest it. But families carry inherited abilities and traits that manifested through generations.

She wasn't the first person in her family to have an affinity to spirit. The difference between the two was, the Power she was born with felt just like a part of her, while this Power felt old.

Maybe it had been part of a person once, someone who had died or been killed a long time ago, and their Power had sheared away. Only, because it couldn't exist without someone to manifest it, it had grafted onto someone else. Then someone after that. The thought felt right to her, somehow true. She felt again the sense of a dark ocean that flowed everywhere but seemed to recede from her touch.

She focused all of her attention inward and reached for it again. It receded again, as if pulling back from her.

Something clicked over in Grace's head, the same way it had when she had heard Khalil talking with the kids in their bedroom or when Chloe had said she was bad.

Oh, no you don't, she said to what had come to live inside of her. *I've put up with a lot of shit in my life because of you. You chose me. Well, that makes you mine. Do you hear me? You will come when I call, because you are mine now.*

Maybe she wouldn't have done it if she had paused to think about it. But she didn't pause to think. Instead, she reached deeper and harder inside of herself, and much as she had with the connection to Khalil, she grasped the Oracle's Power and *pulled*.

She connected. For one wild moment the Power bucked in her hold, stronger and fiercer than she had expected. It rushed up in a roaring wave and threatened to engulf her entirely.

Oh, no, she thought. *You don't own me. I own you.* She wrapped her awareness tighter around it and held on.

It tried to recede again.

No. She would not let it go.

The sunlit meadow disappeared. Everything went dark. She held steady as the Power thundered and crashed in her grip, a feral, undisciplined storm. She got a feeling of immense connectivity again, the dark ocean flowing everywhere, touching everywhere, where the veil of time and space grew thin. Losing her grip and falling into it would be crossing a threshold to drown in a constant state of epiphany. She had heard stories of Oracles getting lost in the Power and babbling madness for the rest of their lives.

And she simply refused to do that. If nothing else, she was stubborn. She had dishes in her sink that needed to be washed. She had to change the oil in her car. Max and Chloe needed to be tucked into bed that evening. There was also something else she had said she would do. She couldn't think of what it was, with all the crashing and heaving going on in her head, but she knew she had promised to do it, so she wrestled the Power down.

As she did so, she glimpsed a ghost.

She stared, confusion tumbling through her thoughts. She could "see" ghosts, such as the elderly women in the kitchen. They looked like indistinct, transparent smudges overlaid on normal reality.

Oracular visions were an entirely different experience. Those streamed directly from the Power, and like the vision that came for Cuelebre, they overwhelmed her regular senses.

Seeing this ghost felt like a true vision. It was another anomaly. According to what she had learned, the Oracle's visions came for other people, but at the moment no one else was around. Wasn't anything going to go the way it was supposed to?

The ghost certainly wasn't Don and Margie's father either. It was either Wyr or Demonkind, a strange creature with a face like a human female's, except its features were too sharp and elongated, and it had more of a snout than a nose. The face flowed back to a hooded cobralike flare of a neck before falling to the body of a serpent as thick as a man's waist.

Grace felt a pulse of recognition that went deeper than knowledge, past instinct. It came from the Power she held. She said to the ghost, *This was once yours. This Power came from you.*

The ghost stared at her in astonishment. Then it gave her a merry, feral smile. *Very good, child. Very, very good.*

She knew the ghost did not speak English, but she still understood every word. Blood thundered in Grace's ears, or maybe it was the sound of the dark ocean. The ghost came clearer, and Grace seemed to see her in a cavern. Struggling with astonishment and an odd sense of betrayal, she said, *I thought we were human.*

You are, said the ghost. *Mostly. Your many times greatgrandmother found me after an earthquake on Mount Parnassus. My body had been crushed from tons of falling rock. She tried to help me, but it was too late.*

Grace asked, *How did we inherit this*?

The ghost's smile widened to reveal long, sharp fangs. *I gave her the serpent's kiss as my thanks. I meant to give her the Power to walk the night, but I died while I kissed her. I gave her all of my Power instead.*

Another vision came to Grace. Although the image was born from a far distant past, it was also as sharp and clear as if she were truly present. Grace watched the serpent creature convulse in death throes as she bit a screaming human woman.

Grace said, *We're an ACCIDENT*?

You are a thing of beauty, the ghost whispered. *Although your ancestress went a little mad.*

Good gods. Grace shuddered and almost lost control of her hold.

The serpent-woman ghost coiled on itself. *Your grandmothers created a history of prophecy and service out of the legacy I gave them. You should feel proud.*

I don't need you to tell me how I should feel. Grace noticed how the Power pulled toward the ghost. She said, *You didn't mean for any of this to happen, so you never really let go.*

The ghost came up to her. *You're strong. You pulled the Power up in daylight, and you called me to you. You're very strong for such a young one.*

Well, I didn't call you on purpose, Grace told her. Gripping the Power while talking with the ghost took all of her strength. She didn't know how much longer she could hold on without it sucking her into that dark, endless sea. She said, *I wanted to see if I could pull the Power up in daylight, but since we're having this nice chat, you really need to let go now. Or take it back. I don't give a shit which one you do, just do one thing or the other.*

The ghost turned away, and her coiling grew agitated. *What if I can't take it back? I'm no longer alive. I cannot contain my own Power.*

Then let go, dammit. Your connection to it is too strong.

I can't get full control while you hold on. Grace injected all her strength into the words. In the back of her mind, she was turning frantic. If she couldn't get control, she didn't know if she could release it safely.

The serpent woman looked at her. Her smile had faded away to be replaced by something much darker. *What if I don't want to let go? My Power is alive in you. As long as my Power is alive, something of me is alive as well.*

Realization struck. *You're the reason why the Power doesn't bond with any one person, why it jumps from Oracle to Oracle,* Grace said. *It's because you won't let go. But you're not alive. You're dead. You're only pretending.*

While they were speaking, she searched for how the Power connected to both her and to the ghost. Now that she knew she was haunted, she could try to get rid of the ghost in the ways she had been taught, but she didn't know if she could do that while she still held on to the Power. She might have trapped herself with her own impetuousness. Dumbass.

Holding on is the only thing I have left, said the ghost.

Fury welled. Grace said, *You didn't "kiss" my ancestor. You didn't mean to give her a gift. You just fucking bit her.*

The ghost hissed, *I give life to all of my children!*

Grace had begun to shake. Her grip was close to slipping. *We're supposed to be your CHILDREN?* she gritted. *No decent parent I know would ever put their child in jeopardy.*

I haven't put you in jeopardy! the ghost roared as she recoiled. *You did that to yourself when you tried to control something you were never meant to control!*

Really? said Grace. *You mean when I tried to take what had come to me, what was supposed to be mine? That doesn't sound like much of a gift to me.* She grew calm as she told the ghost, *It's not too late. I'm sorry you died, but you died. Maybe you didn't mean for this to happen, but you can still make good on the gift you tried to give my ancestor.*

The serpent woman stopped coiling on herself, and that feral, beautiful face turned wistful. The ghost asked, *What would you, a mere mortal, do with an immortal Power?*

Don't you think it's time we find out? Grace said. If she couldn't persuade the ghost to let go, she was going to have to take her chances and exorcise it, whether she was struggling to deal with the Power or not.

The serpent woman's wistfulness grew. She held a hand out, as if she would caress Grace's cheek. *You're not only strong. You're more impertinent than the others were.*

Grace didn't know what to do. She wanted to cry or laugh or scream. She said, *Maybe I'll grow out of that. I'm still pretty young. Give me this chance. If I am really supposed to be one of your children, let me become your heir.*

The ghost's hand dropped. She faded away. Grace felt the ghost let go.

Instinctively, she braced herself. Afterward, she realized that might have saved her sanity and maybe even her life as the dark sea rushed toward her in a tidal wave. She threw everything she had at it, straining to hold on. All thought burned away in a gigantic, formless roar.

Gradually the roar quieted as the tidal wave receded. The darkness in her mind faded until she could see sunlight again.

She looked around wildly, soaking up the sight of the meadow drenched in sunshine. Then she bent at the waist, shaking as she drew in deep gulps of air, as wrung out as if she had just sprinted a mile.

She realized she could hear voices. Don and Margie were still talking just inside the tunnel door. The entire conversation with the ghost, along with her struggle to get control of the Power, appeared to have taken place within the span of a few moments.

Goddamn. She wiped her sweating face with the back of one hand. She couldn't tell if she felt euphoric or flat out nauseated. Just, goddamn.

"Miss Andreas?" Margie said behind her. "Are you all right?"

"Call me Grace," she said, her voice hoarse. She straightened and turned. Margie and Don looked at her with nearly identical expressions of discomfort and concern. "I'm fine," she told them. "I got a little warm, that's all. Have you made a decision?"

Margie said, "We have, and I'm sorry for wasting your time. I'm just not comfortable with this."

"Please don't worry about it," Grace told her as gently as she could. She considered the two. Don appeared to be struggling with disappointment, while Margie had clearly been crying. She realized she had promised Don and Margie she would help them, and that had been part of what had helped her to hold on.

In the meantime, everything in her head seemed to have quieted down and her heart rate was returning to normal. Cautiously, she reached deep inside herself. Was it just her imagination, or did the Power feel closer? No, it was definitely closer. She made contact with the dark sea, and it rose readily to her touch.

Right there, in broad daylight. It rose to her touch, because it was hers.

Hers.

God*DAMN*.

There was no mistaking her euphoria that time. She kept a stern grip on the emotion, as she said, "If you don't mind me asking, what makes you most uncomfortable? Is it actually speaking with your father or the thought of going underground to do it?"

Margie glanced at her brother then said, "I don't mind you asking. It's both things, really. I—you were right, it's too soon for me. Then the thought of having to go down in some dark cave is too much like going into his grave."

Grace winced at the imagery and the pain so evident behind it. "I'm sorry," she said. "Remember, you can always come back when you're ready."

"I'd like that," Don said. "Maybe we'll be in a better place in a couple of weeks."

"Just e-mail me if you would like to come back. Maybe next time we can try to connect with your father without going into the cavern," Grace said. "As long as you keep in

mind I can't promise anything, I'd be willing to try if
you are."

Margie's eyes filled. "Thank you," said the older woman.
"Thank you so much."

Grace nodded, feeling awkward in the face of so much
raw gratitude.

Looking as awkward as she felt, Don handed her an envelope. She could see cash through the paper. She gave him a
small smile as she folded the envelope and slipped it into the
pocket of her capri pants.

Then they walked back to the front of the property,
mostly in silence. Neither Don nor Margie seemed inclined
to small talk, and Grace had more than enough on her mind.

She needed to digest what had happened, to consider
what it might all mean.

The ghost had said the woman she had bitten had gone
mad. Had the woman been too mad to comprehend what had
really happened or explain it to her children? How many of
Grace's family traditions were because her ancestors didn't
understand where the Power had come from or why they
couldn't control it? Had any of them tried to exorcise the
ghost before and failed? Would Grace be able to call the
Oracle's Power at will? She needed to practice, to see how
much control she could establish over it. Now that it was
hers—really hers—did that mean it wouldn't pass on to
Chloe or to some other child? Would it die with her? What
did a mere mortal do with an immortal Power?

Was she . . . still mortal? The possible implications were
enormous.

They reached the driveway. She said good-bye to Don
and Margie, and watched as they climbed into a Ford pickup.
When they pulled onto the road, Grace took a deep breath
and turned to the house.

That was when she sensed Khalil. His presence seethed.

He was in the house. With Therese. And he was very,
very angry.

Well, crap.

≈ EIGHT ≈

Grace hurried to the house and climbed the porch steps as fast as she could. As she reached for the screen door, Therese was already on the other side, slamming it open. Grace jerked back. "Whoa, easy there!"

Therese was a pretty woman in her midthirties, and usually she had what Grace privately liked to call Snow White coloring—very dark hair, pale skin, and a full mouth Therese emphasized with red lipsticks. At the moment the older woman's creamy skin was flagged with two bright spots of hectic color.

"You have a Djinn in your house!" Therese hissed. "I heard one showed up the other day, but I thought he had left!"

Like any other small, tightly knit community, witches gossiped. The percentage of humans who were born with Power was low, and often the ability tended to run in families. The number of those who pursued and received training for their Power was even lower, even in their own demesne. At the last census, those who claimed to have received training in witchcraft were under six thousand.

The coven grapevine was notorious, so Grace shouldn't have been surprised Janice had talked about Carling, Rune and Khalil, but Therese's acidic tone roused Grace's own temper.

Grace looked inside. Khalil stood with his feet planted apart and his arms folded. He was still in the black tunic and trousers from earlier, his eyes incandescent. He looked enormous and murderous.

"He is a friend of mine," she said sharply. "And I knew he was stopping by. I just forgot to tell you." She had meant to say she was sorry for not remembering to tell the other woman, but she would be damned if she apologized now.

Therese cast a wide-eyed look over her shoulder as well. She switched to telepathy. *And you allow him around the children? Are you CRAZY?*

Khalil wasn't the only one suffering from a touch of bigotry. Grace snapped back, *Stop talking about him like he's a wild dog or an infestation.*

Therese's eyes flashed. *Fine. I would have thought you had more sense than that, but suit yourself. They're not my kids.*

That last was so callous, Grace's expression turned cold. She said between her teeth, "I'm crossing you off the roster. Don't come back."

"Don't worry," said Therese. "I won't."

As the other woman flounced down the driveway to her car, Grace looked inside again. Max sat at Khalil's feet, fingering Khalil's black shoes curiously. He was oblivious to the tension between the adults. Also oblivious, Chloe was busily looking through her new pile of library books on the living room bookcase.

Khalil's eyes blazed. He said to her, *I caught that woman going through your things.*

Caught totally off guard, Grace blinked. *What?*

He repeated, *When I arrived, the woman was rifling through the papers on your desk.*

Digging through her things? What the hell.

Even as he spoke and Grace tried to process what he said, Chloe grabbed two of the books. She ran back to Khalil, chattering. "See what I got today? I can read them if you help."

Grace watched again as a remarkable transformation happened. Khalil looked down at the children, and his elegant face gentled. His rage vanished as though it had never existed. He told the little girl, gravely, "I would be honored to assist you."

Chloe beamed at him. "Does that mean you'll help?"

"Indeed," said Khalil. He bent down to pick up Max. His tremendous hands were exquisitely careful as he handled the baby.

A new surge of fury and outrage clogged Grace's throat as, behind her, Therese's car door slammed.

Digging. Through her things.

Beyond the outrage was a sense of violation, a trust that had been broken.

She checked to make sure Chloe wasn't watching her. Then she put her hand behind her back and stuck out her middle finger. Fuck you, Therese.

Therese's car peeled out of the driveway with more force than was necessary, or maybe Grace imagined it.

She looked at the kids. She thought of them playing innocently while Therese snooped around. What else had the other woman done? Grace's hands clenched, and a muscle in her jaw began to tick.

She opened the door and stepped inside. She tried to move as carefully as she could, because it felt like her rage was flowing off her body in waves. Max greeted her by blowing a happy raspberry. The smile she tried to give the baby felt more like a grimace.

Khalil glanced at her as he sat in the armchair. He settled Max on one leg and lifted Chloe, books and all, into his lap as well. Chloe folded her body up, perching on his other leg as naturally as if they had read together thousands of times before.

She could have hurt them, Grace said to Khalil. *She could have done anything.*

Khalil said, *She did not. They are well.*

The little girl eagerly opened her top book and pointed to the page. "What does this say?"

Khalil bent his head and began to read.

Grace watched them for a moment. They were a strange yet wonderful sight. If she apologized to anyone, she felt she owed it to Khalil for forgetting to let him know Therese would be babysitting. But she had only found out about Therese snooping because she had forgotten and Khalil had shown up unannounced.

It's not just what the hell, she thought. It's *why* the hell?

She didn't have any money for Therese to steal, and the other woman would have known that. Grace certainly didn't have any secrets. It wasn't as though Therese was a teenager, with a teenager's sometimes irresponsible sense of boundaries. Had it been pure, simple nosiness?

Forcing her muscles to unknot, she moved quietly through the living room into the office.

As she studied the room, she tried to remember exactly how everything had been. The stack of papers on her desk was a hodgepodge collection of bills, photocopies of journal articles for her unfinished school projects and various drafts of her resume. The papers seemed slightly disarranged—or was that only because she knew Therese had gone through them?

She rubbed the back of her neck. The truth was, her desk wasn't all that neat, and she would never have noticed anything if Khalil hadn't caught Therese. Her computer was on, and she distinctly remembered turning it off earlier. But again, if Khalil hadn't said anything, she would have shrugged it off, thinking perhaps Therese had wanted to check her e-mail.

Maybe none of it meant anything. Maybe Therese *had* checked her e-mail. Maybe she had dug through the papers because she had been looking for a pen and a blank piece of paper.

She had been awfully outraged at Khalil's unexpected appearance.

Was that really bigotry, or was it anger that she had been caught?

Caught doing what, exactly?

Grace and Therese weren't friends, merely acquaintances. Therese belonged to one of the local covens, and Grace had met her a time or two—enough not to question having her on the babysitting roster or think twice about leaving her alone with the children. But Grace still felt angry and unsettled, betrayed and hurt.

And she wasn't even sure if she should.

Except for Therese's callousness. As far as Grace was concerned, even if the other woman had reacted out of anger, what she had said and how she had said it were unforgiveable. Grace went back into the living room, to the bookcase where she kept her purse. She looked through the contents. Car keys, identification, checkbook, a packet of gum, one of Max's pacifiers. She had the same amount of cash in her wallet that she'd had earlier, sixteen dollars and fifty-three cents. As far as she could tell, Therese hadn't taken anything.

Grace turned and studied the living room, her hands on her hips. It was the same as her office area, untidy and lived in.

Khalil glanced at her again from under his brows. He asked, *Are any of your possessions missing?*

His expression promised trouble for Therese if there were. Grace shook her head, her mouth a tight, unhappy line.

I do not care for this babysitting roster if other people like Therese are on it, he said.

I don't either, she told him. *I really don't.*

If she couldn't rely on the people on the roster, what the hell was she going to do now? She rubbed the back of her neck and added it to the growing list of shit she needed to think about.

And thinking wasn't going to make the kids supper. She walked toward the kitchen.

As she passed the armchair, she asked, "Will you stay for supper?"

The smooth flow of words in Khalil's low, pure voice halted.

He said, "Very well."

. . .

Friend, Grace had called him.

Khalil resumed reading to the little ones, while he mulled over the word. The baby sucked his thumb and leaned back so he could look up at Khalil's face. Chloe rested light as a pixie against Khalil's other side and fingered the edges of the page as she listened to him. Her blonde hair floated like dandelion fluff around her head. His daughter, Phaedra, had not been, even at her youngest, as fragile as these two humans were. These baby birds were warm, soft, openhearted and open-minded. So trusting.

When he had caught Therese digging through the papers on Grace's desk, Max and Chloe had been in the living room. Max had been chewing on a stuffed animal while he watched Chloe pull toys out of her toy box. Khalil had felt a rage so deep at Therese, the only reason why she remained unharmed was because the children had been present.

Friend.

Over the last day, Khalil had been busy with his own life. He hadn't accomplished everything he wanted to do. He still wanted to discuss Grace's vision with one of the first generation Djinn of his House. He was too disturbed to dismiss the experience. Even if the vision had been Cuelebre's, Khalil had heard the voice too. "Global," Grace had said. And "elemental." Perhaps the Oracle needed to distance herself from the visions that came for other people, but he did not.

Other matters interfered with his goals. He ended up talking through the night with certain members of his House about an issue that had arisen with House Shaytan. House Marid had convened this morning to decide how they would, as a collective, respond to certain actions made by Shaytan members. When the folk of the air gathered en masse, they did so over oceans or deserts, because their energies swirled like gigantic tornadoes and endangered those who were bound to flesh.

He had been bored by House Shaytan's actions and had found the discussions and arguments made by his own House just as dry and uninteresting. Why must everything always be balanced, down to the most precise equation? Grace was right; they had become a pedantic lot. Perhaps House Shaytan had meant to cause offense, and offense had certainly been taken, but nobody had actually been attacked or injured.

When it came his time to speak, he urged his House to ignore the whole idiotic thing and get back to the business of living their lives. The other Djinn were startled and disturbed. Grudgingly, one or two admitted that the issue might not be as urgent as had been first believed. Then a few others agreed, and eventually the whole assembly had disintegrated into disgruntled mutterings.

The entire process had been a colossal waste of time, and that was not a phrase an immortal being, who had all the time in the world, bothered to use that often.

After that, because the Djinn were part of the greater Demonkind collective, Khalil traveled to the Demonkind demesne offices in Houston.

Demonkind were like the Nightkind in one regard; they were the only two Elder demesnes in the United States that contained a variety of creatures, for the Wyr, despite their immense variety, were all essentially two-natured beings.

However, for the Nightkind, Vampyres had long since become the dominant race, and their demesne was ruled by a Vampyre monarch.

The Demonkind demesne was unique among the U.S. demesnes. Like the human U.S. government, and also like the Djinn, the Demonkind demesne was the only one that governed by consensus, through representatives of each Demonkind race: the Djinn, devils, the medusae, ogres, monsters (those creatures who did not develop a Wyr form, such as the Sphinx) and, unfortunately, the Goblins.

Everyone considered the Goblins unfortunate.

Djinn elders from the five Houses took turns acting as representatives in the Demonkind legislature. Khalil was currently serving his two-year term. It was not an especially onerous task, although it was time consuming. When he reached his own offices in Houston, he assumed his physical form to spend the afternoon reading through papers and answering e-mails.

At midafternoon, he took a break. On impulse he Googled "Grace Andreas" and "Oracle." He discovered the Oracle's website and read all the information posted there. The history of the Oracle was long and rich, even by Djinn standards.

Friend.

His world was vast and intricate, and built on associations upon associations. His House. The Djinn. The different creatures of the Demonkind. The Demonkind demesne's various alliances and antagonisms with humankind and the other demesnes. Favors granted and favors owed.

In all of his associations, Khalil thought, very few would call him friend.

How had Grace known to align her energy with his yesterday? Her surprise seemed to indicate she had done so by accident. He had dismissed her so cavalierly at first. He was shocked at how much there was to discover about her. He thought of how she had felt, her psychic presence resting against his, feminine and complex, with layers of Power, both old and young. It had been delicious, exotic, surprising and enticing. Sexual.

Remembering it, he held himself under tight control.

Pleasant supper smells wafted through the shabby, comfortable house. Chloe grew restless and wriggled out of his lap to run to the kitchen. She announced, "I'm hungry!"

"Hello, Hungry, I'm Grace," said Grace. "Nice to meet you."

Chloe giggled, and Khalil smiled. He rested his cheek on the top of Max's head. The boy had a strong, light energy and a kernel of Power that was like a rosebud waiting for the right season to unfurl. His wispy tuft of hair smelled like clean baby. Khalil approved of this little man. Very much so.

Grace said behind him, "Dinner's ready."

He nodded, set the children's books aside and carried Max into the kitchen.

The room was complicated. He paused to take it all in. The table was set simply with three place settings. Each plate had a few slices of apple. There was a fragrant central dish that, if Khalil didn't miss his guess, looked like broccoli, rice and cheese. Chloe's place had a small glass of milk. The other two plates had glasses filled with ice and a brown, clear liquid. A bowl had been set on the table in front of Max's high chair. It was filled with different colors of goop. Khalil had no idea what was in that bowl; he assumed it must be food.

Khalil turned his attention to Grace. Her red-gold hair was disheveled, and her cheeks were touched with a healthy faint blush, a far better color than her chalky complexion of the last couple of days. He guessed her earlier paleness had stemmed from exhaustion. The shadows on her face had eased as well. She was barefoot and wore a yellow tank top, along with short, dark green pants that just covered her scarred knees. The pants emphasized her slender ankles and arched, graceful feet. She was not wearing the knee brace, so her leg must not be not causing her as much discomfort. He was glad to see that.

Really, she was well formed all over, with high, small breasts, a long, narrow waist and a flat stomach that flared gently into rounded hips. All in all, her physical form was entirely pleasing to gaze upon.

He remembered how shapely her lean, muscled legs had been, except for the livid red scars. He was suddenly angry on her behalf. The physical damage from the accident might be permanent, but it had been wholly avoidable, if only she'd had access to Powerful medical care. Now she would have to suffer some kind of limitation, if not outright discomfort or pain, for the rest of her brief life.

Then he remembered another thing. She had said, *I didn't have health insurance or the money to pay for that kind of treatment.* He looked around with a new perspective, noting the signs of age and wear in the furnishings. He remembered the page on the Oracle's website that explained donations. It even had a PayPal button. Why did Grace not have enough money?

He had visited often enough now to realize that, while at times the house might be cluttered with the business of dealing with small, active children and daily life, underneath the clutter, it was clean.

His scrutiny must have grown too prolonged, because her pretty, fine-boned face grew self-conscious. She gestured awkwardly at the table. "I know you said you don't need physical refreshment," she said. "But you seemed to enjoy nibbling at things and drinking coffee yesterday at breakfast, so I set a place for you."

She was not only poor, she was generous. He smiled at her. "Thank you," he said.

Her gaze widened.

He murmured, "Maybe that phrase isn't quite so bad after all, as long as it isn't overused, as some people are wont to do."

"I can't believe I just heard someone use *wont* in a sentence with a straight face," she murmured back.

He laughed. "Will you show me how to fasten Max into his seat?"

Her vivid eyes sparkling, she did just that. He slipped the baby into place and secured the fastening. Chloe had clambered into her seat. She was already eating a slice of apple. Grace gave the girl a strange look. However, she said nothing. Instead she picked up the serving spoon and served Chloe first. She offered a spoonful to Khalil, who nodded. He was curious to taste what they would be eating. Grace served herself last. She sat in her chair by Max and began to feed him bites of the colorful goop.

Khalil tasted his own small serving of supper. He was correct. It was creamy cheese, broccoli and rice, simple and actually quite tasty. He took another bite and said telepathically to Grace, *I did not understand the expression on your face just now as you looked at Chloe.*

She glanced at him, eyes dancing. *Little Miss is on her very best behavior. You should feel flattered. She's even eating her apple slices. Holy moly, she just took a bite of broccoli. Pay no attention to me while I faint.*

He chuckled and looked at Chloe. The little girl sat very straight. She chewed vigorously with a beatific smile. He said to her, "I like libraries too."

That opened a floodgate. Chloe didn't stop talking. He learned about story time, and somebody named Katherine, and also other people named Joey and Rachel, and something strange he really didn't understand, because it was a person and yet not, and it seemed to have adventures in a castle in the living room.

There was no castle in the living room. This had to be a product of her imagination. The odd person/not-person was a Lalaloopsy—

Grace interrupted. "Wait, your doll is called a Lalaloopsy?"

"Uh-huh," Chloe said.

Grace muttered, "I thought it was Lala Whoopsie."

Well, that explained that. Sort of.

And Chloe took off again. She very much needed and wanted a big bed now, and waiting was terribly hard even for big people, and would Khalil read . . . she meant, would he help her read another book after supper?

"Yes," he said. He exchanged an amused glance with Grace as Chloe bounced in her seat with excitement.

He honored the gift of the apple slices on his plate by eating them. They were crisp, crunchy and tart. Then he drank the brown liquid. He discovered that it was iced tea, refreshing and cold. Max dribbled goop out of his mouth and giggled. Every once in a while, Grace looked at Khalil. She did so surreptitiously, out of the corner of her eye, as if she didn't want to be caught showing any kind of interest.

Each glance reminded him of how entertaining it had been to flirt with her, tease her and indulge his sense of mischief. He could sense feathery, delicate touches as she reached out psychically to touch his presence. She always withdrew again almost immediately. She didn't appear to realize that he could sense every time she did it, and she couldn't possibly know how erotic that was. It was as if she trailed her fingers very lightly along his bare skin. Aroused, he clenched down hard on himself, and his self-control turned fierce.

And he loved all of it.

Somehow the evening slipped away. He was not quite sure how it happened. At one point he looked down to discover his small serving of supper had disappeared from his plate. Max accidentally knocked over his bowl of food. The expression of openmouthed surprise on the baby's face was so comical, the rest of them burst out laughing. Grace cleaned up the mess. There wasn't much to clean up, since Max had been close to the end of his meal anyway.

Then supper dishes were washed, children bathed, the toys picked up. Chloe did not forget about her story. Khalil settled back in the armchair to read to her about an irritable boy who had a terrible, horrible, no good, very bad day. Khalil quite liked that boy. He was sorry when the story ended. Grace stretched out on the couch, and Max lay on top of her, kicking a foot lazily in the air as he sucked his thumb and his eyelids drooped.

Through the open windows and screen door, the evening shadows grew long, while the sunlight turned a heavy gold and the green of the foliage darkened. Khalil could hear traffic sounds, but they were distant and muted. The place was rich with tranquility. He was bewildered at the intense surge of his response. He had already promised his protection a couple of times, first to the children and then to Grace.

Now he actually felt the need to protect them. Whatever quality this quiet, shabby place held, it was more precious than the treasure of kings. He said to Grace, his telepathic voice edged, *You will call me whenever you need someone to look after the children, do you understand?*

Grace stirred. She had been looking relaxed and sleepy, but now she stared at him with wide, surprised eyes. *I can't expect you to be available every time I might need a babysitter.*

He set his teeth. *I want you to burn that roster.*

I can't. She sighed. *But I need to go over the list again. I think I should ask for references too. I just thought everybody who was on the roster would be all right.*

Her relaxed, sleepy expression had vanished, and she looked troubled again. He said, more gently, *Checking references will take time. In the meantime, I will be careful. I will not do anything with the children you would not wish. And I want you to call me. Please.*

Her expression softened, and there it was, luminous on

her skin, that quality more precious than the treasure of kings. She nodded to him then said aloud, "Bedtime."

Chloe said, "No."

"Baby girl, you must," Grace said, with the kind of tiredness that seemed to indicate there had been many repetitions of the same conversation. "If you don't go to bed, tomorrow can't happen."

Chloe clutched the library book. "We have to keep reading. We can't stop." She sounded close to tears.

Maybe the child didn't want to let go of this precious thing either, Khalil thought. Chloe had already suffered more loss than many children would ever know. He patted her delicate back. "May I come back to help you read another time?"

Chloe turned to look at him. Her wide gaze searched his face. "Will you come back tomorrow?"

Khalil looked at Grace over the girl's head. Grace had eased upright carefully, so as not to jostle Max, who was almost asleep. Grace met his gaze easily enough, but her expression was guarded, and her energy withdrawn. In that moment, he had no idea what she was thinking or feeling, or if she welcomed the idea of his returning so soon or becoming so actively involved in their lives.

But she had made a bargain. His face hardened. It was of no importance how she felt about the bargain after the fact. Now she must live with it.

He turned his attention back to Chloe and told her, "I will come tomorrow."

With a sudden lurch forward, Chloe flung her arms around his neck. She hugged him so tightly, he could feel her small body straining. He put his arms around her and carefully, carefully hugged her back. First it started as a reassurance for Chloe. Then it turned into something else, something about him, and it was good but it also hurt. He let the little girl go then discovered Grace standing by the armchair, Max in her arms. She was watching him and Chloe, her brows drawn.

He heard himself whisper, "I miss my daughter."

Grace gripped his shoulder hard, her gaze filling with

such pained compassion, he had to look away as Chloe slipped off his lap. Grace said, "I'll be just a minute."

He gestured with a hand. It was of no consequence to him whether she was just a minute or many minutes.

She hesitated then left with Chloe and Max. He stood to walk over to the doorway and look out at the deepening evening. A family of raccoons waddled placidly across the lawn.

There was no reason for him to stay any longer. He had accomplished what he had meant to do and visited with the children. He would go.

He didn't go.

He held himself tensely, trying to soak up that precious something, that invisible treasure. Grace finished saying good night to the children. He listened to her light, uneven footsteps as she approached. He didn't turn around.

She stopped just behind him. He knew she was going to reach out. He sensed her hand hovering in the air at his back.

Before she could touch him, he turned and gave her a silken smile. "Why don't we play another round of the truth game?"

She froze, startled, her hand suspended. Wariness crept into her eyes, and the softness in her expression firmed. "Why?"

He moved away from her and prowled around the room. "Why not?"

She turned to track his movements. "That's not an answer."

Her energy had roused. She was bristling. Good. Bristling was good. He picked up one of her textbooks, read the spine and set it aside. He picked up another. "I don't owe you an answer. We haven't started another round yet."

She put her hands on her hips. "Screw your game and your rounds and your forfeit. Just talk already, like a rational creature. If you have something to say, say it."

"Fine." He slammed the second book down and turned on her. "Why did you call me your friend?"

Silence pulsed between them. He watched her so closely, he saw her blink several times. Her face worked. Pain or laughter or a little of both; he wasn't sure. Definitely a flash of anger. She said, "Because right now you're the closest thing to a friend that I've got."

"Katherine," he said.

"She's very caring. I don't know what I would do without her. She loves the children, and she misses my sister almost as much as I do, but she was Petra's friend. She's not really *my* friend. She and I don't really talk or share confidences." Grace shrugged and looked out the window. Her eyes glittered. "I know," she said, very low and bitter. "You're not really my friend either. We have a *bargain*."

He dissolved and reformed in front of her. She flinched back as he took her by the shoulders. He wanted to shake her for her naïveté. He wanted to shout at her for her foolish compassion and generosity. He wanted to rage through the house and across the land, and tear down this precious invisible thing he didn't understand. He wanted to dislike her again and fight with her and—

She looked incredulous. Then she did something that truly astonished him. "Come here," she said.

As he froze, staring, she put both hands to the back of his neck and pulled his head down with such bewildering confidence, he allowed her to get away with it, if for no other reason but to see what she would do next. He bent, and she put her arms around his neck, and she gave him a full-bodied hug as tight as the one Chloe had given him, until her arms trembled from the strength she put into it.

And she didn't just hug him physically. She hugged him with all of her spirit, her fiery warm presence settling against his, femininity to masculinity, Power to Power.

"I can't imagine how much you miss your daughter," she whispered. "But I know how much I miss my family. And it hurts very much."

He had torn down the stones at the entrance to an ancient pharaoh's funeral temple at Saqqara. He had caused earthquakes, raised hurricanes, leveled mountains. He had waged war with a first generation Djinn, one of the strongest of his kind, and he had won. He could shred Grace into pieces in an instant. He had thought he was so much older, wiser and more powerful than she.

But this. This.

He wrapped his arms and his Power around her. His head was just an illusion. He did not know why it felt so heavy. Still, he rested it on her slender shoulder, and she stroked the back of his head.

"You cannot take it back," he said. His voice was muffled against her skin.

"Take what back?" she asked.

Their bargain. The truths they had exchanged. Her angry, funny quips. The gifts of food, drink, laughter and compassion. Her permission to visit with the children. Her promise to call him so he could watch over them. The claim to friendship.

He raised his head. He said, "Any of it."

Her skin was flush with gentle color like a ripe peach. Her lips looked exceeding soft, full and luscious. She opened her mouth to say something again, to question, argue, prevaricate or to say something unbearably wise.

He decided he wouldn't let her. So he cupped the back of her head, tilted her back and kissed her.

≈ NINE ≈

Grace couldn't remember an evening she had enjoyed more. Watching Khalil with the children was a breathtaking experience, one small, miraculous moment unfolding after another.

Yes, his alien appearance and strength emphasized their human fragility, but their bright happiness at his companionship emphasized his gentleness and the care he took with them, and they blossomed under his attention. Grace told herself she kept a close eye on him to make sure nothing else inappropriate like the doggie-cat incident happened again. But that was such a bad lie, she couldn't fool herself. She was watching him so closely because he was such a pleasure to watch.

He learned fast with the children, and now he asked questions when he wasn't sure about something, instead of arrogantly assuming he knew the answers. And it was such an unexpected pleasure to share a laughing glance with him whenever Max or Chloe did something hilarious or goofy. The pleasure brought with it a bittersweet memory of watching Petra and Niko's exchanged glances of amusement over their children's heads.

Learning to enjoy his companionship was spiced with the

sense of immersion in his male presence. At times she felt like she was swimming in a sea of his Power, buoyed and sustained, all tiredness washed away by his dynamic energy. Then he made his quiet confession about his daughter that was filled with so much pain, her heart went out to him.

Something she did, perhaps the fact that she had the temerity to hug him, made him angry. Or maybe his own pain made him angry.

It was probably dangerous for her to think she might understand him. Dangerous, when he took her in an unbreakable hold and he looked at her so angrily, and she knew that he could crush her without a second thought, and she also knew he wouldn't. He looked at her as if he might hate her, eyes ablaze, his marble face set like stone.

And then. Then.

You cannot take it back, he said. *Any of it*.

Michelangelo's genius took her in his arms. His head arced down to hers, inhumanly fast, his carved features cut with intensity. She had no chance to react before his hard mouth settled over hers.

He did not engage in any tentative, preliminary exploration, as had virtually every other male (boy) she had ever kissed. Khalil's kiss was a hectic, headlong plunge into her mouth. She lost her breath at the shock and the strangeness of it, clinging to his shoulders.

His mouth and body were hot to the touch, his Power scorching. She shivered at the sensations, and the muscles in her legs trembled. She felt his fierce energy slide along hers, and it was extraordinarily erotic, almost more intimate than a physical caress. Her skin felt hypersensitive all over, her arms and her nipples and the heavy, full undersides of her breasts and the private, moistening place between her legs, so inadequately covered by her clothes.

She dug her fingers into the raven hair at the back of his head and hung on, her mouth moving jerkily under his in a clumsy attempt to kiss him back. Fractured thoughts and impressions swirled in her head, blasted by a cyclone. His familiar energy, the exotic sensation of his mouth, the blast of pain, anger and sexuality that roared out of him. His hunger and his need.

He cradled the back of her head in the palm of one hand. His other arm circled her low at the waist. His hold tightened on her until her feet left the ground.

She felt weightless, as if she was floating in him. The fastening that kept his hair pulled back was a simple strip of leather, and it came undone underneath her fingers. The black, silken mass tumbled to his shoulders.

He lifted his head and looked down at her. His expression was tight and remote. The crystalline radiance of his eyes blazed like lighthouse beacons in the darkness, warning of treacherous, storm swept seas. His lips glistened with the moisture he had taken from her mouth. All she could do was stare dumbly at him as she trembled all over, for he was so rampantly glorious, it had stolen her voice.

He eased her down again until her feet touched the floor. She wasn't sure she would be able to stand on her own.

But then she had to, because he let go of her and vanished without a word.

Khalil's kiss burned in her memory that night and through Wednesday. She woke up at night, aroused, her skin damp with a light sheen of sweat, her sheet tangled around her legs. He had used his mouth with such experienced sensuality. Clearly he had taken human lovers before. Realizing that after the fact was devastating. It brought into the forefront of her imagination thoughts of what he might be like as a lover, something that once would have seemed barely conceivable but was now urgently compelling.

Sensations and images flashed through her mind. The feel of his hard mouth taking hers, and the sense of limitless strength in his enormous body. The sheen of his raven hair as it broke loose and framed his ivory, inhuman face and incandescent eyes. The heat contained in his physical form and his scorching, true presence. His regal demeanor, his pain and his anger.

Khalil's pain and anger didn't bother her especially. Grace understood pain and anger, rather more than was probably good for her. But what she did not understand was that he had seemed angry with *her*. What had she done, or not done, to make him angry? She brooded on that the next day.

Her preoccupation made her stupid. She managed to put the salt and pepper shakers in the refrigerator, and when they were out running more errands and she stopped to get gas, she drove away from the pump without replacing her gas cap. Luckily when the cap fell off the hood of the car, it rolled to the edge of the gas station's parking lot, and she was able to find it easily enough when she drove back to look for it.

She also had a difficult time focusing on what had happened in the back meadow, but she forced herself to concentrate. Because of her own impetuousness, she had put herself in danger, and she couldn't afford to do that again so cavalierly. While the children napped, she concentrated on running through the mental exercises her grandmother had taught her. She pulled up the Oracle's Power carefully, and when she let it go again, she did so slowly in a controlled fashion.

By the time she had finished practicing a few times, she was able to call the Power up at any time of the day or night, no matter where she was. While she would never forget how dangerous it could be, working with it had a different quality than it had that first wild, tempestuous time. It no longer strained to flow away from her or bucked to get away from her control.

Early in the morning, she spent over an hour carefully looking for evidence that the strange ghost was still influencing it, but the serpent woman really had relinquished her hold and was nowhere to be found. The more Grace worked with the Power, the more readily it came to hand. Now if she could only figure out what all of it meant, but she thought that might take years or even decades. She made a silent promise to Chloe to work as hard as she could to make it hers irrevocably. Immortal Power or not, she planned to take it with her when she died. Then Chloe, along with any other female descendants Grace might have, would be truly free to explore destinies of their own choosing.

That was Grace's destiny. It was the first thing in her life, including college, that she embraced wholeheartedly.

By the time Khalil showed up Wednesday evening to read Chloe the promised story, Grace thought she had the whole incident with him figured out.

She thought it was possible to sometimes hurt too badly to accept comfort. Maybe by offering him the hug, she had touched something he couldn't bear to have touched. If that was so, she wasn't sure what to do next. It didn't seem quite the thing to apologize or to bring it up so they could talk, but keeping silent felt strange too. She felt adrift at sea, unable to make a decision as to how to move forward.

Khalil did not show up until after supper. By then she had tied herself up in knots. She and Chloe were picking the day's toys up and stacking them in the living room toy box. Max stood at the coffee table, hanging onto the edge while he chewed on plastic toy keys. He was teething and had become obsessed with chewing on anything he could get his hands on.

Khalil appeared in silence, but she could feel his arrival at her back. Her pulse leaped. She turned from the toy box, tangled up in pleasure, self-consciousness, discomfort and confusion.

Whoa. He seemed bigger when she hadn't seen him for a day.

His arms were crossed. He wore plain black. Even though she had seen him assume other colors, black seemed to be his go-to color when in physical form. His hair was bound back again, and his pale, elegant face wore a closed expression. He held his energy tight with rigid restraint. Looking at him was like running full speed into a wall.

Oblivious to the undercurrent of tension in the room, Chloe sang out a happy greeting, skipped up to him and flung out her arms. He gave the little girl a slight smile and picked her up. "What shall I assist you in reading today?"

"The terrible, no good day!" she said.

"That is an excellent choice," he told her. "I would have picked it too."

He carried Chloe over to the bookcase where she leaned over to retrieve the book, then they settled in the armchair. Max let go of the coffee table, fell to his diaper-padded bottom and scuttled over to them eagerly. Khalil scooped the baby up too, and he began to read to them.

Aside from a glance and a nod, Khalil didn't speak to Grace. Her leaping pulse twisted into a heavy sludge, and her own energy clenched into a hurt knot. So that's what it was going to be like, was it?

Fine. Screw him.

Their laundry pile had turned into a mountain. She was determined to catch up before people arrived on Saturday. She went into the kitchen to switch loads, fold clothes and diapers, and carry most of them to the children's bedroom. After she had put their things away, she straightened and dusted, changed their sheets, and then she went into the half bath, which had somehow turned into a disaster area. She cleaned the mirror, scrubbed vigorously at the sink and toilet and mopped the floor. Then it was time to switch the laundry around again and fold more clothes.

The house felt too close, and the fans did little more than push the humid air around. The ghosts sighed and murmured with vague restlessness. Outside, the crickets and cicadas began to saw their nightly symphony. Grace felt toxic with sweat and dust, bathroom cleaning chemicals and anger.

She had been lonely, the kiss hadn't meant anything, and he was clearly regretting it. How many mistakes did that sentence encapsulate in the history of relationships?

She was standing at the kitchen table, slapping folded diapers into a growing pile, when Khalil spoke in that low voice of his that was much too pure to be human. The purity shivered over her skin and through her awareness. Her hands stilled, and she closed her eyes, aching as she listened to it. He spoke with a deep clarion power she imagined renegade angels might use, as they called one another to war with God.

Then she realized the depth of her own foolishness. How

could someone that wild and regal, that immortal and pure, be interested in someone as flawed and uninteresting as her? He was a prince of his kind, while she didn't even know what the term *prince* meant to them. She was the antithesis of her own name, graceless, churlish and rough. She fingered her chapped knuckles, and her throat ached when she tried to swallow.

She hadn't hurt him. She hadn't been important enough to hurt him.

Belatedly, she caught up with what he was saying. ". . . and I thought you would not mind if I put Chloe and Max to bed."

She looked over her shoulder. Khalil held the children in his arms. Max was sound asleep on one huge shoulder, and Chloe had her head down on the other shoulder. She was knuckling her eyes and yawning. Grace met Khalil's gaze briefly to nod an assent before she turned back to the laundry.

He clearly didn't want to talk with her, and she didn't expect him to come back into the kitchen. She finished folding the load of laundry, grabbed a washcloth and went over to the sink to wash her face and the back of her neck. Then she sponged off her bare arms. She was too tired again to climb the stairs for a bath. Tomorrow she wanted to go upstairs while the kids were down for their afternoon nap, and she would run a bubble bath that reached the top of the huge, claw-foot tub in the upstairs bathroom and soak until they woke up.

For the first time, she had worn shorts in public that day and simply ignored the sidelong looks people gave her scarred legs. The cool, moist cloth felt good on her overheated skin. She couldn't twist her bad leg and lift it in the air to wash, nor could she balance her whole weight on it to lift the other leg, so she had to sit at one of the kitchen chairs when she washed her legs and feet. She rinsed and remoistened the cloth, sat down and—

Khalil's tremendous hand came down gently over hers.

She froze. She didn't blink or breathe, and she didn't look up. She just stared at his hand as he eased the cloth out of her unresisting hold.

"You will allow me," he said. Said, didn't ask.

She would?

He knelt on one knee in front of her, an immaculate giant with his regal, severe expression still closed to scrutiny. She blinked as he took her bad leg and lifted it with care. He began passing the washcloth over her overheated skin, from midthigh, down very lightly over her knee to her calf.

"I saw you limping earlier," he said. "You should have put on the brace."

Lightning danced through her muscles. The washcloth felt cool and refreshing as he stroked it along the contours of her leg with a delicate sensitivity that surprised her. She could barely hold herself still. She managed to articulate, "I'm hot and cranky, and I didn't want to wear it."

"That was foolish," he said.

"It was none of your business," she said.

"Have you begun checking the babysitting roster yet?"

"I haven't had time," she said shortly. What did he think she was capable of, anyway? There were only so many hours in a day. Then she realized she had never told him what had happened in the back meadow. The realization felt odd, and it led her to another realization: just how very much she had begun to confide in him.

He didn't seem to take offense at her tone. He merely nodded as he curled the washcloth around her bare ankle. Then a prince of the Djinn washed her foot, set down her leg gently and reached for the other, and she couldn't stand it. She grabbed him by the wrist and told him, "Stop it." Her voice sounded as raw and as graceless as the rest of her.

He stopped and looked at her. Kneeling as he was, their heads were at the same level. She fell into forever again as she looked in his diamond eyes. He looked stern, still rigidly contained and impossible to read. He said to her, his tone deliberately even, "We will play the truth game now, just one more time."

Would they? She was getting tired of being told what to do. She said between her teeth, "I don't hear you asking me."

He leaned an elbow on his upraised knee, his crystalline gaze steady, ruthless. "I can always leave."

Her mouth threatened to wobble. "Why do you want to play?"

"I would have this exchange balanced," he said tersely.

She was bewildered. She didn't understand why the concept of a balanced exchange was so important to him. Maybe it had something to do with control? Then she remembered what he had said before, about wishing for information and not wanting to be beholden to her for it. Her expression tightened.

Well, it wasn't as if she had anything real to lose. She folded her arms and said, "No. We're done with the truth game. Ask me what you want to ask me, and I'll answer or not if I like. I'll ask you anything I want, and you'll answer or not if you like. No forfeit, no control, no balance. No more favors or deals or measuring shit. We'll either have a real, messy conversation, or you can get the hell out."

He grew angry. She could feel it shifting through his energy, slow and sulfurous like slow-moving lava.

She liked it. His anger felt satisfying. It meant he wasn't indifferent to her. So she pushed him harder. "Go on, go."

Ever since he had kissed her, Khalil had felt wrapped in invisible chains.

He had attended to his various duties with a surly attitude, snarling at anyone unfortunate enough to get in his way or to look at him strangely. He sat in on a Demonkind legislative committee hearing because it was his responsibility and he must, but he didn't listen or participate. The committee chair put the subject to a vote, and Khalil looked around at the people with whom he most often shared a common point of view. He raised his hand when they did. Nobody remarked upon it, so he must not have voted for anything too out of character.

He left the legislature and let go of his physical form as soon as he was able to. Then he took to the winds. Releasing his physical form wasn't as satisfying as he had thought it would be. Nothing he did that day was.

He could not seem to put enough distance between himself and thinking about Grace and the children. He wondered what they were doing that day. Finally, in exasperation, he chose to leave Earth altogether. He materialized into his physical form on the moon.

There was no sound, because the moon had no atmosphere. There was no wind, no air. The sun was a piercing roar of flame. The sun's reflected light off the moon's surface was silver white; fragile, unshielded human eyes would have been blinded by the radiance. It did not discomfort Khalil in any way, because his form was a focus. He did not need to breathe. He crossed his arms, staring at the milky green, blue and white ball that was Earth, while he soaked up the blast of inexhaustible energy from the sun.

The moon was as far as the Djinn could travel from Earth without traversing one of the many crossover passages that led to Other lands in other dimensions. Many theories had been put forth about the Other lands, but Khalil thought that the lands were, in the end, either shadows or mirrors, reflections or folds, of the Earth itself.

Around noon, he wondered what Grace and the children were eating for lunch. It would be cheerful, simple and tasty enough to tempt a picky child's appetite.

Bah. He was back to thinking about them again. With a silent hiss he flicked his fingers angrily in the direction of the blue-white orb. Then he dematerialized and went to the far side of the moon. That side permanently faced away from Earth. It was much more suited to his brooding mood. The surface was battered and densely cratered. The moon was halfway through its lunar cycle, so part of the far side was in darkness.

Here light and dark were knifelike. There were no soft, colorful shadows of dusk, as there had been at Grace's house last evening. He chose the darkness and rematerialized to lean back against a boulder and stare at the sharp, bright stars. Away from the Earth's atmosphere, they seemed closer, but they weren't.

He pushed away from the boulder and strode along the moon's surface restlessly. The invisible chains were inside of him. It did not matter where he chose to go. His own thoughts were his cage.

Tasty.

Last night, Grace's mouth had been tasty, succulent with surprise and a kind of honeyed innocence that had nothing to do with virginity and everything to do with the breathless pleasure of new exploration. Her energy had bloomed with arousal.

She was not all sweetness and light. She had thorns, prickly edges and that quick temper he loved to bait into flaring, but the thing that sent him spearing into the night after kissing her was how the darkness of her pain called to his.

While he was not as bigoted as he had once pretended to be with Grace, he had not known many humans very well. He had met those who were just as he had said, conniving and too interested in the search for Power. He had also met some that he enjoyed, and he had taken humans as lovers before.

As lovers they had been toys, a game he had played at, meaningless diversions when he had been bored and looking for a change. He had taken on his physical form for them, because the human lovers Khalil had known couldn't sense his full, invisible aspect. They didn't have the presence or the Power to align with his. They couldn't know what brought him the deepest, truest pleasure, and he always quickly lost interest in them.

Grace had the ability. She was like no other human he had met before. Her Power was, quite literally, unique. She could match him, fit to his presence in the way that Djinn made love to Djinn, share in formless pleasure and arousal. It was bizarre.

It was perfect.

For the first time he seriously wondered what pleasures the actual human senses might have to offer.

His physical form gave him a limited imitation of what humans experienced with all their senses, bound in flesh as they were. But he never really felt the depth of real physical hunger or pain. He never fully tasted, as humans did, the delicacy or nuances of flavor in food, nor did he know to its fullest extent the intensity of physical sexual pleasure. He only played at those appetites, as did most Djinn, sooner or later.

Taking on a physical form took effort and Power. The more real the form that Djinn took on, the more it cost them. To create a fully human form, with the most complicated thing of all, a brain, was an irreversible act. The Djinn called it "falling into flesh." There were between stages of formation that were reversible, but most Djinn only bothered with forming a facade.

If he created a more complete form, with real skin, he could discover what she felt like when he licked her lips. He could truly know why that sensation shivered through her energy and Power, and heightened her arousal to a fever pitch. The effort would be tiring and cost him more Power, but as long as he did not fall completely into human flesh, he could discard the form whenever he chose.

And then he would know.

He returned to Earth with a more settled frame of mind and went through the rest of his day.

Now as he knelt in front of Grace, he tried to initiate a controlled, rational, *balanced* exchange, but she denied all of it. She denied him. Worse, she ordered him to leave.

He usually liked when she dictated, but he didn't like that. He glared at her angry face. Those plush, soft lips of hers were folded into a tight line. She sat bolt upright with her arms wrapped around her middle. She pressed her legs together and turned them to the side. None of that looked promising, controlled or rational. It certainly didn't look balanced.

He frowned and studied her more closely. She didn't just look angry. She looked hurt and resentful, but he would be damned if he would leave just because she ordered him to go. He gritted his teeth. "I kissed you last night when I was angry. I shouldn't have done that."

Surprise changed her expression and posture. Her arms loosened, and her tight lips unfolded. "Are you apologizing?"

He considered. The tricky thing was, he wasn't sorry for the kiss. After a moment, he said, "I don't know."

She watched him. A shrewd spark had entered her eyes. "You were more than just angry."

His own gaze narrowed. He did not reply.

She began to enunciate, as if she were speaking to an idiot. "Here's what you should apologize for: you left last night without saying a word. And you arrived this evening without a word of greeting to me. You wouldn't even look at me."

"I looked at you," he muttered. He couldn't stop looking at her, in between reading the pages of Chloe's book. Grace moved with athletic grace, despite her leg. That was when he had noticed that her limp had become pronounced again.

Her flow of words hiccupped only for a moment. "You were rude. You tell me I can't take back calling you my friend. Well, let me tell you something, Khalil. Friends don't treat each other that way."

He felt as if she had punched him between the eyes. Not because she had told him off—she had been lecturing him since they first laid eyes on each other. He tried to think back. He was almost certain that this was the first time she had ever said his name. That changed something, somehow. It was . . . more intimate.

"Grace," he said, experimenting. She had a lovely name. He watched her face change and grow uncertain; she must have felt it too. "I have had much to think about. I am sorry for leaving so abruptly and for coming back so—" Conflicted. Convoluted. Contrary. He finished, "Complicated. And I don't want to be friends."

She flinched, and said sarcastically, "Oh, so I can't take that back, but you can?"

"I don't want to take it back," he said, putting emphasis on the last word. "I want to change it."

She froze again. "What do you mean?"

"Last night you kissed me too," he pointed out. His eyelids lowered. "I want you to kiss me again."

She sucked in a breath. Color flared into her cheeks. "What? W-why?"

He cocked his head. "Why do you think? I want to know if you would like to kiss me again. Am I too strange for you to enjoy?"

The color in her cheeks deepened. She looked perplexed, flustered, all of her vivid colors bright, from the azure-jade honey of her eyes, to her strawberry blonde hair, and that dark red flush that highlighted her cheeks so beautifully. Then her gaze fell. She said in a strangled whisper, "I loved kissing you. Couldn't you tell?"

He smiled, surprised by the pleasure her honesty had brought him. "I was busy at the time. I thought so, but I wanted to be sure."

"I don't know about kissing you again, though."

That jolted him. He didn't like it. He came up on both knees and grasped the seat of her chair, on either side of her slender legs, and came nose to nose with her. He said, "Explain."

She looked at him directly. When she spoke, she did so with evident difficulty, and there was no denying the truth in her words. "Times are hard for me right now. I have things I've got to do. I don't know how I'm going to get some of them done, and the kids must always come first. If you're saying what I think you're saying, I . . . Khalil, you've said you're sorry, and I accept your apology, but you hurt my feelings, and it made my day harder. I just don't think I should get tangled up in something that does that to me. It's not fair to the kids. Poking at you and indulging in the truth game for a little while was about as much foolishness as I dare to indulge. I've been too impetuous lately about a lot of things, and I need to be more careful. I think friendship is all I can offer you."

He had to give her credit. She very clearly drew a line he had not foreseen, and it was a sensible, responsible one. He should be relieved. Maybe he should be offended. He was certainly chagrined. He had spent all that time today considering whether or not he would take her as a lover. It had never occurred to him to spend any time considering whether or not she would take him. So, he should go.

He didn't go.

Instead he took her hands in his. They were so much smaller than his, fine boned, the fingers slightly reddened from her hard work. Gravely, he raised them up to kiss them, first one hand then the other. "I will not make things harder for you. I said I would protect you and the children, and I will, in this way too."

She nodded. Was that resignation or disappointment that flashed in her eyes?

Then he leaned forward and kissed her mouth. This time he did so lightly, and just as they had last night, her pretty lips fell open in surprise. He caressed them with his, enjoying their soft, plush terrain. He pulled back and said to her firmly, "I have heard you, and I respect your reasons, but you should not say no. I have apologized and you have accepted it. That means we should put that behind us and look to the future."

She looked down at their hands. Her expression twisted with uncertainty.

He said firmly, "Grace." Her gaze flashed back up to his. He cupped her cheek and told her, "I am busy tomorrow. But I will come on Friday to read to the children. And you should say 'we'll see.'"

"You should not tell me what to say," she said, scolding.

He stroked his thumb over her lips as he raised his eyebrows. "And?"

For a moment she looked undecided. He braced himself for another argument. Then a reluctant smile broke over her face, and her dimples appeared again. "All right. We'll see."

≡ TEN ≡

Grace was busier than ever on Thursday and Friday. Aside from the usual activity involved in daily caretaking for Chloe and Max, getting ready for a group work day involved as much work as the work day itself did.

The morning after her talk with Khalil, she woke up before the kids did, with a course of action already settled in her mind. The ninety-day grace period for a new Oracle was a custom, not a law of physics or magic, or some kind of sacred covenant with a god. It wasn't even a bargain, and like calling up the Power in the daylight, Grace couldn't think of a single reason why she couldn't change it.

Isalynn LeFevre, acting in her capacity as Head of the witches, had been the one to order the babysitting roster staffed by volunteer witches. A tall, striking, African American with an ageless beauty, Isalynn looked like she could have been thirty, but Grace guessed she was closer to her midfifties, for she was not only one of Kentucky's longest-serving, most popular senators, she had also been Head of the witches' demesne for over twelve years.

"After all," Isalynn had said to Grace at Petra and Niko's memorial service, "the Oracle is not only one of our demesne's resources and strengths, but it is our heritage too, and it is our responsibility to support you."

Before Grace had time to rethink things and back out of her decision, early on Thursday morning, before the children got up, she sent an e-mail to Isalynn LeFevre's office.

Dear Senator LeFevre,

Due to unforeseen complications, I will be unable to take petitions as the Oracle for at least another month, and I ask that you put out a public notice to this effect. I will also post a sign at the end of my driveway. I'm sorry for any inconvenience this may cause to petitioners.

Also, while I am grateful for the roster your office put together, I will require babysitting references from each person on the list before resuming my duties.

Thank you for your continued support.

Best regards,
Grace Andreas

She sat in a clench for several minutes afterward, her awareness locked on the Power that rested so deeply inside. If she was wrong, it might still abandon her and go to Chloe. *I claim you, and I will hold on to you*, she said, as she called it up. *You will stay with me. You're mine.*

As it had before, the dark sea welled up readily at her command, still immense, still dangerous, but no longer bucking against her control.

Okay. She relaxed slowly, and the Power settled back into place again. Another hurdle accomplished. She turned her attention to the children and breakfast.

She had expected an e-mail reply from one of LeFevre's aides, but when the phone rang at twenty after eight, the caller turned out to be Isalynn herself. "Hello, Grace." The senator had a strong, warm, confident voice. "I hope I'm not calling too early."

"Good morning, ma'am," Grace said. The Head of the witches' demesne did not have any other honorific. "Or should I say Senator?"

"Please call me Isalynn," said the senator. "I was concerned when I read your e-mail. How are you and the children doing?"

Grace took a deep breath. She had no idea how she was supposed to answer. She said, cautiously, "It's been challenging."

"I can imagine," said Isalynn. "You have had a lot on your plate. My office will put out a public notice for you later today."

"Thank you."

"In the meantime, is there a problem with the roster? It was my understanding that all the names you were given had already been cleared."

"Yes, there has been a problem," Grace told her bluntly. "The last babysitter looked through my papers and got on my computer without my permission. Maybe there's some kind of innocent explanation for that, but I'm not comfortable with what happened, and I don't want her back in my house. Without any better information, I also don't feel good about calling anybody else right now."

"I see," said Isalynn. The warmth in her voice dropped to an icy, clipped anger. "What an unfortunate thing to have happen. I apologize, Grace, and I promise you, I will look into this issue personally. Who was it that behaved so inappropriately?"

I am a vindictive bitch, Grace thought, and I'm going to hell for enjoying this. "Therese Stannard."

"Thank you," said the senator. "I will follow up with you soon. Is this why you feel unable to take petitions?"

"It's one of the main reasons," Grace confessed. "I've also experienced some shifts in the Oracle's Power itself. I think I'd better take some more time to work with it before I expose other people to it."

"Shifts in Power," Isalynn said slowly. "Interesting. Did you know that I've consulted with the Oracle several times through the years? I petitioned your grandmother when I first thought of running for senator, and then again when I became Head of the witches' demesne. I also petitioned your sister when she became Oracle five years ago."

"I had no idea," Grace said. Max had climbed to his feet while holding on to her leg, and she ran her fingers gently through the soft tuft of baby-fine hair at the top of his head. "But then you know we're supposed to keep petitions confidential."

"Yes." The anger in Isalynn's voice had been replaced with warmth again. "Your sister had quite a different voice from your grandmother. I think each Oracle acts as a different lens for the Power. You will bring your own strengths and abilities to the experience."

"Seems like it, anyway," she muttered, scratching the back of her head. Grace hadn't interacted much with Isalynn. Not only was Isalynn much older, but she was a true Power broker on the world stage, and they didn't move in the same social circles. But Grace really liked her.

"I intend to petition you too, as soon as you are able," Isalynn said. "In fact, since your three months were up, I was going to petition you next week."

"I see," she said, biting her lip. What if she didn't take any more petitions? What if she could quit and still hold on to the Power? What would she do with her life then? She had the impulse to confide in the other woman but held back for now. "I'm sorry."

"No need to apologize," Isalynn told her. "Just keep in touch and let me know when you're ready for consultations again. Since you've had Power shifts, it might be good for your next consultation to be with an experienced witch, anyway. I can provide that for you or get someone else to do it, if you'd like."

"Thank you," Grace said, startled at the thought. "I think that might be a really good idea."

"In the meantime, I'll look into the issue with the roster and get back to you."

Grace hung up thoughtfully after the call ended. She and

Max looked at each other. She said to him, "That conversation didn't suck."

"Fffft," he said.

"I agree," she told the baby as she picked him up. "You are a wise young man."

He put his head on her shoulder and patted her.

Later that morning, she finally turned her attention to washing a load of her own clothes, which was when she rediscovered the envelope in her pocket from Don and Margie. With Khalil's arrival and her unexpected clash with Therese, she had forgotten all about it. When she opened the envelope, she found five twenty dollar bills inside. She bit her lip as she considered the cash. Whatever else happened, whether she continued to act as the Oracle or stopped altogether, she would have to honor her promise to them.

That afternoon, she had another surprise phone call. The kids were down for their nap when the phone rang. She lunged to answer before it could wake them up. It was Jaydon Guthrie. He wanted to discuss the details for the Saturday work day. She had met Jaydon a few times, although she did not move in the same social circle as the Guthries either. Both Jaydon and his wife—Melinda or Melissa—had attended Petra and Niko's memorial service, along with virtually all the dignitaries in the witches' demesne and many from the other Elder demesnes as well. Most of what she knew about Jaydon, she had learned from Petra, who'd had more of an acquaintance with him through attending demesne functions. (Grace really wasn't looking forward to those. She wore cutoffs, not cocktail suits or dresses.)

A tall, dark-haired, lean man in his late thirties or early forties, Jaydon was a criminal prosecution lawyer, with an inherited multimillion-dollar house in affluent Mockingbird Valley and a model-gorgeous blonde wife. He was also head of one of the oldest, most established covens in the demesne. He had run a few times unsuccessfully against Isalynn LeFevre for Head of the witches' demesne, but Isalynn proved to be an impossible candidate to beat.

Jaydon came from a moneyed family and was Harvard

educated, while Isalynn attended the University of Kentucky College of Law. A Powerful witch in her own right, Isalynn had learned her craft growing up in a poor small town in southern Kentucky. She had a strong grassroots appeal coupled with a sophisticated legal mind, and she balanced all the layers of her dual legislative roles with seeming effortlessness.

The last rumors Grace had heard from Petra were that Jaydon had given up for the time being on trying to beat Isalynn in the witches' demesne elections, and he might be running for District Attorney in Jefferson County during the next election, while Isalynn's supporters were urging her to consider the next gubernatorial race.

A few weeks after Isalynn had set up the babysitting roster for Grace, Jaydon initiated the quarterly work-day volunteer effort on her behalf. When Grace heard of it, she first thought Jaydon's long-standing rivalry with Isalynn was still going strong. Then she felt embarrassed, because it seemed mean-spirited of her, especially when both plans were meant for her benefit. And the Guthries were well-known for championing community service. Jaydon's wife worked actively to fund-raise for the local Humane Society and sat on the Board of Trustees for the Jefferson County Library System.

Still, Grace hadn't expected to hear from Jaydon personally. He confirmed that eighteen witches from several covens had signed up for Saturday. A full coven had thirteen members, so like Isalynn's babysitting roster, Jaydon had achieved cross-coven support. Eighteen people would be a great turnout for a volunteer work day.

"I'm sorry Melissa and I will not be able to make it," he said. "We have another function we need to attend, a fund-raising luncheon for the library that Melissa's been working on. She has three guest authors flying in for readings and book signings. I'm afraid she volunteered us to act as hosts for the authors before consulting me."

A little taken aback, Grace said, "I understand." She didn't understand, not really. Neither Jaydon nor his wife had attended the first work day either, and Grace frankly hadn't expected them. Mowing, whacking weeds, moving furniture and repairing fences didn't exactly sound like their schtick. "Thank you anyway."

"Brandon will be attending." Brandon was one of the witches in Jaydon's coven, and he had supervised the last work day. "He can help with who does what."

"That's great," she said. "I thought I would buy sandwich things and make a salad for lunch. Get some fruit, something for dessert, and have iced tea and coffee for everybody. I might cook a casserole or some spaghetti, as well."

Jaydon said, "It's supposed to be ninety-six again on Saturday. People are going to be hot, busy and sweaty, and you're going to have your hands full as it is. There's no need to heat up your kitchen further or tire yourself out by trying to cook something for everybody. Sandwiches, a salad and plenty of cold drinks will do nicely."

That sounded sensible to her, and she was more than happy to cross one more thing off her to-do list.

On Friday afternoon, when she had finally finished getting everything ready for Saturday, she found herself in the half bath, humming and putting on makeup. Mentally she called herself a few choice words while she did it. "Crackbrained idiot" headed the list. Khalil had, after all, kissed her when she had been a total mess. Twice.

She paused, mascara wand poised in midair. That was a good thing, wasn't it?

Anyway, it was too warm to put on much makeup. She settled for a light dusting of blush, a tinted lip gloss and a few brushstrokes of mascara. And she might have fluffed her hair a bit. And put on a light print summer skirt, along with a spring green tank top.

Was the skirt too much? She thought it was; she just couldn't help herself.

After all, "we'll see" meant taking a good long look at . . . possibilities. Right?

No. The skirt was too much. Too hopeful. She wasn't hopeful; she was cautious. She had told Khalil no more kissing or . . . or whatever for a reason. She took off the skirt and yanked on shorts. Then she washed her face. By the time Khalil appeared, the house was clean, the children fed and bathed, and she was freshly scrubbed and scowling. She and Chloe were busy stacking the day's toys into the toy box, while Max hung onto the box's edge and peered at the contents with interest.

Khalil's presence eased into the living room before his physical form appeared. Intense, male, sensual, he curled around her with lazy intent. The tiny hairs along the back of her neck and arms rose. Goose bumps broke out over her skin. She stood frozen in the middle of the living room floor, while Chloe, once again oblivious, trotted around the room and chattered.

Invisible arms came around Grace. Her mouth fell open, and her thoughts stuttered. Large, unseen hands stroked up her arms, along her shoulders, and trailed up the back of her neck. Long, strong fingers slid into her hair. He tilted her head back, and hot lips caressed her lightly. Then his tongue eased into her mouth. He kissed her deeply, and his energy tightened around her, heating with lazy arousal.

She stared at the ceiling blindly. This had a stealthy wickedness beyond anything she could have imagined. Her whole body trembled.

"Why are you doing that, Gracie?" Chloe asked.

Slowly, unhurriedly, the pressure on her mouth eased, and his touch slid away. Grace managed to close her mouth and swallow hard.

"Huh?" Chloe asked. Small fingers poked Grace in the stomach. Chloe stood in front of her, peering up at the ceiling in curiosity. "Why are you looking up like that?"

"No reason," Grace wheezed. He totally destroyed her capacity to think, and she couldn't seem to get her breathing under control. A low chuckle sounded in her head.

"Rachel has clouds in her bedroom. Can we have clouds too?"

Grace tried to concentrate. Aside from how much it might

cost to buy blue and white paint, she didn't know how to paint clouds. Even if she taught herself how, the project would take hours of standing on a stepladder.

"Honey, I don't think so," she said. She watched Chloe's face fall, and her heart twisted. There were so many things she couldn't afford to do for them. A thought occurred to her. "Tell you what. We'll get some glow-in-the-dark stars. I saw a package the other day at the toy store when we bought coloring books. Would you like to look at stars when you go to bed?"

"Yes!" said Chloe happily.

As Grace and Chloe talked, Khalil materialized in front of Max, who was still hanging on to the toy box. Khalil wore undyed linen again. The gentle beige color emphasized his pale, elegant features and the raven sleek sheen of his black hair. He gave Grace a sparkling, wicked glance over one wide shoulder.

Grace's pulse started a helter-skelter race, hurtling through her veins. Max crowed, his little mouth making a rounded "O" in surprise. He started to squeal in delight.

The baby let go of the toy box and took two tottering steps toward Khalil before he fell on his diapered bottom. He scuttled over to Khalil as fast as he could on hands and knees.

"Oh, my God," Grace said. "*Oh, my God!* Did you *see* that?"

Three very different sets of eyes turned to regard her with mild surprise. Khalil had already knelt to pat Max's small back in greeting. At Grace's exclamation, he frowned fiercely and looked around, as if searching for hidden dangers.

Grace hurried over and plucked Max out from under Khalil's hand. "What a smart, big boy you are!" she exclaimed. She swung the baby high, and he shrieked with laughter. "You're so clever!"

Khalil rose to his feet. Both he and Chloe still looked mystified. "What happened?"

"He *walked*! He let go of the toy box and took his first two steps toward you!"

A bright, keen smile broke across Khalil's face. "I saw it, but I did not realize those were his first steps. He is young for this?"

"He's nine and a half months," Grace told him. Grace beamed up at Max as she held him high. "That's a bit young to start walking, but we were all early walkers—I don't know about Niko, but Petra, Chloe, and I started when we were around nine or ten months old. It'll take Max a while to really get going."

Never one to miss out on a good party, Chloe started hopping around the room. "Yay, yay, yay!"

Just as suddenly as the euphoria hit, Grace's face twisted. She snatched the baby close, hugging him tight as her eyes swam with tears.

Suddenly Khalil was right beside her, his expression sharp. *What is it?*

Grace said, *Petra and Niko aren't here to see him.*

Khalil's gaze darkened with sympathy. He put an arm around her and drew both her and the baby close. Grace turned her face into his wide shoulder. She told herself she hid her face because she didn't want to disturb the children, but she might have leaned on his straight, strong figure a little bit.

Khalil's arm tightened on her. He distracted Max by talking to him while Grace pulled herself together.

Clearly ready for the next good thing that involved her, Chloe started shouting as she ran around the room. "It's story time! It's story time!"

Grace straightened and pulled away from Khalil's hold. After one searching glance, Khalil let her go. He smoothly took Max away from her. "Get your books," he said to Chloe.

She stopped running laps. "Would you help me read as a horsie?"

"No," Khalil said.

"A doggie or a cat?"

"No," he said again.

Chloe's eyes narrowed. "I don't see why not," she said, turning truculent.

Uh-oh, thought Grace as she wiped her eyes. Chloe and Khalil assessed each other like two gunfighters in a Western movie. Grace could almost see the dirt street they stood on, with the white steeple of a church in the background. The classic theme music from *The Good, the Bad, and the Ugly* whistled in her head. She could have sworn a tumbleweed blew by. There was going to be a shootout at the O.K. Corral, and it wasn't going to be pretty.

But Khalil proved to be more than a match for their contest of wills. He turned away from Chloe with a casual shrug. He said, "It is quite all right if you're not interested in me helping you to read this evening. I can always read to Max."

Outrage dropped Chloe's mouth open. The tiny gunslinger drew her gun and started firing. "*No!* That's not fair! He's just a baby!"

"Suit yourself," said Khalil calmly. He sat in the armchair and settled Max on one side of his lap. He raised his eyebrows at Chloe. "Are you bringing your books or not?"

Chloe clenched her fists. She appeared to be conducting a mighty internal battle that lasted all of three seconds under the cool challenge in Khalil's gaze. Then she broke down and ran for her books.

It was perfect, thought Grace. He took Chloe out with one, well-timed shot.

Laughter threatened to take Grace over as she watched Chloe fold herself into the other side of Khalil's lap. Khalil made no further comment. He merely chose a book from the pile, opened it to the first page and began to read.

Grace wandered into her office/bedroom and sat at her desk. Her amusement faded.

Shocked arousal. Surprise and euphoria. A surge of grief and then laughter, and all of that occurred within—she checked the time on her computer—a fifteen-minute span of time. No wonder she felt punch-drunk.

She had found a few job postings throughout the week that she ought to apply for. Clicking on the electronic folder that contained her employment documents, she opened a draft of a cover letter, but trying to concentrate on the details proved to be a waste of time. In the end, she sat quietly in the shadowed room, hands in her lap as she looked out at the evening twilight and listened to Khalil's perfect voice as he read to the children.

Then he fell silent. He said to her telepathically, *The children are asleep.*

Okay. Thank you. She stirred.

Do not trouble yourself, he told her. *I am capable of putting them in their beds.*

The springs in the armchair squeaked, then his footsteps sounded as he carried the children to their room.

She should move or do something, but for the life of her, she couldn't think of what she should do.

She could feel when Khalil's attention turned her way. This time he did not enter the room as a formless presence. He walked down the hall toward her. She listened to his footsteps as he approached. There, he rounded the corner to the living room. Now he stepped into the office. He was just fifteen feet away, then ten. Then five. She pushed her bangs off her forehead. Her fingers were shaking.

His presence enveloped her even as he turned her office chair so that she faced him. He glanced over her shoulder at the cover letter document open on her computer screen. He paused and frowned. His gaze darted to the stack of red-inked bills at one corner of the desk. She felt the impulse to squirm and squashed it. She had already told him times were hard, and she was not ashamed of or embarrassed by anything on her desk.

He knelt on one knee in front of her, which brought them face-to-face again. Leaning one elbow on the arm of her chair, he braced his other hand on the edge of the desk and looked deeply into her eyes. His ivory features were somber, those crystalline eyes grave.

"I would very much regret," he said quietly, "if somehow I managed to make your day harder again today."

Surprise took her over. Did he think he was somehow responsible for how close she came to tears earlier? She smiled at him. "You didn't make my day harder today, Khalil," she said. "You made my day better. It was really wonderful to see Max take his first steps today. It was even sweeter to see how excited he was to see you. Both Max and Chloe enjoy your visits so much. I just wish—I wish Petra and Niko . . ." Her throat stopped up. She made an inadequate gesture with one hand.

He studied her. His proximity was unsettling, but she didn't want him to move away. After a moment, he said, "Lethe was Phaedra's mother—Phaedra is my daughter. Lethe was a first-generation Djinn who was born when the world was born. I am a second-generation Djinn, so I am old and Powerful, but I was not as Powerful as Lethe. We were both from House Marid. I discovered that she had broken her oath to someone who was Powerless to call her to account. I exposed her lack of honor and had her driven from our House, and so she became a pariah. In retaliation, Lethe captured and tortured Phaedra."

Grace tensed as she listened. Khalil spoke quietly and simply. Somehow it underscored the unfolding horror in his tale. "How could she do that, torture her own child?"

"I do not know," Khalil said. "To me it is an insane thing. But when Djinn turn bad, we are very bad."

"Humans are too," Grace whispered.

He continued. "I was not strong enough to fight Lethe on my own, so I gathered as many Powerful allies as I could. Carling was one of them. This happened a long time ago, when pharaohs still ruled Egypt." His gaze was stern and distant as he focused on that ancient battle. "I finally paid the last of my debt to Carling when I brought her and Rune here the other night."

"That's why you were with them," Grace said.

"Yes," he replied.

"And you stayed that night because there could have been danger," she said, finally linking it all together in her head. "You stayed because of the children."

He gave her a small smile. "Yes."

The lump was back in Grace's throat. She couldn't have known any of it, of course, and Khalil had been arrogant and abrasive. It was fruitless and stupid to feel regret about how they had clashed that night. She asked, "What happened next?"

"We went to war against Lethe." His expression turned savage. "Our last battle tore down a mountain range and destroyed a crossover passageway. The last was unintentional. It is the one thing I regret. Whoever or whatever lived in that Other land is now cut off from the rest of Earth forever."

She put a hand on his arm. It seemed like a useless gesture, when everything had happened so long ago, probably as useless as her hug had been, but she couldn't help herself. "You said your daughter survived?"

He looked down at her hand as if it were a strange phenomenon he didn't understand. Then he covered it with his own. "She did," he said. "We trapped Lethe and destroyed her, and we freed Phaedra, but she was damaged. Now she is the pariah. She will not make associations with any Djinn House, and she attacks if I—if any of us—come too close. So far we have had no evidence that she has caused harm to others." When he spoke next, it was so quietly she had to lean closer and strain to hear his words. "I very much hope I never have to hunt her down and destroy her too."

"I'm so sorry," Grace said as gently as she could.

"As I said, this happened a long time ago," he said. "You are so spirited I forget sometimes how recently you suffered your own loss."

"We all lost," Grace said. "Me, Chloe and Max, Petra and Niko."

"Yes," Khalil said. "But you have to shoulder the burden for all the rest." He raised her hand to kiss her fingers. "I will come again tomorrow, with your consent."

She smiled. "That would be terrifi—no wait, that won't work. I won't have the children tomorrow. Remember, I mentioned Saturday was a work day? Katherine is taking Chloe and Max tomorrow. They're spending the night at her house."

He frowned at her. He was silent for so long, she fell silent too and began to wonder what she might have said.

"Grace," said Khalil, and her name had never been spoken so purely before in her life. He gave it an unearthly, haunting beauty. Just listening to it made her want to be better, more worthy of being called something so wonderful. If he ever sang, she thought, the song would be so unbearably gorgeous, it would soar over spires of stone and steel, and pierce the hearts of humans and other creatures, and he could rule the world.

If he ever sang to her, she would go anywhere with him, anywhere at all.

He had paused. "Why do you look so stricken?"

"Never mind," she whispered. "Go on."

"I no longer come just to see the children, you know," he said. "When do your people leave tomorrow?"

"I—I don't know, around five, maybe, or six," she stammered.

"You will call me when they leave," he said. His gaze was intent.

The thought of them alone in the house caused a slow, sensuous heat to spread over her body. He knew it, damn him, and the smile that spread over his ivory features was just as slow and sensuous, and unbelievably wicked.

She was sliding dangerously fast down a slippery slope, if she went from "no kissing" and "we'll see" to him coming over when the children were gone. She cast around in her mind for something, anything, to stop her headlong plunge.

She blurted out, "Do Djinn date?"

He blinked. "That is not something to which I have given much thought," he said. "Perhaps some Djinn might date some . . . creatures . . . some . . . times. Dating has not previously been a habit of mine."

She nodded, too rapidly, and forced herself to stop. "I just wondered."

"Humans like to date," Khalil said thoughtfully. Then he turned decisive. "That is what we will do tomorrow. We will go on a date."

Suddenly she was dying. She didn't know from what exactly: repressed laughter or mortification or perhaps a combination of both. She managed to articulate, "You don't dictate a date."

"I do not see why not," said Khalil, his energy caressing hers with lazy amusement. He tapped her nose. "Humans require air. Breathe now."

She did, and a snicker escaped. "If you order a date to happen, it's no longer a date. It becomes, I don't know, a meeting or kidnapping or something."

"What is the proper procedure?" he asked. "For a date."

His low tone was sultry. It brought to mind all kinds of heated images for the concept of procedures and dates. Now he was definitely teasing her. She said firmly, "If you are interested in spending time with someone, you ask them. You don't tell them."

"Will you go on a date with me?" he asked promptly.

She did want to see him, and it shouldn't be alone, in the house. It just shouldn't. "Sure," she said. "What will we do?"

"I have no idea," he said. "You are the dating expert. I am sure you will figure it out."

She, a dating expert? She shook her head. This conversation was surreal. "I'll come up with something," she told him. What on earth would it be? "It won't be fancy. You might want to dress casual."

He nodded. "Call me when you are ready." He vanished.

A date. She stared at the empty place where he had been a moment before as his presence faded. "I am never going to see Damascus, am I?" she whispered to herself. "Not in this lifetime."

Then his presence returned, and he curled around her caressingly.

"I forgot to say good-bye," he murmured in her ear.

Instinctively she held up her hands, fingers questing through the air, but his physical form did not reappear.

Not quite.

Instead invisible fingers trailed down her face, stroked her throat, traced the edge of her T-shirt's neckline. She couldn't see him, touch him. She felt hungry, bewildered and blind.

So she reached for him the only way she could, psychically, and felt herself align with his presence again. Power to Power, spirit to spirit. Feminine to masculine.

Astonishment and heat roared out of him. She felt it as a sheet of flame washing through her. Her breasts felt hypersensitive, nipples distended, and sexual hunger speared between her legs, sharper and harder than anything she'd ever known. Her head fell back against the office chair.

His energy rippled with something like a physical shudder. He hissed, "*Good night.*"

Then he was truly gone, and all she could do was whisper, "Holy fuck."

And all she could think was: we really do have to get out of the house tomorrow.

≈ ELEVEN ≈

Caught in the last moments before Khalil had left, Grace had a difficult time going to sleep. The warm humid summer night pressed against her skin. She kept reliving the rush of heat that had roared out from him, flashing over her psyche. It altered her understanding of pleasure and desire. She did not think she would ever be able to respond to a mere physical embrace again.

Would he climax during lovemaking, as humans did? Her body throbbed. She kicked off her sheet, curled on her side and slid a hand between her legs, pressing against the hungry, empty ache. When she finally slept, she dreamed of his huge, invisible hands sliding down the contours of her body, easing her own hand away. Long, clever fingers dipped underneath the shorts and panties she wore and caressed along the folded lips of her labia, at the edge of her clitoris.

Her hunger spiked, reverberated back and forth between the physical and the psychic, the one intensifying the other. She needed to climax so badly. It had been so long since she had felt pleasure, and she had never experienced anything like this before, but she needed his physical form too, needed him sliding into her, filling that empty ache, moving with the kind of rhythm her body craved . . .

She plunged awake before completion and struggled with disorientation. For one heart-pounding moment, she balanced between a frenzied hope that Khalil was really there and a shocked need for him to not be present, to not have taken his lack of human sensibilities to that extreme.

She cast out her awareness, searching for him—and he wasn't there. The quiet, darkened house was serene, and she was quite alone. Her dream had just been a dream. That left her to settle into disconcerted disappointment. She didn't want him present, but she still ached with emptiness and wanted his touch. She tossed and turned for the rest of the night.

Early Saturday morning, when the children woke, she started another long, full day feeling disgruntled.

The temperature had already reached eighty-six by the time she drove Chloe and Max over to Katherine's at eight o'clock. Katherine gave Grace the phone number of someone who had a twin bed and was interested in exchanging it for Chloe's toddler bed. Grace also took all the serving plates with the lids, along with the set of four heavy linen napkins, to give to Katherine, who was overjoyed.

Katherine was also intensely curious, and Grace's explanation for how she had gotten them took a good twenty minutes. By the time she returned home, it was a quarter to nine.

Brandon was the first to arrive. He was a stocky man with pale blue eyes that seemed to weigh everything. Grace didn't especially care for the sensation. It left her feeling like he was judging her and found her lacking. That feeling intensified in their first conversation that morning.

"We only have twelve people coming from a smattering of local covens," Brandon said. "Not the eighteen we'd originally thought. Apparently there's a rumor going around that you've had a Djinn hanging around." He studied her coolly. "He isn't here now, is he?"

Taken aback, Grace muttered, "Not that it's any of your

business, but no, he's not. I can't believe six people canceled because of that."

Brandon shot her a sidelong glance. "Djinn are Powerful and unpredictable. They make folks nervous."

"Folks need to get over it," she snapped.

He shrugged. "Maybe. Maybe not."

Her ready temper flared, but before she could say something she might possibly regret later, Brandon asked her for a list of projects. Since he was about to spend the day working on her property, she decided it was probably best to just let the subject drop. For now.

It was the height of summer, and everything was overgrown. She hadn't had the time or the energy to keep up the fenced-in backyard. As a result, the yard was too unkempt to take the children out to play. The main issues, she told Brandon, were mowing the property (not an insignificant task, since it took a good ten hours for a single person to sweep through the open areas on a riding mower), moving a dresser downstairs to the office, and getting the backyard in shape so she could take the children out to play.

She said, "We used to keep more of the property mown, but right now I'll be grateful to have the area around the house, the main path to the back, and the grass by the driveway cut down."

He nodded as he listened. He had turned his attention to studying the house. "A couple of the guys are bringing their riding mowers," he said. "We can get the whole property done this time around." He pointed at the roof. "Got some tiles missing. That roof won't make it through the winter."

Her shoulders sagged. "I know."

That earned her another assessing glance. "Well," Brandon said after a moment. "Winter's several months away yet."

Then a couple of cars turned into the driveway, and the work day began.

It was a sticky, sweltering, tiring and sometimes strained day. Several of the witches would barely speak to her. One or two others treated her with a smooth, smiling courtesy that seemed even worse. Her Power bristled, as it had when she had explored trying to sell part of the riverfront, but just as it did not pay the monthly bills, it also didn't mow the lawn, so she shoved it aside irritably. For some reason the ghosts in the house were agitated too, which added to the undercurrent of tension, although Grace was fairly certain she was the only one who could sense them.

She was grateful to see someone she really liked, a quiet witch in her thirties named Olivia, who worked as a reference librarian for the Ex Libris Library in Louisville. Ex Libris was the major repository in the United States for resource materials on or about humankind's witchcraft, Power and magic systems. The library also had one of the largest collections worldwide. Olivia belonged to a coven of professional academics, teachers, professors and other librarians.

Olivia gave Grace a genuine smile in greeting. Grace found herself gravitating toward the librarian as the day went on.

Once tasks were allocated, people dispersed and got busy, and the underlying tensions dissolved somewhat. Grace was constantly being pulled from one question to another. Which dresser did she want brought downstairs? Where did she want it put in the office? Did she want all the clothes that were in the dresser brought down too, or did she want them left upstairs? Did she care if the rosebushes out front were trimmed, and would she like them watered? Did she know there was a hole in the backyard fence? The hole would need to be repaired before she took the children out to play again. Would she like that done today?

Then late morning, as Grace and Olivia arranged the lunch on the table, the house phone rang. Grace picked it up.

The caller was Brandon on his cell phone, from the back meadow. Cell phones didn't work on the property very well, so their connection was spotty, but he managed to ask Grace to come to the back to give the men some advice. "If it isn't too much trouble," he said through the crackle. "We were hoping you and Olivia might bring some iced tea too."

"Sure," she said, looking at the full, heavy pitcher and

glasses with resignation. She hung up and told Olivia, "I've got to go to the back meadow. Would you mind helping me carry drinks back for the guys?"

"Of course," Olivia said. She surveyed the table. "We're done here anyway. People can help themselves to lunch whenever they're hungry."

They collected everything. Olivia grabbed the full gallon of iced tea before Grace could. She didn't say anything, just picked up the glasses, and they headed out. "I have to admit," Grace said. "I'm relieved to get away from everybody else for a few minutes."

"They're a charming lot this morning, aren't they?" Olivia said, snorting with scorn.

Grace darted a glance at her. The librarian's short chestnut hair gleamed with honey highlights in the sun, and her gray eyes were vivid with intelligence. Olivia had a quiet Power that ran deep; she worked daily with books and resources of Power, so she must be proficient at her craft. Usually witch librarians were symbologists who could read, control and infuse words and images with Power.

Grace said, hesitantly, "I didn't expect how people are acting today. Everybody except you, I mean. There are people from several different covens here. I thought they would be more, I don't know, talkative and happy to get to know each other. The last work day was a lot noisier."

Olivia raised her eyebrows. "I keep forgetting, you're not part of a coven, are you?"

"No."

"Well, covens are like professional guilds with networking opportunities and regular continuing education in various magical disciplines," Olivia said. "A witch might not necessarily have any close friends in her coven. People can have stronger ties to their bowling leagues, their churches, their reading groups or any political party they belong to."

Grace frowned. "Okay, that's a good point, and it's not something that would have occurred to me. How does that apply to people here today?"

"When I look around at who is here today, I don't see people who are silent because they don't know each other," Olivia said. "To me, they look like they're not talking because they know each other very well."

Grace stopped walking. "What are you saying?"

The librarian shrugged. "I don't know exactly. I've seen some exchanged glances and raised eyebrows, like there was an unspoken conversation going on. I thought people were acting standoffish because of me. Early this morning I got a phone call from Brandon who said they had more than enough people showing up, so they didn't need me. It seemed a little too high school for me, like I was disinvited to a party, so I decided to come anyway, because I wanted to see how you were doing and to say hi."

Grace said slowly, "That doesn't make any sense. First Jaydon called Thursday and said eighteen people were going to show up today. Then Brandon arrived this morning, and he said—at least I thought he said . . ." Under Olivia's intelligent, attentive gray eyes her voice trailed away, and she scowled as she tried to remember. "Okay, maybe he didn't actually say what I thought he said. He said twelve people were coming, not eighteen, and then he asked me about a rumor of a Djinn hanging around. I just thought the two things were connected and that people were backing out of the work day because of Khalil."

Olivia's eyebrows rose. "You have a Djinn hanging around?"

"Yeah." Grace stiffened. "What of it?"

Olivia grinned. "Nothing, just cool. I've met exactly one Djinn in my life, and she was pretty freaking spectacular."

Grace looked at her sidelong. She could feel the skin in her face start to burn. "We're going on a date tonight."

"You're *dating* a Djinn? That's even better." The older woman laughed. "I've heard stories of—never mind."

"I have to say, your attitude is refreshing," Grace muttered. "Most of the people I've been talking to have been pretty negative."

"You've been talking to the wrong people," Olivia told

her. "Pay no attention to what Brandon says or tries to imply. He's one of the biggest bigots I know. You do know he was one of Jaydon's strongest supporters, when Jaydon ran against Isalynn LeFevre in the demesne elections, don't you?"

"No, I didn't make the connection," Grace said. She shrugged, somewhat impatiently. "I'm not really into politics."

Olivia started walking again, and Grace did too. "Isalynn's a conservative about some things," Olivia said. "That's part of her long-standing appeal. She's an advocate for less government. But she's a moderate when it comes to dealing with the Elder Races demesnes. Jaydon has argued for a stronger federal government and less sovereignty for the seven demesnes. He has a strong support base of people who are anti–Elder Races entirely. It doesn't matter what race— Vampyre, Wyr, Djinn, Light or Dark Fae, whatever. The group wants the Elder Races out of Kentucky and out of the federal government."

"But we're part of the Elder Races," Grace said.

"To some people we're not," Olivia replied. "Sure, we're witches, but we're human. A lot of them want the inhuman Elder Races to move their governments to an Other land and be treated as foreign countries."

"That isn't feasible," Grace said, still frowning. "They're as much a part of our society as the fifty states. None of the demesnes are going to uproot and change their locations."

Olivia shrugged. "That isn't stopping people from trying. Anyway, things got pretty heated in the last election, with lots of demonstrations and name-calling. Just something for you to think about when you're dealing with Brandon."

Grace shook her head. She still didn't see how any of that applied to her. As the Oracle, she was supposed to remain neutral and treat all petitioners alike. Of course, that didn't mean she couldn't have personal opinions. But she couldn't imagine anyone would care about what she thought about politics. "Well, I know the witches' grapevine is very active. If they all know each other, maybe Brandon's attitude has influenced the others."

"Maybe." Olivia gave her a slight smile. "I'm not sure I'm

the best resource for you to ask, since I don't belong to a clique and I don't gossip. Clearly I'm not part of the 'in' crowd today."

Grace sighed. She said bluntly, "I like you."

The other woman laughed. "I like you too. What's more, I respect the hell out of you for what you've taken on with the kids. A lot of young women your age wouldn't have done it."

"I had to," Grace said. "I love them." She was also the only one who could pass on to the children what she had been taught about their family and heritage.

"Well, still, kudos to you. If you ever get away from the munchkins, stop by the library some time for coffee."

Surprised pleasure bloomed. "I'd like that. Thanks."

Grace and Olivia reached the back meadow. Four men had taken on the chore of mowing and had gotten roughly half of the meadow finished. Brandon was using Grace's riding mower, and the other three had brought their own, hauled behind pickup trucks and SUVs on small flatbed trailers. At the moment all four mowers were quiet and abandoned, the engines turned off. The men were standing and talking in a cluster near the door to the cavern, which stood open.

Either Grace's Power bristled again, or she did. She swiped the back of a hand across her warm, damp forehead as she and Olivia reached the men. "That door wasn't unlocked and open when you found it, was it?" she asked tersely. She had been tired and preoccupied when Don and Margie had come, but she hadn't been *that* careless, had she?

"No," Brandon said as the men clustered around the two women for glasses of iced tea. "We unlocked it. I was going to wait and go down with you, but then I went ahead and checked the tunnel and cavern's ceiling and walls, myself. It looks fine from the inside for now. Did you notice how much erosion has occurred on this side of the path? It's developed a fissure down the side of the bluff. You need to keep an eye on this and check the tunnel and the cavern on this side after a strong storm."

"I think you should put some stones or tree stumps along that," said one of the other men. "Make the path safer in the dark. If you use the path much in the dark."

"Well, no," Grace said. "But occasionally it's unavoidable, and an accident would not be good."

She had been aware of the fissure erosion and had been keeping an eye on the path, although it had not occurred to her to watch the tunnel and the cavern from the inside. Brandon could have waited to talk about this until he got back to the house. It wasn't urgent enough to warrant the effort it took her to make the trek. Probably the whole point behind asking her and Olivia to come out was to get cold drinks brought back while they stood around and talked for a half hour. She felt a surge of irritation, which was totally unreasonable, given how much time they were volunteering. When Brandon offered to haul a truckload of stones over next week to shore up the widening gap, she felt like even more of a bitch.

Olivia and Grace collected the glasses when the men had polished off the last of the gallon of tea. Grace took one last look at the open doorway.

"Don't forget to lock that," she told Brandon.

"We won't," Brandon said, his blue eyes watchful.

But he was always watchful.

She could still feel him watching as she turned to leave.

The group finished all their projects and called the work day to an end just after five thirty. Everything on Grace's list had been accomplished and the hole in the backyard fence repaired. Despite whatever personal tensions might have existed throughout the day, she made a point of thanking each one individually when they left.

"Call me sometime next week?" she said to Brandon as he was leaving.

"What?" He looked blank.

"You were going to bring a truckload of stones over?" she prompted.

"Oh, right. Sure. I'll call you."

Well, that didn't sound promising. She stifled another surge of irritation. Dammit, she hated it when people threw out offers but didn't follow through.

The last to leave, Olivia gave her a quick hug. "Stop by for that coffee," Olivia said. "Or give me a call sometime if you think you can get away for lunch. I just need a few hours' notice."

"Thank you," Grace said, warming to the older woman all over again. "I will."

Then Olivia was gone as well, and Grace was left alone with her thoughts.

She didn't even have to clean up the kitchen. Somebody had already done it for her. The house was clean and silent, and the main issues on the property were taken care of, at least for now. As far as the roof went, she had a few months to try to figure something out. She looked out the kitchen door window. Most importantly, the backyard was trimmed, tidy and useable again.

She would stop at the toy store tomorrow morning before she went to pick up the kids and use the rest of the hundred dollars she had gotten from Don and Margie to buy a small plastic pool and some glow-in-the-dark stars for Chloe and Max's bedroom.

For now, she could relax. Maybe she could take that bubble bath she had been promising herself for a week, before she called Khalil and went on a date.

Holy gods, a *date*. With a *Djinn*.

Grace was almost positive she had hallucinated that part. She thought instead of relaxing, she might tie herself up in knots instead. She knew Khalil had only decided to go on a date on a whim, because the thought had amused him. Whereas she would either get ready for the *date* in a complete panic or take the smart route and call the whole thing off.

She couldn't explain the impulse that gripped her next. Instead of relaxing, panicking or cancelling, she strapped on her knee brace, slipped out of the house and for a second time, she walked the length of the property to the back meadow.

Without distracting conversation, she could hear the wind sighing in the trees. The land seemed to doze in the early evening heat. She smelled freshly cut grass. She looked along the edges of the clearing, along the path, studied the eroded area carefully.

She didn't know what she was looking for. Something.

Why would Brandon call Olivia to tell her she wasn't needed today? Did he do that with the other people who hadn't shown up? And if so, why did he tell her in such a way that implied the others had cancelled? It didn't make sense. The day would have gone a lot quicker with more people. Unless he was trying to cherry-pick volunteer hours for his buddies?

That didn't make sense either. Part of the function of the covens was to keep track of a witch's service hours. It was a lot like paying union dues. Since the Oracle's entire function was service oriented, Grace was now exempt from the tithe, but the community service tithe wasn't onerous, just five hours a month, and there were always plenty of ways a witch could volunteer.

Now that everybody had left, her Power was quiescent, the ghosts tranquil. Back in this area by the river, the ghosts she sensed were American Indian. Occasionally through the years someone would find a few arrowheads or maybe a flint knife. She suspected a tribe might have once lived here.

Taking the key from the coffee can on the lintel, she unlocked the old wooden door, pocketed the key and stepped into an area large enough to hold two sturdy Rubbermaid cabinets. She felt in the air above her head for a dangling cord, and when she had found it, she switched on the naked lightbulb that hung from the ceiling.

The Rubbermaid storage cabinets held old blankets, jackets, packages of batteries and flashlights and a couple of old-fashioned oil lamps, along with boxes of matches in zippered plastic bags to keep them from getting damp.

There was also one other item, wrapped in cloth. Grace took it out of a drawer and leaned back against the cabinet as she uncovered it. The cloth fell away to reveal a plain gold Greek mask, with stylized features, and holes for the eyes and the mouth. The face was androgynous, beautiful and blank. The style of this mask was far, far older than Agamemnon's famous gold leaf mask that had been found at the citadel of Mycenae.

Grace regarded the mask wryly. *Stunning*, Carling had said when she first laid eyes on it. But Carling had seen it by flashlight, from a distance. She might have called it something else if she had studied it in the light of day.

Funny, how no one ever tried to steal the mask of the Oracle. If they had, they would soon discover it was not made of real gold, nor was it very old. Instead it was a very pretty fake. The Andreas family had sold the original mask in Europe, to the Queen of the Light Fae in Ireland, who had long had a fascination with auguries of any kind.

Her family had used the proceeds of the sale to finance their relocation to the States, to buy this land and to build on it. The only thing Grace regretted was that she didn't have the original to sell again, because even in a depressed economy, she felt sure the original mask would sell for enough to solve all of their money problems for years.

Whereas the sale of the fake mask probably wouldn't bring in enough to fix the roof.

Although come to think of it, that might be worth checking. Maybe somebody would like to buy the fake mask for novelty's sake. It was a decent replica of the original.

She wrapped the mask in the cloth again, tucked it under her arm, took one of the stronger flashlights and went down the tunnel, picking her way carefully on the uneven floor to the perfect black of the cavern below. She shone the flashlight over the walls and ceiling as she went. Finally she admitted the truth: that she had bristled at Brandon going into the tunnel and cavern to check them without waiting for her. She didn't like him poking around by himself, but her reaction was irrational. The cavern wasn't off-limits to people, it was just off-limits to children, and that was for their own safety.

She still couldn't explain what she was looking for.

She was just looking for something.

Was Therese anti–Elder Races, like Brandon? Was that why she had reacted so badly to Khalil's appearance? Grace had thought it was because Therese got caught snooping. Had Therese been snooping because she had heard a rumor about a Djinn hanging around? What about Janice? Had this whole thing begun with her, because *attracting a Djinn's interest is generally not considered to be a good thing, Grace*?

Spinning in circles like this made her head hurt. Worse, it made her angry. If quarterly work days were going to make her feel like this, she wanted to tell them all to fuck off. But she couldn't do without them or the babysitting roster, unless things changed.

It all came down to the Oracle's Power. How she used it. What she made of it.

And that came down to her.

She reached the cool, spacious cavern. After walking around and checking the entire space, she turned off her flashlight and let her eyes adjust. She had left the door propped open on the surface. A diffuse shaft of light from the tunnel cut through the absolute blackness.

Many people had a problem with caves, but Grace didn't. She liked it down here. The cavern itself was beautiful. Not only did it call to the Power that lived inside her, but it was utterly silent and peaceful. In the darkness, it felt womblike, filled with the potential birth of limitless possibilities.

The Oracle's moon was soon, perhaps tonight or tomorrow. She could feel the approach, especially here in the dark. It felt like a convergence, all times, the past and all possible futures, coming together.

She had been taught that she could only access the Power deep in the earth, yet it had come in daylight, and not just once. She had called it up several times now.

She'd also been told that the Oracle could not consult the Power for herself, but only for others. Yet she had called the ghost of the serpent woman and had talked with her.

What else had she been taught that was wrong, or at the very least incomplete?

Each Oracle acts as a different lens for the Power, Isalynn had said. *You will bring your own strengths and abilities to the experience.*

Which was exactly what? She wished she could ask her future self for advice.

She let the cloth fall away from the mask, and she held it

up to her face, pretending she was a petitioner. How did they feel when they faced the mask? This time she barely touched the Power before it welled up, more readily than ever before.

The Power felt good in the dark, filling her to the brim and then spilling out into the cavern, an endless witching sea. She sensed thousands of sparks in the sea like distant glints of moonlight on water, and all the sparks were ghosts. She searched for ghosts she recognized, Petra, her grandmother, the serpent woman, but she didn't see any of them.

Visions normally came when the Oracle used the petitioner as a focus as she called up the Power. Cuelebre had been an inferno of Power; perhaps his ferocious energy had been what had drawn the Oracle. The serpent woman had been an unusual ghost, attached to the Oracle's Power and to Grace. For Grace to get any specific vision now, she needed more of an outside focus. Disappointed, she let go of the dark sea. She wrapped the mask up again as it began to subside.

Then something else Powerful flowed down the tunnel to join her in the dark. It was a Djinn, but unlike any Djinn Grace had met thus far. This presence was jagged with razored edges. It radiated a discordance that cut at her awareness. She held herself utterly still, thinking hard.

Then she turned on the flashlight.

The form of a tall woman, dressed in black, stood in front of her. The Djinn's form had a lethal grace. Her ivory face was regal and fierce, a feminine version of a handsome, inhuman visage that had already become so dearly familiar to Grace. Crimson hair flowed like blood past her shoulders, and her eyes were two black, crystalline stars.

She said into the cavern's absolute silence, "Hello, Phaedra."

This time on Saturday nothing would interrupt Khalil's agenda.

Djinn were cursed with a terminal curiosity. It was often their worst weakness, and sometimes it was their downfall.

Khalil was no exception. If a door was open, he peeked through it. If it was closed, it made the peeking so much better. If the door was locked, well. There was a natural progression to this sort of thing.

Things weren't adding up, and he didn't like it. The ancient social contract between Oracle and petitioner, the PayPal link on the website, the general shabbiness of Grace's home, the lack of repair. Her inability to access premium health care when she needed it the most, the unpaid bills, a cover letter to apply for a job, when she already had to do too much, had to meet too many responsibilities, was too alone.

He called in one of the multitude of favors owed to him, this time from a Djinn who had a particular facility with accessing information via the Internet. The information Khalil was interested in wasn't particularly hard to find. Grace's bank account balance was abysmal, and the money that the website drew in was hardly worth the breath it took to mention.

That was when Khalil grew angry. He searched for his old ally Carling and her lover Rune. They weren't in hiding, so they weren't particularly hard to find either.

They were in a beachside villa in Key Largo.

More specifically, Carling Severan was under house arrest in Key Largo. By association, Rune Ainissesthai, the Wyr gryphon who had recently been Dragos's First sentinel but had now become estranged from the Wyr demesne, was under house arrest too, because Rune had mated with Carling and would not leave her.

Carling was a very old, very Powerful sorceress, and a Vampyre in the late stages of the disease. The Elder tribunal had judged that the fluctuations in her Power made her too much of a danger to others. The tribunal had placed Carling under a kill order. Carling and Rune made a compelling argument for suspension of the sentence, for they claimed to have found a way to put her in partial remission.

No one wanted to execute a kill order prematurely. The social and political ramifications would be enormous. Carling had once been Queen of the Nightkind; most recently she had been a Councillor on the Elder tribunal itself. Not only that, but Rune would fight to the death for her. As a result, the Elder tribunal placed Carling under quarantine and observation for three months in order to verify the truth of their argument. Carling and Rune had just finished their first week.

So Khalil went to sunny Key Largo. The villa had an acre-length private beach. Two-story windows along one side of the main house overlooked an infinity pool beside the ocean. The property also had two guesthouses where the Elder tribunal Councillors who were Carling's observers and jailors stayed. The prison was altogether luxurious.

The villa was shining with Power as Khalil approached. He studied it from high in the air. The Demonkind Councillor Soren, a first generation Djinn who was also of the House Marid, was one of Carling's two wardens. Her other warden was the Elven Councillor Sidhiel. Wards had been placed all around the borders of the property, ostensibly, Khalil assumed, to keep Carling contained and not to keep others out.

But caution in the face of unknown wards was always the wisest course of action. Despite his anger, Khalil slowed as he came closer.

He was unsurprised when Soren noticed his arrival first.

The Councillor arced up to meet him. To Khalil, Soren's presence was a hot blaze, but it was not formless. Rather, it was patterned with aspects of Soren's personality. Soren had set aside involvement in House Marid concerns when he had taken his position on the tribunal. Khalil had not seen him in some time. Like Khalil, Soren was very male. The two Djinn stayed a respectful distance apart from each other. Carling had once remarked acerbically that male Djinn were like betta fighting fish and flared in aggression if they got too close to each other. Khalil had to admit, the Vampyre did have a point.

Councillor, Khalil said in greeting.

House Marid, Soren replied. *What brings you to this place?*

Khalil's reply was edged with his anger. *I would speak with Carling, if she is allowed visitors.*

She is allowed visitors, said Soren. *But she may not leave this place.*

I have no interest in that. Khalil thought of Grace's vision. He said, *I would also speak with you afterward, if you have the time. It is a matter of some importance.*

Certainly, said Soren. The elder Djinn's courtesy was impeccable. *I will be waiting for you in my living quarters. Until later.*

Soren cared for courtesies, so Khalil spoke the traditional parting phrase. *May you enjoy peace this day.*

And you, Soren replied.

Soren withdrew, and Khalil plummeted to the earth.

Now that he had gained access from one of the wardens, he did not bother quite so much with being quiet or courteous. He arrowed into the villa's great room with enough force to rattle the two-story windows, and in a whirl he created his physical form. It knocked the sofa and chairs around the room and the artwork hanging on the walls askew. His violent entrance was an expression of his extreme displeasure, and all the forewarning Carling and Rune would get.

Rune raced into the room, followed closely by Carling. They drew up short when they saw Khalil. He studied them coldly. The couple, he thought, were a surprising match.

Carling had been ancient at the time of the Roman Empire, but she still had the face and figure of a thirty-year-old human. By modern standards, she was an average height for a woman, with a slender, exquisite bone structure; smooth, luminous skin the color of honey and a sensual mouth. Until recently her dark hair had been long, but now she wore it short. The choppy style emphasized her patrician Nefertiti-like neck; long, almond-shaped, dark eyes; and high cheekbones. She wore soft, gray trousers and a sleeveless shirt, and was, as her usual habit, barefoot.

Carling's new mate, Rune, was barefoot too and bare-chested, as he wore a pair of denim cutoffs. Rune was an immortal Wyr. As such, he carried an intense furnace of energy that rippled the air around him. He stood six foot four, with sun-streaked, tawny hair and the body of a natural swordsman. He had sun-bronzed skin and lion-colored eyes that were normally smiling. Khalil noted Rune's smile was absent. His handsome face showed the marks of recent strain.

He had also been Dragos's former First sentinel for a reason. He looked at Khalil, his face hard, but he kept his voice even. "Came in a little rough on your landing there, Khalil. Care to tell us why?"

Khalil ignored him. He had no interest in conversing with the Wyr. He looked at Carling and spat, "In all the years of our long association, I never thought I would be calling you honorless."

═ TWELVE ═

Carling's expression sharpened. Even though Rune had not moved, his Power spiked with aggression.

Khalil did not mind that in the slightest. His own Power flared into battle readiness.

Carling's hand shot out, and she gripped Rune's muscled bicep. "Easy," she murmured to him. In a louder, calm voice, she said to Khalil, "Clearly I have caused offense to you when none was meant. I would be grateful if you would instruct me on the nature of my transgression, so that I may make amends."

"You don't owe amends to me," Khalil said. "And I am not your keeper."

Rune had begun a low, barely audible growl. Carling whispered to him, "Stop it, please." She looked at Khalil. "The only way I could have become honorless to you is if I did not meet my side of a bargain. Khalil, I want you to hear me on this. Rune and I have been under a lot of strain."

"That holds no meaning for me," he snapped.

"I know. The Djinn keep an immaculate accounting of favors owed and favors paid. But you and I have had an association that has been filled with honor for many centuries.

We struck a bargain a long time ago, and yes, you paid me three favors, but I helped you first with something so dangerous I might not have survived to collect. I'm asking that you remember that and let it weigh against your anger. Please understand, at times these last few weeks, my thinking has not been very clear. If I owe someone, it is a mistake, not a choice to live without honor. I want to pay the debt."

He struggled to hear what Carling was saying. She was right, his sensibilities were outraged. For the Djinn, only pariahs behaved in such a way, but Carling was not Djinn. And the Djinn might suffer from damage, but they did not suffer from disease. He could not calculate or fully understand what effect that may have had on the clarity of her thinking.

The Oracle's website had explained everything perfectly. Khalil didn't know who had created the content, but the webpage devoted to donations had been gracious and well written. A short paragraph described the history of the ancient social contract and the reasons why the Oracle would not speak of such matters whenever someone came to make a petition.

The tradition was very like those found in certain American Indian nations. The elders gave their teachings and healings to the people, passed down oral histories thousands of years old, and they often provided a place where sacred ceremonies were held. It was the people's responsibility to support and honor them. Like any church or social service, it cost money to provide the space and time for sacred ceremonies. Mortgages, rents and utilities had to be paid. Lawns had to be mowed, firewood cut, properties maintained and food bought.

As the unknown writer explained, often petitioners were grieving or otherwise preoccupied with important issues and challenges in their own lives when they arrived to consult the Oracle. The experience could be overwhelming. It often left one with a sense of epiphany, so it was important to come already prepared to fulfill the contract.

No matter how nicely the webpage was phrased, Khalil thought, the underlying message was plain. Don't forget to make your offering, because the Oracle won't bring it up.

His respect for Grace grew. It took a particular kind of strength to hold true to one's side of a bargain, no matter what. Most Djinn did not bother to find that out. If someone reneged on a bargain, they took revenge.

And he could not quite let go of all his anger, as he glanced around at the spacious villa that was, by anyone's accounting, extremely luxurious, and he compared it to Grace and the children's situation. If anyone should know better, it should have been Carling, who was so well versed in bargains, payment and balance not only in the culture of the Djinn but also in matters of magic.

So he chose to explain but not hold back the bite in his tone. "What exactly do you think you owe the Oracle for your consultation?"

Rune moved suddenly, his aggression ebbing. Stricken awareness flashed in Carling's long, dark eyes. "Oh, damn," she said. She and Rune looked at each other. Something passed between them, a troubled shadow from the recent past.

Rune said in a quiet voice, "We owe the Oracle everything."

"She is in need," Khalil told them. "You will pay her what you owe."

"Of course we will," Carling said. "And offer our deepest apologies. Thank you for telling us, Khalil." She looked at him oddly. "You are still in contact with her? I—would not have expected that to go well."

"She is my friend." Khalil crossed his arms. "We are going on a date tonight."

Silence filled the villa. Both Carling and Rune stood frozen.

Khalil had nearly forgotten one detail. He added thoughtfully, "I am to dress casually."

Rune's suntanned skin darkened dramatically. He broke into a convulsive fit of coughing. "Excuse me," he whispered. "I need a drink of water."

Both Khalil and Carling watched Rune stride rapidly out of the room. Carling's face was rigid as she watched her lover leave, but her gaze held an expression that looked, to Khalil, peculiarly pained, as if she had been betrayed.

Carling turned back to Khalil. She raised her eyebrows. "So what are you going to wear?"

He didn't have a clue. He hadn't planned that far ahead. He said, "I thought I would Google for images of casual wear in Louisville."

Carling had begun to relax. At that she went rigid again, closed her eyes and shook her head. "No, Khalil."

"No?" He frowned. "Perhaps I should wear a garment like the one Rune is wearing then."

Carling said, "No."

A half hour later, Khalil strode toward Soren's quarters in the north guesthouse. His business with Carling and Rune had gone much better than he had expected.

He had arrived prepared for a confrontation. When he walked away, he had a check written to Grace, along with a handwritten note of apology from Carling.

He had also received impromptu dating advice from Rune, of all people. Rune and Khalil had come very close to becoming enemies in the past. As far as Khalil was concerned, they were still not that far away, so he listened impassively as Carling called Rune back into the room.

"I'm going to write a quick note to Grace and write her a check," she told Rune. "You need to tell Khalil what to wear for a casual date. Be specific." Rune gave Khalil a sleepy-looking smile. She smacked Rune in the chest with the back of her hand and added sharply, "And be serious." She pointed at Rune as she said to Khalil, "Pay attention to what he says. He's dated quite extensively, and he's been quite successful at it."

Carling strode out of the room. Khalil and Rune regarded each other warily. Khalil remembered again how Carling had described male Djinn. He thought her metaphor probably applied to him and Rune as well. They were two betta fighting fish flaring their fins with aggression while talking about dating. It was an oddity.

When the silence had stretched between the two males for too long, Khalil finally said, "Speak."

"Jeans. T-shirt. Either boots or sneakers," Rune said. "Pay for everything, and open doors for her. Dating's simple. Listen to what she says, tell her she's beautiful and make her happy."

Dating did not sound simple, except perhaps for one thing. Khalil looked at the Wyr quizzically. He said, "Grace *is* beautiful."

That caused the other male to pause. For the first time in their spiky acquaintance, Rune gave him a crooked, yet real smile. "Dude, let her know that with the same kind of sincerity. You will make her happy, and it doesn't matter what you do. You can go to a movie, take a walk in a park, hold hands, go to a restaurant for a meal or to a bar for a drink, sit on a beach and watch the sun rise at dawn or stand on your head—it's all just variations on the same theme."

Khalil had never been called "dude" before. He was fairly sure he didn't like it.

Then Carling walked back into the room, and the moment passed. She handed an envelope to Khalil. "Neither of us has access to all of our accounts at the moment," she said. "So this is what I can do for right now. Let me know if she needs more, and I can do more later. The Oracle should not be hurting for money."

"Agreed," Khalil said.

Then Rune and Carling looked at each other and shared a short, apparently private and rather incomprehensible conversation. "I've been reading diving information online," Rune said. "I think all the cave systems in Florida are underwater."

"They are for now," Carling replied. She pursed her lips. "That doesn't mean we can't find a suitable cavern somewhere, block it off and pump all the water out."

"Inconvenient," said Rune. "Time-consuming. But possible."

"I wonder if she would like Florida?"

Jealousy stirred. Khalil said, "Why are you talking about trying to move the Oracle to Florida?"

Carling and Rune looked at him, both wearing the same mild expression. Rune said, "We decided we might turn collecting underutilized resources into a hobby. It's kind of fun."

"The Oracle is an underutilized resource," said Carling. "A very Powerful one who has fallen somewhat out of fashion in the last century or so. It is a shame Grace has become so isolated."

"And Max is cute as hell," said Rune. "I'm sure his sister is too."

Khalil demanded suspiciously. "What are you planning?"

"Dude, we don't have any agenda in mind," Rune said with a blink. "It's not like we synced our electronic calendars with some kind of overarching evil plan."

Khalil decided he definitely didn't like being called that word. Having done what he came to do, he deemed it was time to leave. Remembering what Grace said about leaving without a word, he said to Carling, "Good-bye."

"Keep in touch," Carling told him.

"And you, as well." In the end Khalil was glad he chose to meet her halfway. Perhaps Carling was, after all, one of the few creatures he might call *friend*.

Then Khalil looked at Rune. No. He was not prepared to go that far.

Rune raised his eyebrows. He gave Khalil another one of his sleepy-seeming smiles. "It's been so special."

"Don't call me 'dude' again," Khalil told the other male, as he strode toward the sliding glass doors.

Khalil found Soren reading in the guesthouse he had taken for his quarters. Soren's physical form was tall and lean, with craggy features, white hair, and piercing stars for eyes. As Khalil approached the open door to the small house, Soren said, "Come in."

Khalil stepped inside slowly. The living and the dining rooms were all in one great room that was filled with fashionable furniture suitable for a beachside residence. Other than several books, stacks of file folders and a high-end laptop on the dining table, the place looked uninhabited, but then Soren created his own clothing when he created his physical form, and he didn't have any bodily needs.

"Please have a seat," Soren said. "I hope your visit was productive."

Any first-generation Djinn had a presence so intense it took a while to grow accustomed to being in proximity to one. Khalil braced himself as he took the lounge chair opposite Soren's. He replied, "I accomplished everything I intended to accomplish."

"Did you," said Soren. "I understand you have befriended this beautiful human Oracle and are looking forward to your date tonight."

Khalil was not unsurprised to find that Soren had listened in on his conversations with Carling and Rune. Jailors often did monitor their prisoners. He said nothing.

Soren set his book aside. "If you were less mature, I would be concerned that you may have become too fascinated with the lure of those bound in flesh. I mourn whenever the folk of the air fall prey to this fascination. It is a sad thing when a Djinn falls to his death."

Soren referred to when Djinn made the irrevocable decision to create a completely human form and fall into flesh. It was a rare occurrence. Khalil had never had a close association with any Djinn who had chosen to fall.

Djinn could only choose to be mortal. They did not have the Power to create one of the other long-lived Elder Races who were bound in flesh. It cost too much Power for a Djinn to fully transform. They could not create a cage of living flesh for themselves and also make it immortal. He had always wondered what might prompt a Djinn to make such an extreme sacrifice. He could not imagine a Djinn who might do so just as a rejection of who he was. As Soren said, there had to be a lure, something they fell toward.

Unbidden, the memory came to mind of soft little bodies sleeping so trustingly against his shoulder. That memory was followed closely by another one, the delighted joy on Max's round face as he took his first two steps toward Khalil. He thought of the peculiar satisfaction in watching how Chloe's forming, questioning mind worked, and of that ineffable, precious thing he had touched as he stood looking out the porch screen door at a tranquil summer evening.

Finally his mind turned to what he had been avoiding for most of the day, the most addictive memories of all. The softness of Grace's lips, the way she kissed him, molding her mouth and body to his as she molded her presence to him. As he thought of it, the intensity of heat that flared inside him was blinding.

He shook with the urge to contain it, to keep it hidden from Soren's too perceptive gaze. Djinn understood that knowledge was power, but it was also dangerous. They played a game of truth, balance and forfeit for a reason. The light of epiphany was a flame that burned like no other. He didn't know all that he and Grace might share or how far they could take this unique new terrain that lay between them. *He didn't know.* And the need to know drove him beyond anything.

He would coax out of her everything she had to give. He would finally understand the mystery of what it meant to be flesh to flesh while sharing the indescribable passion of spirit to spirit.

Silence had fallen. Outside the ocean murmured. Quiet Elven voices sounded in conversation from the other guesthouse. From the villa itself came the sudden, startling peal of Carling's laughter.

"You wished to speak of something," Soren said at last.

Khalil gathered his composure and his thoughts together. He told Soren of hearing the voice in Grace's vision. He took his time, careful to impart every detail and impression, and Soren did not rush him. Finally Khalil fell silent.

"'Not form but Form, a prime indivisible,'" Soren repeated. The elder Djinn had grown intent, his entire focus on Khalil's tale. "And 'all things were set in motion from the beginning.' Those are the Primal Powers."

The Elder Races honored seven gods, the Primal Powers that were the linchpins of the universe. Taliesin, the god of the Dance, was first among the Primal Powers because everything in the universe was in motion. Then there was Azrael, the god of Death; Inanna, the goddess of Love; Nadir, the goddess of the depths or the Oracle; Will, the god of the Gift; Camael, the goddess of the Hearth; and Hyperion, the god of Law.

"That seems logical," said Khalil. "But it sounded to me as if this voice claimed that Lord Death was not a Primal Power but a part of . . . it, whatever it is. And it also talked of Cuelebre as though he is a Primal Power. Your memory goes back to the beginning of the world. Have you ever heard of such a thing?"

Soren spread his hands. "I have not. But I do not remember the beginning of the world. To remember that, I would have to have existed before the world did. I do not know that any of us who came first remember that. As far as I have ever heard, we only remember coming into a new world. If the Great Beast is indeed a Primal Power, as your voice said, he would remember the beginning of the world."

Cuelebre—a god? Khalil wanted to scoff at the idea, but he found that he couldn't. The idea was too disturbing. "Do you believe such a thing is possible?"

Soren gave him an indecipherable glance. "It is more accurate to say I do not believe it is impossible. It is a curious thing, that the older one becomes and the more knowledge one acquires, the more one realizes what a mystery the universe is, after all."

"Whatever the reality may be, the speaker believes it," Khalil said grimly. "And it believes it is also a Primal Power."

"It is also quite possible that the speaker is entirely insane," Soren pointed out. "With your permission, I will pass word of this occurrence on discreetly to others to see what they may think."

Khalil spread out a hand. "Be my guest," he said. "Grace thinks the vision came for Cuelebre, but I heard it too."

"In the meantime," Soren said, "it turns out that you taking an active role in the Oracle's life is the wisest course after all. I think it is smart to befriend her and coax her into growing comfortable with your presence. Forgive me. I should not have voiced any concern about your involvement with her until I heard everything you had to tell me."

Khalil remained silent. He had no desire to confess anything to Soren regarding his own newfound need and growing struggle. Soren might feel obligated to approach the other elders of their House to voice his concerns, and Khalil would not risk that.

Djinn could be imprisoned. Lethe had imprisoned Phaedra. Even the most Powerful of Djinn could be imprisoned if enough of his fellow creatures joined in the effort. A serious thing to consider at any time, imprisonment was an especially terrible thing to do to the folk of the air.

He had heard of such a thing before, one group who took it upon themselves to imprison a Djinn who was in danger of falling. They held him prisoner until the object of his fascination died.

Khalil did not know what had happened to the Djinn after that.

He became aware of how late the evening had progressed. It was almost nine o'clock, and Louisville was on the same time as Key Largo. He frowned. He would have expected Grace to call him for their date by now.

He stood abruptly. "I must go."

Soren nodded to him and reached for his book again. "I enjoyed seeing you again. Peace be with you, Khalil."

"And you, father."

Khalil released his physical form and arrowed toward Louisville and Grace's house. As he came nearer, he noticed that her car was in the driveway but the lights in the house were off. Perhaps she had been too tired, and she had fallen asleep.

He entered the house quietly and checked from room to room. It was unoccupied, tidy and silent. Not even the fans were running. He frowned at the empty little beds in the children's room. He disliked how the house felt without any of them present. By the time he had reached the narrow futon where Grace slept, his frown had turned into an agitated scowl.

He whirled out of the house and rampaged across the land.

She was not in the meadows. Nor was she near the river. He could not locate her anywhere, and the light was failing fast. His sense of urgency turned to frenzy. In fifteen, twenty minutes at the most, it would be full dark. Her eyesight was limited, and her knee was not strong.

She was so fragile. She was only human.

Then he saw the door set into the side of the hill. It stood open. That would be the tunnel that led to the place where the Oracle spoke.

He dove. He didn't waste time assuming a physical form. Instead he roared down the tunnel to the cavern.

≈ THIRTEEN ≈

The female Djinn gave Grace a smile that looked eerie in the flashlight's sharp beam, elongated shadows filling in the hollows at cheeks, temples, underneath her black starred eyes. "Very good, human," Phaedra said. "How could you tell?"

"You choose a physical form that has something of Khalil in it," Grace said quietly.

Phaedra walked close to circle Grace like a prowling cat. "My physical form has something of both my parents," said Phaedra. "I do not want to forget anything they did for me or to me."

Grace held very still and tried not to let her unease and sadness show. She might wish with all of her heart that it was not so, but dark, angry spirits really did tend to be dark and angry because they held on to things.

She said, "Khalil told me how your mother kidnapped and tortured you, and how he had to go to war with her to free you."

As Phaedra circled around, she trailed fingers along Grace's back and across her arm. "Did he tell you it took him five hundred years to free me?"

Khalil always felt hot when Grace touched him. By contrast, Phaedra's touch was oddly cool. Goose bumps broke out over Grace's chilled flesh. She cleared her throat and said softly, "No, he didn't say. I'm so sorry."

"I spent five hundred years trapped," said Phaedra. "Five hundred years because he was too *cautious* to fight Lethe on his own. No, he had to take his time, build allies, create an army. Clearly it was not an issue of some urgency to him."

Grace struggled to reconcile that information with the pained sadness she had sensed in Khalil whenever he referred to his daughter. She said gently, "I don't know what to say."

"I used to dread Lethe's visits," Phaedra said. "Then I looked forward to them, because as much as they hurt, anything was better than the dark, empty, airless hole she kept me in. Then I learned that was just a phase too, as I became the dark."

Grace couldn't imagine what such a lengthy, profound deprivation interspersed with torture might do to a mind, inhuman or otherwise. What would it take to recover? Djinn might not need physical food but they gained nourishment from Power and energy sources like the sun. Had Phaedra actually starved? Was there anything left of her that was salvageable?

"Khalil said he thought Lethe was insane," she said.

"Did he?" Phaedra thrust her face close, black eyes blazing. *"Then why did it take him five hundred years!"*

"I don't know," Grace whispered.

Just like she did with Khalil, she felt surrounded by Phaedra, but this time there was no pleasure from a warm, male presence. She felt surrounded by razors, any one of which might cut her at any time. She knew Phaedra was trying to frighten her. It was crude and obvious, like playground bullying.

It was also working. She thought she had felt alone at times before, but she had never felt as alone as she did right then. She patted the thread that led to Khalil. The connection felt so insubstantial, it seemed like a mirage. She kept part of her mind focused on it tensely, but she did not tug on it.

Phaedra cocked her head, unblinking. The purity of her white face was pitiless, stark. "Why don't you ask him sometime, since he apparently likes to talk to you?"

"How did you know to come here?" Grace asked.

"You mean, how did I know he comes to see you and your cute widdow famiwee?" Phaedra said. "His new human toys? It's been remarked upon." Phaedra opened her eyes wide and said in a pseudo-confidential tone, "I don't have friends, but I do have sources."

"What do you want?"

"Why do I have to want something to be here?"

"Because you wouldn't be here if there wasn't something you wanted," Grace said. Her gut had tightened into a knot without her permission, as if her instincts knew to expect a body blow. She had no one to ask for advice and no backup. All she had was the training her grandmother had given her.

Phaedra lifted her head and looked around. "I like it here. It reminds me of old times. Don't you like it here?"

Grace said, "I do."

That brought Phaedra's black sparkling gaze back to her, a quick glance that told Grace she had surprised the Djinn. Phaedra gave her a sarcastic smile. "Aren't you going to offer to try to help me?" she said mockingly. "Like everyone who tries to find and talk to me?"

"Nope," said Grace. "I didn't try to find you. And I can't help you."

She had surprised Phaedra again. Phaedra's expression grew ugly. "I thought it was your *job* to help people."

"It is my job," Grace said, as gently yet as firmly as she could, "to give people who ask the chance to consult with the Oracle. You have to want to help yourself. You have to make the journey here, you have to ask for the consultation, and it's up to you whether or not you make anything good out of what the Oracle gives you. I'm not a doctor. I don't make house calls. I'm not going to try to be your friend, and this isn't therapy. I will not presume that I know what you need or what you don't need. That's on you. I'm sorry about what happened to you. I can't imagine the horror you went through. I also can't imagine all the gifts and talents you have, not least of which is immortality, and my God, just the sheer amount of time you people have to get over shit. You're the one who owns your life. It's your responsibility what you make of it."

Halfway through, Phaedra turned her back and stood rigid. Grace finished speaking to that bloodred fall of hair. Even though her heart was pounding, the chill of the cavern was seeping into her bones. It was a strain to stand so long. Her muscles quivered with tiredness, and her knee ached like a son of a bitch.

Then Phaedra laughed angrily.

Well, what the hell, Grace thought. Let's throw that useless little sanctuary law out there. Just for shits and giggles.

"And should this matter to you," she said quietly, "if you do anything to hurt me, you violate inter-demesne law. I don't know who would be sent after you then. I doubt it would be Khalil. So did you want a consultation with the Oracle or is this a social call?"

Phaedra turned to regard her, bloodred eyebrows raised. Phaedra's expression was so cold, Grace shuddered. She staggered as her bad knee threatened to give. She might have fallen if she hadn't worn the brace.

Along with the useless little law, Grace readied herself to throw what was probably a useless little spell—the spell of expulsion she used to get rid of a dark spirit. It felt like getting ready to throw a cupful of water on a bonfire, but she couldn't just stand there and do nothing.

Phaedra was staring curiously at her legs. Then she looked up with a razored smile. "I will not be beholden to you for a consultation."

Grace blinked. What a Djinn-like thing to say. Did Phaedra still have a shred of honor, a sense of what balance was supposed to be? Maybe Grace shouldn't make too much of it. Maybe it didn't mean anything.

And she was so damn tired of worrying about the boundaries she wasn't supposed to cross as Oracle. The Power was still roused from when she had called it up. She held on to it tightly as she said, "If that's the only thing stopping you, you don't have to owe me a favor. Really, it's quite okay to send cash."

A heartbeat. Then another.

Well, hot damn. The dark sea that filled her didn't so much as even quiver when she mentioned money. It certainly didn't give any hint of retreating or leaving her. Maybe the part where the Oracle was forbidden to ask for money had been just another legend.

Or maybe this was a whole new ball game, now that the ghost of the serpent woman wasn't acting as a backseat driver.

Phaedra laughed. "Prophecy from a crippled Oracle. I might like that. I will think about it. Perhaps I will return."

Grace held her breath as Phaedra stalked close. The Djinn trailed a finger down Grace's forearm again. A moment later, Grace felt a sharp, slicing pain. She stared down dumbly. Her arm was bleeding. Phaedra had cut her.

"Oh, don't worry," Phaedra whispered with a smile. "It's just a small payment for your lecture. I didn't really hurt you. Much."

"You goddamn, freaky bitch," Grace said, because, hells bells, it had been a righteous day, and all of a sudden, *pow*, her temper was done lost and gone.

She pulled on everything she had and threw the expulsion spell. She meant to reach for the Power she had been born with, but her anger got in the way. Both Powers jettisoned out of her. She felt the spell strike Phaedra full on.

The force of it lifted Phaedra's physical form and hurled her across the cavern. She struck the wall and slammed into the ground.

"Oh, shit," Grace said. *Oh, shit.* She limped over to Phaedra's prone figure as fast as she could. The Djinn was sprawled on her stomach, dark red hair covering her face. "Are you all right?"

Phaedra began to laugh as Grace reached her. "The crippled Oracle has quite a punch. I didn't see that coming."

"I didn't either," Grace said. "You pissed me off and I lost my temper."

Phaedra pushed her hair back. A champagne-colored liquid trickled from the corner of her mouth. As Grace watched, the liquid faded back into the Djinn's skin. Awkwardly, Grace struggled to kneel on her good leg, as she said, "You're not *bleeding*, are you?"

Phaedra came up on her hands and knees to face Grace, her expression mocking. "Don't tell me you care."

"Don't confuse who you are with the rest of the world," Grace snapped. "I do care. You're the one who doesn't."

The mockery faded from Phaedra's face. Grace kept her guard up and both Powers at hand as they stared at each other. As she focused on Phaedra, something roused in the dark sea. She held her breath and concentrated.

She said, "If you ever do want to petition the Oracle, there is someone who would like to see you."

Rage and curiosity warred for supremacy in Phaedra's expression. "Who is it?"

Grace said, "A ghost."

She watched as the rage won. Phaedra bared her teeth and spat, "My *mother*?"

"No," Grace told her. Balancing on her good knee was more tiring than standing. The muscles in her thigh began to tremble. "It's someone else."

Phaedra's anger faded slowly, until what remained was feral and bewildered. "I don't know any other ghost who would be interested in talking with me."

"Suit yourself," Grace said. "Just know the offer is there if you want it."

The Djinn flowed to her feet with the same impossible grace as Khalil had, and Grace fought to rise. She couldn't leverage with her bad leg. Phaedra watched her struggle with an unreadable expression.

"Come on, Freaky Bitch," Grace said irritably. "Give us a hand."

The last thing she expected was help. If anything, she expected her snark to be the impetus that drove the Djinn away, and really, by that point, good riddance. Instead Phaedra held out her hand slowly.

Grace stared at the outstretched fingers. Just as slowly, she put her hand in Phaedra's grasp. She was braced for an attack. Instead, Phaedra pulled Grace to her feet. She muttered, "Thanks."

But Phaedra dematerialized even as she spoke.

Grace found herself alone in the cavern. She stood with her weight on her good leg, straining to hear past her own stressed, noisy breathing as she cast her awareness out. Heavy, cool silence pressed against her eardrums. She could not sense the Djinn anywhere on the land. Phaedra had really left.

Tension leaked out of her quivering muscles. She realized the only light she could see was from the circle cast by her flashlight. The pale, diffuse sunlight that had streamed down the tunnel was gone. She sighed heavily, collected the mask from where she had dropped it, tucked it under her arm and braced herself for the upward trek through the tunnel. Climbing the uneven floor was more challenging than climbing stairs, and her muscles were already cold and tired.

The only way she was going to make it happen was to just fucking do it. She limped over, and with one hand she clutched the flashlight, while she used the other to brace herself against the wall. She started to climb, using her strong leg to go up, and she leaned against the wall and balanced on her bad leg on the opposite step. Inelegant, but it worked.

Or at least it did until a wild maelstrom of Power roared down the tunnel.

The Power blasted into her, and she staggered. She felt her precarious balance go, clutched first at the wrapped mask and cried out as she lost hold of the flashlight. The light careened wildly as the flashlight bounced down the tunnel. Then all illumination cut out abruptly, and she fell back into the absolute darkness.

Oh, shit, this was going to be a bad one—

She flashed on ripping out all the painful repairs on her still-healing knee, more expensive doctor's visits, maybe even more surgeries.

Khalil's warm, fierce energy enveloped her even as strong arms formed around her and broke her fall gently. The rest of his body formed next. He said, "Easy. I've got you."

Her heart was racing like a crazy thing. Her feet still rested on the uneven tunnel floor, but lightly, for he had taken all of her weight. She grabbed him and said unsteadily, "Goddamn. Watch where you're going next time!"

"I'm sorry." For the first time since she'd met him, his voice sounded discordant and harsh. He drew her upright. "It's late. I couldn't find you, and I got worried."

"All right." It seemed to be the most natural thing in the world for her to turn in his arms and lean against him. Some of the day had been good, but the bad bits had been downright rotten, and maybe if she had thought it through, she wouldn't have chosen to do what she did. But she didn't think; she never thought things through the way she should. She just put an arm around his long, lean waist and buried her face against the wide, steady support of his chest.

Mmm. He seemed bigger in the dark.

He stood quietly, holding her, one massive hand cupping the back of her neck. Something rested on the top of her head. His cheek.

"I sense blood," he said. His voice had turned dangerous. "You are injured?"

She shook her head, her mind racing. "It's just a shallow cut on my arm."

"What happened?"

What should she tell him? She couldn't think straight. She hadn't had time to process Freaky Bitch's visit for herself, let alone consider how he might react. She said, "Later. I'm cold and tired, and I really want to get out of here."

His reply was to swing her into his arms and stride up the tunnel. His energy still remained edged and unsettled, but always with that addictive undercurrent that was powerfully male, uniquely him.

A small part of her couldn't help but notice his long, smooth effortless stride. She could usually control that part, but it was harder to do when she grew tired and emotionally out of balance. She wished she could flip a switch and turn it off, because it was small-minded and whiny. It didn't care that he was inhuman and there could be no meaningful comparison between the two of them and their abilities. It only took note of how strongly and evenly he moved and whispered poisonously to her, *I could do that once.*

She turned truculent. "I didn't mean for you to carry me."

"There is no reason for you to struggle when I can transport you with ease," he said shortly.

"Whether I struggle or not is beside the point," she said, just as shortly. She kept stiff in his arms. "The fact that I can and will do it is the point."

"Do not be stupidly prideful," he told her. "We both know you can do it. There is no reason for you to wreck yourself proving it."

Was that what she was doing? She fought with her conflicting instincts. He must have moved more quickly than she had thought, for suddenly he strode out the tunnel doorway into the warm night.

The warmth was a welcome relief from the cavern. The western part of the sky was still tinged with color, although the sun had set. After sunset, the land got very dark without streetlamps or neighboring houses to illuminate the night. In another half hour or so, it would be too dark to walk without a flashlight. Khalil's ivory face looked edged in the shadows.

"Stop," she said. Then, more sharply as he ignored her, "Khalil, stop!"

He shot her a sparkling look, his jaw tight, but he stopped. "What do you require?"

"I have to put this away," she said, indicating the mask in its wrapping. "And shut and lock the door."

After hesitating a moment, he carried her back to the cavern entrance and eased her to her feet. He waited with his arms crossed as she tucked the mask back into a Rubbermaid cabinet, locked the door and put the key in its usual place in the coffee can on the lintel.

When she turned around, he reached to pick her up. She slapped a hand onto his chest and stiffened her arm. He grabbed her wrist, so inhumanly fast, she jumped. But he did not pull her hand away. He just held her forearm in a gentle, unbreakable hold. She felt his Power probe along her skin.

"Where are you bleeding?" he asked.

His face was tight. Staring up at him, she held out her other arm. He stroked his fingers lightly along the cut. She felt a slight flare in his Power, and the trickle of blood stopped. The annoying nag of pain vanished too. She tilted her arm up, squinting in the last of the light. It looked like the cut had scabbed over. "Thank you."

"I'm not a healer," he said. "That's the extent of what I know to do."

"What you did is great."

"Sorry," he had said. And "worried." She would never have imagined a week ago that he would admit to such things, let alone that he would say them to her. The wild agitation in his energy was calming down. She stroked his hand that still held her other wrist. His hold loosened, and as she turned to walk back to the house, he fell into step beside her.

The scene was so like, and yet unlike, her dream. The night was full of shadows, and the wind caused the trees to whisper secretively. She looked up. There was still the barest sliver of the waning moon. The Oracle's moon must be tomorrow. It was an especially Powerful time to prophesy, if anyone knew to ask for it.

Khalil might be in his human form, but his immense body still moved with impossible, fluid grace. He watched her with that same diamond gaze as piercing as the emerging stars, but instead of jarring her, she found it comforting.

She thought of how Petra and Niko would face each other, no matter how hard the conversation became. She couldn't pretend nothing had happened either. She said, "I have something difficult I need to tell you."

Khalil gave her a frowning glance. "Difficult for whom, you or me?"

"Probably both," she said, sighing.

"Very well."

Feeling trapped, she fumbled for words. How could she say it? What would make it better? She was no good at this kind of shit. She stopped walking and said bluntly, "Phaedra came to see me."

His response was electrifying. After a moment of standing frozen, he whirled and grabbed her by the shoulders. His face was savage, and his eyes blazed. He snarled, "*You should have called me.*"

She stammered, "I-I'm sorry. I know how badly you want to see her, I just—"

"Did I not warn you pariahs are dangerous?" he hissed. He actually shook her. "What did she do?"

She stared, too shocked to protest his manhandling. He was angry because Phaedra was dangerous? "We talked. She was unpleasant."

He stopped shaking her. She tried to read his expression. There was ferocity and loss and something else. Something vulnerable. "What did she want?"

"I'm not sure. I don't think she knew. She sort of . . ." Grace's voice trailed away. Struggling to understand one Djinn well enough in order to explain her to another was wreaking havoc on her communication skills. "She's angry at you," she said finally. "She's really angry that it took you so long to come after her. She said it took you five hundred years."

His chest moved, as if he took a deep breath, even though he had no real need to breathe. He dragged his long fingers through his hair, dislodging the plain tie that held it back. It fell about his pale hard face.

"I couldn't go after Lethe alone," he said harshly. "She would have destroyed me, and then there would have been no one to go after Phaedra. By the time I gathered enough allies, Lethe and Phaedra had disappeared. I spent most of that time searching for them. I didn't rest. I didn't stop. Not until I found them."

Moved to compassion, Grace reached up to touch his cheek. "She doesn't understand that. She couches it in a lot of sneering and anger, but I think at the bottom of all that, she's hurt."

He covered her hand with his. "What else did she say? How did she know to come here?"

"I asked her that. She said your attention to us and this place has been noted and remarked upon, and that she has 'sources,' whatever that means." She shook her head. "I think—Khalil, you should weigh what I say carefully, because I'm no kind of expert on Djinn behavior, but I think she's not only hurt, but she might be jealous of the time you've started to spend here."

"She doesn't want anything to do with me," he said bitterly. "How can she be jealous?"

"That's a rational question," Grace told him. "She doesn't want anything to do with you, but then she keeps tabs on what you're doing? I don't think 'rational' applies here. And she might be damaged and refuse to build associations with others, but I'm not sure she's a pariah, exactly. At least not the way I understand pariahs from how you described them. I asked if she came to consult the Oracle, and she said she wouldn't be beholden to me for a favor. From what you've said, I don't think pariahs would care. They would take the consultation and just not fulfill their part of the bargain."

He frowned. He hadn't calmed. His energy was still volcanic under her fingertips, but he had become better controlled. "Perhaps you're right. Perhaps not."

She asked hesitantly, "What's wrong with her? I mean, I can see and feel how very different she is from you and the other Djinn I've met. She feels jagged and sharp. I just don't understand what that means."

He rubbed the back of his neck. "It's hard to explain. We each have an innate understanding of our own identity, the patterns and energy signature that makes us who we are, and we carry that with us no matter what form we assume."

"I think I understand," she said. "I always know who you are, no matter what you look like."

He glanced at her. "When we sustain an injury, we heal ourselves by remembering who and what we are, and we . . .

realign ourselves to that identity. Sometimes it's exhausting. The deeper the injury, the harder it is to align, and we sometimes have to rest for a long time afterward. And sometimes Djinn are damaged so badly, they don't have the strength to realign, or they can't remember how they were before they were damaged so they can't heal themselves. We have no healers for these kinds of injuries."

"That's terrible," she said quietly. "All the time you people have to get over shit. Except when you can't get over shit." Remorse twisted inside. "Isn't there anything to be done for damaged Djinn?"

"Not that we know of." He looked grim. "And terrible or not, Phaedra's still dangerous. You still haven't told me why you didn't call me."

Grace's shoulders sagged. "She seemed undecided and volatile. I was afraid if you showed up, it might make her worse. I didn't want you to have to fight her, because if older Djinn are more Powerful, I thought you would be stronger than she is and you would win. But she might push you hard enough that you would have to kill her to do so."

He cocked his head. From what she could see of his shadowed face, he was looking at her with a curious expression. "You were protecting me?"

She gave him a twisted smile. "I was trying to, anyway. How'd I do?"

"You did foolishly," he snapped.

Her smile disappeared. Her fuse was short enough at the best of times. As strained as her day had been, it flashed hot and bright again.

"Oh, yeah? Fuck you too." She turned and headed toward the house again. "I'm so done with the bad bits of today. I've changed my mind about that date. It's the most goddamn ridiculous thing I've ever heard of. Go away."

"*Gracie*," he said between his teeth.

For crying out loud, he didn't just call her that. That was her nickname, the one that her family called her. Chloe was the only one who ever called her that anymore. She pivoted on the heel of her strong leg back to him and gritted, "*What*?"

Suddenly he was right in front of her. He tilted up her face with both hands. When she felt his fingers shaking, the bottom seemed to drop out of her stomach. His gaze was a stern, furious blaze. "You could *die*. You could be *gone*. All it might take is one blow, one fall, one stab to the heart. One accident." He stopped and tilted his face up at the waning moon. For one moment his regal features looked desperate and searching. When his gaze came down to hers again, it was like watching stars fall. He said, with a naive surprise, "You scared me."

Damn him. Damn him.

Khalil stroked her cheeks as he told her, "I figured out what to wear on the date."

Her mouth opened and closed. No words came out. She didn't know what to say. She jerked away and headed toward the house again. "It's got to be late," she said over her shoulder. "After nine at least."

He said nothing. He didn't have to. She could feel him, full of scorching intent, prowling at her back.

She snapped, "I'm tired and filthy. I haven't had any supper. Forget that, I didn't get any lunch. I haven't eaten all day, and I haven't even showered yet."

"I have a present for you," he purred.

She stopped abruptly. He didn't run into her back but reformed in front of her. His long black hair fell about his face like a velvet curtain. He was smiling. She bit her lips and tried to stop herself from asking, but then the question came out anyway. "What is it?"

"You will shower first," he said. "Then I will tell you that you are beautiful."

"You'll *what*?" She stared, astonished all over again.

"Then we will go somewhere for supper and a drink and a walk on the beach, but I refuse to stand on my head, and I forget all the rest," he said. "But you won't get your present until we go out."

"There aren't any beaches nearby," she said, dumbly. Stand on his head? Where the hell had he gotten his information on dating?

With one hand, Khalil made a gesture grand enough for the most accomplished of stage magicians. "That is a minor inconvenience only, since I can transport us anywhere we may wish to go."

With that, he opened up a whole different vista in front of her. The possibilities were staggering.

This whole Damascus business had turned into quite a trip. If only she had realized, she would have packed some bags.

"We'll go somewhere local," she said, almost dreamily. No witches' haunts, not with the kind of chilly reception she had been getting all day. "There's a pub in town that caters to a wide clientele from the Elder Races. I'll eat something and maybe have a drink." Maybe she would have a stiff scotch. "A quick, quiet date. No drama, no fuss, bed by midnight. And you'll give me my present."

He gave her that slow, mischievous smile of his, the one that oozed sin and sensuality. "Absolutely."

"Okay, then," she said. She looked around. If she was giving in, she might as well chuck away her whole stance. "You can transport us anywhere?"

His smile turned into a grin. "Why, where did you want to go?"

Was it bad for her to ask? Or was that the Darrin in her talking? She said, "The bathroom on the second story of the house."

Before she could change her mind, Khalil snatched her up and a whirlwind embraced her. She lost touch with the ground or with anything solid or familiar other than the strong, confident hold of his arms and his lean, hard chest. She threw her arms around him, shrieking as though she plummeted from the top of a cliff.

Then the world reformed around them. Squinting up, she saw his long hair whipping around his starred eyes and elegant face. He was smiling. They were standing in the deep shadows on the second-floor landing of the house, just outside of the bathroom.

"Think I'm going to take a bath," she croaked. The main reason was she didn't think she could stand upright.

"Please yourself," Khalil said. "I'll change and be waiting for you downstairs."

He dematerialized. She couldn't blink as she watched him go. It was a spectacular sight, no matter how many times she saw him do it.

What was he going to change into?

And what was her present?

She sighed and let the rest of the day fall away. Then she headed to the bathroom. Bubble bath. It might be a quick one, but it would still be freaking awesome.

She didn't care what she put in the bath, as long as it foamed. After starting the water, she grabbed the first bottle that came to hand. It was Sesame Street Wet Wild Watermelon Bubble Bath. It sounded divine. She dumped some under the water and went to her bedroom to grab something to wear.

She didn't have time to dither. She wouldn't let herself have time to dither. The red glowing numbers in the clock upstairs read nine thirty-five. Ready by ten o'clock, home by midnight. This was the only way she would date from here on out. She would put herself on a ruthless schedule and stick to it. Not that she would get all that many opportunities.

But it was good to have rules.

Climbing into the bathtub was bliss. No matter how she might wash everything at the kitchen sink, it just didn't feel the same as total submersion in water. She scrubbed everything, lathered her hair twice, rinsed and dried and dressed in the skirt she had put on so briefly the other day. It was bright and patterned with deep, rich orange, pink and purple flowers, interspersed with green leaves.

The colors should have clashed. Instead, the shades had been cleverly chosen, and they complemented each other. She paired the skirt with a light green tank top. The bright outfit brought out her own colors, the peach of her skin, the different flecks of color in her hazel eyes, and the red-gold hues of her strawberry blonde hair. She could wear her knee brace and nobody would notice. She slipped on flat, pretty leather sandals.

There was hardly any time for makeup, which was another good thing. A swish of blush, a swipe of gloss, and a few brush strokes of eye shadow, and badda-bing, badda-boom, she was ready to go by nine fifty-seven, and feeling calm and virtuous to boot.

All of that was a good thing, because the date really was the most goddamn ridiculous thing she'd ever heard of. The sooner she went on it, the sooner she could collect her present and come home and go to bed and get on with the business of living the rest of her real life.

Because she needed every scrap of her strength and attention on meeting each challenge as it arose. There wasn't any room in her real life for dating or her growing obsession with a haughty, child-loving, mischievous, kick-in-the-head-sexy prince of the Djinn.

She told herself she was all right with that.

And listened to the silence.

≈ FOURTEEN ≈

Grace descended the stairs carefully, holding on to the banister. Her wretched knee decided it didn't like the strain of carrying her weight while bending in the downward motion, so she had to go down lopsided, the same way she had climbed the tunnel. Khalil had turned on a few downstairs lights. Her pulse was racing too much as she opened the gate at the bottom of the stairs and rounded the corner to the living room.

She told herself she was being idiotic. After all, it wasn't as though she hadn't seen Khalil . . .

Hadn't seen Khalil a hundred times . . .

A tall man stood in her living room. It was Khalil; she knew it was. She could feel the familiar blaze of his Power coming from the man, although it felt peculiarly muted at the moment, as if clouds had drifted over to obscure the sun.

But this man *looked* completely different. Well, not *completely* different. He was still very tall, well over six feet, and massively built. He still had pale skin, long, raven black hair pulled back in a simple leather tie and regal, elegant features.

That was where the similarity with the old Khalil ended.

This man wore a black T-shirt that strained over the wide, broad muscles of his chest and thick biceps, faded jeans and black boots. His features and his skin . . . His skin was human, with the kind of paleness that went with black-Irish coloring, and a slight, dark shadow of beard along his lean cheeks and jaw. She edged closer, staring. There were even slight laugh lines at the corners of his mouth and eyes.

Then he turned to look at her, and all semblance of humanity ended. For lack of a better description, she tried to call the color of his eyes gray, but that wasn't right; for even though the strange crystalline-like quality of his gaze was muffled like the rest of his Power, they were still starred with too much radiance.

"You're so different," she breathed. Fascinated, she edged closer. Did he have pupils? She couldn't tell. His eyes seemed to take in and multiply the amount of light around him.

Khalil's lean face creased with a keen smile. "You *are* beautiful," he said with evident pleasure. His pure, gorgeous voice sounded the same. "Clearly bathing suits you."

She choked on an unexpected bubble of laughter. Khalil had quite a way to go in the learning-how-to-give-compliments department, but she wasn't about to bring that up, when he spoke with such sincerity.

She reached out to touch his forearm then hesitated self-consciously. "Do you mind?"

"No," he said.

She laid her fingers on him. His skin not only looked human, but it felt like human skin too and warm to the touch, not quite as hot as usual. She stroked lightly down his arm. He made a surprised sound and looked shocked. She snatched her hand away. "Did that hurt?"

"No," Khalil breathed. He looked down at his arm, at her hand. "It felt incredible," he said. His voice had deepened. "Do it again."

She held her own breath and tentatively touched him again. This time she curled her hand around the back of his elbow. She drew her hand down the underside of his lean forearm until she reached his broad palm. He hissed at the contact, and a shudder went through him. That simple touch and his intense reaction were unbelievably erotic. His long fingers curled around her wrist, and he held her tight.

"You've never felt that before?" she asked faintly.

"Not with such intensity, no," he said, his voice unsteady. "Creating a more humanlike form is complicated. The more complex a form is, the more energy it takes to create and maintain. I have never been interested enough to descend this deeply into flesh before."

"How real is this?" she asked.

He stared at his own arm curiously, as if he wasn't quite sure of the answer himself. "Real enough to feel how pleasurable your touch was," he said. "Real enough to sustain damage. Cuts and bruises would hurt." He frowned. "And I do not think I can transport us anywhere while I am bound this deeply in flesh."

He spoke of his body as if it were a cage. The concept was oddly disturbing, although she could see how flesh would be a cage for him, although he could still discard it anytime he chose.

The whole conversation had created far more intimacy between them than she had expected or welcomed. It had also raised more questions in her mind. She pulled away.

"We'll have to see that you don't get damaged tonight," she said lightly. "And I can drive."

"In a car," he said, his frown deepening.

He did not look entirely enthused at the prospect. Suddenly amused, she grinned. "Yes, Khalil. In my car."

"Very well," he said. "But I am paying for everything and opening all the doors."

She rolled her eyes as she went to the bookshelf to grab up her purse. "It sounds like you have quite a well thought-out agenda," she said. "I would love to know who or what your dating resource was."

"I went to Florida today," Khalil said. "Carling and Rune are being held in quarantine in Key Largo."

She glanced at him. "How are they doing?"

"They're fine. Rune told me a few things about dating.

I must say, I didn't quite trust all that he said, but his suggestion for a casual outfit seems all right."

"It's great," she said, rather more huskily than she had intended. But then anything he would have worn would have been kick-in-the-head good. She decided it was past time to get out of the house, and she headed for the door.

He might not be able to dematerialize and reform as instantly as he had before, but this new, more humanized Khalil could still move with lethal speed. Suddenly he was in front of her, unlatching the screen door and holding it open. She flipped on the porch light and turned and locked the front door after he stepped out after her. He watched everything she did with an extra-close attention she found unsettling.

She smoothed her hands down the sides of her skirt self-consciously and muttered, "I feel like you're studying me to take notes."

"Things acquire more significance in this form," he said. "You must pay more attention to your physical surroundings when you're bound in flesh." He followed her to her car. He opened the driver's door and closed it after she slid in. She strapped herself in.

When he had climbed in the passenger seat, she waited. He waited too. She told him, "I never drive anywhere unless everybody in the car is wearing their seat belt. It's a thing of mine."

He shook his head and looked mystified. She sighed and leaned over him to fumble for his seat belt strap. It brought her breasts against his arm and the left side of his chest, and she caught his scent. He smelled like clean, healthy male. She caught her breath and tilted her head back to look up at his face. He was watching her intently, eyes blazing.

"Sorry," she croaked, pulling back.

He gave her a keen, bright smile that had every bit as much mischief as it did in his old form. "Don't apologize. Really."

"Just pull that strap around and buckle the two parts together, like mine." She gestured, and when he had done so, she started the car and backed out of the driveway.

Almost every metropolitan area in the States had at least one bar or pub that catered to a mix of Elder Races clientele. Louisville had two, both under the same ownership, although they were located in very different parts of town. Grace drove to the nearest one, Strange Brew, a pub that was located about fifteen minutes' drive away on the edge of the historic district of Old Louisville.

Old Louisville was located north of the university and south of downtown. While it was not actually the oldest part of the city, the area had a large collection of pedestrian-only streets and almost all of the architecture was Victorian. Historically, it had housed some of the area's wealthiest residents but had suffered several declines over the last hundred years. Now it held a diverse mix, including large professional and student populations, and some areas were more fashionable than others.

Strange Brew was the area's original Elder Races bar, and it was not located in one of the more recently fashionable areas of the neighborhood. An immigrant Light Fae from the Seelie Court in Ireland had opened the pub in 1878. The second bar, Deep Waters, was located on the riverfront, near the Waterfront Park and the river cruises. That one tended to attract the out-of-town tourists.

Strange Brew was more of a hangout for locals. So far, it had successfully weathered all the many changes the area had undergone. It was located at one end of a block-long, utilitarian brick building. It had a storefront entrance on the street, an alleyway entrance that led to a pothole-filled parking lot and a long mishmash of different levels and rooms in between, including a basement bar. The pub was wildly popular on St. Patrick's Day, although to the best of Grace's knowledge, it had never boasted a visit from a real leprechaun.

Grace was already rethinking the whole excursion when she turned down the side street that led to the packed parking lot. Going to an Elder Races bar had sounded good in theory, but the reality was, at ten thirty on a Saturday night the pub would be crowded and noisy and probably filled with more than its fair share of students.

"Maybe this wasn't such a good idea," she muttered. She cruised slowly, searching for a parking spot. The lot was full. She pulled out and looked along the street for a space.

"I do not see why not," Khalil said, looking around with curiosity and interest. "You require supper and a drink. This seems popular enough. People must approve of the nourishment."

She bit back a smile. He had his own kind of wisdom and deep knowledge, but he didn't have a real connection to some things. Maybe the difference had to do with being embodied. It would be easy and potentially lethal, she thought, for someone to mistake that difference for naiveté.

She said, "I don't think people really come here for the food."

He glanced at her, amused. "Then why did you want to come?"

Good point. Khalil knew of Janice's and Therese's reactions to his presence, but he wasn't aware of how the other witches had acted earlier that day.

She was tired of tensions and difficult conversations. She rubbed her face. She had told him about the one conversation that would really matter to him. The rest, she decided, was irrelevant, at least for tonight.

She settled with muttering, "You've never been on a date. I just wanted you to be comfortable."

"You have succeeded," Khalil informed her. "I am entirely comfortable. And now that we are here, we might as well go in."

Up ahead, she spotted a car pulling out of a space. The timing seemed like kismet. And it was really too late to go anywhere else and still try to stick to her timetable. She pulled into the spot.

Khalil said, "Piloting a vehicle is more complicated than I would have expected. You appear to handle yours with proficiency."

She burst out laughing. "You drive a car; you don't pilot it. You pilot boats and planes."

"Then I must learn to drive." Khalil gave her a wicked smile that was highlighted in the yellow glow of nearby streetlamps. "I lied," he said. "I do not have a present for you. I do, however, have something for you from Carling and Rune." He dug into the back pocket of his jeans and handed her a folded envelope.

"What's this?" she asked, unfolding it.

"I reminded them of their obligation to you as Oracle," Khalil said. His smile had disappeared, and something edged and dangerous took its place. "And that they had been derelict in fulfilling their part of the bargain."

"You did?" She blinked at him, astonished. "I didn't think they were derelict. Carling healed Max's ear infection and saved us a trip to the doctor."

He shook his head. "No, Gracie. She did not do that as an offering to the Oracle. She did that because he was a baby and he was sick."

She wasn't sure what moved her more, Carling's act of healing, or Khalil acting on her behalf. Or how he called her Gracie.

"Open it," he said. "See what she sent for you."

She tore the envelope open and pulled out a note and a check. She looked at the check first.

And started counting zeroes. Her hands began to shake.

No. This couldn't be right. She started counting all over again, and then again. Her mind refused to move beyond an incoherent stutter. She said, choked, "Oh, my God. Oh. My. God."

"Is that good?" he said, watching her sharply.

She looked at him. "This check is for two hundred and fifty *thousand* dollars."

He reached up and wiped under her eyes carefully with his thumb. That was when she realized tears were pouring down her cheeks. "She said it was all they could do for now, but you are to let them know if you need more."

Property taxes. A roof. A better car. Her student loans and medical bills paid off. She could focus on the children, her own healing, and finishing her incompletes. If she was very careful and frugal, she wouldn't have to worry about getting an outside job for several years. She could get the children things they needed and things she wanted them to have. Maybe she could hire a babysitter occasionally and get out of the house. Maybe she could see a movie now and then.

"This is incomprehensible." Her lips were shaking too. "It changes everything."

"For the better, yes?"

"Holy shit, yes." It took her several tries to tuck the check back into the envelope, but she managed it at last. "I can't believe they gave so much."

"It is fitting," Khalil said in a quiet voice. "Carling and Rune remember the old days, when emperors and kings would lay treasure at the Oracle's feet. As Rune said, they owe you everything. I was very angry with them when I pieced all of it together and realized that they had not fulfilled their end of the contract."

She remembered the tense scene in the clearing, as Rune and Carling faced off against the Elder tribunal. She felt compelled to point out, "They were fighting for their lives."

His face hardened. He said in a cold voice, "That is no excuse."

"Well," she said, rather inadequately. Khalil was Djinn, after all.

She looked at the note, written in a bold, feminine hand. It was a simple missive. Carling offered an apology and said she would be in touch soon. Overcome again, Grace slipped the note back in the envelope, along with that precious, mind-numbing check, and tucked the whole thing securely into the bottom of her purse.

"I don't know how to thank you," she said from the back of her throat. "I just don't know what to say. This is one of the most important things anyone has ever done for me. For the kids."

"Hush," he said gently in that renegade angel's voice, and he leaned forward and kissed her.

She didn't even think to hesitate or pull away; that's how much things had changed between them. Instead she wrapped an arm around his neck and kissed him back. His lips were warm and firm yet moved on hers with exquisite sensitivity. She felt again that ache of arousal, only this time it was a gentle blossoming, like a garden coming to life after the long, bitter season of a killing winter.

He brushed her lips lightly, back and forth, as if learning their softness and contours for the first time, and he groaned. He sounded shaken. Then he pulled back and stared at her as he stroked her face. His hands were shaking too, and his regal, elegant features were stricken and marveling.

It was such a beautiful expression she had the impulse to look around to make sure it was meant for her. "It was good?" she asked.

He whispered, "Holy shit, yes."

A nearby raucous laugh jolted her. Khalil put a hand on her shoulder protectively as he looked around. She looked too. Six young men, around twenty or twenty-one years old, were walking leisurely in their direction, talking and joking. Khalil's eyes narrowed. He said between his teeth, "I want them to go away."

She started to laugh. "It's a public street. They're not doing anything wrong."

"I have no interest in that," he said.

She took an unsteady breath. She had been worried about going from friends, to kissing, to possibly other things with Khalil, but somehow she had slid headfirst into a foreign landscape she couldn't have foreseen. That slippery slope was a treacherous thing.

"We're here," she managed to say. "And as you said, we might as well go in."

He gave her a glowering look. He said, "I have no interest in doing that, either."

The problem was, neither did she.

Which was all the more reason, she thought, why they should.

· · ·

Djinn didn't get drunk. Alcohol had no effect on them.

But other things could, and Khalil was reeling from a bombardment of physical sensations. Djinn were highly sensitive, but in their original state, what they were most sensitive to was the ebb and flow of Power and energy.

The full range of physical sensation was an entirely different spectrum of experience from anything he had ever known.

The slight friction of the aged denim jeans on his thighs. The stretchy give of the cotton T-shirt across his chest and shoulders. The insubstantial lick of the summer breeze against his cheek.

He was euphoric, disturbed. He thought this must be what intoxication felt like. He wasn't altogether sure he liked it.

And then Grace came carefully down the stairs, and she was such a feast of color, all he could do was stare. Her skin looked burnished, and her outfit made him think of a bouquet of flowers. Her short, damp hair glinted with red-gold highlights, and when she neared him, her multicolored eyes rounded with wonder. Then her scent wafted over him, a clean, light fragrance that he thought must be unique in all the world.

And then she touched him.

Just that one thing, just that simple touch on his arm, and he went into shock. Her flesh, touching his. When she did it again, her gentle hand slid along the contours of his arm to his palm, and he *felt all of it*.

Intensely. Ecstatically. Intimately.

Hungrily.

He followed her out of the house in a daze, where he encountered so many more new sensations: the texture of the screen door's wooden frame, the scents of a summer night, the rough rhythm of chirruping insects. He climbed into her car. His fingertips learned the smooth, hard metal of the car doors, and the soft, worn passenger seat. When he turned to look at Grace, he caught the shadowed gleam of her smile.

Would he ever see another smile as gorgeous as hers?

And the deadly seductive thing was, he could sense how the physical evidence of her pleasure spread throughout her psyche. He could *feel* her smile as well as see it. It lightened the crackle of her spitfire personality.

Then came more sensations. The blast of air swirling through open car windows, the feeling of movement through space as they drove into the city, the pressure of his seat belt against his collarbone and torso.

When she cried at the check she had received from Carling and Rune, he felt the wetness of her tears on the softness of her cheek as he wiped them away.

Then he kissed her.

And it was the first kiss, the only kiss.

The only one in the entire world.

She embraced him, and there was more friction, this time from her warm arm sliding along the back of his neck. She molded her soft lips to his, and the kiss became a sensitive and searching dance as they shifted and caressed in response to each other's movements.

They parted, and he discovered more colors: the darkened rose of her lips and the blush in her cheeks. Her eyes shone with a lustrous sparkle, and her energy flared with brilliance.

He had once believed he knew desire, from the things he had witnessed and the lovers he had taken. Desire, he had thought, was an artifice, an educated exchange in pleasure.

The roar of agonized hunger he now felt seared him. There was nothing of artifice in this. It was raw and edged, and he barely held it in control.

He had existed for so long he had never bothered to count the years. The numbers and the accounting had no meaning for him. But he remembered living them all. He measured the span of his life by events, and he had never experienced desire like this, as a complete desperation.

She felt it too; he knew she did. She ached with just as much hunger as he did. The raw burn of it was spiced with the complexity of her thoughts and feelings.

And she still preferred to go into that establishment.

He could come to only one conclusion. Clearly she had not found the kiss as compelling as he had.

That meant he would have to work harder the next time he kissed her, so that she did.

Frowning fiercely, he climbed out of the car when Grace did. As she locked the doors, he gave the six approaching, noisy youths a hard glance, warning them silently to keep their distance, and he made sure at least a few of them saw it.

One of the youths gave him an amiable grin. The young man said, "Hey, dude . . ."

He decided right then and there, he hated that word.

"Where did you get those contacts?" The young man strolled over, peering at Khalil in fascination, and a few of his associates followed. "Your eyes are wicked awesome."

"Do not call me 'dude,'" he said coldly. The entire group was human. He attributed their extreme foolishness in approaching him to that. Any young Djinn would have taken the hint at his first glare and would have disappeared by now.

"Anything you say, du—uh, mister," said the young man. One of his friends sniggered quietly behind a hand. "How did you do that thing with your eyes?"

"What thing?" Khalil asked impatiently. "Tell me then go away."

The male gave him a loose smile. "They kinda glow in the dark. Do you have special contacts that reflect the light?"

"That is none of your business. Now do as I told you. Go away."

One of the male's associates scratched his chin. "I've heard some drugs can make your eyes look funny, but I thought that mostly meant they just dilated or something."

Khalil grew angry and his Power bristled. Behind him, Grace said, "Khalil, they don't mean any harm. They're probably just college kids, and they're a little drunk."

He glanced behind him. Grace stood on the other side of her car. Her eyes were dancing, her face alight with amusement. "Very well," he muttered. He would not have minded taking his frustration out on a foolish someone. Or a few foolish someones.

"I'm not drunk," one of them said. "I only had four or five beers. I just can't drive."

"Dude, you're totally making that up," his neighbor said. "You had more like seven or eight."

Khalil considered that one's use of "dude." Since it had not been directed at him, he decided to let it pass.

"Well, I had nine, and y'all kept up with me," said a third. "That's why none of us are driving."

"What are we doing, again?" said a fourth.

"You are getting out of my way," Khalil said. He pushed through them as they started talking over each other.

Then the original youth made a mistake. He laid a hand on Khalil's arm.

"Hey, about those contacts—"

The physical sensation of being touched without his permission was a thousand times worse than when another Djinn male came too close. Hissing, he whirled on the youth, whose somewhat silly face rounded in an *O* of surprise.

Suddenly Grace shouldered into the midst of all of them, pushing the young men away, and inserting herself between them and Khalil.

"Go on, guys," she said with cheerful firmness. "You're interrupting my date."

One of them grinned at her. "Sorr-ee."

Khalil watched malevolently as the one who had dared to touch him edged away to the other side of his group. "Didn't mean anything by it," the young man grumbled. "All I wanted was to know what he did to his eyes. Thought I might go to his ophtha . . . ophtha . . . Is it ophthalmologist or optometrist?"

One of his friends exclaimed impatiently, "Oh, it doesn't matter, numbskull. Eye doctor."

Arguing now and shooting wary glances at Khalil over their shoulders, the group edged down the street. Khalil watched them until they had gone half a block away, and he was sure they wouldn't be back. Then he turned back to Grace. Her arms were crossed, and her eyes were narrowed. The sparkling expression of pleasure had disappeared from her face. He sensed storm clouds gathering in her energy.

"What was that all about?" she asked.

His face stony, Khalil said, "He touched me."

She took a deep breath, and the storm clouds dissipated somewhat. "You must make allowances, Khalil. Peoples' decision-making skills are impaired when they're drunk. They didn't mean any harm."

He still didn't have to like it or allow it. But as he walked over to put his arm around her, he took her point to heart.

Intoxication could make one do foolish things, even intoxication of the senses. He would do well to remember that.

Grace sighed and slipped her arm around his waist. Together they crossed the street, and he opened the door. A blast of chaotic light and noise assaulted all of his senses as they stepped into Strange Brew.

⟨ FIFTEEN ⟩

Grace had been in Strange Brew perhaps a half-dozen times since she had turned twenty-one. The interior of the pub was the same throughout, bare brick walls and lots of wood—wooden bars, floors, stools, tables and chairs. There were three bars: one at the front of the building, one toward the back and the third in the basement. They all had a patina of age that darkened their surface. They were scarred from years of use and glossed from countless polishing.

The basic decor was original and bright, with colorful posters and prints hung on the walls, gathered, Grace had heard, throughout the years from the owner's travels. There was also a thoroughly modern sound system installed, which was currently blasting the Rolling Stones over the speakers.

The pub was packed, of course, with people shouting to be heard over each other and the pounding music. Grace paused to get acclimated.

Sparks of Power blinked throughout the crowd like fireflies. Several human witches were in the room. She could sense them by the feel of their Power, although she didn't recognize anyone. Through the brick archway that led to another section, she saw a couple of Dark Fae standing close in conversation. A dwarf headed toward the back rooms shoved her way aggressively through the crowd. Grace caught a glimpse of the dwarf's craggy face. Her beard hung to her short waist in several braids and was threaded with colorful beads.

Grace didn't see any Light Fae. Perhaps the owner was in another room, or he might be at the other location. Grace couldn't remember what his name was, but she would bet he was wealthy enough that he didn't have to work on a Saturday night if he didn't want to.

Further down the bar, she noticed a male Vampyre. Like most Vampyres, he was attractive, although somewhat disheveled. He leaned against the bar as two humans, one male and one female, hung off his shoulders. All three were flushed and looked inebriated.

Grace's forehead wrinkled. Either they were all on a date, she guessed, or the Vampyre was a bottom-feeder. A few Vampyres couldn't give up drinking. Vampyres couldn't feel the effects of alcohol through direct consumption, but they could if they drank from intoxicated humans. Nicknamed bottom-feeders, they trolled bars and looked for willing participants, offering to buy drinks in return for sips of the humans' blood in a kind of quid pro quo.

Usually they found no lack of willing participants, as drinking increased the sense of euphoria caused by a Vampyre's bite—or so Grace had heard. As long as the humans were of legal drinking age, the transaction was entirely legal, although it could get dangerous. Continuing to drink on top of blood loss also increased the effects of intoxication for a human, and if a Vampyre grew impaired, he lost his ability to gauge when to stop feeding.

She shook her head at the sight of the trio, turned away and shouted at Khalil, "I want to go to the bar and ask if they're still serving food."

"As you wish," he said. That was when she noticed how rigid he had become. His expression had turned stony again, and his eyes blazed with a brilliant, sharp-edged light.

She paused, staring up at him. She had no idea what Khalil

was thinking. *Djinn are Powerful and unpredictable*, Brandon had said. *They make folk nervous.* Shoving that unwelcome thought aside, she asked Khalil, "Are you okay?"

He had been surveying the room, his mouth tight. His gaze came down to her. "Do not trouble yourself with concern over me," he said. "Order your food."

"All right," she said. She glanced around again. "I didn't think about how hard it might be to find a place to sit on a Saturday night."

"I will locate a seat," Khalil said shortly.

She hesitated again, searching his expression. Finally she said, "We don't have to stay, if you don't like it here."

That brought his gaze back to her. "This place is . . . an adjustment," he said. "And I am still adjusting. I will let you know if I need to leave."

"All right." She sighed. Apparently this venture was not going so well. What else had she expected from a goddamn ridiculous date? But her stomach was so empty, the hunger pains felt like they were shooting through to her spine. Maybe she could grab a quick sandwich, and then they could leave.

Khalil strode through the crowd. His height and natural arrogance were such that people automatically moved out of his way. Feeling much less effective, she wiggled her way through the crowd and actually managed to reach the bar.

Two bartenders were working hard. She waved as one whisked past her to deliver tall mugs of foaming beer at one end. She waved again as he passed, this time carrying a tray of empty dirty glasses. He gave no sign of acknowledging her presence, and she scowled.

Over the sound system, one song ended, and another one by the same band began. It must be Rolling Stones night. The raucous lyrics pounded in her eardrums.

Someone came up behind her, his body brushing against her back. She stiffened, already aware that it wasn't Khalil even as she began to turn. A low voice said in her ear, "Hello, darlin'. Lemme buy you a drink."

She cast a leery glance over her shoulder. A handsome

male smiled down at her. His eyes were glazed. Ugh. It was the bottom-feeder. "I'm with someone," she said, loudly enough to be heard over the music. "And he's going to be right back."

The Vampyre said, "I'll buy 'im a drink too. We kin all have a party. I'll s'ply the likker." He leaned forward confidingly. "Know what the best thing is about being me?"

"I have a feeling you're going to tell me," Grace said.

"The high we can all get is entirely legit, 'n for you guys it's free. You're welcome." He braced a hand on the bar, effectively trapping her with his body, as he looked her up and down. "Shew," said the Vampyre, his southern accent slurred. He swayed. "Yer all dressed up like a garden. I'd love to pick yer flowers."

Grace dropped her head over her hands and groaned as she leaned against the bar in an effort to get away from him. She said, "I cannot believe you just said that to me."

"You smell good too." The Vampyre dropped his nose into her hair and sniffed noisily. "Kinda like watermelon. I think. I dunno, it's been so long since I've eaten food, I forget."

Ugh! She twisted around and shoved at him. It was like trying to shift a planted tree. "Seriously? My companion isn't friendly. You need to go away now."

He grabbed at her hands. "Anybody ever tell you, yer so purty you could make a dead man come?"

She stared at him in shocked affront. "*The hell* did you just say to me?!"

At the same time, one of the bartenders yelled, "Earl! Don't make me come after you. Back the truck up, buddy, or I'm tossing you out!"

"C'mon, it was just a joke. Don't you get it?" With a sloppy grin, the Vampyre shuffled back a step. He pointed at one of the speakers. "Vampyre—Rolling Stones—the end of 'Start Me Up'? A joke's no good if you gotta explain—"

Two massive hands clamped down on the Vampyre's shoulders. Grace looked past the Vampyre to Khalil's furious face. The renegade angel was gone, replaced by an expression of such glittering malice, Grace knew things were not going to go well for Earl in the near future.

"I'm not going to get any dinner," she said to the man next to her at the bar.

The man didn't respond, probably because he didn't hear her. He was too busy staring along with the rest of the bar, as Khalil took the Vampyre by the back of the neck and belt, lifted him overhead, twisted and threw him through the arched doorway, across two rooms. The Vampyre struck the brick wall with a crack that was audible even over the blaring music. He disappeared as he slid to the floor. Conversation stopped.

A nearby woman said huskily, "Someone get that guy a superhero costume with really tight tights."

Yes, Grace thought, as she stared at Khalil. He is magnificent. And he seems so much bigger when he's enraged.

And this has got to be the most cursed date in the history of . . . ever.

The commotion began. Where the Vampyre had fallen, a growl sounded, and a wave of people scrambled back, like a wave rippling outward. Khalil smiled a calamitous smile. His hair had slipped out of the leather tie again and fell about his face. He looked entirely anarchic. He strode forward.

Grace turned back to the bar as the sounds of destruction began. "Do I have to do anything about this?" she asked herself. "I don't think so. This isn't one of my problems."

She saw a bowl filled with peanuts and popcorn nearby and pulled it toward her. If only she could reach that bottle of beer, sitting on the counter behind the bar. It wasn't what she normally liked to drink, but beggars couldn't be choosers. She stood on tiptoe and strained, and managed to hook her two longest fingers around the bottle. She wiggled it her way. Then she dug in her purse, found a ten-dollar bill and dropped it on the counter.

Behind her, chaos spread. When she looked over her shoulder, people appeared divided into two groups, those that pushed for the door, and those that moved toward the chaos. Either the second group thought they could help in some way, or they were going to join in the fight. Some of them, no doubt, were touching Khalil without his permission. None of them had realized what Khalil really was. If they had, they would all be racing for the door.

Grace made sure she had a firm hold on her purse with its precious contents. Then, carrying the beer and the bowl of snacks, she headed toward the group working to get out the door.

She had only limited success, but she would take it. She lost a third of the beer and half the peanuts and popcorn by the time she reached outside. Inside, the music had stopped. Sounds of shouting, cursing and splintering wood replaced it. Outside, most of those who had exited the bar, talking to each other or on their cell phones. A few were laughing. Sirens sounded in the distance.

Grace took a couple of healthy pulls off the beer before setting the bottle on the sidewalk next to the building. Then she ate the peanuts and popcorn while she walked to her car. It wasn't what she had hoped to get for supper, but it stopped the noisy hunger pains.

The car was quiet when she drove home. No sexy, distracting, unpredictable Djinn, no chattering Chloe, no *whees*, *hoots* or other random, cheerful noises from Max. No unexpected kicks in the head from anybody. The house was quiet too when she unlocked the door and let herself in. Peaceful. It was nice to be alone for a little while.

To tell the truth, she missed the children, but it would also be nice to have the rest of the night without them. Maybe for once she could sleep past the crack of dawn.

She set her purse in its spot on the bookcase by the front door. She had the impulse to cook herself something real for supper. A warm meal sounded good. But cooking seemed like too much effort. Instead she ate one of the nectarines left over from lunch.

Including travel time, the date had lasted just under an hour. She had been on some pretty bad dates, but that was a record even for her. Forget about a midnight deadline. She could brush her teeth and be in bed by quarter after eleven.

So she took off the flower garden. (*Pick yer flowers.* Ha!)

She slipped on a pair of shorts, washed the makeup off her face and brushed her teeth. Then, because the whole evening had taken on a surrealistic quality, she had to look at the check again. That gorgeous, unbelievable, life-altering piece of paper. She sighed with happiness as she tucked it away. Her problems and challenges hadn't vanished, but she was starting to see a way through them, and the relief made her feel so buoyant, she realized just how much of a crushing weight had been on her shoulders these last few months.

That was when Khalil arrived. He exploded into the house in a blazing rush and formed in front of her. He was back to his original form. In black. His hands were on his hips, his eyes shone like supernovas, and he was glowering.

Oh dear. Himself did not appear to be happy. Grace was fairly certain that was not her problem either.

"I looked for you," he said. "You were not in the bar's immediate vicinity."

"No, I wasn't, was I?" she said. "Did you have fun on your first date?"

"I do not believe that is how dates are supposed to go," he informed her.

"Is that so?" She sat on the couch. "How do you believe dates are supposed to go? And what do you think went wrong?"

"That son of an ass put his hands on you," he said edgily. "He insulted you."

She shook her head. "Nope," she said in a calm voice. "That's not what went wrong. Would you like another shot at answering, or should I just tell you?"

He remained silent, watching her.

"Okay, here we go," she said. "You were wrong. I was wrong to go out with you. The date itself was wrong. We made the decision to go out, and it all snowballed from there. Of course the date was a disaster. It was going to be a disaster no matter what we did. We are about as different as two different creatures can get. You're a prince of the Djinn— and I still have no idea what that means. . . ."

"It means nothing," he snapped. "It's an honorific. All the

male elders in the five Houses are princes, and the female elders are excellencies. They're titles of respect, that's all."

"All right," she said, letting go of that. "So what, it doesn't matter. None of it matters. I'm mortal. You're not. I'm human, and you're not. We come from very different cultures; we have different expectations, abilities, and goals for our lives, and—"

"Stop," he said. "You're wasting time."

Again, he caught her openmouthed. "What?"

"We're still on our date, and you're wasting time." He glanced at the living room clock. "We have forty minutes to go before midnight."

"You can't be serious," she said faintly.

"I am completely serious," he said. He prowled close, took her hand and yanked her to her feet. "You made a bargain. You're going to stick to it."

"Khalil, no," she said.

"Yes." He looked ruthless. Worse, he looked about as calm as she had felt mere moments ago. "Not everything that happened was a disaster. You had fun up to a certain point. You laughed and were happy. I was watching you. I understand the stories your face tells so much better than I did before. I know what your happiness looks like now."

She shivered as his intense male energy slid against hers, and they aligned again. That strange thing they did together felt more than good. It felt incredible. She struggled to ignore it and whispered, "That doesn't mean I'm wrong."

"You're wrong," he said, with such confidence it shook her. It really shook her. "The kiss wasn't a disaster. It was perfect."

She swallowed hard. She didn't want to think about that kiss, because he was right, it had been perfect. His wonder, their tender exploration. "I . . . don't think it counts when you weigh that against everything else."

"Of course it counts," he said. He stroked her cheek, down her neck, and along the edge of her neckline. He watched where his fingers trailed, his expression turning hungry. He told her huskily, "I had to release my other form so I could transport back. I do not have the Power to create it a second time in one evening. Although I want to, very much."

Grace's heart started to pound. She swallowed hard and whispered, "I shouldn't have left you like that."

"I shouldn't have left you alone at the bar," he whispered back. His fingertips trailed down her bare arms, then his hands settled firmly on her hips. He lowered his face to hers, slowly, eyes intent.

"We should have left as soon as we saw how busy it was." Her eyelids felt so heavy. They fluttered shut.

"I should have kissed you a second time in the car. And a third time." His mouth settled over hers, and he kissed her deeply, in a spiraling aggression that she met with her own escalating urgency. He growled at the back of his throat and muttered against her lips, "This is not the same. But it is still *so damned good.*"

Arousal pulsed through her in a gush of heat, agonizing and delicious. Her nipples peaked, and the delicate, private area between her legs ached. Khalil hissed against her lips, and his energy roared in response, a flash fire of raw sexuality.

"Is it . . . less?" she asked.

"No," he murmured. "It is different, that is all. But I want to know what it is like to make love to you the way humans do. I have never made love to anyone like that before."

Never?

She whimpered. "Make love?"

He ran his hot mouth over her cheek and down her neck. "Make love," he said against the tender skin at the base of her throat. "I want you to teach me everything you know. I want us to teach each other. I want you to show me how good it can feel to be skin to skin. But right now, Gracie . . ." He lifted his head and looked down at her gravely. "Let me show you how I can make love to you."

She didn't even think to say no, because that was how far he took her in a single conversation, how much farther they had come since they had first met. Instead, she looked up into his starred eyes as she slipped her fingers into his midnight hair, pulling it free from the tie as she told him, "Yes, please."

He smiled as he stroked her face. Then he kissed her again, and all his aggression and intensity came roaring back as he drove deep into her soft, inviting mouth. His sexuality danced along her skin, and her hunger for him flashed hotter, brighter. He groaned, or she did. The silk of his long hair tangled in her fingers as she fisted it, kissing him back with jerky, out of control movements. Then he lifted her up.

Not with his hands.

His presence intensified, and her feet left the ground.

It took a few moments for realization to sink in. Breathing heavily, disoriented, she stopped kissing him. "Wait— are you . . . ?"

"Wait, what?" he asked, cupping her face in both hands as he nipped gently at her lips. At the same time, his large, strong hands spread across her back. "Am I, what?"

What?

She dragged her mouth away and looked around wildly.

She was suspended a few inches off the floor, completely supported in midair. Her feet didn't dangle. Her knee wasn't strained in the slightest. Khalil watched her expression with a heavy-lidded gaze, his lips curved in that sinful, sensual smile.

As his hands—*both his hands*—slid under the hem of her top and spread around the sides of her rib cage, resting against her skin.

And long, hot fingers slid through her short hair, cupping and massaging the back of her head.

And two hands slid down her thighs, to the sensitive skin at the back of her knees, cupping them firmly.

She stared at him, blank with shock. "Khalil."

His smile widened, a tender, mischievous look. "Relax, I've got you," he murmured. Then his smile was burned to vapor by the incandescence inside of him, and all that was left on his elegant face was savage hunger. "My gods, I can feel you everywhere."

Because they were aligned, Power to Power, male to female, his presence surrounding and sustaining her. Her lips trembled as she whispered, "I've never felt anything like it, like you."

His diamond eyes blazed. *"Good."*

His head drove down, and he took her mouth again, hard, and she lost track of everything. Her thinking burned to ash.

His hands were everywhere at once. Literally. Clever fingers teased her tank top up and caressed the underside of her breasts, trailing in decreasing circles until they reached her pink-tipped nipples. He rolled the sensitive tips between thumbs and forefingers.

While clever fingers edged their way under the hem of her shorts, tracing the crease where her buttocks met her thighs, easing around to the front and teasing the sensitized skin of her inner thighs before they burrowed gently underneath the elastic of her panties.

While the clever fingers supporting the back of her knees coaxed her legs apart.

And he kissed and kissed her, hungrily, gently, changing the tempo and the pace and the depth as he dug in deep with his tongue, and then he eased back to lick lightly at the corner of her shaking mouth.

At the same time, his hot, moist lips ran along the back of her neck, and he licked the racing pulse at her throat.

And his mouth followed up the curved line of her ribs as he unfastened her bra. He squeezed her breast gently as he took her nipple in his mouth and suckled.

As he squeezed and kneaded her other breast gently and took that nipple and suckled, nipping at it carefully with his teeth.

Oh, my gods, he was suckling both her breasts.

At the same time.

While he tore away her shorts and panties, and growled into her mouth as he kissed her, and drove his tongue onto the soft, fluted flesh of her labia, and licked his way to the stiff little bud of her clitoris. She flung out her hands, groping uselessly, desperately for something of him to hold on to, and he clasped both her hands in his warm, firm grip as he worked her everywhere.

And even as he drove her to the most intense, mindless frenzy she had ever been in, she felt him press a tender kiss at the base of her spine.

It was beyond perfect.

He was everywhere, everywhere, hard edged and hungry, exploring the most private areas of her body with tender greed. She flung her head back and shrieked, muscles trembling from the strength of the passion that poured out of her. It poured into him and came back, stronger and harder, only then it was his passion, driving into her.

He said against her lips, "*I've got to come inside of you.*"

"Then get the hell in here," she screamed. She sounded like she felt, completely insane.

He pressed at her swollen, aching entrance, and it felt good and right, a thick, hard cock pushing into her emptiness, filling her up, while at the same time he flicked at her clitoris with his tongue and licked at her labia and sucked on her nipples and stroked so gently down her back and held both of her hands like he was her very best friend. Somebody was swearing raggedly, an incoherent stream of profanity, and she thought it might be her . . .

And he said, "Grace." Just that.

Even at the height of her insanity, the sound of his pure voice pulled at her. She opened her eyes.

He had lost his physical form and any semblance to being human. Black smoke swirled around her. She rested in the center of the cyclone. His crystalline eyes were right in front of her, glowing with Power and emotion. She thought she caught a glimpse of long black hair, blowing across a hint of his elegant face.

The queen of all epiphanies cracked her wide open. She was driven beyond thought, language or all sense of her own form.

That was when he came inside of her, in a furious blaze of incandescence, and she could tell this was his true climax.

Both of her Powers, the one she was born with and the one she inherited, rose up to claim him, even as he blanketed her with his own bright, immortal Power. As they tangled together, closer than lovers, she felt her own physical body peak. The most exquisite completion of pleasure rippled out of her. She felt his presence shudder as it hit him.

His ravenous aggression transformed to reverence. She could feel every nuance of emotion in him, from an intense male satisfaction that he had brought her such pleasure, to his own shocked wonder at their joining and a deep wellspring of caring.

There was no way to hide anything from each other. She was so purely naked, she felt helpless as a newborn. She fell back into the shell of her physical body and realized she was shivering spasmodically. His physical form solidified as she came back into herself. He was naked and on his knees, his cock still pressed inside of her. She sat in his lap, legs splayed wide, her arms resting limply around his neck. His arms clenched tight around her.

"You destroyed me," she whispered as she shivered. The words never even struck her as histrionic because they were so true. She was back in her body, but she wasn't yet in control of it again. She wasn't even the same person.

"I've got you," he whispered into her hair. He rocked her. "I've got you."

She put her head on his shoulder. She got a sense of movement as he took her up the stairs. She was fairly certain he didn't walk. Then they reached her bedroom. Her long unused bed was simply made with sheets and a bedspread. He eased her down on the bed. She turned over to curl on her strong side.

He settled into place behind her and wrapped an arm around her, spooning with her.

He didn't have to. His presence was absolutely in her bedroom, with or without his physical body. He must have wanted to. He must have known she needed it. She felt his lips against her shoulder. Then he put his face in her hair.

He rubbed her thigh gently. Eventually her shivering stopped.

They didn't speak. She, for one, had nothing to say.

She had learned another thing she couldn't unlearn now

that she knew it. Her slippery slope hadn't thrown her down a hill. It had, instead, shoved her into an entirely different dimension. She had always scoffed at people who fell in love when they had sex. She'd always been convinced that they confused an intensity of experience with the real emotion.

But Khalil had shattered her understanding of what it meant to make love. She had reformed into someone else, a humble stranger to herself.

That stranger knew beyond a shadow of a doubt that she had been falling in love with him for a while. And she could not imagine ever wanting to make love with anyone else again. He had taken all of her desire with such complete effortlessness she had not even been aware at the time that she was giving everything she had to him.

She closed her eyes and fell asleep.

Even in her sleep, she felt the last miniscule shift in the lunar cycle that brought the Oracle's moon.

≈ SIXTEEN ≈

Grace slid into a dream. She walked the property at night. It was so dark she couldn't see where she was going. She had lost her flashlight. The stars fell and surrounded her with light. Then she was swimming in a dark sea, and the stars that surrounded her were the bright sparks of countless souls.

The water carried her forward, faster and more powerfully than she had expected. She was caught in a riptide. When she looked to either side, Petra and her grandmother were swimming alongside her.

You're going the wrong way, Petra told her. Her sister sounded the same as she ever did, full of exasperated affection. *You've got to turn back.*

I don't know how, she said. *I don't know where I'm going. I only know where I've been.*

You're almost out of tuna, her grandmother said.

No, I'm not, Grace said. *I just bought two cans.*

Don't stay in the house when you bake the casserole. It'll get too hot. Her grandmother smiled at her.

Gram, why don't you come to see me? Grace asked. *You*

would enjoy hanging out in the kitchen with the other women, and I'd really like to talk to you.

But her grandmother was gone. Then Petra was gone as well, and the water pushed Grace faster and faster, until she was tumbling down a black tunnel. It was like being born, except she was going the wrong way, into the cavern, not out of it. Then the water spewed her onto the cavern floor at someone's feet.

A tall woman knelt in front of her. She held the gold Oracle's mask in front of her face.

As soon as she looked at it, Grace knew that mask wasn't a fake. It was the real deal, down to the tiny scratches from countless ages on the shining, precious surface. She studied the eyeholes, trying to figure out the identity of the person behind the mask. But there were no eyes. The holes were black but not empty. Instead, they were filled with something unbelievably vast and Powerful.

She said, *That's weird.*

The vast woman considered her. *What will a mere mortal do with an immortal Power?*

I don't know, Grace said. *None of this is going the way I thought it would. Will you help me?*

The gold mask's perfect, inhuman lips curved into a smile. *I will, but in order to reach me, you have to go the wrong way. You can only find me if you go very deep.*

You're Nadir, Grace said. *Of course you are. Where else would the goddess of the depths be? How far down do I have to go to reach you?*

Try drowning, said the goddess. The dark sea filled Grace's nose and mouth, and she thrashed. *Don't worry about that,* Nadir told her. *You left your body once tonight. You can do it again if you want to badly enough.*

"Grace," said Khalil. And she felt it again, the conviction that when he called her in his unearthly, pure voice, she would go anywhere with him, anywhere at all.

Nobody should have been able to follow her, but Khalil could because he had no body. Black smoke swirled through the cavern, out of which crystalline eyes like stars focused only on her. He ignored Nadir completely.

The goddess looked amused. *You're right*, Nadir said. *He isn't friendly.*

Burning hands reached for Grace and pulled her out of the sea.

Grace plunged awake. She was lying on her back. Khalil must have turned on the bedside lamp. It threw a soft gold light over everything. He leaned over her. Black hair fell around his face. He was frowning sharply and shaking her by the shoulder.

"What's wrong?" she asked blurrily, as she stared at him.

She had not really seen him nude before when they made love. Or perhaps she had, since she had seen his real form. This body he chose to wear was perfectly fashioned, from the heavy ripple of muscle across his wide chest and shoulders, to his tapered stomach, lean hips and long legs. Her gaze fell to his groin where his genitals were as perfect as the rest of him, his penis lying in a graceful curve over the twin mounds of his testicles.

She stroked a hand down his smooth, hot chest as she realized that, except for the shining, black fall of his hair and the slant of his eyebrows, he had no body hair. He was completely, inhumanly beautiful, his ivory skin gilded with the soft gold light from the bedside table.

In sharp contrast, her body was imperfect in almost every way. The pink of her nipples were still a darkened rose from his suckling. A bruise was forming on her hip bone where she had banged it on the corner of the kitchen table earlier that day. She had a long, thin scab on one of her forearms from Freaky Bitch. And yes, of course there were the scars on her knees, yada yada, and she smiled to realize how little they had come to matter to her.

The peach tint of her human skin looked shockingly rich against Khalil's marblelike hue. The soft, fine tangle of her pubic hair was a darker red-gold than the hair on her head. In her own way, she realized with a trace of embarrassment, she was as beautiful as he was. They were especially beautiful together.

You are my lover, she thought, as she blinked at him. She swallowed hard. My lover. At least for this one night.

What a calamitous, incredibly spectacular first date. And why in the world would she have expected anything else from him?

Her heart squeezed, or maybe it expanded. Whatever it did, it wasn't behaving normally at all. She felt light-headed and giddy, truly happy for the first time in she couldn't remember when, and absolutely, utterly terrified.

His long fingers came underneath her chin. He tilted her head up. "Pay attention, I'm talking to you," he said irritably. In contrast to his tone, the expression in his gaze was concerned.

"So that's the noise I keep hearing," she said. She glanced at the bedside clock, which read 1:42 A.M. She hadn't even slept an hour and a half. She yawned hugely until her eyes watered, and her eyes drifted closed as she sank back against the pillows. While it was wonderful to stretch out on her bed, and frighteningly awesome to be in bed with him, the upstairs of the house was stifling, and he was far too hot.

Hey, she had a check in her purse. She could afford a higher electric bill. She muttered cagily, "I'll have sex with you again if you close all the windows and turn on the air-conditioning."

She was trying to bargain away something she would beg for anyway. For someone who always chose the dumb route, that was actually pretty smart thinking. She turned her face into his bicep and sniggered, even as her eyes watered more.

Oh gods, what he had done. Even more than the sheer physical impossibility of the lovemaking, he had broken her wide open.

He hissed a curse. She jumped as all of the upstairs windows slammed shut, and the ancient air-conditioner unit that was propped in her bedroom window clacked on.

Her eyes flew open as he took her by the shoulders and hauled her upright. "I said pay attention," he snarled.

He looked entirely disturbed, and despite their nudity, not at all loverlike. Suddenly she felt wide awake. "I'm paying attention," she told him. She frowned as her mind kicked into gear. "I was having a weird dream before you woke me up."

"I woke you up," he said between his teeth, "because you were acting weird."

"What happened?"

"That old Power you inherited. You know how you said it sits deep at the edge of your consciousness?" She nodded. Now that she was really paying attention to him, his hard grasp on her relaxed. He smoothed back her hair. "I can sense it. It feels just as you described, very deep, like it sits at the edge of thought. While you were asleep, it . . . rose up."

She frowned at him. "What do you mean, it rose up?"

"It filled you up like you were an empty glass. Then it spilled out of you and filled the room. That's when I woke you." His sharp diamond gaze searched her face. "What happened?"

She rubbed her forehead. "I don't know. I just had a dream."

"About what?"

"It's hard to describe. It was very dreamy."

"Try."

The air-conditioner was running at full blast. The window unit blew frigid air on her exposed skin. Shivering, she pulled the bedspread and top sheet down and climbed under the covers. After a second's hesitation, Khalil joined her. He pulled her into his arms, and she settled against him gladly and rested her cheek against his smooth, hot skin.

It wasn't just that his heat had suddenly become welcome. He chose to hold her. Maybe he did it for her, but he did it unasked, so he must have done it for him as well. His presence wrapped her up as securely as his arms did, and he didn't try to take her strength away. He offered her a chance to rest against his, and it felt so good.

Once she started talking, she didn't stop. She started with the dream and worked her way backward, and she told it all wrong, because everything came out in a tangle.

The dream. The goddess. Hitting Phaedra with an expulsion spell that knocked her across the cavern. How everyone acted earlier that day, everyone except Olivia. Either Brandon or Jaydon or somebody had lied, or she simply didn't understand, or maybe she had misheard, but it was strange how the story had shifted from eighteen people who had planned to come to work that day to twelve. The talk she'd had with Isalynn, postponing her duties as the Oracle, practicing with the Power until she could call it up at any time, whether it was daylight or not, no matter where she was.

Talking to him was as beyond perfect as his lovemaking had been. It was such a relief to unburden herself. Although he occasionally asked her for clarification, he didn't rush her or appear impatient in any way, and he didn't try to stop her.

At least not until she told him about the ghost of the serpent woman.

His physical form dissolved, and caught by surprise, she fell forward. Her nose squashed in the pillow he had been leaning against, and the hair at the back of her head whipped around as a cyclone rampaged her room. Cautiously she braced herself on one elbow and lifted her head to look around.

She had never been very interested in knickknacks, and earlier her small jewelry box had traveled downstairs along with her dresser. That was probably a good thing, since her bedside clock, along with three somewhat dusty paperbacks and the lamp, crashed to the floor. The window curtains blew into knots, all the upstairs doors banged shut then blew open again, and the windows rattled.

Somehow the lightbulb in the lamp hadn't broken. The light shining from the floor threw elongated shadows over everything. The familiar surroundings looked ominous and strange.

And he felt absolutely furious.

Was he having his version of a shit fit?

She sank back down on the pillows and put an arm over her head. She said to the cyclone, "I hope you know you're picking everything up again and replacing anything you break."

He cursed, and the light flickered wildly as the lamp jerked off the floor and landed back on the bedside table. "You tell me that your sanity and your life might have been in danger, and I find this out *days later*?"

Yep. Shit fit. She told him, "Stop yelling."

Still disembodied, he plummeted down on her. The entire cyclone seethed with rage on the space of her double bed. The air felt heavy, far too dense, and the change in pressure made her ears pop. Was this her problem? Yeah, she thought this one probably was. She pulled the covers over her head.

He yanked them down again. "Gods dammit, Grace, how could you do something so dangerous? Why didn't you call me? You're supposed to call me!"

Her nose prickled, and a tear leaked out. She swiped at it with the back of her hand. She said, "You're making some pretty big assumptions."

He snapped, "Like what!"

"I didn't know it would be dangerous," she said softly. "The petitioners were having a problem with going into the cavern, and I just thought if the Power came out once in the daylight, I could make it come out again. I had no idea the ghost existed until she showed up. By then it was too late to do anything but deal with the situation. I certainly didn't have time to think about calling you or anyone else, and even if I had . . ."

"And if you had?" he prompted when her voice trailed away.

"Even if I had thought of calling you, it wouldn't have done any good," she said. "Because you wouldn't have been able to do anything. Nobody would have. Everything that happened, the conversation with the ghost and the whole struggle was internal. By the time I had anything to say to anybody, it was all over."

He took form behind her on the bed and turned her so that she lay on her back. His hands were so gentle that when she opened her eyes, she was completely unprepared for the severity of emotion that transformed his face. He said coldly, "I'm calling in the favor you owe me."

Jolted, she said, "What, right now?"

He interrupted her. "Are you able to pay your debt?"

"Of course," she told him. "As long as it doesn't affect the kids—"

He cut off her words by simply putting a hand over her mouth. Eyes blazing, he leaned closer until the only thing she could see was him, and the only thing she could feel, all around her, was him.

"You will call me," he said. "For the rest of your life, you will call me. I don't give a shit whether or not you're in the mood. I don't care if your cause is useless or if I am too late or if you can fix the whole damn problem by yourself or if you just get scared. You will call me, Grace. *You will call me.*"

Her eyes widened. He was not quite in control of his physical form. It rippled, or his hand simply shook with the same emotion that shook through his voice. His eyes weren't just blazing. They were too bright, even for him. She listened to not only what he had said, but to what he had not said. Underneath his anger was another emotion.

You scared me, he had said earlier, and he wasn't used to experiencing fear. He was too arrogant and Powerful, too accustomed to the complacency of living a very long life.

She curled her fingers around his wrist and urged his hand away from her mouth. His jaw worked, but he allowed her to shift his hold. The tips of his fingers stroked across her lips.

"I love you too," she said, because her sense of direction for picking out all the dumb routes in her life was pretty much infallible. She watched as the impact of her words changed his expression drastically, and she started to babble. "I know it's stupid. I thought the age difference between Hugh Hefner and his girlfriends was bad. And who has time for this sort of thing, right? I think it happened when you put Max on your lap for the first time. . . ."

She never finished the sentence. Khalil slid his hand to the back of her neck. He lifted up her head as he lowered his face, and she got caught in the middle, as his mouth settled over hers, and it didn't matter if the Oracle wasn't supposed to be able to prophesy for herself, because in that moment Grace knew she would love him unconditionally for the rest of her life.

He kissed and kissed her, like he had before, gently, hungrily, spearing into her with his hot tongue, and she burned everywhere he touched her, all over her body and deep in her soul. "You will call me," he said against her lips. "Swear, Gracie. I cannot stand it if you do not call me."

"I swear it," she murmured. She felt desire take fire in him again. He had cracked her wide open before, and it was too soon, too much for her to reach that insane, intense outpouring of passion again. She wasn't ready for it, but at the same time she needed it and him. She dug her fingers into his hair and started to shake.

"Shh, be easy," he said. He gripped her by the hip, gently, as he rested his forehead against her collarbone. His desire remained steady, banked. "Your Power is still roused. I do not like how it has been dangerous for you."

His own stern control helped her to find hers. She rubbed her face as she checked the strange landscape she had become. "It doesn't feel roused," she said. "Maybe it feels stronger to you because today is the Oracle's moon. The Power flexes with the lunar cycle."

He lifted his head, frowning down at her. She could feel him scanning her carefully. It felt delicious, like he was physically running his hands gently down her limbs. Underneath the weight of his body, she stretched and sighed. "You're right," he said. "It is stronger than it was last night. But it's more than that. It's different. I don't think that difference is because of the lunar cycle."

She confessed, "I'm starting to lose the sense that it's something separate from me. It feels like we're knitting together."

His mouth tightened as he shifted to her side. He settled his body alongside hers and propped his head in one hand. "You are."

She watched his face curiously. "How does it look—or feel?"

"It's beautiful," he said with obvious reluctance. "But then you were beautiful before. It's a dark vein marbling your energy. If this continues, I don't see how it will pass on to Chloe or to anybody else." He met her eyes. "That was what you wanted, wasn't it?"

She smiled. "Yes. That's exactly what I wanted."

"It's changing you," he said. His own gaze was shadowed with worry. "Are you sure that you're all right with that?"

"It changed me the moment it left my sister and came to me," she told him. "I've kicked against it, cursed and yelled at it, then finally accepted it. Now I've claimed it, and I want to know what I can make of it. And what it's making of me." She bit at a fingernail. "That means I need to keep experimenting. That expulsion spell I threw at Phaedra was meant to get rid of dark spirits. I only threw it at her because I lost my temper and got desperate. That spell never would have had the strength to physically throw anybody before. She bled a light-colored liquid that soaked back into her. I didn't know you could bleed."

"We don't, at least not in the way humans bleed. When the bodies we create sustain damage, the part of our Power that has become physical leaks until we fix it." His hand resting on her hip tightened. He growled, "You don't experiment alone anymore, do you hear me? Forget that, you don't experiment without me. In your dream your grandmother and sister said you were going the wrong way. You need someone else present to help you in case things get out of control again."

She nodded as she curled against his side. Her eyes felt dry and gritty. She closed them and turned her face into his chest. He cupped her head, holding her gently against him. "That might have been what they meant. I've certainly been doing things differently from how I'd been taught."

"I see another truth," said Khalil quietly. "You're discarding the rituals your family has used for generations. You exorcised the ghost, or at least you persuaded the ghost to leave you, and you claimed the Power. It is as though the

Oracles that came before you needed all the rituals and the steps in order to access the Power, because they were substitutes, while you are actually becoming the Oracle."

She held her breath as she considered his words. Was he right? She couldn't tell. Exhaustion weighed her down again. She muttered, "I'm tired of thinking about all of this right now. Khalil, I had a long day, and I need to get some more rest. I have to pick the kids up in the morning."

"Then stop thinking." He kissed her forehead. "While you pick up the children, tomorrow morning I am going to do what I should have done before this."

She pressed her lips against the smooth skin of his chest. "What's that?"

"I am going to find out where Therese lives," he said. A stiletto of malice crept into his voice. "I would like to know how she enjoys it when someone looks through her things. I'm also interested in what I will find when I do so. And after that, I think I will find this witch Brandon. I might even introduce myself to Jaydon Guthrie. Then we will see what tale this Oracle's moon tells."

She snorted, a small exhalation of air. "I have another human saying for you," she said drowsily.

"What is that?" he asked.

She smiled and told him, "Just let me know if I ever piss you off, so I can have a chance to apologize."

Amusement danced through his energy. "Sometimes you have made me very angry," he said. "And I have not noticed that you are overly eager to apologize for that."

"Mmm." It might be time for a strategic distraction. She stroked his presence with hers in a lavish, languid caress.

He caught his breath then whispered, "Go to sleep, dearest."

Her heart kicked and pleasure rippled through her at the oddly archaic, beautiful endearment. Then she sighed and did just that.

⇒ SEVENTEEN ⇐

I love you too, Grace had said, and that was a far more radical thing than simply calling him friend.

Too.

As if she had already known something he hadn't.

Khalil held himself tensely while he watched Grace sleep. How had this young human woman become so precious to him so quickly? It had happened in less than two weeks. A mere handful of days.

He had been at war with Lethe for longer than some civilizations had existed. Often he had taken years to decide where he might go on vacation. When he had met Leo Tolstoy in 1906, the Russian novelist had intrigued him so much, Khalil decided he would consider reading *War and Peace*, and he had still not yet made up his mind. It wasn't that he was indecisive; he simply had no reason to rush anything.

He had never bothered to count time before, but he started to now, and it began with counting each breath she took. He watched the gentle rise and fall of her chest in agonized amazement. She would take only a limited number of breaths in her lifetime, and then she would stop breathing forever.

Max and Chloe, those bright-eyed baby birds, would live for such a short, short while.

Once he had thought they lived such small lives, outside of politics and world concerns and violent struggles for dominion and Power. Now he realized how big their lives really were, because their lives were everything that mattered. They were the only thing that mattered. The joyous surprise in each discovery they made together was more precious than the treasure of kings, more suspenseful than the most spectacular of car chases, more beautiful than the most exotic of landscapes.

He studied Grace with meticulous care. As uneasy as it made him, the patterning of her light, fiery energy entwined with the dark Power really was quite beautiful. The pattern flexed and breathed, a part of her living presence, flowing through her life. He had been worried that the darkness would taint the Power she had been born with, dull the bright strength that was so uniquely hers, but it didn't appear to be doing that. In fact, it looked like the dark Power reinforced what had already been there.

How would it change her? Was he right? Was she actually becoming the Oracle in a way that none of the others that came before her had?

As he had told her, he was no healer, nor was he any expert on human physiology, but he still examined her body as carefully as he knew how, to see if the Power changes might be toxic to her in any way. She appeared perfectly healthy to him, her young body strong and filled with vitality.

Her cheeks were flushed with a soft rose. He noticed that her thick eyelashes were a rich, tawny mink, darker than her short, fine red-gold hair and eyebrows. Her hair would probably never lie down in a sleek cap, because she was always running her fingers through it. The rucked bedsheet was only partially tucked around her torso, exposing a generously rounded, pink-tipped breast.

He let his gaze trail along the graceful dip of her spine to where it disappeared under the cover, noting how the sheet followed the swell of her round, firm ass.

He remembered the taste of her desire, the feel of her delicate, stiff little clitoris against his tongue, the exquisitely curved petals of her labia, and how she sucked in those precious shocked breaths of hers as he ravished, sucked, licked her everywhere, everywhere, and the interplay of her physical pleasure with the vibrancy of pleasure in her spirit was so goddamn beautiful it was symphonic, ineffable. Then her remarkable spirit had opened wide as he had pushed into her welcoming body, and he had fallen into her so far he could not imagine how he would ever wish to come out again.

And he needed to know, *needed to know*, what it was like to take her, human skin to human skin, but he had squandered too much of his energy earlier on foolish, useless things, and he would not be able to fall deeper into flesh again until he had rested and fed.

He wanted to stroke her all over, but that would disturb her sleep, and she needed to rest. He held his hand a few inches over her head and imagined, remembered, what the silk of her hair felt like. Then he clenched his hand into a fist and struggled to tamp down the desire raging through him, because it was really quite extraordinary that she could sense that too, and if he didn't control himself, he might wake her up that way as well. She was the most alive and sensitive creature he had ever met.

Even though he tried, she still sensed something. She stirred and murmured. Without fully waking up, she reached up to take his hand and pull his arm around her. He sank down, wrapping his body around her while surrounding her with his presence.

You destroyed me, she had said.

If that was true, she had destroyed him as well.

He was too old to have allowed just anybody to do so. He did not think he would have allowed her, except that those incredible, loving children had acted as a stealthy vanguard and stole their way into his heart. When he dropped his defenses and opened up to them, Grace somehow became the engine that drove his existence.

He buried his face in her flyaway cloud of hair.

I love you too.
Love.
Too.

He drifted, resting until the sun broke over the horizon. Then he began to absorb energy from it. He could get more nourishment faster if he shifted out into direct sunlight, but he felt too lazy and comfortable to move.

Grace shifted and sighed, and her presence came to alertness. At least somewhat. "I might have figured."

Excellent. Now that she was awake, he let himself do what he had been wanting to do for hours and hours. He stroked down the curve of her back. "Might have figured what? I didn't wake you, did I?"

"No," she murmured. She rubbed her eyes. "With the kids gone, I thought I would be able to sleep past dawn for once, but I think they've got me trained too well."

She felt so warm and soft. He pressed a kiss to the sleek curve of her shoulder blade. "Do you want to try to go back to sleep?"

She shook her head and reached behind to stroke his hair.

Desire lit a slow-burning fuse. "Good," he muttered. "Because I've been waiting such a long time to do this." He cupped her breast and flicked the tip of his finger over the distended tip of her nipple. "Hours and hours. And hours."

She groaned and arched, pushing herself into his grip. He squeezed and caressed her as he ran his teeth along the sensitive cord at the base of her neck, and she shuddered all over. He felt her go into a meltdown, the core of her gushing with molten heat. Her presence twined around his, and her hunger for him was so damn sexy it incinerated every one of his intentions for going slowly and gently.

He rose over her as he pulled her onto her back. She wound her arms around him, her fine features etched with passion, and *gods*, it was such a damn fine thing to have a hard cock to push inside of her. He had the presence of mind to make sure she was moist and ready for him, and then he entered her, and she was tight as a fist, and he *need, need, needed* to know what that felt like when he wore a more human skin.

But for now he dug in as deep as he could, and he couldn't wait to go slow. Because he had to take advantage of the things he did have right now, and he was so damn greedy for everything she could give him, he licked on her nipples, and yanked at her hair so her head tilted back, then he bit at her neck and suckled ravenously at that exquisite little bud at the core of her pleasure while he thrust his hard cock into her.

Then she screamed again. It was the sweetest sound he'd ever heard. Her climax convulsed her body and threw her spirit wide open. He dove into her, a silent spear of need, and then his own cascade of pleasure took him over.

For an endless, pulsating moment, he couldn't see or hear. When he came back to himself, slowly, she was sucking in air in rapid gasps as she clung to him. Her gaze was unfocused and tears streaked from the corners of her eyes. He sank a fist into her hair and kissed her while he ground against the gorgeous, swollen flower of her body, and she squealed, a helpless, surprised sound, and climaxed again.

The fabulous pleasure rippled out of her, into him, and he sent it back into her, growling.

Again, he said in her head.

In her head, in her body, in her spirit. In. He pushed in.

She shook all over. "I can't—I can't—"

You can. Gracie, give it to me again. He bit her neck and sucked her hard and washed over her in a sheet of flame, and this time she sobbed out loud when she came.

He came with her. He came with her every step of the way. Power to Power, presence to presence. For an uncounted amount of time they floated together, entwined. Then she fell back into her body, and he returned to himself, wrapped around her again, with her and yet alone.

She huddled against him, and he covered her. She was shivering. He went with her there too, as the muscles in his body quivered. He realized his fist was still clenched in her hair. He would probably have to do something about that sometime. For now he held on.

"I think I went blind that time," she whispered.

Her lips were swollen and trembling. He covered her mouth with his, caressing her gently. He wished he knew how to describe to her what he felt.

I started counting time for you.

I want to change who I am for you.

You are my Grace.

He was too full, and there weren't enough words.

He said, "I did not know I needed grace until I met you."

Then as she held him tightly, he knew that what he said had been enough.

He settled back against the pillows and pulled her into his arms, so that her head was on his shoulder. She hooked her leg up, resting it across his hips. He drifted that way, and she dozed until close to eight o'clock. "I have to get moving," she said. "I told Katherine I would pick up the kids around ten."

"There's plenty of time," he said lazily.

She groaned and rolled onto her back. "No, there isn't. I want to go to the store before I pick them up. I promised Chloe some glow-in-the-dark stars for their ceiling, and I want to buy them a little inflatable pool so they can play in some water today. They've been too cooped up in the house lately."

He sighed, stretched and accepted the inevitable. "That sounds like a good day," he told her. "And I have people to see and things to discover."

"I would say be careful, but . . ." She rubbed her face and looked sideways at him. "Maybe instead I should say, please don't start an inter-demesne incident."

He smiled.

She pointed at him. "That's what I'm talking about."

He snatched at her hand before she could pull away, and he kissed her finger.

In the bathroom, water started to gush in the tub. Grace startled and frowned. Khalil told her, "I started a bath for you."

Her mouth opened. Then shut. She said faintly, "Thank you."

"You're welcome," he said. "Do not fret about me. Pick up the kids and enjoy your day, and I will see you later, if that is acceptable. May I use your computer while you bathe?"

"Of course," she said, smiling at him. Her multicolored eyes glowed in the morning light. She looked so beautiful in that moment, unself-conscious in her nudity. The sheet was tangled around her legs, her hair stood up in feathery tufts, and her face was marked with sleeplessness, but this time she was not, by any means, pale. Her smile turned into a grin. "Do you know, I think that 'thank-you' sailed totally past you this time."

He cocked his head as he considered her words. "Indeed."

He kissed her fast and paused just long enough to watch pleasure bloom in her expression before he created clothing for himself, another pair of jeans and a black T-shirt this time, and he strode downstairs. It didn't take him very long to find out where Therese lived. He checked Grace's babysitting roster, memorized Therese's phone number and used a reverse phone lookup to get her address.

He turned off Grace's computer, then he dematerialized and streamed out of the house. Once outside, the sun was so bright and hot, he drifted for a while and basked as he soaked up the plentiful nourishment. When he felt quite energized again, he went in search of a certain nosy human.

A human who disrespected the bargain she had struck with *his* human. His lover, his Grace.

And if there was one thing Khalil hated, it was when someone disrespected or reneged on a bargain.

Therese lived in a modest-sized house with a fenced-in backyard, in a neighborhood with tree-lined streets. Khalil wasn't very familiar with Louisville, but he did recognize in the distance one of the famous spires from the Churchill Downs racetrack. He surveyed the house and immediate area from above as he floated down. The driveway was empty. Therese appeared to be gone. Her house winked with flecks of Power.

It was as unwise to rush into a place filled with unknown magic as it was to rush into a place filled with unknown wards. Either Therese was a competent witch, or she knew someone who was, because all of the entrances to her house were spelled, front and back doors, her windows, even the chimney.

He studied the spells thoughtfully. They seemed like they might be sensitive enough to be triggered by his presence. He didn't think they would hurt him so much as alert someone if he triggered them.

He was interested to know who they might alert. He was even more interested in the fact that the spells felt bright and shining, like newly minted coins. Why would Therese recently feel the need to spell her windows, doors and even her chimney?

Perhaps Khalil had not made a favorable impression on her when they met.

He lowered down and slowly circled the house from a few feet away at the ground level. The house was not so new. However, both it and the detached garage were nicely maintained, and the flowers and shrubbery in the yard were quite charming and well tended.

There. A small vent for a clothes dryer protruded from the exterior wall, a few feet above the ground. It was covered with a grill and an aluminum flap, but those barriers did not matter in the slightest to him. The vent was not covered with a spell. He thought perhaps someone should tell Therese about that.

He attenuated his presence and flowed into the vent, through the dryer, and materialized in a small laundry room. There were no living presences in the house, so he strolled out of the laundry room and found himself in a kitchen filled with a great many things.

The walls were covered with hangings and framed pictures. There was a rooster clock and a smiling creature made of cloth with denim clothes and straw for hair and button eyes. There were cartoon cows interspersed throughout. A red-and-white checked cloth covered the table where two small ceramic chickens sat, one with the letter *S* and the other with the letter *P*. A pink jar fashioned like a pig sat on the counter. The word COOKIES was printed on its round belly.

Really, he did not understand the pig thing.

The jar had a lid shaped like a puffy white hat. He lifted the lid and looked inside. It was, indeed, filled with cookies. How logical. He took one, sniffed it and tried a cautious bite. It was brown, sweet, and had a spicy kick.

He ate the cookie as he walked through the house. He paused in the hall by the front door to flip through Therese's mail—bills, cards, clothing catalogs and a solicitation from a political group called the Humanist Party. Therese liked stinky colored leaves and dried flowers that she kept in a bowl on the hall table. She had a small computer station in one corner of the living room, and a large flat-screen TV in another corner. He turned on the laptop and left it to power up as he continued his search.

Therese also liked a lot of pillows, and she had a lot of dolls. She really had a lot of dolls. Dolls on shelves, dolls in glass cabinets. Dolls with curly blonde hair and frilly dresses, cloth dolls, plastic dolls, baby dolls, porcelain dolls, dolls both new and old. He lost interest in counting them after he reached a hundred. In her bedroom, she had twenty pillows on her bed of varying shapes, sizes, colors and patterns, and over thirty dolls were arranged in front of them. Some of the dolls sparked with magic.

Khalil was inclined to think this was strange. He was almost bored, and he really wanted to go back to Grace and watch the kids splash in a small pool, but he was also curious. Down the short hall, he found a bathroom (there were dolls in the bathroom too, which he found totally incomprehensible), and a half-closed door that led to a darkened room that held most of the Power in the house. Carefully he eased the door open further and looked inside.

There were so very many dolls. By this point he was beyond surprise. There was a workbench with a tall stool and a lamp, and parts of dolls on the bench, along with clay, jars of powders and liquids, bowls and measuring implements, a pestle and mortar, dried herbs, and candles and a smudge bowl with something half burned in it.

Ah. No wonder Therese had a thing for dolls. She worked sympathetic magic, and she made poppets. Khalil stepped closer to the workbench, studying everything without touching it. While he was no expert on human magics, it appeared Therese was accomplished at her craft. Someone could do a great deal of damage with poppet magic, and also a great deal of good. Several human cultures had magic systems that used poppets, from early Egypt, to West African fetishes and New Orleans voodoo.

Had Therese collected anything of Grace's or the children's to use in poppets, when she had snooped through their things? Just the possibility made Khalil want to raze her house to the ground so completely that not a single cornerstone was left standing.

Tires crunched on gravel outside. He blew to the window nearest the driveway in time to see Therese climb out of her car. She collected her purse and a few grocery bags from the trunk. As she headed for the front of the house, he flowed into the kitchen, materialized to lean against the counter and waited for her. He helped himself to another cookie as she unlocked the front door. He chewed and listened to her heels click on the floor.

Then she rounded the corner, caught sight of him, dropped everything and screamed.

He took a last bite of cookie and said, "Hello, Therese."

She whirled to run. He stood in her way. She screamed again and spun to lunge for the back door, only suddenly he stood there too, blocking it. He watched her coldly, his arms crossed. A nice man probably would have felt bad at causing her panic. But Khalil remembered her digging through Grace's things, and he wasn't a nice man at all.

Therese flushed a deep red then turned pasty white. Her hands shook, and her eyes darted around. "H-how did you get in? All the entrances were spelled!"

Someone ought to tell her about the dryer vent, but it wouldn't be Khalil. He said, "I should have followed up with you before this, but I've been busy. You might not know it to look at me, but I do have a day job."

"You're going to be sorry you broke in," Therese spat.

"Am I?" He regarded her, almost with interest. "Probably not before you're sorry you dug through Grace's things. What were you looking for?"

"Nothing!"

"The thing about panic," said Khalil, "is that it lessens one's ability to lie, especially to someone who has an exceedingly well developed truthsense."

"My gods, I was just looking for a pen and a piece of paper!"

In the next moment, he held her pinned by the throat against the wall. He hissed, "You would not be lying unless the answer mattered."

"I was only looking for information!" she sobbed. "That's all, I swear it!"

"What information?" Max and Chloe—*his babies*—had been playing innocently the whole time.

"I was looking to see if Isalynn LeFevre had contacted Grace!"

He was so angry, and it would be so easy to close his hand tighter and crush her windpipe. He barely held himself in check. "Why?"

"I don't know why." Something must have shown on his face or maybe his fingers started to tighten, because she screamed, "I don't know why! Gods damn you freaksome bastard, someone asked me to check!"

"Who?"

"Brandon Miller!"

Brandon, from Grace's work day yesterday. There was the connection to follow, and it wasn't even difficult. His hand relaxed. "How convenient," Khalil said. "He was next on my list."

She regarded him with equal amounts of loathing and fear. But he was not at all interested in that, and now he had what he wanted from her.

"I like your cookies," he told her as he tied her to a kitchen chair. He didn't bother with a complicated binding since he didn't plan on leaving her alone for long. He dissipated and flowed out the dryer vent, and as soon as he had rematerialized, he tugged on the connection that led to Ismat.

The other Djinn streaked toward him and formed in front of him. This time the Djinn chose the form of a dark-skinned, stocky male, with hawkish features and a twinkle in his starred eyes. "If you keep up this impetuous spending spree," said Ismat, "you will convince all the younger Djinn that the sky is falling. Everyone will rush to call in all their favors, and our venerable society will collapse."

Khalil didn't smile. He said, "I'm asking you to agree to an open-ended favor that will cancel out the rest of what you owe me. I trust you, and you're one of the few people I would call friend. I need you to help me, and I'm not yet sure what that means. Are you willing and able to pay your debt this way?"

The other Djinn's merry expression faded. "Of course. What's wrong?"

"I don't know," he said. "But it involves Grace and the children." He explained rapidly. "I need to find out where Brandon lives, and somebody needs to do something with Therese. I don't know what, question her to see if she knows anything else or take her to the witches' sheriff's office, except I'm not sure yet if she's actually broken any laws. I almost killed her, but Grace asked me not to start an inter-demesne incident."

Ismat turned toward the house. "I'll take care of her."

Khalil started to dematerialize then paused. "I almost forgot—you'll want to enter the house through the clothes dryer vent. She has all the doors and windows spelled. I'm not sure who would be alerted if the spells are tripped, but I prefer not to broadcast our intentions."

"Got it," Ismat said. "Good hunting."

It took Khalil longer to find Brandon Miller's house than it had for him to find Therese's. He called his Djinn associate with the facility for information gathering on the Internet, and he did something he rarely did any more—he bargained away a favor for information.

His contact got back to him quickly. Brandon didn't live in the city. He owned a twenty-five-acre property about a half hour's car drive south of the Louisville International Airport. As soon as Khalil had the details, he took off.

It took some effort to locate the property. While he searched, Khalil's sense of unease deepened. Grace had said that Olivia thought the other witches from Saturday had known each other very well. If Olivia was correct, what did that mean? Why would they all wish to work on Grace's property together?

Why would they wish for other witches to stay away while they did so?

Why did Brandon want to know if Isalynn LeFevre had contacted Grace?

Even though Brandon's property wasn't marked with so much as a mailbox, Khalil finally located it. A long gravel drive led back through a tangle of old-growth forest. The day had turned into a bright afternoon, and a fierce humid heat lay heavily across the land like a dense fog. He traveled through the forest carefully, all his senses wide open for sparks of Power that could be traps.

He found plenty of them. The land was layered with traps overlaid on traps. There were so many magical and physical traps, he stopped trying to gain information by slipping through the forest. Instead he soared over the land until he spotted a small cluster of buildings well away from the road. A large vegetable garden bordered the buildings, along with a chicken coop.

He drifted down as gently as a snowflake, spreading his presence so thin, almost nobody would have been able to sense him. Nobody except for his extraordinary Grace.

There were three older, rusted vehicles near the buildings, but none of them looked like they were in drivable condition. The main building was the house. He slipped close and listened, but he didn't hear anyone stirring. It appeared Brandon was not at home. As he circled the house, he glanced in the windows at a cluttered interior. One room had several brightly colored signs stacked against the wall and piles of posters and buttons on a table, all with the American flag rippling in the background. Some signs had the slogan: THE HUMANIST PARTY. Others read: JAYDON GUTHRIE FOR HEAD OF THE WITCHES.

A couple of large dogs napped on a covered porch. He took care not to disturb them, in case someone was actually in the house where he could not see them. Some dogs and certain other animals were very sensitive to a Djinn's presence.

He slipped away and scouted out the other buildings. One was an unused barn with a roof that was falling in. Another was a toolshed filled with a variety of implements and machines, and an aluminum ladder lying on the ground against one outside wall. Even that building had wards glowing on it. Brandon cared for his possessions. The only building that didn't have wards or other sparks of Power was the rotting barn.

Khalil twisted in a circle, his attention sharpening. The barn really was the only building without sparks of Power glowing on it somewhere. Was there nothing in the building that Brandon wanted to protect?

Khalil really had no reason to go looking in the barn except for his terminal case of Djinn curiosity. He slid inside through a gap in the wooden wall. The interior was deeply shadowed. Cobwebs floated in the air. The bones of yet another vehicle sat inside. The metal lines of its body were heavy and rounded. It had no engine, wheels or seats. Thick dust coated the vehicle and the barn's pitted floor, along with mice droppings.

A wooden ladder with broken rungs led to a loft. He floated up, intending to exit the barn through the hole in one corner of the roof.

That was when he discovered the loft wasn't dusty or empty.

He whipped toward it. The repairs to the loft floor had not been visible from below. Fresh planks of wood covered the old floor in places. A new workbench was pushed against one wall made of wood planks as raw as the repairs to the floor. There was also a stool and battery-operated lantern, but that was as close as it came to any resemblance to Therese's work area.

This workbench was littered with a variety of hand-tools, a blowtorch, wires and other bits of knobby, oddly shaped metal. Nothing felt magical. Khalil materialized in front of the bench. Frowning, he picked up a length of thin, flexible pipe and turned it over in his hands.

How did the human get into the loft in the first place? He saw no point of entry for an embodied creature unless it had wings. To one side of the loft, there was an opening in the wall, covered with a large wooden flap, but that looked as dilapidated and unused as most of the rest of the barn. The only other point of entry was a filth-streaked window.

He walked over to look closer and discovered fresh scratch marks on the sill. Looking out the smudged pane, he could see one end of the nearby toolshed. A corner of the aluminum ladder was just visible.

He returned to the bench. To say that he was not mechanically minded would probably be one of the biggest understatements anyone could make in a year.

Something had been constructed. Or perhaps something was going to be constructed. But what? He didn't have a clue.

And why go to all this trouble to hide it?

≡ EIGHTEEN ≡

When Khalil disappeared, Grace wobbled her way to the upstairs bathroom. She felt like a drunken sailor. Gods, what he had done to her.

Every private place on her body felt hypersensitive, and her inner thigh muscles quivered. She touched a dusky area on the side of her breast. It was a suck bruise. She thought of him working her everywhere, and intense arousal pulsed through her. It was followed immediately by a forceful wave of emotion. She covered her eyes.

I did not know I needed grace until I met you, he had said.

I'm turning into some weird hybrid creature, she thought, like that crazy homicidal chick from *Species*. And Khalil Bane of My Existence told me that he needed me. Today's forecast calls for free steaks and flying pigs.

Probably all it means is that Djinn males can get caught up in the moment just like human males do. I shouldn't make too much of it. But I did learn that he likes sex. He likes it a whole lot. We haven't enjoyed it in a leisurely fashion yet, but he did devote all of his attention to it.

And I already crave it and him.

She tried to lasso the part of her brain that had decided

gibbering was a good thing to do before coffee on a Sunday morning. She didn't have much luck, as she slid into the bathtub, washed her hair and soaped herself all over.

Everything was so sensitive, her body well used and pleasured hard. Even in the middle of their frenzy, he had been so careful with her knee. It hadn't been strained in the slightest. She still thought she'd better wear the brace for a while, until the rest of her got used to standing upright again.

All of her casual summer clothes were now downstairs. She wrapped herself in a towel and went down to the office and dressed in a tank top and another pair of soft, unstructured shorts. Then she turned on the air-conditioning unit that was fixed into one of the living room windows, and she walked through the house, closing all the open windows. One larger unit was downstairs, and two smaller units were upstairs. With all three running the big, old house should be comfortably cool for the first time that summer. Yee-haw.

As she turned away from closing the window over the kitchen sink, she felt the Djinn enter the kitchen.

Her hackles raised as Phaedra formed in the middle of the room.

Oh damn.

Even though Khalil insisted she call him, every reason she had for not calling him the first time Phaedra showed up was still valid. But she had promised.

He didn't actually say *when* she should call him. That was splitting hairs, and frankly, it would be a toss-up whether his Djinn sensibilities could accept that reasoning or if he was going to be royally pissed.

Who was she kidding, he was going to be royally pissed.

But she was still going to protect him, and he would just have to forgive her. She readied the expulsion spell as she said, "Hello, Freaky Bitch."

Phaedra stared at her, black eyes burning. "Who is it? Who is the ghost?"

Grace studied her, mouth level. "Okay," she said. "But just so you know—if you ever come uninvited into my house again, or if you come anywhere near my kids without my permission, I pinky swear I will knock the living shit out of you." Damn, it felt good to have an offensive spell, or at least one that worked on Freaky Bitch.

Phaedra looked as if she hated Grace. *"Just show me who it is."*

Grace touched the Power lightly and it flooded her. It really was like drowning, she thought, as the dark sea filled her to the brim and overflowed. She no longer tried to hold herself back from it, because that would be like trying to hold back from herself.

Come on, she whispered into the sea. *Show yourself again.*

The ghost heard and arrowed toward her. Grace held out a hand, and the ghost took it, eyes shining like the brightest of stars. Somehow she lifted the ghost out of the sea or pulled it into the present, for she was a doorway. She thought she would act as a channel, but instead, with a grateful look, the ghost stepped through her and into the kitchen.

Then Phaedra from a far distant past came face-to-face with the Phaedra she had become. The present Phaedra stared, her expression stricken.

The ghost of who she had been stared back wonderingly. Their forms were identical. They both had regal ivory features and bloodred hair, but they were far different from each other. The Phaedra from the past was transparent, but even so she had a brightness of spirit, a light in her face. She felt straight and strong and beautiful, and Grace knew this was who Phaedra had been before Lethe had imprisoned her, before she had become the dark.

In contrast, the present Phaedra's razored edges and black center felt especially wrong. There was nothing wrong with the dark, Grace thought, as she considered the living sea inside of her. Darkness can be a beautiful thing, and the night had a velvet embrace that the day could never hope to match. But darkness was an entirely different thing from this brokenness.

The present Phaedra's face contorted. She screamed, and the sound was so full of rage and pain, so full of shattered glass and catastrophic ruination, that it almost doubled Grace over.

She was horrified at what she had initiated. *I'm so sorry,* she wanted to say. But before she could find her way to the words, the ghost sprang, faster than thought, and wrapped around the present Phaedra.

Who screamed and screamed, beyond anything a human could produce. The strength of anguish behind it finally had Grace clapping her hands over her ears as tears streamed down her face. How could anybody survive with something like that inside of her? It was intolerable. No creature should reach a place of such pain that caused a scream like that.

Underneath the screaming, Grace began to hear something else.

Choose me. Choose me. All but inaudible, heard only in the mind, the ghost said it over and over, *Choose me.*

The screaming stopped. What it left behind was a pounding silence.

The ghost sank into Phaedra, whose body shuddered and rippled. Grace felt Phaedra flex convulsively. Then with a concussion that rattled the house, her presence *snapped* into a different alignment.

Oh, please let that be a good thing.

Grace wiped her eyes. When she could see again, Phaedra's form was barely visible. The Djinn's presence felt fragile and fundamentally changed. Grace said, "Tell me what I can do to help you."

I must rest. Then Phaedra said slowly, *Call on me when you have need, and I will come. I owe you a favor.*

Grace felt something settle into place as the Djinn's presence faded. It was a tiny, barely perceptible thing.

A thread of connection.

She turned, braced her elbows on the counter and leaned there for a while until her racing heart slowed. She couldn't wait to tell Khalil what happened. Either that, or she dreaded it. Maybe both.

Phaedra had felt so paper-thin and delicate before she disappeared, hardly capable of surviving.

But there was a connection.

Grace wanted to pack it in cotton and wrap it in a bow. She could stare at it all day, hovering and fretting, except she had things to do.

The Oracle's moon was a nexus, as the veil between times and worlds thinned and possibilities converged. It could be unpredictable and dramatic as hell.

So that was done and over with, right? Because she was calling a moratorium on unpredictable drama for at least a couple of weeks. Well, as long as she was calling a moratorium, she might as well make it a decade. She would insist on no more unpredictable drama until both the kids hit eighteen, but Chloe was going to reach puberty well before then, and Grace just hoped she had benefits at that point because she thought she was going to need a therapist to get through those years.

Khalil's reaction was going to have to wait for now. She had to pick up the kids.

She made coffee, filled a travel mug and started her errands. The first order of business? Make an ATM deposit at her bank with that insane check before she did something stupid, like dump coffee all over her purse. She started laughing as she punched in the right sequence of numbers and watched the machine suck in her deposit envelope. Yeah, that was probably going to mean a phone call from some startled bank employee tomorrow.

Then she drove south to the nearest superstore and spent the last of her cash on a small, inflatable, rainbow-colored kiddie pool, bright plastic waterproof toys, a red bucket, two packages of glow-in-the-dark stars and children's sunscreen.

When would Khalil come by? Like the love-struck fool that she was, she missed him fiercely. She wanted him more than ever, and she hadn't eaten a proper meal since yesterday morning, and she already needed a nap. She was exhausted, terrified and euphoric, running on caffeine and an overabundance of dumbfounded endorphins. She instinctively knew they had only begun to touch on all the sensual possibilities they could share, while she barely comprehended what they had already done. What he had done to her.

Huh. He really was the bane of her existence. She just hadn't realized that might be a pretty spectacular thing.

As she pulled into the driveway at Katherine's house, Chloe raced squealing out the front door, blonde hair floating around her head like dandelion fluff. Laughing, Grace stepped out of the car. Chloe beamed and threw her arms around Grace's middle. "Max missed you so much!"

"Did he?" Grace hoisted the little girl onto her hip and hugged her tight. "How about you?"

"I was a big girl." Chloe put her head on Grace's shoulder. "I was fine. But overnight is an awfully long time."

"It is, isn't it? I wasn't a very big girl. I missed you like crazy." Grace kissed her cheek. "I bought you presents."

Chloe's head popped up. She looked electrified. "What is it?!"

"You get to see when we go home." Grace set her on her feet. Katherine's children Joey and Rachel had run outside too. When Chloe shrieked and skipped in circles, they joined her. Grace went to talk with Katherine and collect Max and their overnight bag.

Katherine met her at the front door with Max on one hip. When the baby saw Grace, he squealed and tried to fling himself forward. Laughing, Katherine handed him over. "They were great, as always. Chloe struggled a bit last night and cried to come home, but other than that I think she had a good time. How did yesterday go?"

The babbling part of her brain almost got control of her mouth, but as Grace received a slobbery baby kiss, she managed to wrestle the internal babbler into silence. She was not up to dropping bombshells that would kick off a three-hour visit of explanations. That could come at a later time. For now she said simply, "Very productive. We got a lot done."

Katherine told her, "Well, you look good but exhausted. Everything all right?"

Grace smiled. She couldn't believe the older woman didn't hear the whistling fireworks rocketing through her head.

"Everything's great. I'll call you in a couple of days. We should set up a time when I can take Joey and Rachel, so that you and John can get away for the weekend."

Katherine's pleasant face lit up. "That would be awesome!"

"Why don't you talk it over with him and figure out some possible dates then let me know what you come up with?"

"Absolutely!"

By the time Grace got the kids home, she had reached a crisis of hunger that mere coffee couldn't stave off any longer. She needed a hot meal, but the leftovers from the Russian Tea Room were gone, and all they had in the freezer were Tater Tots, packages of peas, broccoli and corn, and concentrated juice.

Meanwhile Chloe was in a frenzy over the presents. Grace looked wryly into Chloe's agonized face and said to herself, yep, I walked right into that one, didn't I?

Life narrowed and became one foot in front of the other again, one step at a time. Her higher thought processes took a hike. Even the babbler fell silent. She blew up the inflatable pool until she was dizzy, put it in the backyard in the corner near a shady tree, and yanked the old leaky hose over to add water to it. Not much. Enough for them to splash and have fun, but a small enough amount so that the sun could warm it quickly.

She put towels and sunscreen at one end of the table, and gave Chloe the task of ripping the packaging off the plastic water toys and stacking them in the red bucket. Chloe set to work with single-minded intensity. Grace turned her increasingly cloudy attention to lunch. A hot meal, dammit. Nothing fancy; they didn't have anything fancy in the house. Simple comfort food.

What did they have to work with? She started grabbing things out of the cupboard. Egg noodles. Mushroom soup. Tuna. Great, a tuna casserole. Quick to throw together, easy to bake, and maybe she could sneak some peas past the food Nazi in Chloe's head. That girl, that girl.

Chloe sang under her breath. Max scuttled around on the kitchen floor, dragging his love object/baby blanket along with him. Grace blanched noodles, threw everything together in a bowl, splashed some milk into it.

All her thoughts bled together in a jumbled mishmash.

Khalil's hands. His mouth, working her with such gentle urgency. His presence, everywhere.

What was she forgetting?

Gram, swimming beside her in the dark sea. *You're almost out of tuna.*

Was that actually what Gram had said? Tuna? Or time?

Gram really would have liked the kitchen ghosts, but they were loud today and restless. Chloe was loud too and getting louder, her singing escalating up the music scale.

Phaedra, screaming. That fragile, rare connection.

Grace filled the casserole dish. Set the mixing bowl in the sink, and filled it with water to wash later. Forgetting something. Oh, duh. She hadn't turned on the oven yet. Good thing the air-conditioners were on. Otherwise the old oven would heat the house up terribly.

She had left her body when Khalil made love to her. Not figuratively. She really had left her body.

That was unusual.

You left your body once tonight, the goddess had said in her dream. *You can do it again if you want to badly enough.*

She needed to remember that. It might have meaning.

Forgetting. Dammit, the oven. Food would help to clear her head. Then she would take the kids out to play in the pool. She turned the oven on and pulled out a chair to sit down with a sense of relief. Soon the next step would be to eat something. That one was easy.

Don't stay in the house when you bake the casserole.

Grace smiled as she remembered seeing Gram, even if it had been just a dream.

Actually, the house did get pretty hot when the oven was on, even with the air-conditioning working. She looked into Chloe's agonized face. She would never get the little girl to eat, unless they went outside first.

She asked, "Do you want to play in the pool while lunch cooks?"

"Yes!" Chloe screamed. She hit a perfect high *C*, which was like a needle going into the brain. She grabbed the bucket's handle and raced out the back door.

Grace and Max looked at each other. "Come on, you too, little man," she told him. She scooped him up, grabbed the towels and the sunscreen, and went outside too. She stripped Chloe down to her panties, left Max in diaper and diaper cover, liberally sprayed both of them with sunscreen and then sprayed herself. The kids went into the pool with the toys, while she eased down onto a towel.

She could actually relax for ten minutes or so while the oven preheated. Yowzer.

Max's wonder and Chloe's delight were a joy to watch. Grace let her mind fill with clouds as she watched them play in the pool. She caught herself up with a jerk as she almost fell asleep. Ugh, dammit, not when the baby was in the water. He was only sitting in a couple of inches, but still.

Time to put the casserole in the oven. But not without the baby.

She stood first and pulled him out of the pool. Max, who was normally so placid and easygoing and an all-around cool guy, stiffened in outrage and yelled. "Whoa," she said. "It'll only be for a minute, buddy."

Unfortunately he didn't have the language to understand, but he did have object permanence, and he had developed some mad love for that little pool. He kicked and screamed. The sound scraped against her already abused eardrums. She said loudly to Chloe, "We'll be right back."

Chloe nodded without looking up. Grace walked toward the house while she tried to control Max's chunky, protesting body. She couldn't even hear herself think, let alone figure out why all the ghosts of the old women rushed at her, their indistinct, transparent forms loud with distress—

You're going the wrong way.

Which was ridiculous. That was from her dream. She was only going to the kitchen.

The wrong way.

Confused, she stopped, looking down at Max's reddened

little face while she tried to sort through the clouds of hungry tiredness in her head.

Wrong.

An enormous, invisible fist punched her. She lost her hold on Max and slammed into the ground. The back of the house disappeared in a rolling ball of flame that blew out an inferno of boiling heat. She thought there was sound too, a gigantic roar, but maybe that was all inside her head.

Max.

Oh gods, she had dropped the baby.

With an immense effort she rolled onto her stomach, looking for him. He lay on his stomach too and pushed himself up on stiffened arms. He looked utterly panicked, his mouth wide open and his face purpled as he screamed.

She came up on all fours and lunged for him. Burning pain flared in her knee. She snatched him close and ran her hands down his arms and legs then clenched him tightly, twisting to put her back between him and the ferocious blaze.

Chloe. Grace looked for her. The swimming pool was thirty feet or so farther away from the house. Chloe sat frozen in the water, clutching her bucket. She stared at the fire, her face contorted. Grace couldn't hear anything aside from the gigantic roar, but she could clearly read the little girl's lips.

"I need my mommy! I need my mommy!"

Grace fumbled. There had to be a connection somewhere in her ringing head. She swept out with her mind, did a wide, blind scoop, and yanked with all of her strength.

That was when the earthquake hit Louisville.

⇒ NINETEEN ⇐

A supernova blasted toward Grace. The sense of oncoming destruction blocked out everything else. She huddled around Max, trying to cover him with her body.

Later she would find out that her property was the epicenter of an earthquake that registered 5.8 on the Richter scale. She never even felt it. Nearby streetlamps warped and bent like they were sticks made of soft wax, trees fell, the cavern caved in and her car was thrown to the street, where the pavement buckled. Luckily, the surrounding area was not as developed as more urban areas and damage was minimal, although a roof and part of a stone wall collapsed at a nearby cemetery. And it was luck, not intention: that was how out of control Khalil had been.

Instead of destruction, what she felt was a gentle black smoke that swirled around the yard, blanketing her and the kids. It blocked out all the heat and noise. At the same time Khalil covered the burning house with Power. The fire died with an eerie suddenness.

Grace gripped Max in one arm and glanced around, dazed, as she tried to scoot awkwardly toward Chloe, hampered by having only one free hand and her goddamn useless knee.

Strong arms lifted her and Max. She blinked as Khalil formed around them. His expression was stark and shaken. Her gaze lowered to his moving lips. She made out his words. "Stop. I've got you."

"Chloe," she said. She couldn't hear herself speak, and the only way she could control her dizziness was by tilting her head. She tried to say Chloe's name again. With both her and Max in his arms, Khalil spun toward the swimming pool.

He froze, staring.

A Djinn was wrapped around a sobbing Chloe, the presence so gossamer thin she was transparent. It was Phaedra. When Grace called Khalil, she must have pulled both connections by accident.

Max's body was rigid and shaking in her arms. She turned her attention to him. He was still screaming with such lusty energy his face was a darkened red.

She decided right then and there that screaming was awesome. Screaming meant you were alive. If you had the strength to scream, hopefully you had the strength to recover. But *still*.

"We need a doctor," she said to Khalil.

He looked at her again, a sparkling crisis in his eyes, while his jaw flexed.

She was making sound when she talked, wasn't she? She put more force into the next words. "A pediatrician. Tell them it's an emergency."

His Power flared. A strange Djinn appeared. Khalil said something in a sharp whip of a voice that she heard as if from a distance. After one wide-eyed glance around, the Djinn nodded and whisked away.

Oh, good. That meant a doctor would be coming. She looked at Max again. He wasn't bleeding. That had to be good too. She had no idea what to do for him. There were classes for that sort of thing, what were they called? Whatever they were, she should take some. Her head was pounding, her ears hurt, and her skin and knee felt like they were on fire.

Then Khalil knelt, and Chloe was there, still sobbing and wrapped in towel, and he simply enfolded them all. Grace leaned against him while she wrapped her arms around the children, and Khalil put his face in her hair. She thought he and Phaedra said things to each other, but she wasn't sure, because it was such a strain to focus on anything, so she just concentrated on holding those poor, scared babies.

Black clouds like smoke filled her head, or maybe it was the dark sea. This time the vision came to her so softly, it was as if she fell into a dream.

She was surrounded with people.

Petra touched her hand and looked at her with such gratitude. *Thank you for looking after them.*

Of course, Grace said. *What else would I do?*

Gram smiled proudly and said, *I knew you would figure it out.*

Then a strange, angry man told her, *Check the insurance again. I would never fall asleep at the wheel.*

Grace stared. She recognized him from photographs in the newspaper. He was the independent trucker who crossed the meridian line and caused the head-on collision. *But that's what I was told.*

It's a lie.

The trucker faded back into the sea, and suddenly the world snapped back into place. Khalil knelt in front of her. He cupped her face, handling her with a tense care that was in sharp contrast to the banked violence of emotion in his elegant face. She startled badly when she realized the kids were no longer on her lap. She grabbed his wrists.

He shook one of his hands free to hold a vial up to her mouth. She watched his lips as he said, "Drink it."

She could feel the magic in the vial even in her dizzy confusion. It was a "cure-all" healing potion, expensive and rare. When she opened her mouth to ask where the kids went and how he had gotten the potion, he tilted the precious contents of the vial between her open lips, and she had no choice but to swallow.

An intense golden glow filled her body and drove back

the dark sea. The Power from the potion pulsed in her skin, her knee and her head. Khalil wrapped an arm around her shoulders and nudged the rim of another vial between her lips. "Drink another one," he said.

By that time her dizziness had lessened, and she heard him for real. She didn't waste time on asking how he had gotten them or how much they cost. Instead she drank, and that time the Power in the potion blew away the clouds in her head. She said, "The kids."

"Right over there."

She looked where Khalil pointed. Somehow the backyard had filled up with people. Max was lying on a stretcher, attended by a man and a woman, EMT equipment on the ground nearby. Chloe sat on another stretcher, wrapped in a blanket. She was being examined by another man. Four Djinn stood nearby, watching the EMTs alertly.

Power swirled behind her. She glanced over her shoulder. At least two other Djinn were in the blackened wreckage that had been the back of the house, although they weren't in physical form. As she turned back to face Khalil she caught sight of a seventh Djinn, who wore the form of a muscular ebony-skinned male. He stared fixedly at her.

Whatever was up with that particular Djinn, it was definitely not her problem. She had enough on her plate at the moment, thank you. She turned away from the puzzle. As she focused on Khalil again, he said, "The kids are all right."

"Are you sure?"

His jaw was clenched, diamond eyes filled with radiant wetness. She put a hand to his face, and he snatched her to him so tightly she grunted. "Yes," he said hoarsely. "You're all going to be all right. But gods *damn,* you almost weren't. *Gods damn*, I saw my daughter. I talked to Phaedra. She said you healed her."

"I didn't heal her. I just showed her who she used to be." She leaned against him, resting her head on his chest. "She made the choice, and—I don't know what else to call it—she repatterned or realigned herself. I didn't mean to call her when I called for you. I just couldn't tell what I was doing. My head was all fucked up."

"The EMT said you had a concussion, and Max probably did too." Khalil ran a finger lightly down the bare skin of her arm, and his mouth twisted in a quick sharp spasm. "And first-degree burns. A pediatrician is with him now."

Grace glanced gratefully over at the people working to help the children. She said, "Phaedra looked so threadbare after she changed, I was really worried about her. She said she needed to rest. Is she still here?"

"As soon as other help came, she left. She needs time, maybe a lot of time, and nourishment, and I don't think she can ever be quite the same as she was. But her essence is true again, not warped. She made a connection with you, and she answered it." He glared. "You were supposed to call me if she showed up again."

"I remembered," she told him, truthfully enough. "I just got busy."

"We will talk of that later." He bowed over her. She could feel what a maelstrom he was of out-of-control emotion, pain, a terror that was too slow to fade, and a twisted up, overwhelmed sense of wonder. He could barely hold on to his physical form. "Do you realize what a miracle you are? *You scared me so much this time.*"

A glowing drop of liquid streaked down and landed on her dirty T-shirt where it lay like a shining jewel for a moment before it was soaked into the material. "I'm sorry," she whispered. She touched the small damp spot wonderingly. It still had a tiny spark of his Power that slowly faded. "I didn't mean to."

Someone approached; it was the woman who had been examining Max. She knelt beside Grace with a smile. "I'm Dr. Lopez. You're looking better."

"I'm feeling better, thanks," Grace said.

"I scanned you when you were a little out of it earlier. You've strained your knee, but I don't think you've done any further lasting damage. Wear your brace for a couple of weeks and baby that knee. Hot and cold compresses, and ibuprofen. I'm sure you know the drill. Be sure to see your orthopedic surgeon if it gives you any trouble."

"I will." Grace twisted around to look at the kids. One EMT rubbed Max's stomach, talking soothingly while the baby sucked his thumb. The other EMT smiled at Chloe, who was showing him the toys in her bucket. "How are they?"

"They're doing really well," Dr. Lopez said. "Chloe had a shock, and she's still shaken. I don't see or sense any evidence of injury. Max had a couple of healing potions like you did, and he's calmer and feeling better. The pink to his skin is gone, and his concussive symptoms have disappeared. I don't sense any further injury when I scan him, no pressure or swelling in his head or spine. If you would feel better, we can admit him to keep an eye on him overnight, but to be quite honest, I don't think it's necessary."

"Who are you and where are you from?" Grace asked. She glanced at Khalil. He looked focused and suddenly calm.

The doctor's direct gaze was friendly and understanding. "I work at the Children's Hospital in Boston."

"She teaches at the Harvard Medical School," Khalil said. "We wanted to get the best."

Like pancakes from the Russian Tea Room? Grace gripped Khalil's forearm. "And the EMTs?"

"They're from the Children's Hospital in Boston too." Dr. Lopez did not quite smile, but she looked like she might want to. "Our trauma unit does not often see several Djinn appear to demand medical care for two human children."

"Try never," said one of the EMTs from behind the doctor. He had walked over hand in hand with Chloe.

Dr. Lopez said, "They volunteered to come."

Chloe flung herself at Grace and Khalil. She wailed, "Our house broke!"

"I know, sweetie." Grace snatched her close, and Khalil's arms closed over them both tightly, while Grace kissed and rocked Chloe. So fragile, so precious. A spasm of shaking rattled Grace.

Gram, I don't deserve your pride, she thought, because even with the dream and all the ghosts yelling at me, I almost didn't figure it out.

"Do you think you could give me some big-girl help?" she said in Chloe's hair.

Chloe said timidly, "I dunno. It might be too big for me."

Oh, ouch. Grace's throat closed up, and for a few moments she couldn't talk. She felt torn in two.

Khalil put a hand to her back. *I'm right here. Tell me what you need.*

Her two pieces aligned, and she grew calm and clear-headed. She said to him, *The children need to be with some-one they feel safe with tonight, and it can't be me because I have things I need to do. Normally that would mean Katherine, except right now I want them out of Kentucky altogether.*

Why is that? Khalil asked. He looked sharp, and for the first time since she had met him, truly predatory.

She met his gaze. *Because the trucker that caused the car accident in the spring didn't fall asleep at the wheel.*

Arrangements for the children happened much quicker than she thought they could. Two of the Djinn took Dr. Lopez, the EMTs and their equipment back to Boston. Khalil sent a third spearing into the air to find Katherine and John and explain what had happened, and what was needed from them. Grace hated for Katherine to find out everything that had happened that way, but she needed to focus all her attention on the children. The fourth Djinn made travel arrangements for a suite to be made available for Katherine, John, their children, and Chloe and Max at the Four Seasons Hotel in Houston, in the heart of the Demonkind demesne.

That caused Grace to pause as she tried to figure out how to finance the trip for all six. The check from Carling and Rune hadn't cleared the bank, and she didn't have a credit card. While she knew Katherine and John would do any-thing to help, she certainly couldn't expect them to foot the hotel bill. Sitting with her back against a shade tree while cuddling Chloe on her lap, she brought the question of financing up with Khalil.

Khalil held the exhausted baby against his shoulder. He paced slowly, so he didn't wake Max up. He had chosen, of all things, to wear jeans and a T-shirt again. The outfit brought to mind their date, which seemed like it had happened ages ago, except now the clothes looked shockingly exotic against his more inhuman physical form. He held his energy under such tight control, it made Grace's bones ache just to look at him.

Max wasn't aware of any of that. The baby had begun to snore. He sounded like a squeaky toy. Khalil put his cheek against Max's head, rubbing his small back.

"Do not trouble yourself in the slightest over paying for the trip," Khalil told Grace quietly. "It will all be taken care of."

Grace jerked as suddenly the ebony-skinned Djinn appeared and knelt beside her, diamond eyes intent. The strange Djinn said, "I will pay for all of it."

If anything, Khalil grew even quieter, yet this time a thread of steel ran through his voice. "Now is not the time, Ebrahim."

"I understand," the other Djinn said, just as quietly, while pain flared in his expression. "Just know I will pay for everything." He looked into Grace's eyes and whispered, "Anything you need."

"Thank you?" Grace kissed Chloe's temple and tilted her head sideways to see the little girl's face. Chloe was sleepy but still awake, and sucking her thumb. Grace said to the Djinn in a gentle, perky voice, "You need to back up and give us some space now. Actually, if you really want to help, you could get the children something to eat since our kitchen blew up." Grace murmured to Chloe, "Are you hungry?" Chloe nodded. "What would you like to eat?"

Chloe slipped her thumb out of her mouth. "Cheese."

Ebrahim looked at Max.

Khalil said promptly, "Similac formula. Not the powder. Ready to feed bottles with nipples. A package of Pampers disposable diapers, a dozen jars of stage two baby food—get a variety of things, and remember, he loves applesauce—and a small spoon, some baby wipes, and a diaper bag. A soft stuffed toy suitable for a nine-month-old and a cotton blanket. That should meet his immediate needs."

Grace stared at Khalil, her mouth open. If she hadn't fallen in love with him already, that would have done it. Twice.

Ebrahim's intensity had splintered into confusion. Khalil told him, "Ask a store attendant to help you pick it all out. And hurry."

The other Djinn dematerialized and blew away. Grace asked, *He was a bit intense. What was that all about?*

Khalil told her, *His mate is damaged. He saw Phaedra and heard us talking. He is hoping you can help his mate. I didn't remember that when I called on him to pay his debt.*

She pushed the heel of one hand against her temple. *Oh, criminy. I can't promise anything to anyone. Khalil, what I did was a fluke. Honestly, Phaedra did most of the work.*

He squatted in front of her. Max looked so tiny nestled against his chest. *I know. And now really isn't the time. But when the time does come, would you at least be willing to try—for him or any of the others?* He gripped her shoulder. *No matter how you answer, I will support your decision.*

And if she hadn't already fallen in love with him, that would have made the third time today. *Of course I'll try*, she said. *I couldn't say no.*

He looked into her eyes, took her hand and pressed his lips to her fingers. *Indeed.*

Just then the two Djinn that had been exploring the house assumed physical forms and walked toward them. They wore the shapes of identical women, tall, blonde and strong looking. Grace looked at them with her mind's eye. Their presences were almost an exact carbon copy of each other; they really were twins. Khalil's expression darkened as they came near, his face hard. He asked, "What have you discovered?"

"We have shut off the gas," said one of them. "There is nothing magical in the ruins."

"And the cause?"

The other twin held out her hand. In her palm was a piece of damaged metal. "We think it was this piece of the stove. It is part of the gas regulation and ignition process called a flame failure device. It appears quite faulty."

Grace said, "We used that stove hundreds of times, and it worked perfectly."

Khalil looked at Grace. "This was the first time you used the stove since yesterday's work day, wasn't it, when you had so many people over?"

"Yes." She went a little numb.

The twins looked at each other. One of them asked, "Did you leave the house for any length of time?"

Twelve people, not including Olivia, who knew each other well. They looked her in the eye and ate her food and mowed her lawn. Did *twelve people* do this?

She nodded and whispered, "For about forty-five minutes."

Khalil's rage flared red-hot against Grace's senses. His face was vicious. "Brandon Miller has metal devices like this in a hidden workshop. Along with tools with which to alter them."

Chloe knuckled her eyes. "Did our lunch break the house?"

Grace's arms tightened. She shook her head at the others, silently warning them to stop the conversation, as she said, "It seems so, baby girl."

The Djinn returned from their various errands. The first to arrive were the two who had gone to Boston. Then came the one who made the travel arrangements. Ebrahim was the fourth, laden with packages. He had the new diaper bag, stuffed with everything Khalil had requested, and a large plastic shopping bag filled with three different kinds of cheese, crackers, juice, pudding, fruit and animal cookies. Grace opened packages of food so Chloe could nibble, and she ate too, mechanically, because she needed the fuel.

The messenger to Katherine and John was the last one to

return. The Djinn wore the form of a reed-thin girl with a gleaming fall of chocolate-colored hair.

"They are coming," she said, her voice as light and airy as a flute. "Katherine told me to tell you, of course they will come. She is shocked and saddened and extremely angry."

Khalil said, "Make sure they arrive safely."

"Yes." She vanished again, and two of the others went with her.

Khalil spread out the new cotton blanket beside Grace and Chloe, and he eased the sleeping Max onto it. Then he went with the rest of the Djinn to look at the house. He returned soon with her knee brace, the hated cane, and Chloe's Lalaloopsy doll.

"They will see what is salvageable of your possessions, and if possible, they will work on repairs," he said to Grace, his voice softer than ever, for Chloe had fallen asleep too. He set Chloe's doll on the blanket beside Max and knelt to help Grace buckle the brace into place.

"They must be in a lot of debt to you if they're still working to cancel it out," Grace said.

"None of the Djinn owe me anything anymore," Khalil said. "Now they're working for you."

Her eyes rounded. "No pressure, right?" she muttered. "That's a hell of a burden of hope they're piling on my shoulders."

"I have been talking to them. I promise you, nobody will expect anything more than you can give." He brushed at her face lightly with the tips of his fingers, eyes burning. Then he leaned forward to kiss her with tautly controlled passion. His hand dropped to circle the base of her throat. *I think this time you scared the immortality out of me.*

I'm sorry, she said again.

He leaned his forehead against hers, and he said in her head so softly she barely heard him, *Grace, you almost died. I don't want to know what that's like.*

She didn't need to say that she was going to die sooner or later while he wasn't, because the fact hung over their heads like the sword of Damocles that dangled by a single hair. She stayed silent and stroked his face, her eyes closed, and absorbed the hot comfort of his presence.

But because the Oracle's moon could be a freaky bitch too, it didn't care if there were only so many epiphanies a girl could take at a time. The endless day wasn't done with her yet, as the dark sea took her again, the riptide filled with beginnings and endings, all potential futures and the past.

This time the vision that took her was sharp as a blade's edge, and she saw that the real sword hanging over their head was not her mortality, but something else entirely. Image upon image of possible futures bombarded her. She flinched back with a gasp.

Khalil grabbed her shoulders. His touch snapped her back into the here and now. He studied her with a sharp concern. "What's wrong? You've gone completely white."

She stared at him, heart pounding, then her expression turned grim. "No," she said. "One thing at a time. Right now we've got enough on our plate."

"Gracie," he said between his teeth.

Gods, she loved it when he called her that, with his perfect blend of exasperation and tenderness. She put the knowledge of the vision behind her for the moment and opened her eyes wide at him. "I don't recall when I said I would tell you every little thing that went on inside my head. I sure don't remember you bargaining for it."

He looked infuriated and unpredictable and actually a little evil, and there it was; she tumbled head over heels in love with him for the fourth time that day. She thought she would really love to spend whatever time she had in this life, tumbling head over heels every time she looked into his eyes and fell into forever. Always loving, always falling.

"I will get it out of you," he growled, so very softly over the heads of the tired, sleeping babies.

"Wow, you really can't stand a secret, can you? Are you going to spend Christmas with us? Teasing you about presents is going to be a *blast*."

He let go of her, slapped his hands on the tree trunk on

either side of her head and leaned over her. He looked fierce, like he might explode, except she could feel his emotions in truth. Sparring with each other had become a game they both loved to play. All of his real rage was directed elsewhere. "You are such an impudent and disrespectful human."

"Indeed, that is what you are wont to call me." She grinned at him. "See what I did there?"

One corner of his sexy mouth twitched. She stroked her presence along his, aligning with him softly.

His hands slipped on the tree trunk. He sank a fist into her hair and just held her, looking into her eyes with a steady promise. Her home might be in ruins, her life forever changed, and the sword might fall and cut them, but right in that moment, she had never felt so alive.

He let his fingers loosen and stroked down the back of her neck as he turned his head. Then she heard voices. Katherine, John, their kids and the Djinn escort had arrived to take Chloe and Max safely away to Houston. Khalil gathered Chloe off Grace's lap. Using the cane, Grace levered herself to her feet.

Katherine had clearly been crying, and John, who had loved Petra and Niko too, was grieving and enraged all over again. They stared in grim, shocked silence at the ruined back of the house. When they collected the sleepy kids, they did so with a special tenderness. As John and Khalil carried the children to their minivan, Katherine squeezed Grace's hand so hard it hurt. "John told his boss he had a family emergency, and it's true. Don't worry about the kids, all right?"

"I won't." Grace squeezed her hand in return.

The older woman's eyes glittered. "Get their killers. Get all of them."

"I promise you, we will."

She walked around the house with Katherine and gave her a fierce hug good-bye. Then she stood beside Khalil and watched them drive away with the last of her family and with four Djinn as invisible guards.

That was when Khalil released his iron grip on his temper, and his rage whipped the air in a vicious whirlwind.

He turned to her, his face stern and deadly, and she knew what would happen if he sent his renegade angel's voice ringing through the sky in a call to war. She had seen it in the vision as one of the possible futures. It would bring the sword down on them.

He had so very many connections. His call would be answered. Djinn would appear like meteorites that slammed into the ground to became tall, shining figures. Tens of Djinn, then scores, then hundreds. Their numbers would be dotted with a few rare figures that shone with a radiance that was especially piercing. She had recognized one of them.

Soren, the Elder tribunal Councillor for the Demonkind and a first-generation Djinn.

That would be the beginning of the end for her and Khalil. Soren would slash the fragile hair from which the sword hung. And the sword would fall and slice them apart. If they were to have a chance at any time together, Khalil couldn't send out that call.

His Power compressed in readiness. She grabbed his arm. "*No!* You mustn't. Khalil, please don't."

He looked down at her, his expression hard, as the wind howled around them. "Tell me one reason why I should not."

She projected all the urgency and conviction she could into her voice, because she could tell his attention was already slipping away from her.

"Because if you do that, we may never see each other again after today."

═ TWENTY ═

He stared at her. If anything the howling wind worsened as his expression turned cold and remote. For a terrible moment she thought he had already slipped away emotionally and she really had lost him. She started howling inside a little bit, too.

Then he pivoted in a circle, spitting curses savagely. She watched him, her gut in a twist. He seemed to reach out and grasp his rampaging Power and haul it forcibly back under his control. She had to lean hard on the cane as her muscles shook.

She whispered to the quieting storm, "Thank you."

He spun back to her. "That is what you saw," he said. "Earlier."

Her attention dropped from his incandescent eyes. He held himself so tightly, the clenched muscles in his biceps twitched. She tried to speak in a way that might be calming to an adult, not to a small child. It wasn't something she was good at. "That's one of the things I saw, yes."

He inhaled, shuddered, and the maelstrom of energy pulled back into his body. "Okay," he said as he strode over to her. "What do you think we should do?"

She had just realized her car was no longer in the driveway. She cocked her head, looking around. The Honda was tilted on its driver's side several yards away, by the road. She wondered if the car would be drivable if they tilted it back over and added it to the list of things to do as Khalil joined her.

"We can't create an inter-demesne incident," she said. "If you call Djinn to help hunt down the people who did this, that's what would happen."

"The sanctuary law is an inter-demesne law," he snapped.

"Yes—*inter-demesne* law. Not Djinn law. No matter how tempting it is, don't send Djinn swarming all over Kentucky, because nobody will react well to that. We have to work with the witches' demesne. Offer help. This has to be justice, not revenge. We need to talk to Isalynn LeFevre. After that . . ." Her voice trailed away as visions threatened to take her over again, and she drifted, lost in a tangle of thought and shifting possibilities.

He gripped her shoulder. "After that, what?" he prompted, watching her with close attention.

Once again his firm touch anchored her back in her body. She gave him a grim smile. "We'll have to see where we are after that."

Suddenly Ebrahim stood right beside them. "The Oracle's life may still be in danger. I will go with you and help to protect her."

Khalil's eyebrows rose. "I will not allow anything to happen to her. But if you wish to add your presence, that is acceptable."

Grace had jerked back at the other Djinn's sudden appearance. "You've got to stop doing that!" she said to Ebrahim. "Pretend I'm surrounded by a ten-foot bubble, and you can only materialize outside it. Then *walk* toward me."

Ebrahim contemplated her, curiosity in his radiant gaze. He said finally, "As you wish."

Khalil asked her, "Are you ready?"

"Almost," she said.

She turned to face the house. It looked undisturbed from

the driveway, even peaceful. She had lived her whole life in that house. She had played jacks on the porch and kissed her first boyfriend at the front door. While she went to college, she had daydreamed about getting a place of her own one day. Once she had been excited at the thought of leaving home—but that excitement was with the understanding that home was always going to be there for her to come back to when she needed it.

With Khalil close behind her, she walked inside. The sight of the black ruin that had been the back of the house punched her. The blast had taken out not only the kitchen, but the portion of the second floor above it. That meant the bathroom and probably the back bedroom—her bedroom— was gone as well. The living room was not unscathed either. The force of the explosion had blown furniture across the room and broken lamps and picture frames.

She found her purse under the bookcase, which had been knocked over. Khalil lifted the bookcase so she could pull her purse out. She looked for the black, spiral-bound phone book and finally found it between the upended coffee table and a wall. Some pages were creased, some torn. Her grandmother had written some of those numbers. So had Petra. Grace smoothed the book shut, tucked it carefully in her purse and set it to one side.

Afterward she turned and stared at the remains of the kitchen table. Nausea roiled. She and the kids would have been sitting right there. Beside her, Khalil stood quietly with every appearance of patience, but his tall form felt compressed and dangerous.

A cyclone arrived in the middle of the chaotic living room. Grace recognized the Djinn. It was Ismat, wearing a male form, his arms wrapped around Therese from behind, one hand clapped over the witch's mouth. Therese's gaze darted around at the devastation. She appeared frozen in horror.

Ismat gave Khalil a fierce smile. "Therese is part of a secret coven that belongs to an anti–Elder Races political group."

"The Humanist Party," said Khalil. He sounded ice-cold. "They support Jaydon Guthrie."

"Yes. The coven is broken into three cells. Therese only knows the identities of the witches in her cell, like Brandon Miller. She might not have known why Miller wanted to discover if Isalynn LeFevre had contacted Grace, but she knows enough to have made some educated guesses."

Grace asked, "Which are?"

Ismat looked at her. "The coven's real target is Isalynn. Therese isn't clear on what the coven leader plans to do, other than remove Isalynn from power."

Grace started to shake. She had lost count of how many times she had lost her temper in the last twenty-four hours, and whoopsie-daisy, it was starting to skip out on her again. "How does this involve us?"

"The Oracle's prophesies are too unpredictable, too dangerous. All it would take is the right question or the right prophecy for everything the coven is working toward to be uncovered." Ismat's smile had disappeared, replaced with an expression of dark sympathy. "Therese knows how to do some interesting things with sympathetic magic," he said. "For example, if you made a poppet of a truck driver and timed things just right, you might be able to control his driving long enough on a rainy night to radically change his course. . . ."

When Ismat said "truck driver" a formless roar filled Grace's ears. She whispered, "Let go of her."

Ismat raised his hands immediately. The twin investigators formed on either side as he stepped back from Therese. Khalil moved behind Grace while Ebrahim joined the group. The two women stood in a circle made up of watchful, waiting Djinn.

Grace's heartbeat pounded in heavy, hard slugs. She gestured to her bad knee and said hoarsely, "You did this?"

Therese's Snow White beauty was gone. "You're going to take *their* word for it? They're so alien; they don't even have bodies."

"Your bigotry is not my issue," Grace said. *"Did you do this?"*

"It's not bigotry!" Therese said. She looked terrified and

ashen, her lips bloodless. "All the Elder Races occupy positions of power and prestige. Their lives are filled with a sense of entitlement. They have more Power, more money, more influence in government, and they live so long they get deeper entrenched into everything they touch!"

"I'm standing in the ashes of my own house," Grace spat. "Your political rhetoric doesn't have a hell of a lot of meaning to me at the moment."

Therese's voice picked up speed and desperation. "We're second-class citizens in our own country, Grace! You can't believe just anything they say—"

Grace screamed, *"Did you kill Petra and Niko?"*

Any composure Therese might have retained splintered. She screamed back, *"You bet I did, and I would do it again if I had to!"*

"Maybe it's time to start experimenting with my Power now," Grace said to Khalil, as her breathing turned ragged. She pulled all of her rage and pain together and threw the expulsion spell.

Therese flinched and gasped, but other than that, the spell seemed to have no effect on her. It did, however, slam into Ismat, who was standing just behind her. The spell threw him back against the wall. Ismat fell in an ungraceful sprawl on the ground then looked up at Grace, wild-eyed.

"Shit, I'm sorry," Grace said to him, as he climbed slowly to his feet. "That must only work on Djinn."

Khalil said, "I will teach you fighting spells."

"Fine, but for now, I know something else that's offensive," she said between her teeth. She strode up to Therese and ducked as the other woman swung wildly at her. Then she threw her full body weight into a roundhouse punch. The blow connected. Therese's head snapped back, and she dropped like a stone. Grace wiped her wet cheeks with the back of her throbbing hand as she looked at the woman sprawled in front of her. Khalil gripped her shoulders from behind. She turned to him and whispered, "Okay, maybe we can get a little bit of revenge."

"We will go to find Isalynn now," Khalil said. He looked

entirely merciless. "And we will hunt down all the others who did this."

"I will take this creature to the witches' sheriff's office," Ismat said as he reached down for Therese.

"Join us afterward," Khalil said.

"That will be my pleasure," Ismat told them.

One of the twins said, "We will continue the work here."

"Thank you," Grace said to them. She turned into Khalil's arms. He held her tightly. She leaned against him as the cyclone took her.

Her sense of their impending separation was growing. It settled as a heavy knot of dread in her middle.

She thought she had changed that. Instead that future felt closer.

What were they doing—or not doing—that brought them forward to that place?

Would Khalil *want* to say good-bye and leave? He had stopped earlier, when she had asked him. More than that, she could feel his emotions and the profound, fierce pull of desire he felt whenever he looked at her. She recognized the feeling. It was the same way she felt when she looked at him. She could never have enough time to assuage her hunger for him.

What had she missed? Why would that damn sword fall?

After a formless time, reality took shape around her again. The ground grew solid. Khalil held on to her arms as she gained her balance and looked around. Ebrahim took form beside them.

She had known Isalynn lived in Indian Hills, an affluent neighborhood of Louisville, but she had personally never been to the house. They had arrived in front of a spacious two-story colonial brick home, highlighted beautifully by the afternoon sun and positioned attractively on a large land-scaped plot of land. A Lexus and an Acura sat in the drive-way, while a more humble, older model Ford Focus was parked in a space beside the garage.

This house did not glow with Power, as most witches' homes did. Perhaps Isalynn practiced her craft away from her house, but Grace suspected it was more likely that the

Head of the witches was simply that adept at containing the evidence of her Power.

The front door opened as Grace and the two Djinn approached the house. The Head herself stood in the doorway, dressed casually in slacks, sandals, simple gold jewelry and a red blouse. She was striking even from a distance, with her long, strong body and bold, sensual features and rich, cocoa skin. A sharp intelligence glittered in her eyes. She was joined in the doorway by an older Hispanic woman, along with a lanky teenage boy whose features and expression identified him as Isalynn's son.

Isalynn's frown deepened as she looked hard at the two Djinn and at Grace's grass- and dirt-stained appearance. "I felt your arrival," Isalynn said to the Djinn. She turned her attention to Grace. "And I see that something has happened. Please, come inside."

Grace stepped into a large, gracefully proportioned foyer, followed closely by Khalil and Ebrahim. Although the interior was as attractive and peaceful as the exterior, neither Djinn relaxed his vigilance.

Isalynn led the way through the house, her demeanor calm and composed. "You will have to excuse us, Malcolm," she said to the teenager. "Judith, please bring iced tea to the sunroom. After that, you may leave for the day."

Judith nodded, and both she and Malcolm disappeared.

They reached the back and stepped inside a sunroom that was as wide as the house. Comfortable furniture was interspersed with potted plants. A laptop, files and a cell phone were set at one end of a table. Books and magazines filled the surface of a side table by a cushioned chair and ottoman. The sunroom looked over a large backyard with several strategically placed flower and herb beds, and a tennis court half hidden by bushes.

"This is my sanctuary," said Isalynn, as if they were simply visiting. "I work as much as I can back here when I am at home. Please sit."

Grace tried to hide how her hands shook as she took a seat.

The separation. It was almost here, almost final.

Was it death? Her death? *His?*

Her mind raced frantically through options of what to do, how to avoid it. She must not have hidden it very well, for Khalil watched her sharply, his face hard, and he took a seat as near to her as he could. Ebrahim continued to stand.

The simple truth of the matter was, Grace realized, she couldn't avoid the separation if it was something Khalil chose.

"Now then," said one of the most Powerful legislators in the country. "What has happened?"

Grace said, "A secret coven rigged my house to explode. My sister and her husband's murderer is being taken to the witches' sheriff's office. And we think you're in danger."

At that, despite all her best efforts, the whole affair became an inter-demesne incident after all.

Isalynn sat, still as stone, her face chiseled. "Tell me everything," she said, and so they did. She interrupted just once, to pick up her cell phone, punch in a number and say, "Thomas, the Oracle has been attacked. Send a security detail to my house and an investigative team to Grace's. You had better notify the Elder tribunal and the other demesnes as well. We're on highest alert."

The whole time, Khalil seethed. The anger that had built up, the fear he had felt when Grace had pulled so hard on their connection, all boiled underneath the surface of his skin. He seethed, fighting to hold it in, to control the urge to race after the bastards who dared to hurt Grace and the children.

Wait, she said. Justice, not revenge, she said. Because of some mysterious reason, some vision she saw that she wouldn't tell him.

That was when he realized he was angry at her too. She made him feel things he had never felt before, a desire so keen it sliced at the heart of him and a need that bound him like chains, when he had never been bound before by anything. By anyone.

He *would not* be bound.

He had done as she asked. Now it was time to do as he wanted.

"I want Brandon Miller," Khalil said to Isalynn.

"What a coincidence, so do I," said Isalynn with a sharp smile. "I want every one of those coven members. By all means, go after him—as long as you bring him to me alive."

He returned the witch's smile, his own flicking out like a switchblade. Alive did not mean happy or comfortable. "As you wish," he told her. He glared at Grace as he let his form dissipate to smoke. Nothing she could say would hold him back this time.

Grace said nothing. She sat without moving. Her face was colorless, her wide eyes filled with a dark sea as she gazed at internal vistas visible only to her.

He hesitated. "Grace."

Her gaze snapped into focus. "I will not be the reason you are trapped. Leave."

Ebrahim was staring at him coldly. For some reason the other Djinn was not happy with him, but he was not at all interested in that. Ebrahim had already said he would stay to protect Grace, and Isalynn's security detail would arrive momentarily. Khalil blew out of the house and arrowed through the sky, furiously eager for the hunt and already planning what he would do.

He would burn that cursed barn and scatter the ashes and trigger every trap on the property to do the maximum damage possible. No matter how much Power Brandon Miller had or where he might turn, there was nowhere for him to hide now that Khalil was after him. By the time Miller saw justice, he would be screaming for it.

Khalil had reached south of Louisville before he pulled to a stop.

I will not be the reason you are trapped.

Why did Grace say that?

He curled around on himself in the deep gold afternoon sunlight, thinking hard. She might have been able to sense his emotions, just as he could sense hers, but she could not have known what he had been thinking. Not that he had been thinking rationally. He had been reacting to his own fear and mentally lashing out at everything, including her. He had never been so afraid, and he loathed that feeling.

But Grace had never once tried to trap him. If anything she had tried to shove him away. After that day when he had felt wrapped in invisible chains, she had told him to go. Last night at the bar, instead of trying to stop him or control what he did, she had chosen instead to simply leave.

So she hadn't said it because of what he thought or felt.

She had said it because of what she had seen.

She was protecting him from something again.

Like she had protected him when Phaedra had come to see her. Twice. Even after she had promised him something else entirely.

Suddenly neither justice nor revenge mattered anymore. Swearing, he roared back toward Indian Hills. When he reached Isalynn's house, he plummeted.

Ebrahim shot up to meet him. Khalil veered to avoid Ebrahim—and the other Djinn veered with him. They collided in midair with a concussion that shook the ground beneath them. Khalil twisted to disentangle himself. Ebrahim held on to him. He fought to get free, roaring furiously, *What are you doing?*

What I bargained with the Oracle to do, said Ebrahim.

Grace had bargained with Ebrahim to keep him away? Rage detonated. Khalil snarled, *You can't win in a fight against me. BACK OFF!*

I have to try, said Ebrahim, who hung on grimly. *Because you can't win in a fight against your father.*

Soren. Khalil spun, sharpening his senses.

Isalynn's backyard zoomed into focus where Soren and Grace stood facing each other. They were alone, Isalynn somewhere inside the house. Soren's Powerful white blaze of a presence all but obliterated the image of his physical form. In contrast, Grace's figure was slight and excruciatingly fragile. She looked tired and dirty, and she listed slightly as she leaned on her cane.

Soren glanced up and Grace did too, both clearly aware of Khalil's presence.

"Young Oracle, you are playing a game you are much too young to play," said Soren in a gentle voice.

"I wasn't aware that I was playing a game," Grace said.

"You cannot keep me from my son." The gentler Soren sounded, the more dangerous he became. "And it is beyond foolish for you to try."

"I know." She tilted her untidy head. "Once the explosion occurred, I kept seeing you in visions, and I couldn't get you out of my head. Every course of action we took. All those pathways to possible futures. They all led to you. I kept trying to think my way out of this. Then I realized I couldn't."

Khalil felt crazed. Soren was the head of the Elder tribunal and one of the strongest Djinn in the world. He could break Grace with a single flex of his Power, and if he deemed it necessary, he would do so without hesitation.

Let go of me now, he hissed at Ebrahim. *Or I will tear you apart.*

I have a message from Grace, Ebrahim said. *She thought you might return quickly.*

That was possibly the only thing the other Djinn could have said that would make Khalil pause. He snarled, *Speak fast.*

She asked for us both to trust her, no matter what she said, Ebrahim told him. *And she said when you came, you should call the Djinn now.*

What was she doing?

Khalil did trust her. Her temper was too rash, and she said foolish things, and she had terrible impulse control, which he was going to talk to her about just as soon as they were alone again. But she was wise beyond her years, compassionate and strong too.

And when she loved, she loved with all of her fiery heart. That was a warm, giving place to be, surrounded by her love, the only place he wanted to be. When he realized it, all the chains and sense of restriction were gone.

All right, he said.

Ebrahim let him go.

Khalil pulled connections as he dove to earth. He plunged to Grace and wrapped himself around her so tightly he was a dense, dark, protective veil that covered her from head to foot. As he surrounded her, he could feel her exhaustion and the determination that stiffened her spine.

I love you too, he said to her. Joy pierced her, bright as the morning. It beamed out to him. He took it and doubled it back to her.

Ebrahim joined them, standing battle tense at their side. The other Djinn Khalil summoned began to appear until they filled the entire yard.

Soren took a long, thoughtful look around. Then he turned back to Khalil, ignoring Grace. Soren's expression was pained. He said, "I heard your attachment to the human had grown too strong."

"According to whom?" Khalil growled. "My attachment to Grace is nobody's business but ours."

"She will pass, Khalil," said Soren. "They always pass. It's inevitable, and it happens too quickly, and while that is a shame, we cannot grow to love them too much."

"That is your definition. Those are your limits," Khalil told him. "They are not mine."

"Pay attention," Grace said. She raised her voice. "All of you, pay attention. I am the last Oracle. There will not be another. The Power will not pass on to my niece or to some other female descendant when I die. However long or short my life might end up being, this is it. For the people in your Houses who are damaged, I am their one chance at healing. I am *your* one chance at healing, if you become too damaged to heal on your own. Do you understand? I can't guarantee anybody's healing—but I know you won't get another shot when I'm gone."

Ebrahim said, "The Oracle speaks the truth. She healed Khalil's daughter Phaedra earlier today."

A profound silence filled the yard. The gaze of every Djinn locked on her.

"Back to you," Grace said to Soren. "I offer you a bargain."

"Which is what?" Soren bit out the words.

"I will do everything in my Power to heal any Djinn who comes to me," Grace said. "No reservations, no matter when, no matter what the issue, I will give to each person everything I possibly can."

"What do you require in return?" asked Soren. He had frozen, a pillar of white ice.

"I want the life of your son," said Grace. "I want Khalil, free and clear. I want him to live in whatever manner he may choose, whether that is with me or not. Whether he chooses to fall into flesh and live a mortal life, or not— Yes, I've seen that is a possibility. I've seen other possibilities too, because nothing in the future is fixed. You will not imprison him. You will not try to stop his choices in any way, because if you do, I will never help any of you." She turned, looking at the surrounding Djinn. "Never. I swear that on my life."

Everything in Khalil leaped at her words, but he never took his attention away from the real threat, his father. The rage on Soren's face was blinding. "That isn't a bargain, that's blackmail."

Khalil flattened farther around Grace, tightening his Power in case of a blow. She said, "Call it what you like."

"You're talking about his death!"

"I'm talking about protecting his right to choose whatever he wants."

"We do not sacrifice our people!" Soren took a step toward her, his hands clenched.

Every other Djinn moved forward too, their attention locking on Soren. Ebrahim stepped in front of Grace and Khalil. It was an entirely brave thing to do and, if Soren chose to strike, entirely suicidal.

Khalil dared to loosen his hold on Grace enough to rise over Ebrahim's head and face his father. "It appears that no one else agrees with you," he said. "Enough of this. You will not hamper me in any way from doing what I want with my life. Strike the bargain."

Soren met his gaze. "Khalil, don't."

"Strike it." He didn't waver, despite the look in Soren's

eyes. Soren in pain was more dangerous than ever, but Khalil also knew that once Soren agreed to the bargain, the older Djinn would be honor bound to keep it. "And for the love of gods, keep peace between us."

Soren looked around at his people, and his expression grew bitter. "Yes," said Soren. Then he vanished.

Grace sagged. Quicker than thought, Khalil took form and snatched her close, and as he counted her precious breaths, he knew that every other Djinn would be doing so as well, watching and helping her in any way they could.

"You've just gained an entire race of bodyguards, nurse-maids and babysitters," he said in her hair.

She clutched him so tightly her arms shook. "Nobody babysits the children until they've read at least three child-rearing books." She whispered, "Even though all the possible futures kept shifting, I kept seeing you in some kind of prison. I kept trying to figure out how to stop it from happening."

She was trembling all over. He tilted her face up and kissed her gently, savoring her soft lips and the core of steel inside her and how she kissed him back.

"I am so proud of you," he said from the back of his throat. "And don't think I've forgotten you never called me when Phaedra showed up, even after you promised. I am still pissed all to hell at you for that."

"Hold on a sec," she murmured. "I might need to gasp and bite my nails."

"Gracie," he said between his teeth.

She buried her face in his chest. "I know, you're never going to let me forget it."

"That's right." He cupped the back of her head and held her. "I have to ask. Are all the Oracle's moons going to be like this?"

She pulled back and stared at him. She looked horrified. "Gods, I don't know. They'd better not be."

⇒ TWENTY-ONE ⇐

After the confrontation with Soren, Khalil had lost his taste for the hunt. Not that it mattered. Once the coven had lost their ability to operate in secrecy, it became a bug hunt. Twelve bugs after Therese were apprehended, and the biggest cockroach was Brandon Miller. Jaydon Guthrie, for whom so many crimes had been committed, had known nothing of the attacks. By Monday evening, all the conspirators were in custody.

Khalil was glad, for Grace's sake, that not all twelve of the people who had showed up for her work day had been involved in sabotaging her house. All but Olivia had been part of the Humanist Party, but only four on Saturday had been part of the secret coven. The other eight had just been unpleasant.

"Somehow that's a bit easier to take, knowing that not everybody on Saturday had been there all day, conspiring to kill me and the kids," Grace said to Khalil with a shudder.

"The ones who did are crazy," Khalil said. "Just like pariahs."

Once the conspiracy had been uncovered, all eight from the workday who were innocent, along with Jaydon Guthrie and many others, called or e-mailed to express their outrage

and grief at what had happened and to apologize on behalf
of the Humanist Party.

One of them was the babysitter, Janice. When Grace
recognized the number on her new cell phone, she almost
didn't pick up, but then she decided otherwise and ended up
talking with the older woman for fifteen minutes. "I have
certain beliefs," Janice said, her voice thick with emotion.
"We all believe in something. But what that coven did
was monstrous, and even though I knew nothing about it, it
hurts my heart to think I had any connection at all with
them."

"I guess it's hard to understand terrorism in any form,"
Grace said. "We just have to learn how to move on now."

Isalynn insisted Grace, and by extension Khalil, stay at
her house for the foreseeable future. Security had swarmed
Isalynn's neighborhood, and her house was large and comfortable. Grace agreed, and that was the last decision either
she or Khalil had to make Sunday evening. After an early
supper, a hot shower and the comfort of soft, old clothes that
one of the Djinn investigators brought, Grace couldn't keep
her eyes open. While Khalil joined her for the companionship, even he was tired enough to rest, drifting and thought-
less throughout the dark night.

Once the authorities confirmed that all twelve conspirators were in custody on Monday, the first thing Grace did
was call Katherine. Even though nobody believed the children were still in danger, Katherine and John agreed to stay
with them in Houston for the week, so that Grace and Khalil
could deal with the aftermath of the house fire.

There were so many details to attend to. The house insurance. Grace also remembered what the ghost of the trucker
had said about his accident insurance. An investigation into
that was set in motion.

Khalil had called it—there was no lack of willing help on
hand. A half-dozen Djinn were available at any given time.
With a few determined Djinn pursuing the issue, they discovered that the trucker had not let his insurance lapse, as
the insurance company had at first claimed. Instead, the

company had made a mistake in processing his payment. Turned out, the insurance company owed his widow and Grace a settlement. It wouldn't be a fortune, but it would be a substantial addition to Grace's growing resources.

In the meantime, while Chloe and Max were in Houston, Khalil arranged for a leave of absence from his duties, and he and Grace tackled the job of sorting out what might be salvageable from the house. They saved some family mementos, photographs, all the historical papers and journals from previous Oracles that were stored in trunks in the attic, the files and computer, some of the children's clothes and toys and the summer clothes Grace had stored in the office.

She chose to keep the rocking chair the children had been rocked in, even though it had been damaged. She wanted to try to repair it, because her grandmother had rocked her and Petra in it as well. Khalil wanted to keep the old leather armchair he sat in to read to the children. It was one of the few physical things he had ever grown attached to. There was nothing else worth salvaging. The structure itself would take an extensive effort to repair, more effort and resources than the house was worth.

On Wednesday afternoon, they sat for a while on the porch, listened to the wind in the trees, and Grace reminisced. Khalil asked her questions, fascinated by the intimate glimpse into her past. He held her as she wiped her face.

"It's kind of a relief," she said. "I feel so guilty about that. And it hurts too."

He could understand it, at least more than he would have been able to before he had met her. This house was where he had stood, looked out the screen door and first felt that magical, precious something.

"You're losing another huge piece of your past," he said.

Grace nodded. "And I don't have to fix the roof," she said.

He laughed. She put her hands over her face and laughed with him and cried at the same time.

When they checked the rest of the property, they discovered the cavern had completely collapsed. Out of curiosity more than anything else, Khalil let go of his physical form and flowed around the crumbled nooks and crannies of the tunnel to the wreckage below. There weren't any pockets of space large enough for a man to stand up in, just shreds of old Power and broken rock. When he emerged, Grace held the one thing from the cabinets important enough to keep, the Oracle's mask, wrapped in cloth.

Meanwhile, the Djinn watched Grace and waited. The numbers of Djinn too damaged to heal themselves were relatively low, but those involved profound injuries. Khalil warned them off, telling them Grace needed time to get her basic needs met and to arrange for the children's welfare before she could start spending energy on trying to heal damaged Djinn.

By Thursday, Grace herself brought the issue up. "I can't stand it any longer," she said to Khalil. "Ebrahim is driving me crazy. I don't think he's stopped working once since he showed up on Sunday."

Khalil rubbed the back of his neck. He, Ebrahim and three other Djinn had been demolishing the house, while Grace watched. Khalil had taken a break for a few moments to join her. "I will talk with him again," Khalil said. "I will tell him he must leave until you are ready."

"No," Grace told him. The day was sweltering, and Grace wore another set of loose, dark shorts made of a soft jersey material that Khalil liked, along with a tank top and sandals. The sun had kissed her skin with color. With her red-gold hair and coppery tan, she looked like a slender, vibrant flame. He approved. "I can't stand that either—the not knowing, I mean. We need to find out if Phaedra was a fluke and whether or not I really can help any other Djinn to heal."

He sighed. "Agreed. But after you try with Ebrahim's mate, you will see no one else for at least two weeks. Katherine and John will be returning with the children on Sunday, and we must still arrange for a place for you—for us—to stay."

Grace looked at him sidelong. The corners of her lips curved upward when he said "us," but otherwise, she made no comment about that. Instead, she muttered, "That's awfully bossy of you."

By then he read her expressions very well indeed. He took note that she looked relieved, not offended. He called to Ebrahim, who winged toward them immediately. Khalil told him, "Get Atefeh."

After one startled look at Grace, Ebrahim whirled away. Khalil watched as Grace braced herself visibly. He laid a hand against her back, and she glanced at him gratefully.

Then Ebrahim returned with Atefeh, his mate. Atefeh was so damaged, she could not create a physical form for herself, and she struggled constantly to soak in enough nourishment. She hovered in front of Grace, her presence dull and skewed.

One by one, the other Djinn quit working on the house demolition and joined them. Others appeared silently. Grace glared at the new arrivals, but she didn't say anything, and they didn't leave. She turned her attention back to Atefeh, and her expression smoothed, her gaze turning inward. Khalil felt the dark Power rise in her. Silence fell.

He didn't know what happened next. He sensed movement that occurred somehow just beyond his awareness.

Atefeh flexed with a gasp and fell forward. Thinking the Djinn meant to attack or overwhelm Grace, Khalil lunged to pull Grace away and wrap her in a tight protection. But Atefeh was focused on something else, something only she and Grace seemed able to see. Atefeh keened, a sharp sound filled with pain. Her mate Ebrahim emitted a strangled groan in response, his face agonized as he watched her struggle.

Let me go! Grace said to Khalil. She shoved him with her Power, and he peeled away. She stepped toward the struggling Djinn. "Don't give up! Don't try to grab her. Stand still and let her come to you. Try to open up—she has to come inside you."

Who was Grace talking about? Khalil couldn't sense anybody but Grace and Atefeh.

Afeteh's presence shuddered and rippled and suddenly flared with brilliance. For a moment, an ebony-skinned woman stood in front of them, eyes incandescent with triumph. She turned to give her mate a fierce smile. Ebrahim lost his physical form and became a piercing white light filled with joy.

All the other Djinn shouted until the sound rang through the open space.

Then Atefeh's smile faded. A moment later, her physical form did too. *I can't hold it any longer*, the Djinn said faintly. *I must rest.*

Ebrahim's fierce white light twined with Atefeh. He said to Grace, *Thank you.*

You are both welcome, Grace said, even as the two Djinn faded away.

Grace turned to Khalil, beaming. He laughed, caught her up and spun her around. Then he stood and held her tightly.

My miracle, he thought. My Grace.

By Friday, Khalil couldn't stand it any longer. "I am putting my foot down," he told Grace at Isalynn's breakfast table. Even though they had spent the last several nights at Isalynn's, they never saw anyone but Judith, who took care of the house. Isalynn and her son, Malcolm, had traveled to Washington, but Isalynn had made it very clear before she left that they were to stay for as long as they needed.

Grace had dressed in capri pants and a sleeveless shirt that buttoned down the front. Khalil chose to form jeans and a T-shirt again. He was growing to like that kind of outfit. Grace rested her chin in her hands as she regarded him. She said, "Putting your foot down?"

"I can have feet when I choose to."

She chuckled. "It's a very human saying."

"Indeed." He folded the newspaper he had been reading and set it aside.

"What are you putting your foot down about now?"

"You make me sound dictatorial," he said. "Finish your breakfast."

She raised her eyebrows pointedly. He smiled at her. He adored his sharp, funny, hotheaded human. "I did not know you had such strong opinions about breakfast." She finished her toast in a few bites. "I ate that because I wanted to."

"No doubt you did," he replied. "You have worked yourself into exhaustion every single day of this week." Each night she had, in fact, barely been able to shower and eat a few bites of supper before falling into bed. He always joined her, sometimes in physical form, sometimes wrapped around her in an invisible embrace. "I am putting my foot down about this evening. Our activities today will be light, and we will quit early."

The sparkle of humor left her face. "The children are coming home on Sunday. I miss them and want them back, but there's still so much to do."

"I miss the children too," he said. "But not everything needs to be done this week. Murderers have been arrested; insurance claims have been filed and investigated; we have gone through all of your possessions, sorted documents, put the salvageable things in storage and taken furniture and your car in for repairs—although I still think you should sell your car. We have demolished your house, established a guarantee of freedom for myself, and you have healed two Djinn. *Enough*, Grace."

"I haven't even started looking at rental properties for a place to stay," she said. Her expression grew shadowed. "We have to have some place to keep the kids when they return. Furniture shopping. Clothes and toys for the kids. Hell, clothes for me. Kitchen supplies, pots and pans, dishes. A coffeemaker. Coffee for the coffeemaker. Cups to put the coffee in."

Speaking of which, he finished his coffee. "Do not trouble yourself in the slightest about any of that. I have arranged everything."

Her posture shifted and she bent her head. Instead of resting her chin in the heel of her hands, she now rested her forehead in them. Looking down at the table, she said, "Khalil, these are not the kind of things people arrange and then tell somebody about them afterward."

"I do," he said. Her head came up, and her lovely eyes

flashed fire. While he most definitely approved of the fire, he took note of the stress that caused it. "At least temporarily. I have arranged for an extended leave from the Demonkind legislature. I can make up the rest of my two-year commitment afterward. We are going on vacation, Grace. The only thing you need to decide is where."

Her expression went blank with amazement. It amused him, but it also twisted him up a little. "But—but . . ."

"No 'buts.' Humans are always in such a hurry." He took her hands and looked deeply into her turbulent eyes. "There is more than enough money. You now have resources in your bank account, and the Djinn will never allow you to suffer a lack of funds. I have funds too, quite a lot, last time I looked. There is more than enough time. There is nowhere you need to go, and nothing you need to do right now unless you choose to do it. You and the children are safe, Grace. You are safe now."

Her gaze flooded with moisture. She looked stricken.

He stroked her hair. "You did not even need to decide what to do with all of your possessions right away or what to do with the house. It just seemed to help you come to terms with everything that happened. I'm only sorry there was so much loss."

"Vacation," she said slowly, as if it was a word in a foreign language.

"Yes. You have three choices. We can join the children at the Four Seasons in Houston. We can check into a hotel suite here in Louisville. I do not recommend that one, since I do not believe you will actually relax if we stay local."

She wiped her cheeks. "What is the third option?"

"Carling and Rune called yesterday evening," he said. "You were so sound asleep, you didn't even hear your new cell phone ring, so I answered it. They have leased a beach house just outside of Miami, with the option to buy. Three bedrooms, two baths, a family room, a living room, a fenced-in yard and a deck that faces the ocean. It's furnished, but Carling said the furniture can be removed if you want your own. They have invited us to use it for as long as we like."

"Beach," she said blankly.

Of all the strange fortune that had befallen her, it appeared that good fortune was what brought her to a total halt. He said in a gentle voice, "Beach. If you like."

"You would come with us?" She searched his gaze.

"I will always come with you," he said simply.

"Where would you like to go?" she asked. "Is there some place you would enjoy?"

He smiled. He liked Paris in the first blush of early morning and snowfall in St. Petersburg on a winter's night. He liked the hot desert winds of North Africa and the wild open spaces of the Colorado and Mohave deserts, where the Djinn went to dance in the sun-drenched air. He adored following the plunge of water over Niagara Falls and swimming along the serpentine twists of the Amazon River, and he loved contemplating the top of the world along the peaks of the Himalayas, where the air grew thin and riotous infinity lay everywhere.

But it would not do to overwhelm her too soon. He told her, "I like the sun."

She frowned as she studied him. "If we go to Houston, you may not get a real vacation either."

He admitted, "That is a good point."

Her frown didn't ease. She said slowly, "I would love to take a vacation, but I also made a promise to a couple of people that I would help them."

His eyebrows rose. "Who are they?"

"You know the petitioners that came the day Therese babysat? They weren't able to go through with the consultation. They weren't ready, and the cavern made them uncomfortable. I told them I would be available if they wanted to return." Grace rubbed the back of her neck. "I need to keep my promise to them. I *want* to keep my promise."

"This is not an issue," Khalil said. "We will get in touch with them. Whenever they are ready, we'll get a babysitter, and I can transport you to wherever these people live. That's assuming you can do without a cavern."

"I really think I can," she said. She met his gaze and

smiled. "I like the thought of being able to make a house call. If, that is, they are open to it too."

They would discover that Grace could indeed make house calls. She had practiced more with Khalil by the time Don and Margie e-mailed her to ask if she might be available for another consultation. Ismat became the children's first Djinn babysitter, and Khalil transported Grace to Margie's home in southern Indiana. Once there Khalil kept a tactful silence and moved into the background as Grace interacted with the middle-aged siblings. Margie invited them into her comfortable home, and they sat at the kitchen table and talked over coffee until both Don and Margie had relaxed. When Grace finally channeled the ghost of Don and Margie's father, it felt like a natural, gentle progression, and the session was quite healing.

She was a natural, Khalil thought, pride swelling as he watched her with the two humans. She was warm and compassionate, and she knew how to listen. More than that, she handled the Oracle's Power with an assurance that had to be a comfort to the others. She had not only taken the Oracle's Power for her own, but now she claimed the position for her own as well.

But all of that came later. For now, Khalil felt a deep satisfaction as he regarded his Grace, who knew the importance of keeping her word, taking care of those who were her responsibility, and holding to her side of a bargain. No matter what.

He told her, "We appear to have narrowed down our choices of where we will go."

A grin broke over her face. "We're going to Florida?"

"Indeed, we must be." He knew that in Florida, Carling and Rune would try to convince them to stay, but he was not at all interested in that. He did not have a preference for a geographical focus and was happy to abide wherever Grace might wish. He tapped her on the nose. "But we will not leave for Florida until the children arrive on Sunday, so for today, I have decided we shall go on our second date."

Her expression froze. "We will?"

"In fact, I know exactly what we shall do."

Her eyes widened. "You do?"

He contemplated her with satisfaction. "Yes, I will take you somewhere special."

She said cautiously, "What do I have to do to get ready?"

"Whatever you like." He paused. "Dress casually."

"All right . . . when do you want to leave?"

His satisfaction dissipated. Really, she did not look as excited as he had expected about the prospect of this date. "Whenever you like."

She looked down at herself, then back up at him. "Maybe we should just go and get it over with."

He scowled. "Fine."

He stood and held his hand out to her. She stood as well, more slowly, and walked into his arms, and they blew away.

Away from Louisville. Away from Kentucky. Away from the Northern Hemisphere.

From Earth.

Khalil had studied Grace's needs and practiced, until he was confident he could keep her wrapped protectively in the right pressurized temperature, provide her with the right UV filter, and the perfect air for her to breathe.

He brought her to the moon with a flourish. The near side facing the Earth, not the far side, since he thought they should take the trip in stages. She turned in his arms to look around at where he brought them.

"W-wha . . ."

"I told you it would be somewhere special," he said, in the invisible bubble he had created for them.

She screamed.

He smiled smugly. Yes, this second date destination was worthy of a happy scream. Very few humans had walked on the moon. He knew how rare this opportunity was. Surely it should make up for what had happened on their first date.

Grace kept screaming. She turned and clawed at him. *"Oh, my God. Oh. My. God. OHMYGOD!"*

His smile vanished. He tried to get hold of her in a gentle but tight grip. That was more difficult than he expected. She seemed to have acquired a half-dozen arms and legs. He informed her, "You may stop making noise any time now."

Somehow she had climbed halfway up his body before he managed to grasp her waist. He plucked her off and set her on her feet. She started to climb up his body again.

"Are you having fun?" he asked suspiciously.

"We're on the fucking moon!" she shouted. *"There's nothing here!"*

He stared at her. "I don't think you're having fun."

"No air!"

He shook his head. "Think about that logically. Could you have possibly said those words if there truly was no air? Of course there's no air or atmosphere outside this bubble—"

"Ofcoursethere'snofuckingairhereorfuckingatmosphere onthefuckinggoddamnMOONyouGODDAMNFUCK- INGCRAZYMORONICDJINN . . ."

"Grace," he roared in her face.

He put so much Power into his shout, her screaming snapped into silence. Her breathing hitched as she stared at him. "Look at me," he said. "Keep looking only at me. There is no danger. You're perfectly safe. I've got you. I've always got you. You're mine. I will never let go. I will always pro- tect you. You are my life now. Do you understand anything I'm saying?"

Her breathing hitched again. "I'm breathing," she whis- pered. "On the moon."

"Don't look away!" he ordered, as her eyes started to slide sideways. Her gaze snapped back to his. "I'm sorry I scared you. I wanted to show you somewhere special that I love to go. I thought you would love it here too. Do you need to leave?"

"I d-don't know, give me minute," she said faintly. "I'm having some serious instinct issues. You always make me feel like Darrin, and I'm *not* Darrin, dammit."

"All right." He rubbed her arms. "But I don't know what any of that means."

"Soon as you said 'date,' I knew something calamitous was going to happen. You are never, ever—*ever*—going to surprise me like this again, or I swear, I will throw my expulsion spell on your ass for a week." Hitch. "And I mean hard, Khalil."

"Never again. I promise you, I am never doing anything like this again. Just tell me if we should leave."

"Hold on."

He watched, bemused, as she took several deep breaths, as if she were about to dive under water. Then she slowly, slowly turned. He pulled her back against his chest, wrapping his arms tightly around her. Her whole body was shaking.

"Oh, my fucking God, I'm on the moon," she said. After all of that, she sounded almost conversational. "No helmet. No spacesuit. No oxygen tank. Just you."

Khalil had learned caution the bitter way. He asked carefully, "Is that a good thing?"

"It's the most." She shook her head and sucked in more air, gripping onto his forearms as they crossed her chest. Tilting her head, she looked up at the immense, graceful orb that was Earth. "It's the most gloriously insane thing I've ever seen. You crazy Djinn."

Well. That had to count for something, didn't it?

He rested his chin on the top of her head with a deep sigh. This whole dating thing wore him to a frazzle.

Grace could only take a few more minutes on the moon. Then after such an extreme adrenaline rush, she felt as if someone smacked her on the back of the head with a two-by-four.

He was speaking, calmly, in that gorgeous pure voice of his, while he rubbed her arms with his hot, big hands. "The far side is pretty spectacular too."

"I will go anywhere with you, anywhere at all," she said. "With a little warning. And in increments. But right now we've got to leave."

"As you wish."

She turned in his arms, clutching his waist as the cyclone took her.

Khalil rematerialized them in the guest bedroom they were using at Isalynn's house. As soon as the ground had firmed underneath her feet, Grace turned away, took three dizzy steps and collapsed on the bed.

"Kiiiick in the head," she said into a pillow.

The bedsprings creaked as Khalil sat beside her. He rubbed one of her legs.

"I love you like crazy," he whispered.

Her breath caught. Like crazy. Yes, that was how she felt too. Crazy outside of herself, like when they had made love and she literally left her body. She reached behind to grip his hand. His long fingers closed over hers, hard.

"What you did with my father—that was bloody magnificent, Grace. Few creatures have been able to face Soren down like that and win."

"I did have something of an inside scoop," she said. "And forty or fifty Djinn to back me up."

For a while on Sunday, the visions of possible futures had never left her. Then they had passed as the Oracle's moon had passed, leaving her anchored where she belonged, in the here and now. But she still remembered some of those possibilities, glittering strange horizons she hardly dared to contemplate.

She sensed him leaning over her, an impression of bulk and strength. Something happened, a tight compression of Power, like when he had pulled all of his rage into himself, only this compression was deeper and harder, a diamond being pressed out of thin air.

Frowning, she lifted herself up on her elbows and started to turn over. He pressed a kiss to her shoulder blade. The sensation lingered on her skin after he lifted his mouth away.

"Promise me something," she said.

He traced the hairline at the nape of her neck lightly with the tip of one finger. "Anything you like."

"Don't change," she said. "Not permanently, not without talking to me first."

His finger stilled. He said nothing.

This time she did turn onto her back.

While he was still dressed in the same T-shirt and jeans from that morning, he wore his human skin again, those regal, elegant features with the touch of beard along his lean jaw, and the trace of laugh lines at the corners of his muted eyes and unsmiling mouth. His long hair was loose, still shining and black, but indefinably different. She put a hand to his chest, and there was the blaze of his Power, hidden deeply inside his body like a gleaming pearl.

She reached up to touch those amazing laugh lines. He shuddered and closed his eyes, turning his face into her palm.

"Promise," she said. "Khalil, you have the ability to fall into flesh, but a goddess in a dream told me I can leave my body again if I want to badly enough."

His eyes flared open. He stared at her, tension in every line of his massive body. He put his hand around her throat, his thumb caressing the line of her jaw. "'What will a mortal do with an immortal Power?'" he breathed.

She lifted her shoulder and said awkwardly, "Well, it was just a dream. I don't know if it could really happen. We need to take time to experiment with all of this. All I know is I don't want to try to become something different from the kids while they're growing up, because they're never going to be able to change, and they deserve the best human life I can give them."

"They deserve you alive," Khalil said. "Gods—if you could change, you would be stronger, harder to kill." He swallowed hard. "You're all so fragile."

"That's part of what being human is," she said. "We're pretty damn tough, too. Besides . . ." She smiled. "I'm perfectly safe, remember? I've got you. I've always got you."

"Please always stay mine," he whispered.

"Always."

She stroked her hand down his back, and he arched and shuddered. He reached behind him, bicep flexing, and grasped his T-shirt to pull it over his head.

Oh, my God, he had a sprinkle of dark hair on his chest.

She ran her palm over it. It was as silken as it looked. He stared at her in naked surprise, and there was the hunger again, washing over her in a sheet of flame.

"Take everything off," she hissed.

He arched away from her to tear off his jeans. She had meant to do the same; she really had. But the sight of Khalil's nude body as he flexed free of his clothing tore almost every coherent thought out of her mind.

Except two. The same—different—the same—they were like two sides of a coin flipping in midair. She saw her lover in every line of Khalil's body, but the newness of his more humanlike form made him almost a stranger. Silken black hair arrowed down his long stomach to his genitals and sprinkled long, muscle-corded thighs. His testicles had drawn up tight under a taut, large erection. She stared at the broad mushroom head and thick length of his beautiful penis.

He turned to her and growled in frustration. "You were supposed to take your clothes off too."

She gave him a stricken look and whimpered, "I forgot."

Laughter and affection creased his lean face before his expression turned sensual and wicked. "Do not trouble yourself in the slightest," he murmured. "I will help you."

He stretched his long body beside her and eased the buttons of her shirt open one by one. She could not stop staring at him everywhere. That cock. She took hold of the warm, hard length in both greedy hands.

A sound broke out of him, a short, sharp cry of shock, and he bowed over her hands almost as if she punched him. Worried, she started to draw back. He grabbed her wrists. "No!" he gritted. "That wasn't bad. That was because *it's so damned good.*"

She flexed her hands along the soft skin that covered his distended flesh. The pleasure of it shuddered through his entire body, and she wanted him so badly she could barely breathe.

Love you.

She gave into the feeling, gave into him. She arched her

back and wiggled haphazardly down the bed, until she reached his waist. Then she rolled toward him and pulled the thick tip of his penis into her mouth. A groan wrenched out of him. Every line of his body, everything she could sense of his presence, roared astonishment. His erection jerked in her mouth. She closed her eyes and felt his hands fist in her hair as she sucked him in.

Love you like crazy.

He pushed his hips, growling as she worked him. She lost herself in his touch, in his taste and rhythm. The sheer physical pleasure of him was blinding.

When he jerked his cock out her mouth, she blinked up at him. His expression was a crisis of need. "Not that way," he muttered. "Not this time."

He hauled her up the bed, she lunged up to a sitting position and together they tore off her clothes until she was as naked as he was. He cupped a hand at the back of her neck, and as he eased her back down, he rose to cover her body.

She spread her legs, and he helped her, so careful with her knee despite how he shook, that she fell in love with him all over again. She was so drenched with desire, he barely had to stroke her before her moisture covered his fingers. He looked at her in mute question, and she nodded. "Get the hell in here," she breathed.

He pushed at her entrance. As he stretched and filled her, his body trembled all over. She held him fiercely, protectively, because no matter how Powerful he might be and as strange as it was, this was his very first time.

Human skin to human skin.

Then he was in her, to the root, and their bodies were aligned. His eyes filled as he stared down at her. There could not be more wonder in his face.

"Grace," he said, and he always said it that way, as if it was not just her name but the most tender and vibrant of stories. He held his big body frozen over her, as if he didn't know what to do next.

"Now kiss me," she whispered.

Leaning his weight on one elbow, he cupped her breast as he brought his face down to hers. His lips closed over hers, and he bowed his shoulders over her with as much reverence as if he knelt to pray in a cathedral, and she never felt more beautiful than she did in that moment as he lost control completely and climaxed into her.

She thought that was it, and it was more than enough, but he surprised her as he always did, for as he climaxed, he ground himself into her, hit her pleasure center just right, and that brought her over the edge with him.

Always loving, always falling.

Like crazy.

The full weight of his body slumped on her in the utter surrender of exhaustion. She spun away into a gentle darkness, for there was no urgency, nowhere she needed to be and nothing they needed to, and it was the most extravagant luxury imaginable.

At some point, he must have stirred and shifted his weight away, but she only woke up when he pulled her with him. She made a sleepy sound as he guided her head onto his shoulder and wrapped his arms tight around her, then she fell back into drifting.

A strange ringing filled the bedroom. Sleepy and confused, Grace rolled onto her back and lifted her head to look for the noise. Her new cell phone danced along the bedside table on Khalil's side of the bed.

Khalil growled, slapped his hand over the phone, flipped it open and snapped, "Speak. Then hang up."

She covered her eyes. No, he was not friendly at all. She whispered, "You could have let it roll over to voice mail."

He scowled at her and mouthed, "Didn't think of it."

She laughed as he listened. His eyebrows rose. "Hello, Cuelebre. No, you can't talk to her. She's busy. What do you want?"

Grace's eyes widened. So much for her moratorium on unpredictable events. She reached for the phone, but Khalil held it away from her. She leaned over his body and made another grab for the phone. Khalil captured her hand, kissed it and held it against his chest.

That brought Grace close enough to hear the strong, deep voice on the other end. The Lord of the Wyr said, "My mate and I are planning another trip to Louisville," Cuelebre said. "We would like to consult with the Oracle."

Khalil pulled the receiver away to look at it in surprise. Then he held it back to his ear. "I thought you don't consult with Oracles."

"Pia convinced me to make an exception," he said. "We need to find out more about that vision Grace had."

"You might have heard that somebody tried to kill Grace and the kids a few days ago, and blew up their house," Khalil told the dragon. "Call back in two weeks. Right now Grace is on vacation."

Cuelebre's voice was edged. "I heard about the assassination attempt, and that she had an abundance of help. I also expect to talk to her directly, not through you."

"Well, dude," said Khalil, "sometimes you just have to get over shit."

He clicked the cell phone shut, threw it across the room and eased Grace onto her back so he could make love to her again.

Turn the page for a special preview of
the next Novel of the Elder Races
by Thea Harrison

LORD'S FALL

Coming soon from Berkley Sensation!

Even though feeling like a drama queen sucked donkey's balls, it was still true—leaving Dragos and New York behind was one of the hardest things Pia had ever done.

What sucked worse than that? Leaving was her idea. She had even argued for it, loud, long and vociferously.

And what sucked the absolute worst of all? She couldn't even pretend she was leaving all her troubles behind, because she wasn't. All her troubles came along with her in a nicely matched portable set, because of course she had to travel with a bunch of psychos.

She had just gotten used to one set of psychos, the Wyr sentinels. Not all of them liked her but most of them had, more or less, accepted her. Now she had to break in a whole new set. All these were fresh and energetic, while she was just goddamn tired and feeling bitchy enough to start tearing off heads for no reason.

That'd win her some brownie points.

Three psychos traveled with her in one black Cadillac Escalade. Three more traveled in another Escalade behind them, also black. In fact, both SUVs quite illegally had the

same license plate numbers and were identical in virtually
every way, in case the group had to split up and one SUV
had to act as a decoy for the other—which would be which-
ever one Pia was traveling in at the time.

In the Escalade following them were Miguel, Hugh and
Andrea. Miguel was nut brown and dark-haired, with a tight
body coiled with lean muscles and dark sharp eyes that never
stopped roaming. Hugh was rawboned and rather plain. He
had big hands, a slight Scottish burr, and a sleepy demeanor
that Pia didn't believe for a moment, because if he was really
that sleepy and slow moving, he wouldn't be traveling with
her.

Andrea looked just like Pia from a distance, which had
been intentional. She had the same leggy five-foot-ten body
type, and the same thick blonde hair that fell past the shoulders and could be pulled back in a ponytail. Andrea's hair had
been carefully lightened so that it matched Pia's blonde shades.

They couldn't pass for each other close up. Andrea looked
to be possibly five years older than Pia's twenty-five, although
with Wyr, guessing someone's age could sometimes be difficult, and Andrea could be as much as thirty years older.
Pia's face was more triangular. Andrea's eyes were green, not
midnight blue.

The three psychos traveling in Pia's Cadillac were James,
Daniel and Eva. James was the tallest of the crew and actually handsome, with dark hair that fell into blue eyes, and a
strong nose and jaw that looked great in profile. With his fine
features and light brown hair, Daniel appeared so boyish
that he looked downright innocent—another impression that
Pia knew had to be false.

Then there was Eva, who was the alpha and captain of
this particular pack of lethal whack-jobs. Eva had the whole
Venus Williams–Amazonian-splendor thing nailed, with
her honed, six-foot-tall body, rich ebony skin that rippled
over strong muscles and a black, bitter gaze that had dissected Pia so thoroughly the first time they met, Pia was not
exactly sure she'd found all the pieces and got herself put
back together quite right afterward.

All six attendants were the Wyr's version of Special Forces. The only Wyr more dangerous were Dragos's sentinels and, of course, Dragos himself.

Her psychos were the strongest and deadliest of Dragos's dogs of war. All were canine Wyr of some sort—wolves, mongrels or mastiffs. They came from the unit that was the most gifted and volatile in the army. They were the first into any conflict and acted as advance scouts, the rangers sent in to places too dangerous for the regular troops. They were the ones that patrolled the shadowed corners and slipped past enemy lines to take down their opponents from behind.

They were not good at conforming. They never wore a uniform, they didn't salute, and they didn't bother to hide their opinions about things. And it was clear they didn't think much either of Pia or of the babysitting job they had been shackled with, which meant they were all in for a shitty trip if things didn't change.

Pia slouched in the back behind the driver's seat, arms crossed as she watched the dirty white, winter scenery scroll by. She could feel Dragos flying overhead, although they didn't talk telepathically. Everything had already been said, shouted and argued out a while ago. After following the two-car cavalcade for about forty minutes, she could sense him wheeling and beginning the return flight back to the city.

She shifted restlessly in her seat. Her head pounded. On the sound system, 2Pac rapped "Ballad of a Dead Soulja." Beside her, Daniel slouched in fatigues and T-shirt, his light brown hair pulled into an untidy ponytail, absorbed in playing a handheld game.

Eva drove while James rode shotgun, literally, with the butt of a late model SCAR (which, Pia had been told, stood for Special Operations Forces—SOF—combat assault rifle) resting on the floor between his boots. Eva's kinky black hair was cropped short, emphasizing the graceful shape of her skull. As Pia looked at the rearview mirror, her gaze collided with the reflection of Eva's contemptuous glance. Pia's already strained temper gave up trying to control her behavior. It slunk away and took her better half with it.

She said, "I want to listen to Kenny G now. Or maybe Michael Bolton."

Daniel's head came up. James twisted to look at her.

"You've got to be fucking kidding me," Eva said. She turned to James. "Tell me she's fucking kidding me."

Pia felt childish, petty and vindictive. The drama queen had turned into a two-year-old, and the toddler was having a tantrum. She said to James, "Change it."

"Woman wants it changed," James said, expressionlessly. He punched buttons. Easy listening music filled the Cadillac.

"That's just fucking great," Eva muttered. "We're going to be stuck in a goddamn elevator for the rest of the goddamn day."

Pia hated elevator music too. She smiled and settled back into her seat. Now everybody else was almost as miserable as she was.

The morning dragged along with the miles that scrolled behind them, and the urban scenery remained the same, dull brick factories, black railroad lines ribboning through dirty snow, rows of houses and the occasional shopping center. Nobody spoke, at least not out loud. The two Cadillacs wove smoothly through interstate traffic, not always staying together, to avoid drawing too much attention, but always keeping within sight of each other. As Pia watched the passing landscape, she couldn't help but think of the last time she had made this trip, seven months ago. The two trips were almost perfect opposites of each other.

Last May she had been on the run, frightened, exhausted and alone, while everything around her had been bursting into bloom. This time she was mated, pregnant—her hand curled protectively over her stomach's slight bump—and surrounded by the Wyrs' most effective, if surly, bodyguards, and it was flipping cold outside, as winter held New York by the scruff of the neck with sharp, white teeth.

January in Charleston would feel positively balmy in contrast, with daytime highs up to sixty degrees and nighttime lows around thirty-eight to forty degrees. Mostly what Pia was looking forward to, though, was the lack of snow on the

South Carolina coast. In late December, New York had been hit with one of the worst blizzards on record, and it would take months for all the mountains of snow to melt.

Ninety minutes into the trip, Pia stirred. "I have to stop."

Eva glanced at her again in the mirror. "Does her?" said Eva in a baby talk kind of voice. "Where would herself like to stop?"

James stirred and said, "Evie."

"What?" Eva snapped. "We barely got on the road, and princess already wants to take a break. And while I'm on the subject, why are we driving and not flying? We could be there in a couple of hours, instead of the trip taking the whole freaking day."

"It's none of your fucking business why we're driving instead of flying," Pia said icily. "And princess here doesn't give a shit where we stop, as long as we do in the next ten minutes. Got it?"

"Sure, dollface," Eva said. "Any little thing herself wants, herself gets."

As Eva signaled and cut right from the fast lane to the exit lane, Pia watched the other woman in the mirror and thought, *Imma have to kick your ass before the day's out, aren't I?*

Yeah, it was shaping up to be a great trip so far.

And they were on a mission of diplomacy.

The other Cadillac cut across traffic to join their SUV, and the two vehicles took the next exit ramp. Their choices for stopping included two gas stations, a McDonald's, a Denny's and a Quik Mart. Eva pulled into the McDonald's lot and parked. Pia stepped out and headed for the restaurant. The other six surrounded her so casually it seemed to happen by accident. The psychos had smooth moves; she would give them that much.

Feeling an increasingly urgent need, she found her way to the restroom, accompanied by Eva and Andrea. So far the seven-month pregnancy didn't show all that much—a fact that pretty much freaked her out if she thought too much about it—and she could keep it completely hidden if she dressed strategically. But the peanut, bless him, was beginning to exert some influence on her bladder. That was going to get much worse before it got better.

The women's restroom was more or less clean and empty. She pushed past the other two women, slammed the stall door shut and enjoyed a few minutes of what was likely to be the only alone time she would get that day.

Resentment and antagonism were two of the troubles that had followed her. Pia hadn't really gained acceptance from the Wyr over the past seven months. Oh, she had from some of the sentinels. All the gryphons had embraced her, and Graydon had become one of her best friends. They also knew what kind of Wyr she was and why she and Dragos kept it secret.

The gryphons were the only ones who knew. Not even the other two sentinels did, although that didn't seem to cause gargoyle sentinel Grym any problems, but then it was hard to tell what he was thinking, since he didn't talk much. And she had achieved a kind of uneasy truce with the harpy sentinel Aryal—at least enough to spar with the harpy on the training mat several times a week, although they didn't share confidences or socialize.

As far as all the other Wyr went, in the early days of her mating with Dragos expectation had turned to puzzlement, and then suspicion as the whispering began.

She didn't reveal to anyone what kind of Wyr she was, because she was stuck-up.

No, she was a fugitive from some other demesne, because Dragos wasn't the only one she had stolen from.

Or, she didn't bother to reveal what kind of Wyr she was, because she was one of the antisocial ones, and she didn't care if she made friends or didn't fit into any of the packs, herds or prides.

For the Wyr, it was hard to warm up to someone who kept something so fundamental to their nature hidden from everybody else. Knowing that and understanding the reasons why it was there weren't much help. The low-level resentment and subtle ostracization still felt sucky.

More than half a year later, Pia still felt like an uneasy guest in what was supposed to be her own home. The only real friends she felt like she had were Graydon, who knew everything; the new Dark Fae Queen, Niniane, with whom she steadily corresponded; and a few people from her old job working as a bartender at Elfie's.

Quentin, the bar owner, didn't need to know all of her secrets, and she didn't need to know all of his. And of course there was Preston, the half-troll barfly, who liked to describe himself as an eight-foot hunka burnin' love, and who really was a sweetie through and through. Preston didn't care if anyone had any stinking secrets. If you were willing to share a dozen orders of baked potato skins, lathered with cheese, bacon, sour cream and chives, and drink beer while watching the NBA playoffs, you were all right by him.

But Graydon was increasingly busy, and letters from Niniane, while fascinating and wonderful to receive, weren't enough to satisfy Pia's social needs, and Pia couldn't hide at Elfie's twenty-four/seven. She could only visit a couple of times a week. As far as she was concerned, there were only two things that made living in Cuelebre Tower worth it. One of them was the peanut—and she really had to stop calling him that, because the little fetus was already so smart, she could tell he thought his name actually was Peanut.

The other was Dragos, who was primitive, Powerful, domineering, calculating, manipulative, infernally clever and tactless, and who she adored with all of her heart. Dragos, who created as many problems as he solved and who loved her too, fiercely, so much so he had mated with her. Their lives had become inextricably entwined, and they had to work for things together now.

Which meant they needed to figure out how to be partners in more places than just the bedroom. (Because Pia was pretty damn sure they had nailed that part the first time they had made love.) Which also meant coming to an agreement about what they worked toward, even if reaching that agreement took months and sometimes felt like pulling giant, dragon-sized teeth.

The Wyr demesne and Dragos himself were facing too many challenges at once to deal with any one of them effectively. Dragos had broken several treaties with the Elves in his pursuit of Pia last May, and those treaties had not been repaired. Border strife continued with the Elven demesne, along with an ongoing trade embargo that had put several New York businesses under and was seriously hurting several more.

Internally, Dragos's multinational corporation, Cuelebre Enterprises, had been hard-hit along with the rest of the world in an ongoing global recession. Diversification, along with aggressively streamlining and retrenching, had the corporation leaner but running strong, but that had taken harder work and more top-heavy man power at a time when Dragos could ill afford to expend the energy.

Then there was the problem of being critically short staffed. Dragos had lost two of his seven sentinels in quick succession last summer, first his warlord sentinel, Tiago Black Eagle, who had mated with the new Dark Fae Queen, Niniane Lorelle. Then Dragos lost his First sentinel, Rune Ainissesthai, who had mated with the Vampyre sorceress Carling Severan. Dragos and Rune had parted badly, and Dragos still refused to talk about it. He had moved two people into sentinel positions as a temporary stopgap, but now he had to go through the process of setting new sentinels into place.

To top it all off, there was the amorphous Freaky Deaky Something that hung on the horizon, the strange voice that Dragos had heard through an impromptu prophesy given by the Oracle of Louisville, Grace Andreas. The Oracle and her family had since relocated to Miami, where Pia and Dragos had traveled to meet with her in a follow-up consultation. Unfortunately, Grace couldn't add much to the original vision since, as she said, prophesies did not repeat themselves.

Grace did offer them a piece of advice. "The person or Power behind the voice from the vision is either already in your lives, or it will be," she told them. "Don't let that knowledge weaken you. There's no point in trying to avoid it, because those actions you take might actually cause you to come into contact with it sooner than you would otherwise. Act from your strengths, and live your lives in a state of readiness. You were lucky. You were given a warning. Most people don't get that."

As Pia exited the bathroom stall and washed her hands, she thought of all these things, along with the added stressor of having just left her mate. Eva and her antagonism shouldn't even be on the list of challenges she had to face.

As Wyr canines, the psychos were a well-trained pack. They would have a strongly defined internal order she didn't yet have a handle on. Each one would be highly opinionated and would make up his or her own mind about Pia, but none of them would go against their alpha, and no doubt several of them would take their cue from how Eva and Pia's relationship developed. Right now Pia was just an annoying, disliked outsider they had to bodyguard. She had to establish a different working relationship with them now before Eva's lack of respect became too entrenched.

The other two women had taken advantage of using the facilities too, first Andrea then Eva, while one remained on guard at the door.

Pia dried her hands deliberately then turned. Andrea guarded the door. Pia met the other woman's gaze. She said, "Get out."

Andrea's blonde eyebrows rose. She glanced at the closed bathroom stall, which opened. Eva stalked out, her whole magnificent body flowing like gleaming black oil.

Pia said to Andrea, "Wrong response."

Eva jerked her chin. "Go on."

Andrea opened the door and backed out without a word.

Pia went to the door and flipped the lock. The *snick* sounded overloud in the silent restroom. It wouldn't keep anybody out who was determined to get in, of course, but it was a strongly symbolic barrier—and the sound would tell any sharp, listening Wyr ears to stay out of what happened next.

She turned, leaned back against the door and met Eva's sardonic gaze. Pia said, "I thought briefly about just kicking your ass, but we would have to take that outside, and I don't feel like getting wet and muddy. Besides, you're not worth it."

Amusement sliced across Eva's bold features, and her

black eyes sparkled. "You are sadly deluded if you think you could take me, princess."

Pia didn't smile, and her gaze remained level. "I can take the gryphons," she said. Eva's face froze. "For the past seven months, I've been sparring with Aryal almost daily. With the harpy, it's more like fifty-fifty, since she doesn't pull her punches. She doesn't give a shit if I'm a female and Dragos's mate. If anything, it makes her hit harder, because she doesn't like me much. So you tell me, Eva. Can I take you?"

Okay, so some of that was bluffing. The other woman was a trained soldier and versed in battle, combat tactics and weaponry in a way Pia never would be. If they were in the wild, engaged in guerilla warfare, Pia was pretty sure that if she didn't succeed in running away from a confrontation, Eva could wipe the forest floor with her. But they weren't in the wild. On a training mat, or in a McDonald's parking lot, Pia didn't have a doubt she could take the other woman. That was the certainty she let sit in her gaze.

"You have two choices," Pia said. "You can either change your attitude completely right now, no second chances, or you can give me the car keys and make your own way back to New York, because I'm not going to put up with your shit. It's pulling my mind off what I need to be thinking about, and not only that, it's unprofessional—from the both of us. We don't have to be girlfriends. We don't have to like each other. Believe me, I'm pretty used to that by now. But if you choose to stay, you've got to come to terms with the fact that, for anything that doesn't involve a combat situation, you're not the alpha in this group. I am. If we're ever facing a fight where you're the clear expert, that's a different story, but until then, you do as I say."

She watched as fury and instinct warred in Eva. The other woman was dominant, and she lived a violent life. Her Wyr side would be much closer to the surface than it was for others. It would be difficult to give up her alpha status without a fight, especially to someone who was an herbivore, not pack. If they were both purely animals, Eva would try to hunt Pia down for lunch.

Of course Wyr were much more than just their animal natures, but even still, some things bled through in subtle and not-so-subtle ways. Predator Wyr often had a condescending attitude toward more peaceful herbivores. Usually that dynamic was nothing more than a social irritation, but in this situation it added more tension.

But Pia would not want to be in Eva's shoes if Eva chose to head back to New York. No doubt that was the deciding factor in Eva's response, along with the fact that the other woman would never abandon her unit. Eva said expressionlessly, "Got it. For this trip, you're alpha. We done?"

Pia poked at her lower lip with her tongue sourly as she noted Eva's specific wording. "No," she said. "I'm not finished." She raised her voice slightly for the benefit of whoever was listening on the other side of the door—which by that point, she reckoned, was all the others. "No doubt you all wanted to stay and watch the Games this week and find out who wins the sentinel positions. And I get that you're irritated, but you people need to change your attitude about this assignment. I don't think you realize how important this trip is or what an honor you've been given."

"We get that you're special, being Dragos's mate and all," Eva said.

"No, knucklehead," she snapped. She might have to take Eva out into the parking lot and kick her ass after all—whatever the other woman said, Pia wasn't sure Eva could really give up her alpha status without it, even if Eva honestly tried. "We're not on some kind of pleasure jaunt or shopping trip, and I'm not just going to have tea and cookies, and go shopping with Beluviel. We're going to try to fix one of the biggest problems the Wyr demesne has right now, repair treaties and better our relationship with the Elven demesne. It's something Dragos can't do, since he's the one who broke the treaties to begin with—the Elves have threatened war if he enters their demesne without permission again, and besides, he has to settle the sentinel issue, which means he has to stay in New York to preside over the Games."

She could tell when Eva stopped sneering long enough to

actually begin to think, and then the shift happened. Suddenly their trip south was no longer an unwelcome babysitting job for an unpopular mate, but had become much more.

She continued, more quietly, "The outcome of our trip matters to a lot of people, Eva. I'm not going to risk failure because you and your idiots don't know how to reign in your snark or take orders from someone who is not pack and is nonmilitary. I get that your more usual assignment involves solving problems that are more of the point-and-shoot kind. If you can't handle this, say so. We'll turn around right now and go home, and I'll start over with another crew that can."

"Okay," Eva said after a moment, relaxing from her rigid stance. "We weren't given the full mission details. All we were told was that we had one objective—travel with you and keep you safe."

"Well, I am special and all, being Dragos's mate," Pia said dryly. Eva snorted, a near-silent exhalation that sounded almost amused. "And by the way, we're not taking a flight because Dragos thought we would have more survival capability on the ground. Incidences involving planes tend to have high fatality rates." Plus nobody in their group had a Wyr form with wings, which seemed to bother Dragos quite a bit. He couldn't imagine flying high in the sky without having the capability to jump out of a plane and take flight if he had to. "Not," she added, "that I plan on explaining every little decision to you in the future."

"Fine," Eva said with a scowl, evidently not liking the sound of that. Then her expression changed. "I would like to ask you just one thing, though."

Pia studied the other woman. She would make more of an ally out of Eva through cooperation than not. Maybe this could be a bloodless coup after all. They might never grow to like each other, but achieving a partnership before they reached South Carolina would be good enough for Pia. So she said, "Shoot."

Eva ran her black gaze down Pia's body as she sucked a tooth. Finally she looked up and met Pia's stare. "You even pregnant?"

Pia's eyebrows rose. She hadn't realized people were beginning to gossip about that as well. "You can't tell from my scent?"

"You have a strange scent," Eva said. "None of us have smelled anything like you before, and we don't know what to make of it."

Pia's face twisted into a wry grimace. Fair enough. She beckoned with her fingers and said, "Come here."

Eyes narrowed in curiosity, Eva stepped forward. Pia reached for her hand, and Eva allowed her to take it. Pia settled Eva's flattened palm over the small bump of her stomach and waited. She watched Eva's face transform into wonder.

The dampening spell that Pia used to camouflage the natural luminescence of her skin also seemed to mask the peanut's presence from others, at least from a distance. That camouflage fell away when someone actually came in contact with Pia's body. Even though the peanut was still very small for twenty-eight weeks, the muted roar of Power at her midsection was unmistakable even for someone who was not medical personnel.

Wonder rounded Eva's eyes. "Holy shit," she whispered.

Pia rubbed her eyes with thumb and forefinger. Yeah. Holy, as it were, shit.

"I'm confused," Eva said, frowning. "It doesn't seem very big, but it's carrying a helluva wallop."

"I'm about twenty-eight weeks along," Pia told her. She could see Eva doing the math.

Eva's frown deepened. "Shouldn't it be bigger?"

"Nobody knows," Pia said with a tired sigh. "The doctor says he's quite healthy, and that's all that matters. Based on his current development, she's estimating a gestation period between 730 and 750 days." She watched the other woman do the math again.

Eva blanched. "You're going to be pregnant for two years."

"Seems likely," Pia said between her teeth. "Did you know elephants have a gestation period of twenty-two months? Apparently dragon babies might be more complicated. And before you think to ask, no, I'm not laying an egg so he can

4

gestate the rest of the way outside my body. No, no such luck. This baby's going to be a live birth."

Eva looked at her in poorly concealed horror. "Won't he have . . . claws? And not cute tiny, puppy ones?"

"We're a little concerned about that," Pia said grimly. "The doctor wants to plan a C-section."

"I see." Eva pulled her hand away and stepped back.

They had roused the baby. Pia felt an invisible presence settle around her neck and shoulders, a bright, fierce, loving innocence. It was a waking version of what she dreamed so often these days, the peanut draping his graceful, delicate white body around her, his long, transparent wings tucked close to his body. Nobody else but her could sense when he did that, not even Dragos. She put a hand to the base of her neck with a small, private smile.

"Guess we better get you to Charleston," Eva said. "You got a job to do."

"I guess we'd better," said Pia.

"I just want to know one more thing," said Eva.

Pia turned to unlock the restroom door. "What's that?"

Eva put her hand on the door and held it shut while she met Pia's gaze pointedly. "Tell me we can change radio stations now."

Pia bit back a chuckle. "Yes, please. Let's get off the elevator."

Eva took hold of the handle and pulled the door open. The other five psychos were hanging in the hallway, looking thoughtful, their arms piled high with food bags and drinks carriers. Daniel was already eating a sandwich.

Reaching a détente with Eva was one hurdle down. Now all Pia wanted to do was reach their rented estate and settle in for the evening. She wouldn't be meeting with any Elves until the next day.

She couldn't wait for nightfall. She only hoped she wasn't so excited that she couldn't fall asleep, because that would seriously screw up everything.